INITIATION

INTO

SPIRITUAL SEXUALITY

The Knowledge, The Secrets, The Journey

By

Ina Laughing Winds

Print ISBN: 978-1-7322834-6-6
eBook ISBN: 978-1-7322834-7-3

First printing, 2022.

Printed in the United States of America.

115 Metroplex Blvd
Pearl, MS 39208
agpearl.com

INITIATION into SPIRITUAL SEXUALITY
The knowledge, The Secrets, The Journey

____

What People Are Saying....

With enthusiasm, I read this exciting novel: a fascinating interplay of a love story, a spiritual journey, and captivating teachings that go far beyond spiritual sexuality.

This journey to oneself with such wise teachings are gifts that open the heart; it touches, invites, transforms, teaches, and gives in a unique way. It shows that nothing is linear. It opens the space for evolution, wisdom, and love to exist beyond time and space. It gives hope that these enriching treasures of knowledge, wisdom, and especially the rites of passage will not be lost and can be made available to all, especially young people.

When Grandmother Spinning Winds starts teaching, a different space opens and it goes right into my heart. I am so curious if others feel this too, like my daughter. The author has a unique and vivid way of taking the reader on a journey to themselves. It is a masterpiece of spiritual teachings and hopefully, the author will write more!

Bettina Steinle-Vossbeck,
BeBliss Verlag/Publisher
Manager of Edition Empirica Verlag GmbH, Germany

____

Where was this book sixty-six years ago when I was combing the Philadelphia libraries and bookstores with so many of the questions and cultural inhibitions Ina Laughing Winds Mlekush has addressed in this book? Oh, yes… Ina was a mere child then…Thinking, yes. Writing, no.

Judy Blume took my generation and my psychology and psychiatry professors into the language, the minds, and the hearts of preteens, young adults, and their elders regarding God, organized religion, menstruation, and oneself.

It took all this time for the next logical questions to be addressed as a very readable novel, Initiation into Spiritual Sexuality—The Knowledge, The Secrets, The Journey.

Sage Wind Dancer's totally authentic 16-year-old voice speaks to the issues of sexuality and relationship and commitment and truth. Her wandering mind and her Grandmother's wisdom weave us through all those areas and more. They seem to wander yet everything is related and relevant. We are 'taught' through a more open and seeing culture spoken through Native American Grandmother Seeks the Truth. We are led away from inhibitions and negative belief systems.

Even after years of counseling individuals, couples, and families, and directing a major New York hospital medical school's Division of Human Sexuality, some of the bluntness was a surprise to me. It became refreshing! It was what I had been looking for in print since my preteen years.

"I recommend this book to teens and adults both female and male. There is so much to be learned here…even through the voice of a very young lady."

Sheila Jackman, Ph.D
Retired Director of New York medical schoo
Division of Human Sexuality
Owner—Director of Sedona Health Wave-
Energy Enhancement System

What an amazing book! Ina has been one of my teachers for almost two decades, and she brings her invaluable Grandmother teachings out through this beautiful story. Especially in this day and age of humanity losing its focus, this book is even more important in demonstrating the rites of passage that should be the focus for boys and girls in their lives. I only wish I had had this knowledge and wisdom as my sons were growing up.

Dan Powers
Executive Director at Beyond the Bedroom
and Pleasure Engineer

With Open Heart and Deep Appreciation

To my mother, who believed in me to accomplish
anything I decided to do.

To my father, who gave me a love of music
and a tenacious work ethic.

To my 48-year-old son, a loving, dynamic man who thinks
his mother is outrageous. I am!

To my husband of twenty years, we agreed to love and challenge
each other to become the best people we could be. By God's good
grace, we have succeeded.

I honor my first Metaphysical Spiritual Teacher, Dr. Vince Corso,
for helping me to discover myself as a single mom searching for a
higher level of consciousness.

To my beloved mentor from the Ancient Shamanic Traditions whom
I met at age thirty-six and continue to learn from his teachings. I
send my love and gratitude. More than any other person, he helped
me become the woman I am today at age seventy-three.

Thank You
Friends, Family, Lovers, Partners in Life,
and Seekers of Spiritual Wisdom.

May you be blessed on whichever dimension you travel in.
You Dance in My Heart!

Ina Laughing Winds

CAST OF CHARACTERS

MODERN TIMES. . . . . ANCIENT TIMES

Sage Wind Dancer . . . . Dances with the Wind

Rose Gregory – Sage's Mother
Rod Gregory – Sage's Father

Grandmother Spinning Winds . . . . . Grandmother Seeks the Truth
Grandfather Strong Bear . . . . Grandfather Standing Bear

<u>Sage's Male Friends</u>

Shane
Michael
Cody
Josh Walks on the Wind

<u>Sage's Female Friends</u>

Andrea
Susie

<u>Sage's Clan Aunts</u>

Aunt Kathy Flowing Heart . . . . Cherry Blossom
Aunt Amy Singing Hawk . . . . Soaring Hawk and others

<u>Sage's Clan Uncles</u>

Tim Fire Hawk
Bruce Quiet Man
Rex

PART I

RITE OF PASSAGE

Chapter 1

I'm Going Crazy! Teach Me!

Today, I planned to visit Grandmother Spinning Winds. She lived about a half-mile from us, and I've walked to visit her my entire life. Before going, I touched the stained-glass image of two hummingbirds and a bumble bee resting on purple and lavender flowers on the front door of our home. Mom had always wanted a special front door made of rich wood and stained glass. Dad made the door himself and hired one of his friends to do the glasswork. It was just what Mom wanted, and I touched it every time I left the house, hoping for good things in my life.

Today, I wanted to learn about sex, and I knew Grandmother was just the one to teach me.

Looking out at the hummingbird feeder in front of our living room windows, I saw two birds at the feeder, one with a ruby-red throat and the other with green and yellow feathers, like the one on our front door. Grandmother Spinning Winds would say that was a good medicine sign.

I smiled to myself. A scientific study said that bumble bees can't fly. I've been told I'm too young to learn about sex. So much for telling us what we can't do!

Grandmother Spinning Winds wasn't my real grandmother, but that's how I felt about her. I had known her and Grandfather Strong Bear for as long as I could remember. I called them Grandmother and Grandfather. Grandmother Spinning Winds had instructed my folks about sacred sexuality, but I wasn't comfortable talking to them about sex because whenever I brought it up, Mom would never answer me.

She'd say, "Oh, Sage, you have so many questions about sex. I know you're mature for your age, but I wish you weren't in such a hurry."

Sometimes she'd look at me with that deep mother's look and say, "Your eyes are so blue. No young man will have a chance once you look at him."

I'd say, "Oh, Mom, I haven't even had a boyfriend yet!"

The last time I tried to talk to her about sex, she said, "You take after me, that's for sure, but I didn't start dating until I was eighteen. Give it a couple more years, honey. You're only sixteen."

She ran her fingers through my long, dark brown hair, brushing it off to one side as she had done all my life. On the one hand, it felt very loving; on the other, it sometimes felt like she was still treating me like a little girl.

It was the second week of September and beautiful outside. I was excited to be going to Grandmother's house. Mom's roses had recovered from the heat of summer, and they were huge. I loved the multicolored roses that bloomed two-toned burnt orange and yellow, but it was the red ones that filled the house with fragrance, and this morning I couldn't resist them. I bent over and tickled my nose with their sweet, spicy scent. I was afraid the petals would burst. If I didn't get some answers about sex soon, I felt like I would burst, too!

When I started down the street to Grandmother's house, my head was filled with the so-called sex talk my parents and I had. They had said very little.

Dad's voice had been stern. "Be sure the boy is a good kid, respectful of his parents! It's not wise to kiss on the first date, or second, or even the third."

I guess I won't be talking to Dad much.

With Mom, a sweet, understanding look came on her face. That look made me think I could go to her for help. Then she said, "Don't be a tease to boys, Sage. They are easily aroused. You know what I mean, Hon?"

I nodded, too shocked to reply. I wasn't used to hearing Mom be so direct.

After that, I knew I needed a different kind of sex talk—not just, "Don't kiss a boy too soon," or "Boys are horny." *Shoot, so am I!* There was something more I needed to hear. I felt it in my heart.

My parents weren't typical. They may have appeared to be the average white, middle-class couple, but they had hungered for a more natural, indigenous way of life. This quest had led them to attend a Spiritual Sexuality workshop with Grandmother Spinning Winds many years ago, so I knew that they knew more than they were telling me, and I had so many questions!

I started walking faster. I knew there was something secret that no one talked about, something I was supposed to figure out when I was old enough.

"I'm old enough!" I blurted out loud. I felt so embarrassed that I quickly looked around to ensure that no one but the trees had heard me.

Grandmother Spinning Winds and I were going to have a medicine heart talk. She always told me the truth, even when I didn't like what I heard. I felt for the tobacco pouch in my pocket and the little box with my medicine gift for her. I never quite understood the gift of tobacco, and I didn't understand why sex couldn't be talked about.

As I walked to Grandmother's house, I heard her voice in my head. *Tobacco is sacred. It's medicine. It has natural healing properties and is strong when used in ceremony or a medicine pipe. I work with a medicine pipe, so I have a direct line to Great Spirit. I have known you, Sage, little one, since the day you were born. Grandfather and I will always be here for you.*

Lost in my memory, and hearing the sound of Grandmother's voice in my head, I was surprised to realize that I was standing in front of her neighbor's garden, which was ablaze with the colors of a dozen ripe vegetables thriving in the hot summer sun.

Why am I looking at this garden? I asked myself. *I've seen it a hundred times before. Surely, I'm not nervous to talk about sex? Nah, I can't be—can I?*

I reached into my pocket and felt the box with the medicine gift. Again I wanted to show Grandmother how important this medicine talk was to me. Holding the box gave me the courage to get my feet moving again. I hoped she liked the rainbow set of earrings I had made for her. I used fifteen different colors so the beads blended, just the way Grandmother had taught me. The design was intricate. Sometimes I wouldn't catch a mistake until I was two or three rows past it. Then I had to go back and pull out those rows to correct my mistake, or it would change the whole pattern.

It took me a long time to make a set of earrings. These earrings were perfect, except for the one bead I had purposely set out of place. That way, someone could see that a human had made them and not a machine. I loved every minute of making them because I knew I was giving them to Grandmother, and I understood the reason why.

I reached Grandmother's house. The front yard was comfortably familiar, with its tall, majestic cactus and white, bleached, horned cattle skull. It was a typical New Mexico desert front yard except for the large, dried-out cholla cactus that lay upon its side. I slowed to look at her Little People's world. I doubt many chollas have crystal cities with Little People's houses nestled into their holes and cracks.

The Little People—elves, fairies, and elementals—lived in crystals and pretty bottles. Grandmother tucked these, plus decorative shells, in and around the skull and dried cactus. There was a whole city of these Little People. I could see them out of the corner of my eye when I wasn't looking.

I tried it, but looking sideways isn't easy. Oh! I thought I saw a flicker of something. Then poof! Nothing. I tried again. You can only see them by not looking. I had trained my eyes to go soft and look the other way while glancing out of the corner of my eye. That's when the Little People would tease me and come out to play. Their gift to those that see them is to teach people how to laugh and not take life so seriously.

I heard laughter on the other side of the front room windows. Grandmother was watching me practice! I realized I was being distracted by playing hide-and-seek with the Little People. "Okay, no more today," I whispered. "I'm here on very serious business."

I took a deep breath and raised my hand to knock on the front door, but the door opened before I could knock.

Grandmother Spinning Winds smiled with laughter in her eyes. "Come in, Sage." Do you want water or something to drink?"

"Water please." I followed her into the kitchen. When she handed me the water, her eyes sparkled as if she had put something magickal into the glass.

Reading my thoughts, she said, "Water is magickal enough without adding magick dust, herbs, or potions to it."

"Yes, Grandmother, I remember. There is stage magic with card tricks, and there is real magick spelled M-A-G-I-C-K!"

Holding her glass, Grandmother headed toward her medicine-talk room, which was also her bedroom. Looking around, I saw sacred items on every shelf: feathers, furs, a warrior altar, a sweet medicine animal altar, a woman's goddess mesa, Little People cities in crystals, and several empty decorative perfume bottles. Her tribal face masks hung on the north wall above the large window. Kachina statues sat on the top shelf of her bookcase on the east wall. This bookshelf held over one hundred three-ring binders of handwritten notes on teachings Grandmother had taken while studying with Thunder Wolf, her shamanic mentor. Feathers from all sorts of 'winged ones' rested on the top of the bookcase on the south wall. To the west, above her headboard, hung her first ten shields from the Ceremonial Dance.

I heard her voice in my head: *These shields provide nagual spiritual protection from their hanging places.* I was accustomed to receiving thoughts from my grandmother in this way.

I saw her gun on the shelf, right above her head and within easy reach when she was lying down. Grandmother had taught me that men and women need good weapons for tonal, everyday protection. She saw me looking at her shotgun.

"I like having my Benelli 12-gauge shotgun next to me in bed, and the STI 2011 9mm with a full twenty-round magazine on the headboard shelf. It's always locked and loaded with the safety on."

Safety first; I had that drummed into me.

"If any bad guys come into my bedroom, the last thing they'll see is one very bad grandma. If you're not trained, never pick up a gun because you have to treat them as if they're always loaded. Never aim one at someone unless you're prepared to shoot them dead. Not many people today have that kind of courage or clarity. No, they'd rather call 911 and have someone come and rescue them. The trouble with that is they can probably get a pizza delivered faster than the police can get there. Their fear of guns makes them victims of their fear."

This was not the first time I had heard Grandmother say these words. I think I could repeat them word-for-word, which is what Grandmother wanted.

"Grandmother," I said as I paused to take a sip of water. "Thanks for helping me get over my fear of guns and for encouraging Dad to teach me to shoot." I reminded her that I was pretty accurate too. Dad was proud of me, and we went shooting once a month. "You and Dad have told me it isn't guns I should be afraid of; it's people who don't know how to properly handle guns or be respectful of them."

Even though it had nothing to do with learning about sex, I couldn't help asking, "What about Grandfather Strong Bear? Can't he protect you? What would he do if a bad guy broke in and was standing over your bed?"

Grandmother looked at me with a twinkle in her eye. "If the bad guy was in Grandfather's room, he'd pick up his gun and take care of business, too."

I was stunned. "You have separate bedrooms? I thought you and Grandfather got along. I thought you were happy together."

She laughed. "Oh, my. You do need to learn about living life as you step into your Rite of Passage. That includes how to keep a relationship healthy with good communication and honest agreements. That is the foundation to keeping a relationship happy and passionate over the long haul. Having separate bedrooms does not mean something is wrong. We sleep together quite often, but there are times when we need our separate spaces, to dream apart from each other, or if one of us is sick. We don't want to get each other sick! Sometimes I have a ceremony I need to do that keeps me up all night. It wouldn't be very polite to expect Grandfather Strong Bear to sleep on the couch or keep him up with my drumming and medicine work, would it?"

That all made sense, and I became even more curious about how to love and live together for a lifetime, especially when you got upset or angry at each other. Mom and Dad shared one bedroom, just like the other parents I knew. This was a new idea that I would have to investigate.

Grandmother put one of her special medicine ceremonial blankets and two pillows on the floor and invited me to sit. "Let's start with smudging ourselves." She picked up the abalone shell, "Do you remember what plants are used in this mixture?"

"Yes. Sage, cedar, sweetgrass, and lavender."

"Very good. Do you remember what the medicine of each plant is?"

"Sage banishes negativity. Cedar brings balance. Sweetgrass blesses. Lavender brings beauty."

"Well done. Repetition helps us learn. Light it, and we'll smudge before we continue our teaching."

The smudge helped, but I was so excited and anxious to begin our talk that I kept shifting my body and couldn't get comfortable. After taking another sip of water, I blurted out, "I know there is something more to sex than Mom and Dad told me. I can't wait any longer. My body is driving me crazy. I have to know the secrets that no one will talk about."

Grandmother laughed, but I knew she held wisdom because she taught adults spiritual sexuality teachings from the ancient ones. "I don't want to wait till I am an adult with all sorts of my problems. I know my folks attended training workshops with you, thank God, or they wouldn't have told me anything about sex. But they left so much out! After studying with you, Grandmother, you would think they would practice more, but they say they get too busy and don't make time for their romantic life."

Grandmother told me she understood why I might be confused and concerned.

My thoughts became a rushing waterfall. "Grandmother, it's hard for a kid to tell her parents that they're stupid. I've never had sex, but I know—as you say—there is something magickal about sex that even my parents haven't discovered yet. I don't know how I know this. I just know there's something more than what my parents are experiencing. If Mom and Dad ever felt that power, I'm sure they would find time to have more sex. Even though they love each other, something magickal is missing.

"Grandmother, you always told me I should trust my feelings. You said that often we carry wisdom from one lifetime to another. So, without knowing how I know something, I just know it. Try and explain that to my parents!"

"It's time for your parents to get more training, learn about their priorities and hungers, and put sex where it belongs—on top of the list! Not fifth or sixth, after the house is cleaned, the yard work done, and the dishes are washed."

I didn't know what Grandmother was talking about, but I knew she sometimes felt frustrated with my parents, too.

She put energy behind her words. "Learning about spiritual sexuality should never stop, no matter how old you get. You can't separate spirituality and sexuality as some religions and cultures have tried to do."

"I know I'm being judgmental of my parents, Grandmother, and I probably shouldn't be, but I don't want to end up like them or my friend's parents, who have no clue as to the importance of being sexual." To emphasize my point, I got up from the blanket and declared, "I promise you, Grandmother, if you teach me, I will never stop learning—that's my promise to you, my vow!"

"Take a deep breath," she said.

"I'm too excited to breathe deep and slow down."

"Sit down, Sage. If you don't learn to breathe slowly, you'll never learn about the magick of sacred sexuality. Do you want me to teach you or not?"

I plopped myself down and slowed my breathing. Grandmother explained that breathing deep and slowing down is one of the keys to opening the mysteries of spiritual sexuality. She said it's the key to opening the body into rivers of orgastic freedom, and most people don't know this life force energy in its fullness.

"Most people, like your folks, experience a little stream and think it's the whole river. People are afraid to push away from the banks of the river to explore the uncharted waters of sexuality. Most people are so grateful for the little bit of sex they get, they never stop to ask if there is more."

I sat silent, listening, mesmerized by Grandmother's honest talk. I felt something awakening inside of me.

"Of course, there's more," she said as she straightened the folds of her long-tiered lavender skirt and sat more upright. "How do you think our universe was created? It was one big orgasm that Great Grandmother and Great Grandfather had. Scientists call it *The Big Bang Theory*, which is not that far off if you see the humor in it."

She told me that our elders have a beautiful creation story like many other cultures have.

"If you can interpret the symbolism, it's all the same story expressed through different cultural myths yet carrying a similar thread."

"Grandmother," I interrupted, "I thought we were going to talk about sex, not theories, or how the universe was created."

"Take a deep breath and slow down," she reminded me.

I would hear this guidance many times in my spiritual sexual training. Deep breathing and slowing down may seem simple, but it's not always easy to do.

"Grandmother, please tell me what kind of orgasm created the universe. I know how babies are made, but universes? You said Great Grandmother and Great Grandfather had one big orgasm? How can that be? Does that mean I create universes when I have an orgasm? Do I need to have an orgasm with a man, or can I create a universe by my own orgasm? Mom and Dad told me about making babies, but I don't think they know how to make a universe with their orgasms. If they knew that, I am sure they would understand the magick of their sexuality and make love more often or longer or—"

I barely took a breath and kept going. "Babies. Where does the soul of a baby come from? Do you have to be in love to have sex? Are sex and love the same things? Do girls have orgasms like boys? Boys have ejaculations. Is that the same as an orgasm? Can girls ejaculate?" I had so many questions that I felt better just blurting them out.

Grandmother smiled and took a deep, slow breath. I mimicked her. She sat calmly and silently as I rushed on, emptying my cup of questions.

"Mom and Dad said sex feels good, but some magazines I've read said it feels great, and you have to practice. But how do you practice if it's not okay to be sexual with someone until you're married or in love? I'm so confused, and no one will tell me the truth. I feel like they're afraid to tell me, like if I know the truth, I'll be out of control and do something bad. I thought the truth sets us free!"

"Slow down, little one, and breathe. All your questions are good ones and will be answered. It will take time. It's not enough to answer your questions; you must be trained so the answers come from your own body knowing."

I was finally quiet and waited to hear Grandmother's teachings.

"There is a way you can begin practicing being sexual, just with yourself."

Cool! I thought. Now, she had my attention.

Grandmother shifted her position and continued. "When you first start discovering the mysteries of the universe, you don't need a partner. You must know your own body first; you must know your breath. You must know your spiritual connection to *The Everything* so that when you decide to engage sexually with another, it is done with respect and integrity, and Spirit is with you. And no, you do not need to be in love or married to be sexual with another. You must love and respect yourself, and it's best to be with someone who respects you as much as you respect yourself. The same holds true for them. There must be honesty between you." She stopped and whispered, "Even if you share intimacy for only one night."

I must have had an intense look because Grandmother watched closely for my reaction.

"Only for one night?" I wasn't sure what she meant. I wondered if she was talking about going to a party, drinking, and getting laid.

"Honesty is needed, and self-love," she said.

I could see that she wasn't talking about what some of my friends did. They told me it was fun, but they weren't so happy when I saw them a day or two later. I nodded slightly in agreement. When my face relaxed a bit, she went on.

"The honesty and dignity of sharing this beautiful expression of your soul's body is the key. It is called unconditional love. Unconditional love is a power so strong in the universe that it can truly move mountains. Unconditional love is different from falling in love. Think of the word falling. Do you like falling off your bike or your rollerblades? Do you like falling when you are snowboarding? No! You fall when you are learning these skills, but the object is not to fall. It is to become proficient, which means being capable and skilled. So why are we supposed to fall in love time after time? Does this mean we're not learning from our mistakes, that we keep making the same mistakes over and over? If this were true in snowboarding or rollerblading, you would soon give up because it would become too painful. Going to the doctor to repair broken bones not only hurts, but it also gets expensive—and so does divorce."

"But Grandmother," I blurted out, trying to understand what she was teaching me, "I fell down a lot when learning how to rollerblade, and thank God for a foot of powder snow when I learned how to snowboard. I didn't just fall, I bounced down the slope, but it was part of learning. I expected to fall. Isn't it the same in learning how to be in a relationship?"

"You have your ups and downs in any relationship," Grandmother said, "and you learn from your mistakes. Eventually, you want a relationship where you can snowboard down the hill together without crashing into each other. When you reach the bottom, you laugh at the skill with which you navigated the bumps and hug each other with joy in your hearts. That's a good relationship."

"So how do I learn to love and not get hurt?" I asked. "How do I practice and learn from my mistakes? I imagine I'm going to have more than one boyfriend in high school, and maybe a few more when I get into college. I don't see myself meeting the man I'm going to live with forever at sixteen. Maybe some people do, but not many stay married. Most of my friend's parents are divorced. I'm not sure that forever is even real. Maybe some couples love each other their entire lives. I hope so."

Grandmother sighed and smiled warmly. "You may get a broken heart— or three! But that will be because you didn't apply what you learned from one relationship to the next. You don't want to jump from one to the next too quickly. Remember to breathe and slow down. You need to take time to consider what your piece of the puzzle is that caused the breakup. For many, it hurts too much to be honest with themselves and admit where they were wrong, so they keep making the same mistakes over and over, blaming the other person for the breakup. That's why we have such a high divorce rate in this country. People are not learning from their mistakes. They just blame the other person and move on."

I definitely didn't want to follow that pattern!

"That's one of the reasons you're seeking to learn about sex and relationships, isn't it? So, *when* you break up, not *if*," she emphasized, "you should consider the time in between relationships as an opportunity to develop your relationship skills."

"I could think of it like snowboarding. I'm just learning new skills," I said.

"Yes, otherwise, your hurts will follow you like a sick puppy. If you keep that sick, dysfunctional puppy around because you feel sorry for it, you are feeling sorry for yourself."

She explained to me that most people deny their dysfunction until the pain gets so great that there's no denying that something is wrong. That's when many people get divorced or become physically ill—especially if they abstain from sex. Grandmother said that's when people go to counseling— when it's almost too late.

My head was spinning with all this information. It was what I wanted, but there were so many new concepts to wrap my brain around.

"What does abstain mean?" I asked.

"It means an individual is not having sex with any lovers, friends, or even with themselves, which we call self-pleasuring, but masturbation is the common word for it. You know, playing with yourself."

I thought I was ready for this sex talk, but when I heard Grandmother just blurt this out, I felt my cheeks heat up. I thought of all the times I had rocked myself to sleep with my pillow between my legs, even when I was a little girl. It just felt good.

Grandmother noticed I was blushing. She quietly asked, "Do you want me to continue, Sage?" Her face was soft, and the love I felt coming from her made me feel safe.

"Yes, Grandmother, please. I want to learn, even if I feel shy sometimes."

"The word masturbation is so cold and impersonal," said Grandmother gently. "It doesn't create the beauty of the experience, the sacredness of loving yourself." Then Grandmother made a face that looked like she had just eaten a sour lemon. "Masturbation! What a word. No wonder you are taught that you will go blind, or boys will grow hair on the palms of their hands if they touch themselves." She told me to remember the term self-pleasuring instead. "This is a much more poetic expression of Great Spirit's wisdom."

Grandmother's face turned serious, and I could tell I needed to pay attention to what came next.

"I know you've studied history in school. You probably learned about the pilgrims coming over from England and settling in the Americas. Do you know why they were called Puritans?

"I haven't a clue Grandmother."

"Here's a good story. The Pilgrims were the true forefathers who brought liberty and freedom to the New World. In 1530, William Tyndale translated the Bible from ancient Greek, Hebrew, and Aramaic into English in England. This was the first time Bibles were printed, and they were used only by the priests for their sermons.

"Gradually, some of the commoners obtained copies of the Scriptures and began to study them and question the Church and the King's rule.

"Although the Church, Queen Mother, and the King were under the rule of the King of Kings, Jesus Christ, the Puritans studied the Bible secretly for fear of being caught, jailed, or beheaded. Anyone caught possessing an English translation Bible was labeled a Puritan and persecuted.

"Today we would call them Patriots. They wanted freedom of worship for all the people. They decided the only way they could have this freedom was to leave England. They tried to escape to Holland first but were betrayed, caught, and jailed. They tried a second time, and only the men made it to Holland. Their ship was the only one out of two hundred that wasn't lost at sea due to a horrific storm. They prayed. I bet your school never taught you this truth!"

"You're right. Please keep going. This is amazing."

"The wives and children were again caught, and it was a year before they could go to Holland to join their husbands and fathers. After twelve years of living and worshipping in a country that didn't allow them to work regular jobs, and seeing their children work to help provide food for their families, they decided to return to their beloved England. From there, they hired ships to take them to the New World, which we now know as America. One ship had to return when it was damaged in a storm. The only ship that made it was the Mayflower. Of the one hundred twenty-one Puritans, fifty-seven lived, and sixty-four died in the violent Atlantic seas.

"It was winter when they reached the new world. The women slept on board the ship, and the men slept on the frozen ground laden with snow. They had no tents or sleeping bags. They had to build shelter and find food. When the ship's captain insisted on leaving, he begged them to return to England with him. They all refused. They had made a covenant with God to find a land where they could worship with freedom, where all men were created equal, and they could follow the guidance of the Bible.

"The women slept on the ground, on top of their children, to protect them from the winter cold. Most of the women died, but the children lived.

"These are the founding mothers and fathers of this country. They established the country of liberty and freedom that we have today. The Pilgrims won their freedom without bloodshed but with perseverance and faith, and they left a monument in Plymouth that still stands today. On that monument are the instructions, words, and statues that tell the story of how the people can fight against tyranny when and if our beloved country should come under attack.

"In that era, the body's naturalness was controlled and repressed. Sex was for one thing only—making babies. Survival and establishing a home that could survive the next winter took top priority.

"The pilgrim's beliefs, which still exist in some religions today, are sexually repressive. Sexual ignorance and inequality were woven into the modern blanket of society, but the pendulum has now begun to swing too far the other way. This, too, is off-balance.

"There is a sacredness in sexuality. I suggest you have a personal conversation with Great Spirit and speak to Him directly. After all, you are loved and provided for by Him."

Grandmother winked at me, and I felt warmth in my belly. I was not wrong. There was something more to sex.

"So, little one, your questions are good," Grandmother continued, "and the time is now because you are asking them now. You can learn from the mistakes your parents and the generations before them made. You'll make some mistakes of your own, but that's normal. They don't need to be as large, and you can learn quickly from them with the right tools to guide you."

"I am so excited I could jump up and down right now. I'm not crazy! I can learn about sacred sexuality, and you are the one to teach me!"

Then as fast as I was excited, I felt my balloon burst, hitting the ground with a hard splat. "Grandmother, my parents fell in love. Do they have a chance to be truly happy?"

Grandmother looked at me sternly. "First of all, I knew your parents when they first met. They lived in California and came to one of my Spiritual Sexuality workshops here in New Mexico. That was a long time ago. They got the teachings and chose to love each other as an act of power. They jumped into love consciously. They did not fall in love. In their ceremony, which I led, they vowed to love each other as an act of power. To support each other to change, grow, and become the best they could be, even if it meant separating because they had different things to learn on different paths that over their life together could require them to be apart. They vowed never to give their power away to the other, but to empower self, life, and others."

Grandmother was on a roll, and I didn't want to interrupt her. I saw my parents in my mind as she continued.

"Relationships are about giving, not what you get. Even when they got upset with each other and didn't like each other, they knew that loving unconditionally meant they were willing to deal with confrontation, rock the boat, and speak the unspeakable. They also vowed that if ever they stopped loving each other, they would separate with dignity. They would never hate each other. No, Sage, your parents came together in a good medicine way. They, and your adopted clan aunts and uncles, have studied the shamanic medicine path for many years. We are your medicine family."

I could tell there was more to their story, and Grandmother was telling me right now to wake up.

"After you were born and had a few years of being a beach baby, they decided to move to New Mexico." Grandmother took a sip of water. "That California trip to Flatrock, New Mexico was difficult, but they are happy now. Flatrock has become your home. Life places demands on them—working, raising a child—it's difficult to find the time for the important things. The little things that matter."

"Like, making love?" I wondered out loud, feeling like I was putting some pieces together.

"Yes, like making spiritual sexual magick," Grandmother said with a twinkle in her eye. "Your parents need more training, that's all. You have to be a warrior in today's world to be a person of power. Remember, any relationship, but especially a sexual relationship, is what you give to it. Good communication, honesty, integrity, dignity, passion, and spirituality are what make a good sex life and a good friendship."

"Oh, at last," I said, "we're talking about sex."

"We have never stopped talking about sex. The problem is you think sex is just about having intercourse, a man and a woman doing the in-and-out thing."

Grandmother made a circle with two fingers and poked another finger in and out.

"Grandmother!" I exclaimed as I felt my cheeks get hot again.

"That's what most folks think. If that were true, then the world as we know it would never have been created."

Chapter 2

What Does Our Creation Story Have To Do With Sex?

Grandmother leaned against her king-size bed and got a faraway look on her face. "You need to hear our Creation Story."

"What are you talking about, Grandmother?" Once again, I felt bewildered. *How can this be helping me learn about sex?*

I think she read my mind because she said, "Remember, a story paints pictures and stimulates your imagination. There are many stories within a story. If you are awake enough, you may hear the hidden story, and the hidden story is about sex."

She had my attention again.

"A good way to be awake for this kind of story is to close your eyes and dream with the story."

Grandmother asked me to help spread another beautiful medicine blanket with red and blue designs on the floor. She said this would help me travel into the story.

"Lie down," she told me.

I shot her a look, and my eyebrows knitted in frustration. "Grandmother, you are so confusing at times. You tell me to be awake, which means sit up straight, open my eyes, and listen hard."

"That's what you're taught in school," Grandmother said. "Do you like school?"

"It's okay but boring."

"That's because you're not being taught to participate—to free think," Grandmother said. "You are taught to memorize and sit up straight. True learning is in the magickal places of the heart, with the mind being curious and going on adventures of discovery. That's where you find the truth. It's not fed to you like pabulum."

"Do you mean baby food pabulum?"

"Yes. They treat you like babies and then wonder why you get so angry. Don't get me started on the school system. Let's just say that when you embrace your sexuality, you'll be a free human being. No one can tell you what Great Spirit says because you'll have a direct relationship with *The Everything*. Every time you have a high-level orgasm, you open the door a little wider, so you can hear Great Spirit talking to you directly. These are teachings that are given in the Level One Spiritual Sexuality workshop. See, you are learning about sex, just not in the way you thought."

Looking deep into Grandmother's eyes, I realized she was teaching me what I needed to learn, but I couldn't stop myself from asking, "Grandmother, a high-level orgasm? Is that like the one Great Grandmother and Great Grandfather had that created the universe?"

"Yes, little one."

"Can humans have high-level orgasms? Are there low-level orgasms, and does anything happen with them?"

"Yes, Sage, humans can have high, middle, low, or even lose energy with their orgasms. The good thing is that any orgasm is better than none. Orgasms keep you connected to your higher self, your soul, and your freedom—even if you fall fast asleep after having a low-level orgasm."

"What about middle-level orgasms?" I asked.

"Yes, middle level comes with following the energy—no script or pattern, being spontaneous. Most people in the world have zero level, where they lose energy and are exhausted after their lovemaking, but we'll talk about that later."

Later, I echoed in my mind. If Grandmother said later, she kept her word. *But how much later*, I wondered. I guessed there was so much to learn I'd be back many times. I had very little patience. I wanted to know about sex now!

Grandmother was speaking to me, pulling me out of my silent complaining. She was preparing me to learn in the old way, the dreaming awake way. This was not a schoolroom, and I was not getting graded. I wanted knowledge, and Grandmother was showing me how to listen to the story inside the story.

"The creation story is an important part of your training about sacred sexuality. Close your eyes, lie down, and relax. Let your mind paint the pictures. Feel the story of life and experience the story inside the story.

"Sage, this creation story comes from ancient teachings. All cultures have ancient stories. Let them teach you."

As I was lying down, shifting my body to get comfortable, Grandmother went to her medicine shelf and brought out a beautiful old shawl with shades of purple and blue flaring into a spinning star. She opened it and swung it around her shoulders. Her eyes softened, and her body relaxed as she sat on the floor next to me.

I closed my eyes.

Her voice was soft and gentle as she began. "As *The Everything's* consciousness awakened to the female and male energies within itself, it catalyzed the mind of the winds and conceived consciousness in all things."

Grandmother paused between each new thought to allow it to enter my consciousness and sprout a new green leaf of wisdom.

"It then catalyzed the spirit of the fires and conceived determination of its evolution in all things. *The Everything's* consciousness then catalyzed the life of the waters, the continuous streams of livingness, and finally, it conceived the Earth and the physical and catalyzed all the bodies of the Earth element. That first Sacred Breath brought the feminine energy and the masculine energy together as one, and out of Zero emerged an absolute unity. It is said that within that unity of female and male dance all the powers of the universe."

I imagined the stars and dark spaces between, and I wondered what this lovemaking of the universe looked and felt like. I could hear Grandmother's voice quietly weaving a blanket of words into a landscape of teachings.

"When the ancient ones of this tradition known as the Zero Chiefs explored exactly how and what happened in the beginning, they discovered that the universe, the Great Spirit, speaks to us about the interrelationship of all things through mathematics. The numbers zero to twenty represent *The Everything*. Zero is the potential for all forms of all things. It is a system to understand the order in the universe. It is a way for us to understand all our dances of all lifetimes, within all dreams."

I was drifting farther and farther away on Grandmother's voice. I felt myself floating as if on a large, white, thick cloud.

I vaguely heard Grandmother say, "We are spiritual beings living in a human body continuing to express this sacred sexual union birthing evolution to this day. We create a cohesive union, and the sexual soul force energy is realized. We become one with *The Everything*."

I whispered to myself, "One with *The Everything*, I am one with *The Everything*."

I began hearing ancient voices talking to me, pulling me, reminding me.

I was no longer in Grandmother's bedroom. I opened my eyes and saw a beautiful bright blue sky with giant, billowy clouds.

Did I just travel here on those clouds?

I was warm and comfortable, feeling the sun on my dark skin. I love the smell of my leather dress when the heat of Grandfather Sun softens it against my skin. It feels so good.

What was I experiencing?

Looking around, I saw teepees with tribal symbols painted on the sides. I knew what those symbols meant, but how could I know this? They were scattered over the land with a wide, slow-moving river flowing off in the distance. Adults and children were walking, talking, and laughing. They were all wearing leather buckskin clothing, decorated with beadwork and colored designs. I thought I was dreaming, but everything was so clear and real.

A tall, handsome, elderly man with long braided gray hair and deeply tanned skin looked at me and said, "Dreams with the Wind, are you dreaming again? Remember what they are teaching you in the dream."

I sat up and blinked. *Dreams with the Wind?* I needed to remember what he called me. He knew me. I knew him in my heart. What was the dream teaching me? Was this a dreaming lesson?

I heard the ancient voices saying, *Remember. Remember the sacred natural ways of your sexuality.*

I am remembering the teachings of our ancient ways. I am with my tribe in ancient times.

I could hear Grandmother's voice, but it was like a whisper in my mind.

"In the ancient tribes, young adults were taught about the power of sexuality and the sacredness of sexual union. Whenever one reached puberty, they underwent a special initiation ceremony: a walking vision quest for boys and an earth kiva vision quest for girls. Each young adult was then brought to a council to determine his or her maturity. If they were ready to study the ways of sexual intimacy, then and only then would they begin to work with a highly-trained medicine man or woman who specialized in teaching this ancient knowledge. The young person would study for years with this teacher.

"This doesn't happen in today's society, Sage. We are talking about ancient times."

Ancient times. I am Dreams with the Wind in ancient times.

Grandmother's soft thoughts of knowledge and wisdom continued to flow into me.

"The young initiates studied with their sexual teachers for several years to learn about energy, proper breathing, alignment with another, and honesty—first with themselves before ever being sexual with another. When the time was right, and they had proven their maturity, they would engage sexually without guilt, blame, or shame. They learned from a teacher who truly cared about them and their development in all aspects: emotionally, mentally, physically, spiritually, and sexually. The medicine person taught them how to direct their sexual energy for they were the next generation. How they learned would be passed on from one generation to another. The Sacred Hoop was strong, and the future seven generations were guided from Sacred Law."

I was physically in Grandmother's room, but these teachings poured through me as I dreamed myself back in time. I longed for this knowledge. I was sitting up, but not seeing people or tepees. My eyes were open, but I was looking deep inside myself.

The ancient ones were talking to me directly now.

You will be initiated and learn many valuable lessons. You will learn the beauty, power, and importance of the balance of the male and female energy inside yourself and with another. You will learn how to merge this energy through breath and, over time, with touch. You will be taught the Energy Breath which can save your life when your energy is drained during conflict or war. This same breath will teach you the beauty of Great Spirit coursing through your body, bringing you joy and internal passion, awakening your soul to your highest potential. You will learn how to merge your wheels of energy with another's energy wheels, allowing your spirits and souls to merge and become one.

As the ancient voices spoke, I felt my body in a new way. I heard them share more teachings with me. *All of this is taught in a medicine way: sharing, practicing, and experiencing knowledge.*

From a distance, I heard a familiar Grandmother's voice. "There were no books with pictures in them, so how do you think they learned, Sage?"

My name was being called as if from far away, but I couldn't answer. I was Dreams with the Wind, dreaming in another space and time. The blue sky, clouds, and teepees are my home. I looked around, breathing in the beauty of what I loved. I wanted to remember this, no matter what happened. I would always hold this in my soul.

I walked to Soaring Hawk's tepee. She was my clan aunt, and this was a special day. She brushed my hair until it was a shiny, black mane touching my backside. She presented me with a lovely white doeskin dress, beaded and decorated. It was the most beautiful dress I had ever seen. Soaring Hawk gently said she had been working on it all year, waiting for this time. She helped me pull it over my head, sliding it into place. It was soft against my skin. I was ready.

I took a deep breath and reminded myself to breathe slowly. I walked to the elder's teepee and stood outside, waiting to be called in. I thought I would be frightened, but I wasn't. This was the circle of our wisest Grandfathers.

The flap opened, and they motioned me in.

One Grandfather in the circle asked me, "Why do you want to learn the sacred ways of man and woman?"

I stood calmly before them. I knew my answer was important. I had heard stories of girls being denied their requests because they were too immature. They had to wait another whole year. They were told they were not ready for the responsibility of becoming a woman, but I was ready.

I heard myself breathing. *Breathe slowly!* I remembered an elder Grandmother teaching me to breathe slowly and speak from my heart.

"Grandfathers, I hear my breath like the sacred winds. I feel the feminine power as I inhale and the masculine strength as I exhale. I know my body has a force that has not yet awakened, though my moon time brings me into womanhood. Something is missing. The Grandmothers in sacred ceremony have opened the veil to my womb, and its mysteries await me. They have been training me to breathe the life-force energy of the Great Spirit into my womb basket. I have learned the energy breath. I feel the mystery of my body. I am practicing what the Grandmothers showed me. My muscles are strong yet supple. They gave me carved *Tipilis*, representing the different sizes of men, thin and thick, long and short, for me to awaken myself and learn how to work with my *Tupuli* muscles.

"The time to share this mystery and explore it with the masculine is now. I have learned much from the Grandmothers and will continue to sit with and seek counsel from them. They say I am ready to be with a medicine man to teach me about the sacred ways of men and women. My body says I am ready to learn these sacred teachings. I stand before you, respectfully requesting a teacher to learn the ways of a man's body and my body in the Ancient Spiritual Sexuality ways."

In the silence, I heard my breath like the soft winds. I instructed myself to slow down, breathe slowly.

Another Grandfather asked me, "What vision is guiding you? You were two days in the Womb of Grandmother in the sacred *kiva*. What was your vision, little one?"

I closed my eyes for a long moment and dreamed myself back into the kiva, the Womb of Grandmother Earth. The vision came to me, thick with images and feelings.

The earth was rich, and I felt the spirits of the other women who have gone before me and those before them. I felt the womb of every woman on the planet. I knew there were secrets in the wombs of women that many have never discovered. Only a few were privileged to receive the teachings and training beyond a certain level. I felt the call of the elders to take my place with them. I was to learn the hidden knowledge.

I knew it was an honor to be called to this training. Tears welled in my eyes as they had that night in my kiva ceremony when the Grandmothers initiated me into their secret society—or was that just a wish? Could I speak of it now to the Grandfathers? Would they believe me? I took a deep breath as the Grandmothers had taught me.

I spoke quietly, with my eyes looking down. "Grandfathers, the elder Grandmothers called me to work with them to learn the ways of spiritual sexuality. They initiated me into the secret circle of the Yellow Moon Society. I have not heard of these Grandmothers or this society before. If this was only a dream of my lower self, please let me know, and I will seek another vision and return a year from now."

My heart spoke silently to me. I didn't want to wait a year! I was ready to learn now, but if my vision was something I had made up, I would be humbled before this council and come back in a year.

The Grandfathers began talking in low voices to each other. I glanced up and saw excitement as they gestured among themselves. I heard one say, "Never before," and another said, "This is a strong vision." The head of the council asked for silence. "We must confirm this vision with the Grandmother Elder. Running Fox, go get the head Grandmother and politely ask her to join us."

Was there yet another circle above these Grandfathers and Grandmothers that I didn't know about? I wondered.

As I bent my head in prayer and fear, my hair cascaded over my shoulders and face.

The head Grandfather asked the head Grandmother to confirm my vision with the Dreamers Circle. He said to her, "I want there to be no doubt as to the future of this little one before us."

I stood silently, listening to my breath. I felt the winds of time and change enter my lungs and escape again as if time itself were an eternity slipping by me and through me. There was a hopeful feeling coursing through me. I was lost in the kiva, remembering, standing before the Grandfather Circle, waiting for the Grandmother to verify my vision with the Dreamers Circle.

I felt my breath release and listened to its sound.

I was lying on the floor of an unfamiliar space with walls and medicine all around me. I heard a Grandmother calling, "Little one. Sage."

I opened my eyes, and before me sat a Grandmother I felt I knew.

She said again, "So, without books and pictures, how do you think you learned?"

I sat up slowly and looked around. I was confused and unsure where I was. Where was my white doeskin dress? I was wearing strange clothing, but it was my clothing. Looking at the Grandmother again, I recognized Grandmother Spinning Winds and remembered where I was.

I took a deep breath and heard the winds of time flowing into me. From deep inside my *knowing*, I said, "After my vision quest, I went to the Grandfather Circle and asked for permission to work with a medicine man who would teach me the beauty of Sacred Spiritual Sexuality—how to breathe and open my heart space to see the soul of another. We would look without shame at each other's bodies and make love. In time, I would explore others, discovering the beauty and magic in different forms. I was to learn the beauty and sacredness so that I could become a teacher for the next generation, and the Sacred Hoop, teachings from generation to the next, would not be broken."

I looked at Grandmother, tears welling in my eyes and streaming down my face. "The Sacred Hoop has been broken. Grandmother, how did the hoop get broken? What can I do to bring the Sacred Hoop back?"

Grandmother Spinning Winds gathered me in her arms. I felt her tears fall on my face, blending with my own.

She whispered, "You heard the story inside the story. You were there."

"Grandmother, was I accepted into the Yellow Moon Society? Can I still learn the teachings?"

"The teachings are inside you, Wind Dancer. I'll help you remember. You learned much, and it's time to remember."

"Grandmother, you just called me Wind Dancer. Is this my medicine name?"

"Yes, little one. Do you know what you just did? You danced the winds of time. For a moment, time didn't exist for you. You were there *and* here. It was a strong vision, and with your vision comes your medicine name: Wind Dancer. You are to go outside later tonight. Your backyard is fine. Wait until you can see the stars and they can hear you. Announce your new medicine name to the four directions, beginning in the south. Do it this way with a voice of power. 'I am Wind Dancer. This is how I will be known in the universe. I am Wind Dancer. Aho!' Then turn to each direction and repeat it."

We were silent for an eternal moment.

With Grandmother's arms around me, I felt safe and protected. I felt the world opening up to me in a way I had never experienced before. I had touched something magickal. I knew there was magick.

Grandmother said, "Drink some water. It is one of the magickal elements on our planet."

It was as if she were reading my mind. I still didn't know how water could be magickal. I knew we needed it to survive, but magickal? I drank and felt the coolness traveling into my stomach. It reminded me of the cold rivers I had drunk from and swam in, but whether the memory was from another lifetime or the present, I wasn't sure. I shrugged, uncertain and not caring. Something had happened that was beyond my wildest dreams. Dreams with the Wind—my name in that other lifetime.

I was Dreams with the Wind then, and I am Wind Dancer now.

Chapter 3

Ancient Rite of Passage

"We need to take a break," Grandmother said. "Fresh air."

This didn't mean the teachings would stop, only that we would shift our space and allow what had just happened to settle deep inside me. I followed her into the backyard. It was only in the 90s with some puffy white clouds floating over us. We walked around her pool, which had a slide. I still had fun with it, even as a teen. Grandmother enjoyed it, too. She would climb up the ladder and laugh because she'd be nude and as high as the rooftop. Then she'd shriek as she slid into the pool with a great splash.

"Never too old to have fun," she'd say.

We both glanced at the slide. It was calling us to swim and play.

Grandmother looked at me, then at the pool. "One slide, one splash, then the purification lodge needs our attention."

We had our clothes off and were up that ladder fast. We laughed and screamed our way into the cool water. With a big splash, we both took in a mouthful and came up sputtering. I knew Grandmother meant what she said, so we swam to the steps and walked out of the pool. Somehow, I wasn't shy or embarrassed. It's what we've always done together—take off our clothes and jump into the pool. She kept a pile of sarongs on a chair. We each took one and wrapped it around our waists. The breeze felt cool, so we didn't cover up all the way.

Her purification lodge was on the far end of her yard. Orange and grapefruit trees grew high against the wooden fence. The purification lodge was on the far end of her yard, in a yard by itself, about three feet lower than the pool area.

We stood in front of the lodge, dripping wet and refreshed.

The lodge frame made of slender trees stood uncovered. You could see every tree trunk bent to create the lodge, and the tall, thinner trees wrapped around it like a woven basket. I had helped Grandmother make other purification lodges, but I wasn't here for this one. Little did I realize the importance of this lodge when I was growing up. As I looked at it now, I thought, *This is such a beautiful lodge—the Womb of Grandmother Earth, as Grandmother calls it.*

"Something special happened in the building of this lodge," Grandmother said. She told me the story as we stood looking at her lodge.

"I put a call out to my students and apprentices to help. As usual, some folks couldn't help due to work or other obligations. It was all men who showed up to build this lodge." She smiled at me; she liked men.

"The men cut some tall trees that grew next to a river up north. They hauled them down, and we put them in the pool to keep them pliable. They had cut them carefully, in a sacred way, of course. I was with them to be sure of that. As the dance chief, it was my responsibility. Usually, we have a balance of men and women. I was concerned at first. The male-female balance is very important." Her voice became dreamy. "But the men built the lodge with such love and respect, every tree arched and touched the next. The hoops around the lodge were made from fifteen-foot-tall trees. They were strong and bent around the lodge, ringing it with intent and purpose. They built this beautiful Womb of Grandmother Earth. This lodge is still strong after six years of use. This is to be your Rite of Passage ceremonial space."

It was so matter-of-fact that I almost missed what she said. "My Rite of Passage?" I repeated.

"Yes, Sage. You need to learn about life. Your Rite of Passage will help guide you into becoming a young adult."

"I love this lodge," I said. "I feel so safe and calm when I sit in it."

"I will speak to your parents about your Rite of Passage Ceremony. The time has come for you to enter the Womb of Grandmother and seek your vision for this lifetime. There will be no hot rocks to make you sweat. You'll be in ceremony for twenty-four hours, which includes preparing the lodge. You must fast without food from sunrise the day you prepare the lodge to sunrise when you emerge from the lodge, but water is permitted. You will stay inside the lodge from sunset to sunrise.

Your mother and your aunts will help you prepare and cover the lodge—the canvas is heavy. You'll adorn the inside with flowers. I suggest you choose flowers that have a nice fragrance."

I stood in shock as I listened to Grandmother describe my first major ceremony in such a straightforward way. I was learning about sacred sexuality, and I would have a Rite of Passage into womanhood. This made sense. I had to experience this ceremony before I could go before the Elder Circle.

Then I wondered, *Where am I? Which lifetime?*

For a moment, I am Dreams With the Wind facing the Elders Circle, then the vision is gone as Grandmother gently touched my shoulder and centered me.

I asked if she belonged to an elder circle here in Flatrock, or did that just happen in times long ago, like in my dream vision?

She smiled but continued talking about my ceremony. "A special ceremony will take place before you go in. You'll say goodbye to your family members." She gazed straight into my eyes. "This is a death and rebirthing ceremony. You'll enter the Womb of Grandmother as a girl and leave her womb as a young woman. We'll have a celebration when you come out. This is an honoring of your womanhood, a gifting from others to you, and you to others, as well as a sharing of food from all the worlds of Grandmother Earth."

I could hardly believe my ears. Grandmother said I was to have a Rite of Passage in the old way. Well, sort of old way. I couldn't go back in time, could I?

I could hardly wait to run home and tell my mother and father. I was so excited. I knew there'd be lots of preparation. I needed to sit quietly and feel what gifts would be appropriate. I wanted Grandmother Bebee, my mother's mother, to be there. She would have to come from Southern California. I liked her. We always had fun together. She was very outspoken and flirtatious for a woman in her 80s.

All my grandfathers had died, but I knew Grandmother's partner, Grandfather Strong Bear, would come. He had adopted me as his granddaughter, just as I had adopted him. I wanted my uncles and aunts to come, too.

My head was swirling, my breath was fast, and I blurted out, "Grandmother, when can we get started? What do I need to do? Will this help to heal the Sacred Hoop?"

She said, "The honoring of the generations, from grandparent to parent, parent to child, will be a part of this needed healing. Like others, you are taking your place in the hoop of time. Yes, it will help heal the Sacred Hoop.

"You will be the teacher of the generations to follow. The sacred teachings will continue from the one to the many. The generations will once again gift the next with wisdom and joy. The Sacred Hoop is the laughter, innocence, and curiosity of the children evolving to the wisdom and knowledge of the elders."

I heard the words, but I was so excited, I didn't understand all she had said. It seemed that Grandmother was talking to herself as much as to me.

"Tell your mother and father that we need to have a medicine talk to properly plan this sacred event."

Hugging her tightly, I said, "Grandmother Spinning Winds, you dance in my heart, *quaheystamaha*." I gave her the tobacco and the small box with the earrings I had made. As she opened it, she gasped. The sun glinted off the tiny cut beads and sparkled in her hand. I couldn't have asked for a better response.

"They are beautiful," she said, turning them in the light. "You must love to bead to make such a beautiful, intricate pattern. You've learned well. I am proud of you, Granddaughter. I'll wear them at your Rite of Passage."

"Thank you, Grandmother. I can't wait to go home and tell my parents. I'll let them know you want to have a medicine talk with them, and they will call you."

I never realized how slow time can move when one is excited for an event to get here. It was months away, yet I knew how fast time passed when there was a lot to do.

As I turned to leave, I saw the slide. I looked back at Grandmother, and she understood. One dip was enough. There was something more important for the moment.

* * *

I don't know if I ran faster to Grandmother's house or back home. It was more than I had hoped. So much happened; it felt like I had been at Grandmother's house for a week, but less than two and a half hours had passed. How did she do that? She always played with time, stepping between the spaces and taking me with her.

I got lost in her voice and eyes. It usually happened when we were in her medicine room. Time would stop for us, and we had all the time we needed. I still had the whole day to do all the other things that I wanted and needed to do.

Grandmother just winked at me when I asked about it. "You'll learn someday that time doesn't exist except in the minds and contracts of mankind. I just make different contracts. That's all."

It sounded simple enough, but I couldn't do it yet. Grandmother always said that lots of things are simple but not easy. I still needed to think on that

28

one. I wasn't sure what she meant.

I burst through the door. "Hey, Mom! Where are you?" I immediately knew she was in the kitchen. She was making oatmeal-cinnamon raisin cookies, and the whole house smelled of fresh-baked cookies. We all loved them.

"In here, Sage," she answered.

I walked to the fridge and grabbed a bottle of cold water and two cookies.

Mom was usually waiting for me when I returned from a medicine talk with Grandmother. I think she got as excited as I did. Grandmother always told me something that was also meant for Mom and Dad. Between bites of my yummy warm cookie, I said, "Mom, I'm ready to burst, but I want to talk to you and Dad at the same time."

She grabbed a cookie and sat next to me.

"Dad will be home soon. If you can wait, Hun, I will hang in there, too."

Looking at the clock, she said, "Sometimes Dad gets home later than he said he would."

I could see we were both ready to burst—Mom with curiosity and me with my need to share. Chewing on my last bite of cookie and taking a swig of water to wash it down, I blurted out, "Grandmother said it is time for my Rite of Passage."

"Aha," she said. "I knew it was coming. I had a funny feeling when you left for your medicine talk that today was the day."

We hugged, and I felt Mom holding her little girl, yet trying to let go and see the young woman I was becoming. It was a difficult thing. She held me tight as her love poured into me. If I had any doubts about her love for me, which I sometimes did—especially when I got mad at her—there was no doubt now. I knew my parents were trying to raise me the best they could, but sometimes, they just didn't know how.

"Mom, I have more to share. I touched magick today. I remembered a past life, and Grandmother is going to teach me about spiritual sexuality."

"Whoa, slow down, girl!" She winked at me.

I wonder if she learned that from Grandmother Spinning Winds, but it worked. I took a deep breath. I saw Mom doing the same thing. "Okay, I'll wait till Dad gets home to tell you the rest."

"I am very excited for you, Sage, and I'm proud of you. Yes, let's wait for your dad."

We both took another cookie and smiled at each other.

* * *

As I waited for Dad, I decided to get my journal and go into the backyard to write down everything I could remember. This usually helped calm me down. I sat under my favorite pine tree. I was writing as fast as I could to capture everything that had happened. Then I stopped and looked around me. I *felt* the big pine tree I was resting my back on—her branches high above me.

"Hello, Grandmother Pine," I said out loud. "I'm here again."

I was thankful for the big Grandmother Pine in our backyard. I could see the pinecones weighing down her branches. Her pine needles were all around me, like wild hair, giving off a fragrance that always reminded me of the mountains. I loved the mountains and pine trees. They were my favorite.

Our pool water seemed unusually blue, and the sky sought an audience to witness its grandeur. I was in love. I felt so expanded. I saw the bigness of everything around me and the details of the smallest pine needle. If this was love, I liked it. I felt special and yet part of everything. Everything was special, and I was a part of *The Everything.*

I wrote in my journal: Ah, Grandmother Pine, thank you for calming me.

My two cats, Ahnay and Kachina, came running out from under a bush and tackled each other. I wished I could do martial arts the way they did. Sauntering over to me, they rubbed themselves against my legs. I reached down and ran my fingers through their soft fur, down their backs, and scratched the base of their tails. They both flopped down and rolled over for more loving and rubbing. So much for writing; my hands were busy. When the cats had their fill, they darted off.

I wished I could get my needs met so easily—getting what I wanted without even talking. Maybe that's what Grandmother meant when she said there were a lot of things that were simple, but not easy.

I reread what I had just written.

Dad slid the glass doors open, and Mom followed him outside. "Sage, I hear you have some good news for us."

They sat down next to me. We had many family talks under this big Grandmother Pine Tree. They told me it was one of the reasons they bought this house, along with the orange, lemon, grapefruit, and tangerine trees.

When I was little and upset, they would take me out to the pine tree and lay with me on Grandmother Earth. It always seemed to calm me. When I got older, they taught me to come out and speak to Grandmother Pine Tree, putting my arms around her and giving my tears or anger to her. It always made me feel better. One day I asked them, "Doesn't it hurt the tree for me to always be giving her my tears, frustrations, and anger?"

"No," they said together.

"To you, they are bad feelings," Dad explained, "but to her, they are energy. She uses them as fertilizer. Energy is energy. You can learn to turn it around and use these feelings for something better if you want to. You don't need to be bothered every time one of your friends gets mad at you, or you don't understand something and it upsets you."

"Do you remember when we told you to ask this old Grandmother Pine Tree the secret of turning shit into fertilizer and growing flowers?" Mom asked.

"Yes! I thought it was funny that you talked like that. But, Mom, it got me to listen, and I started asking Grandmother Pine Tree to teach me how to turn my shit into fertilizer, just like you said." Smiling, I said, "At first, I talked to the tree just so I could say the word shit. As I got older, I realized the word wasn't so bad, and this sweet old tree has taught me. So, to help me change my attitude, I have hugged this tree a lot over my sixteen years. To be honest, there have been times when I've hugged this tree because I've been upset at my own stupidity."

My parents laughed and Mom said, "Yes, we understand that only too well. So glad you discovered it on your own."

My latest tree talk was about my raging hormones. That's when I decided to visit Grandmother Spinning Winds. It was pretty good advice from this Grandmother Pine Tree.

"Hey, girl," Dad said, "do you have some good news for us?"

"So, Mom clued you in?"

He looked at me with such pride that I didn't know which one of us would burst with excitement, but Dad was good about waiting for me to share.

"It's time for me to have my Rite of Passage into adulthood." Beaming, I shared about my time with Grandmother Spinning Winds. I told them about my medicine talk, my vision, and how I touched magick with Grandmother's story.

"Oh, and best of all," I said, "Grandmother gave me my medicine name, Wind Dancer. I have to announce it to the universe tonight."

"That's a powerful name with many meanings," Mom said.

"Grandmother said to call her so you can plan my ceremony properly. I have lots of medicine gifts to make and invitations to send out. Will you help me, Mom? I want my aunts and uncles to share this with me. Do you think they will think this is weird? Will they come?"

"Sweetie," Dad said, "our family is very open and spiritual in our own way. What about your clan aunts and uncles who have adopted you in ceremony? They would all be excited to share this with you. We have purified together in the lodge and even gone on camping medicine journeys. You know, Sage, some of them have done the Spiritual Sexuality training, too. They would be delighted to share this Rite of Passage Ceremony with you. Don't forget about Grandma Bebee."

"Oh, I would never forget to invite her. I like Grandma Bebee. She's so outspoken and funny."

"Is there anyone else you can think of off the top of your head?" Dad asked.

"Of course, I want Grandfather Strong Bear to be there."

"Sage, there's something you haven't thought about. What about boys your own age and girlfriends, too?" Mom asked.

Her question stunned me. "You're right. I haven't even thought of it. I'm not sure I want boys at my Rite of Passage. I have no trouble with wanting some of my girlfriends, but what would the guys think? I mean, I want to learn about sex, but this is spinning me out! I have to think about it, maybe talk to Grandmother again about why they need to be at my ceremony."

"Sage, remember the story that Grandmother Spinning Winds shared with you of tribal times? There is no shame or embarrassment when a young woman begins her moon blood flow. After her vision quest, as a part of the celebration, she stands outside her teepee dressed in her new white buckskin dress, and the young men of the tribe bring gifts and show off for her on their ponies. In a way, it's saying, 'When you are older and looking for a mate, please consider me.' I don't know how Grandmother will create it for you in today's society, but Wind Dancer, she'll want eligible men at your Rite of Passage."

The expression on my face must have expressed my inner voice saying, *Oh, no! I feel trapped.*

What helped was hearing my mother speak my medicine name, Wind Dancer, for the first time. It was so beautiful. My eyes filled with tears. When I looked at my mother, she smiled.

I turned to my dad. "Father," I whispered.

He reached out his hand, and I placed my hand in his. "Your medicine name is beautiful, just like my little, uh, daughter." I saw him catch himself to honor this change, which he knew was coming but was not quite prepared for.

I thought this Rite of Passage was as much for my parents as it was for me.

"Mom, Dad, I'm a little bit scared to have eligible young men come to my Rite of Passage."

We came together in a family hug beneath the big Grandmother Pine Tree. I felt secure in their arms and knew I would be all right with their love and support.

Strengthened, I straightened up, and we all released each other.

"Maybe some of my male friends will like it. Maybe they will want a Rite of Passage, too. We could start a new fad from a very old tradition. I'm going to ask Grandmother if this could heal the Sacred Hoop that has been broken."

"Sleep on it, Hon," Dad said. "It's a lot to take in. You will know the right decision for yourself."

I slept on it for a few days. As much as I wanted the ceremony, it took me a while to get my head around it.

One evening, after four or five days, I told them I was ready to go forward—boys and all. "Actually," I shared sheepishly, "I cheated a bit today in school. I talked to some of my guy friends. They thought it was cool that I'm having a Rite of Passage and doing a vision quest in the purification lodge."

Mom and Dad looked at each other and smiled.

"Go on, Sage," Mom said.

We were at the dinner table, so after swallowing a bite of potato, I said, "They want to know if they can do a vision quest, too. I told them that boys have to go out by themselves into the woods or mountains for twenty-four hours or more, with no food or water and only a knife and a wool medicine blanket. I was sharing the old way with them, maybe to make it sound tough. Shane, Cody, and Michael decided they would let me go through with mine first."

Mom and Dad laughed and continued to eat their pork chops and broccoli. I took another bite and kept talking.

"Shane was the only one who truly seemed interested—almost excited. He told me his father takes him camping and teaches him to hunt and fish, and basic survival skills, so I think he would be more prepared to go without food and water."

Dad smiled and nodded his approval.

"Mom, Dad, I have to admit, I'm relieved they don't think it's dumb. They're excited for me and want to come to the ceremony."

I finished my dinner while Mom and Dad talked. Then I helped with the dishes.

The next day, Mom and I had our work cut out for us—good thing it was a weekend.

After my favorite breakfast of bacon, eggs, and an English muffin, we created a Rite of Passage invitation on the computer. We sent it out to everyone except Grandma Bebee, who didn't use a computer. I mailed hers that day. September was quickly sliding by. October would be here in no time, and my ceremony was in December.

Mom and Dad had their medicine talk with Grandmother Spinning Winds. They shared some of it with me, but some things were to be a surprise.

I got busy making my medicine gifts. My clan aunts and uncles would like something with my beading on it. Grandmother had taught me how to do peyote three-drop stitch. Each gift would be personal and last a lifetime.

I would bead feathers. Grandmother taught me to wrap the feather quill in red cloth, then leather. The final touch was to bead them. The red cloth represented the bird's blood, and the leather was symbolic of the skin. The beadwork was their beautiful plumage. The designs and colors of the beads were my choices—something unique for each person. I loved making the lightning bolt pattern. It was fun, but it took a long time—especially when I made a mistake—but it was worth it. I started beading that morning.

Taking a break from my deep thoughts and beading, I yelled, "Mom!"

"Yes, Sage," she yelled back.

"Are you sure doing my Rite of Passage in December is a good idea? It can be pretty cold in December, which is okay. I like a cold holiday season."

Mom walked into the front room. She looked at me lovingly and said, "I would rather it is a bit colder than burning hot for your ceremony. We picked the first week in December because it will still be sunny. The lodge will heat up during the day, keeping you warmer at night. You'll have your medicine blanket and sleeping bag for warmth. Grandma Bebee lives in California, so traveling here is inexpensive between Thanksgiving and Christmas holidays."

Changing the topic, I said, "With any luck, by the end of December, we'll have snow for a white Christmas. I love the snow for bundling up and skiing. It's been over a year since we've gone skiing."

With a deep sigh, Mom said, "We need to plan a ski trip and invite one of your friends to join us, but not this year."

We laughed together, knowing that my Rite of Passage Ceremony was keeping us over-the-top busy. I spent all my spare time after school and on the weekends making my medicine gifts. Mom had invited my clan aunts to come and help organize the ceremony. I thought we could have waited until after Halloween, but Mom likes to have things planned out. So, I let myself get excited as the doorbell rang and my aunts started coming through the door. I hugged and thanked them for helping. We all sat down around the table, and they jumped right in.

"We're planning to join you early in the morning on the day of your ceremony," Aunt Kathy said. "We'll help you cover the lodge and weave flowers in the roof when the lodge is covered."

Aunt Amy said, "What type of flowers would you like, Wind Dancer?"

I loved hearing my medicine name. "Flowers that have a nice fragrance. Roses from our front yard, especially the red ones. I also love carnations. They smell spicy."

"All right, roses from the garden and carnations from the store," Aunt Amy sing-songed.

My Aunt Amy sang and played guitar. I liked listening to her sing.

Mom said, "Next comes the menu for the celebration feast afterward. We need all the food groups represented: fruits, grain, meat, and dairy. Let's have everyone pitch in and make special dishes. Do we know how many people are coming, Aunt Kathy? You're keeping track, right?"

"Absolutely. I'll let you know when it gets closer to the time."

It was becoming more real! The menu was coming together, and everyone would bring something.

Soon, I would enter my Rite of Passage.

Chapter 4

What If Nothing Happens?

October came and went. It was fun giving out candy to the little kids, but I decided not to go to the Halloween party I was invited to. I was beginning to get nervous.

I made a date to see Grandmother for a much-needed medicine talk.

"Grandmother, just let me get my questions out about my time in the lodge."

"Okay, Sage, go for it."

"What if nothing happens? What if I just sit in the lodge, seeking a vision for my life, and nothing happens? What would that mean? Or worse, what if I sleep the whole time from being so excited and not being able to sleep the night before? Or what if something does happen, like a vision, and I can't live up to it? Do I have to tell everyone what my vision is? Can I just tell you, Grandmother? What about my parents? Will everything change at home? Will my parents treat me more like an adult? After all, I'll still be the same age, just a day older. What could make such a difference by doing a Rite of Passage?"

"Sage, take a deep breath and slow down," she reminded me. "Drop down to your womb, that magickal space for women. The answers are inside you. Trust yourself and stay open to the guidance of Great Spirit. The night before your ceremony, if you need to fall asleep, ask Great Spirit to help you."

Then she explained that when I was in my ceremony, I should let myself listen to the smallest of voices guiding me.

"Spirit doesn't yell in your ear. It whispers to see if you are listening to your inner goofy dialogue or something higher." She also reminded me that I had already traveled the winds of time in this room. "The Womb of Grandmother, the purification lodge, is even more powerful," she said, penetrating this *knowing* in me.

I felt it deep in my heart and womb. "Thank you, Grandmother," I said softly. "I feel calm—at least for now." I reached out for her, and we hugged.

We were moving through November. School activities and homework never stopped, but everything was falling into place. My friends asked me if I was getting excited. Some thought my ceremony was weird; others thought it was cool. The ones I invited said they wanted to see a Rite of Passage. None of them had ever gone through one or even knew what it was, but they were my friends and wanted to be there for me.

I invited my best friends Susie, Andrea, Shane, Cody, and Michael. When Shane asked me how I felt, I told him I was getting nervous. I didn't know what to expect or what others expected of me.

"You don't always know what's going to happen in life," Shane said. "So just go for it."

I liked that. *Just go for it. Don't worry, just do it.* Sometimes Shane was pretty smart. I liked his attitude. He was fun to hang out with.

I love the months of October, November, and December. I had been so consumed with school, making my medicine gifts, and my Rite of Passage that planning Thanksgiving had become a second thought. Mom and I usually planned it together.

Turkey Day decorations had been in the stores for weeks. It was a quick change from Halloween candy and costumes to frozen turkeys, paper gobblers, and pilgrims in the windows.

One weekend, Mom and I were grocery shopping at our Natural Foods.

"Hey, Mom, what are we doing for Thanksgiving this year?"

As she picked up the big organic turkey she had ordered, she said, "I wondered when you were going to ask. I know you love the holidays. What would you like to do this year?"

Pondering for a minute, I said, "Since we are having everyone over for my Rite of Passage so soon after Thanksgiving, doing something small or going to someone else's house with food to share might be nice. We can't go to California to be with Grandma Bebee because I have too much beading work to do, and she'll be coming here soon after. What do you think, Mom?"

"I bought this big turkey because we all love the leftovers. I'm fine with a small dinner at home or going to someone else's house. We'll cook this beautiful bird, and you can help with the stuffing. We can freeze most of it for sandwiches down the road. When we get home, let's ask your dad what he'd like to do. I'm leaning toward sharing time with friends at their home."

"Me, too. Creating two feasts within weeks of each other is too much."

After we unloaded the car and put the groceries away, I heard Mom call to Dad. "Rod, come and sit with us for a few minutes. We need your input about Thanksgiving."

Mother shared our thoughts, and it was an easy decision for Dad.

"We need to share Thanksgiving with one of our friends and save the turkey for the Rite of Passage feast. Let's cut down on our workload. There'll be more to do than we realize."

Before we could get up from the table, Mom's phone rang.

She answered, and after a moment, she smiled. "Yes, Kathy, we'd love to join you. You must have caught our thoughts because we were just discussing it. Let me know what we can bring. All right, love you, too."

"I knew it was Aunt Kathy," I said.

"So did I," Dad said, and we laughed.

When the day came for us to give thanks for all that Great Spirit has provided for us, I was ready to relax and leave my beading work at home. The house overflowed with my aunts and uncles and their kids. After eating too much, we went for a walk in the cool evening breeze.

As the sun began to set, I noticed that the last fall leaves were clinging to the trees, reminding me that I, too, was clinging to my last few days of childhood. Just as spring would mean new life for these trees, my right of passage would see a new beginning for me also. This was a happy Thanksgiving indeed.

* * *

My Rite of Passage was now seven days away. I told my mom it was taking forever, yet I felt rushed. How could that be?

"Sage, set your intention. Do you want time to slow down or speed up?"

"I want it to slow down. I have my medicine gifts made, and Dad helped me get gifts for Shane, Cody, and Michael, but I still feel like I'm missing something."

"You still have seven days to prepare. Next Friday is the eve of your ceremony. Don't count Friday."

"Oh, my gosh, I have six days."

That week moved slowly, just like I intended. I was in class every day. I did my homework and put the finishing touches on my gifts. I placed them carefully in boxes or bags. No wrapping paper for these. Before I knew it, Friday evening had arrived, and we were sitting down to an early dinner.

It was quieter than normal.

"Mom, Dad, I can't believe it's Friday night. After dinner, will you sit with me under Grandmother Pine? I need your support, and I want to talk. The sun is setting, and it's beautiful outside."

"Leave the dishes," Mom said. "Let's catch the crack between the worlds."

After going outside, we uttered a few oohs and aahs at the red, pink, and orange sunset.

"Everything's in place," Mom said. "Your aunts are going to meet you early tomorrow morning at Grandmother's house, and the men have something special they are going to do, as well."

"What is it?" I asked, my curiosity getting the better of me.

"Hey, Hon," Dad said, "the surprise is a part of your ceremony. Just relax. We men don't need to be there early."

"They're the lucky ones," Mom teased. "They don't have to get up at zero dark thirty, before the crack of dawn."

Dad faked a yawn. "Yes, it's nice being a man."

"Sometimes," Mom said.

When they teased each other like this, I knew everything was going well between them. They were happy and not stressed out. We talked as the colors of the sky deepened, but we fell quiet as the night sky darkened.

Mom pointed and said, "Star light, star bright, first star I see tonight. I wish I may, I wish I might, have the wish I wish tonight."

We laughed, and I made a silent wish.

"Sage, it's plenty warm on this lovely desert night. Let's go over the list of what you need for your ceremony tomorrow. As we've said, you need to get up quite early. Be sure and set your alarm."

Dad was resting against Grandmother Pine Tree as Mom was gearing up to review the list.

"My alarm is already set."

"When you enter the lodge, you'll need to wear old clothing from your youth—clothes you used to wear but just hang in your closet now. Have you figured out which outfit?"

"Yes, Mom. I really should have given that outfit away a long time ago."

"After the ceremony, you'll burn it in a fire, a fitting farewell to that part of your life, and a new special dress will be waiting for you."

I was excited because I didn't know which dress Mom had chosen. We had gone shopping months ago, and I had tried on many beautiful dresses. I told Mom I wanted something white like the soft white doeskin outfit I had worn in my vision. It wouldn't look anything like it, of course, but my mother and I would know the connection to my vision. Once again, we fell silent as more stars started to show themselves.

"Mom, Dad, thanks for being my parents. I don't know how this is going to change our lives, if it changes them at all, but I feel really special having this Rite of Passage Ceremony. I know you will try to treat me differently, and I will try and act more grown-up."

Doubt was already creeping in so I silently used my doubt shout from the ceremony Grandmother gave me earlier in the year.

Feeling stronger, I said, "I trust whatever the outcome is."

Dad smiled and said, "You have already shown maturity even in what you just shared."

If they only knew what I just thought, my doubt voice said.

"We're in this together," Mom said. "You will mature into a fine young woman."

Dad added, "Our family and friends have come together in many ways over the years. Your Rite of Passage Ceremony will make us even closer. We have a great family clan here."

He was right. We did, and I took comfort in that.

* * *

Finally, it was the night before my ceremony, and my fear of not getting any sleep seemed more likely. I packed my backpack and checked everything off the list. Following Grandmother's instructions, I smudged myself with the mixture Mom had put in my room when we first decided I would do my Rite of Passage. I used my torch lighter to get the smudge burning strong and fanned the smoke over myself.

Everything will all be okay. I'll just go for it—as Shane said. I will sleep deeply and wake rested. I will sleep deeply and wake rested. This became my chant.

When I awoke the following morning, I was relaxed and refreshed. I glanced at the clock; it was way before dawn. Smiling because I had slept through the night, I turned on my night light and whispered a prayer to Great Spirit, giving thanks for helping me reach this special day.

My thoughts went to Aunt Kathy and Aunt Amy, who were coming over to help cover the purification lodge, but I was up early, so I thought I could do it myself. We could put the roses and carnations in the lodge together.

I had cut Mom's roses the day before, and they were in water. I had a beautiful bouquet of red and yellow roses to weave into the top of the lodge. Aunt Kathy was bringing the carnations.

Snuggled beneath my covers, I felt myself getting excited. The phone rang, and I jumped out of bed. I knew it was Grandmother Spinning Winds. No one else was awake, so I hurried to answer it before it could ring again.

"Well, that was fast," Grandmother said. "You must have been awake. Kinda early for you, isn't it?

"Not this morning, Grandmother."

She laughed.

"We're planning to come over after breakfast. Oops, I'm not supposed to eat breakfast." I suddenly got nervous and felt my stomach tighten as I thought about the ceremony. "I don't think I could eat anything anyway. Can I come over early and put the purification lodge canvas up by myself?"

"It's heavy," she said. "First, though, sit out by the Grandmother Pine Tree, connect to her roots, ground down, feel her calm, and let it become your calm. Breathe down into your belly, down to your womb. This is an important day. I want you to begin your journey in a good way. You need to be strong for the changes and challenges that lie before you. I'll see you when you get here."

I wasn't sure what Grandmother meant, but it seemed ominous. Had I forgotten something she told me? Was I going to be tested?

When I hung up the phone, it dawned on me that I didn't ask Grandmother why she had called so early, but I was glad she did. I took her words seriously.

I slipped into my deep green sweatpants and sweatshirt and pulled on my knee socks and warm boots. Wrapping my long ski scarf around my neck, I headed outside to sit with Grandmother Pine Tree. I took my medicine blanket to sit on and wrap myself in.

It was still very dark and cold. I was glad to have the blanket wrapped around me like the arms of those who love me. I closed my eyes and sent my thoughts down to her roots. The early morning sky was beautiful, and the stars still shined brightly. I sat down to relax, breathe, and feel the calm of Grandmother Earth.

"Grandmother Pine, I give you my nervous, hyper, little girl, frantic feelings. I am ready for the day. My breath is deep and slow."

I had no idea how long I had been sitting under the big Grandmother Pine Tree.

The dawn was barely caressing the new day as my eyes opened. My two cats were sitting on the blanket, looking up at me. When they saw my eyes open, Kachina and Ahnay rubbed against me. I petted them for a long time.

"Today is a special day, my sweet kitties. It's time to review the list one last time—gifts, clothes, and the things I packed in my backpack—just to make sure I don't forget anything."

As I stood to go into the house, Ahnay ran between my legs, almost tripping me. I opened the door, and they flew in, mewing for their breakfast.

First things first; feed my cats.

After a hot, quick shower, which felt good from being out in the cold, I sat on my bed and glanced around my room. "Goodbye," I said. "I will change you soon to remind myself that I am not a child anymore."

I heard my mother moving around outside the door. She, too, was up early. I imprinted the sounds of her moving about the kitchen. I had heard them many times over the years, but they would never be quite the same as this particular morning.

My stomach was growling, "Never mind, not today. Today I begin my fast; I can wait twenty-four hours."

I was half-dressed when Mom gently pushed the door open a little wider.

"Sage, are you awake?"

"Yes, Mom. I've been up for some time. I even visited with Grandmother Pine."

"I'll have hot sage tea ready in a few minutes."

"Thanks, Mom."

She started to walk away, then poked her head back in. "I love you Wind Dancer."

I dressed in multiple layers as it was chilly outside. I slipped into the kitchen and saw my mother gazing out the kitchen window, watching the light of Grandfather Sun awakening the morning sky. She was poised in the type of silence that stops the world, and it was almost as if I could read her thoughts. She had to say goodbye to her little girl. Time wasn't standing still. Tears fell down her face as she turned. She smiled, perhaps a little embarrassed.

"Mom," I said as I hugged her. "A part of me will always be your little girl." She caressed my hair and cheek, and her gentleness touched my soul. Looking into each other's eyes, we laughed.

"Come, Sage Wind Dancer. Have some tea."

"Is it permitted for me to drink tea? I'm fasting today."

"Yes, you can drink water and hot sage tea. Sage tea brings purification to your body. Greeting Grandfather Sun in ceremony brings fire to your spirit and will keep you warm throughout the night. Remember to greet him when you can see his full face in the morning sky."

"I will, Mom. I want to take his warmth into the lodge with me. I don't like being cold."

"Sage, as early as we are up, you can relax. There's lots of time before we meet to help you cover the lodge."

"Mom, I know we didn't plan this, but I want to go to Grandmother's house and cover the lodge by myself."

"The top canvas piece is very heavy," my mother said.

"I know. Grandmother told me that, too. If I need help, I'll wait for you, Aunt Kathy, and Aunt Amy. I really need to do this by myself."

Kissing my cheek, she smiled as if she understood.

"I'll see you at Grandmother's later," she said.

I put on my tennis shoes and a warm jacket. I wasn't sure I needed it, but I was prepared for the desert morning cold. I even grabbed a wool ski hat in case it got colder overnight when I was in ceremony.

I had packed everything the night before, but I did one last check to be sure I didn't forget anything, including my gifts and my old-child outfit that would be burned after the ceremony. My blouse was tight. Guess I had developed a little more than I had realized. Looking at my list, I checked off smudge, fan, lighter, small personal drum, and a ceremonial blanket for warmth and spiritual protection. I had taken this blanket with me to every ceremony I had participated in. My parents had Grandmother Spinning Winds Bless and Awaken it with her medicine pipe to set the intent of ceremonial protection. I would dream under it and seek my vision in the Womb of Grandmother, the sacred purification lodge.

I had everything in my big backpack that straps around my hips. I had the red and yellow roses wrapped in a wet paper towel and aluminum foil in a big plastic bag to keep water from dripping on my blanket. The flowers were the crowning touch, popping out of the top.

"Mom," I yelled, then dropped my voice as it was still early and Dad wasn't up yet. "Grandmother called earlier."

"What did she want?"

"I don't know. We just talked. I was awake anyway and getting nervous. She told me to sit in the backyard and ground myself with the Grandmother Pine Tree. That's where I was before taking a shower. I feel much better, a lot calmer, and ready for the day. I think the sage tea helped, too."

She looked at me with her deep-knowing eyes, a moment passed—an eternity. My childhood stood between us, and my adulthood birthed itself in front of us.

"I'm so proud of you, Sage."

Another moment passed, and something shifted.

"I've seen your maturity. It will be nice to have another adult living here."

Something swelled inside of me. "I wouldn't mind taking on more responsibility in the house, helping to make things easier for you and Dad."

Especially if you treat me more like an adult, I added in my thoughts. *Please don't read my thoughts, Mom.*

Kissing my mother goodbye, I said, "I'll see you at Grandmother's house when Grandfather Sun is shining bright and not just yawning."

I didn't run the mile to Grandmother's house this time. I walked, and everything seemed more alive, the colors more vibrant. The yards I'd passed a million times before were more beautiful than ever. Grandfather Sun was getting stronger, little by little, and he touched my face. I closed my eyes and absorbed his warmth while trusting my feet to guide me. I stopped and greeted Grandfather Sun properly, as Grandmother Spinning Winds had taught me. I felt his warmth sink deep inside me to keep me warm throughout the night.

"Thank you, Grandfather Sun, for your gift of fire and heat," I spoke out loud.

Then my eyes popped open as I remembered the teaching Grandmother Pine Tree had given me. Why didn't I remember it when I was sitting under her? My childhood was like her roots and would always be beneath me, but I must grow tall and mature into adulthood. My childhood is the past that propels me into the future. My inner child would always be accessible when I called her forth. At this point, I started skipping down the street.

My little girl loves to skip. I noted that no matter how old I got, I could take my inner child, which grandmother called my child shield, by the hand and skip down the street. Knowing I could grow up and still embrace my little girl made me feel better.

I saw Grandmother's house. She was out front, watering her flowers and waving at me. I waved back, wanting to run, skip, and throw my arms around her. Instead, I told my inner child we would play again later. I walked with a crisp stride. I stood tall and calmly said, "Good morning, Grandmother. You're watering your flowers very early today."

"I'm up. Might as well. I had to calm someone down earlier today," she said, winking at me.

I smiled back, wondering how she knew to call me. *She has special gifts,* I reminded myself. *She just knows.*

"I'm ready to cover the purification lodge by myself," I told her.

Grandmother chuckled. "You know where the canvas and blankets are."

"Yes, Grandmother."

"That's good. When you need help, your mother and aunts will be here. Go on, get started. Time is flying by."

Walking through the house into the kitchen, I carefully took my backpack off and set it near the sliding glass doors. I got a purple vase from her cupboard, where I know she keeps them. I filled the vase with water and after pulling the flowers out of the top of my backpack, I cut the bottom of the red and yellow rose stems.

"Take a nice long drink because soon you'll be fasting with me. No more water for you, and no food for me until tomorrow morning."

Picking up my backpack, I slung it over one shoulder. Everything was quiet as I walked past the pool, the slide, and down the steps to the second backyard and lodge area. I put my pack down by the lodge and walked over to the shed that held all the gear. I slid the door open and scanned the items for everything I would need.

Putting the canvas skirt on the lodge was pretty easy. I carried these pieces to the lodge and wrapped and tied them onto the lodge frame like a tepee's inner wall or a wrap-around skirt. One piece overlapped the next. I patted the canvas down to the ground so no light could sneak in between the grass clumps or wrinkles in the canvas. I had to make sure the space was dark.

The hardest part was lifting the big piece of canvas that covered the top of the lodge. It was extremely heavy. I wasn't sure I could lift it, let alone carry it from the shed to the lodge. Then I spotted a wheelbarrow nearby. Grunting, I lifted the centerpiece of canvas from the shed and dropped it into the wheelbarrow.

"There," I said out loud, rather pleased with myself.

Pushing the wheelbarrow without tipping it over was the next challenge. As I struggled with the weight of it, I began hoping to see my mother and aunts. I knew I'd have to lift the big square of canvas onto the lodge and center it so it would unfold properly. I parked the wheelbarrow in front of the lodge and walked up the steps to the pool level and to the sliding glass door. I peered into Grandmother's house. No one was in sight. I was on my own.

"I can do it," I said, convincing myself as I walked back to the lodge.

With a heave, I thrust the huge heavy square of canvas onto the top of the lodge, but it was too far to one side.

"Oh, no," escaped my lips as I looked at the crooked canvas. I glanced toward the house, but no one was coming.

Stubbornly, I gritted my teeth, locked my jaws, and started tugging the fifty pounds of canvas into place, careful not to open the big square or snag the frame.

It wasn't easy. Once I unfolded it, I had to ensure that the ends would almost touch the ground. Then it would open like an accordion.

It was bigger than I remembered. Once I got it opened, it looked like a twenty-foot-long, flat, green accordion noodle.

I unfolded two layers and pulled extremely hard to move it near the top, but I couldn't do it. Then the solution popped into my head. I went into the lodge frame and could almost stand up. I grabbed the canvas from inside and pulled hard. To my surprise and delight, it opened easily.

I went back and forth out of the lodge to get it unfolded, over the top, and partway down the sides. I then walked around to the back and, on tip-toes, grabbed the canvas and pulled it to the ground. I was sweating as much from the hard work as I was from worry, but I stepped back and looked at the lodge. "I did it!"

This was the first time I had ever covered the lodge by myself. It was a lot harder than I imagined. I could see why it takes a crew to prepare the lodge!

Now, for the next layer—the gray wool blankets.

I gripped the wheelbarrow's handles and pushed it back to the shed. Piling the blankets high, I surprised myself with how fast I maneuvered the wheelbarrow back to the lodge. The blankets were much lighter than the canvas.

I threw the wool blankets over the top, completely covering the canvas. Then, speaking to the lodge as to an old friend, I said, "I'm tucking you in tight. No light will enter you."

After a moment's rest, I added, "Now, I'll make you pretty." I spun the wheelbarrow around to get the Mexican rainbow-colored blankets.

I created a colorful pattern: purple on either side of the door, then red. I love purple and red together. I wrapped the blue and green blankets around the lodge and placed the melon-color ones on top. My first few flings didn't work. The colored blankets kept sticking to the wool blankets like Velcro. I managed to get the sides wrapped because I could reach them. The top was another story.

Just then, my mother and clan aunts, Amy Singing Hawk and Kathy Flowing Heart, showed up.

"Wow, Sage, you've gotten the lodge almost completely covered," Aunt Kathy exclaimed.

"I need your help—all of you. Your timing is perfect."

Aunt Amy, who was always smiling, said, "Even we can't reach the top of the lodge to spread the blankets. This is a large community lodge. It can hold twenty-four people comfortably. I'll get the rakes."

Aunt Kathy said, "Okay, here's how it's done. Two of us will throw the blankets on top, and two will use the rakes to spread them out to completely cover the lodge."

"With four of us, it's easy," Mom chimed in.

Together it was a breeze, and I would've never thought of using garden rakes!

Mom and Aunt Kathy crawled into the lodge, one at a time, saying, "To all my relations."

I started handing in the colored blankets for the floor of the lodge. I felt Grandmother Earth's Womb calling me to enter. I grabbed the last stack and knelt, repeating, "To all my relations."

Mom told me to cover the grass area in front of the door. I picked up the last purple blanket and spread it out. I wanted it to match the ones around the door. I looked around the lodge with happiness in my heart. The freshly cut grass smelled good. The blankets on the inside reflected the beauty of the blankets on the outside. It was almost done.

I felt the love of my mom and my clan aunts helping me. They were lost happily in their task. I gazed at them with my heart wide open, feeling so appreciative to have these remarkable women in my life.

"We're ready for the flowers," I called out the lodge door to Aunt Amy.

"I'm right here. No need to shout. I'll give them to you in bunches. I also brought your roses down from Grandmother's kitchen."

"Thanks, Aunt Amy."

Mom gently whispered, "Sage, remember to thank the flowers once again for their giveaway to you. Their lives were cut short when you picked them, but that's part of their medicine, their giveaway."

"Thanks for reminding me, Mom. Grandmother had me make a list of all the things the plant world gives us. Let's see if I remember."

Picking up a rose and a carnation, I smelled them. "I love the smell of carnations and roses. Thank you, sacred plants, for your giveaway of oxygen, food, shelter, clothing, and medicine. You give unconditionally. Sacred flowers, I appreciate your giveaway to me and the beauty you bring to my ceremony. Please teach me how to give unconditionally because I need to learn it. Aho!"

Mom, Aunt Kathy, and I wove the flowers into the top of the lodge. I had picked lots of red and yellow roses, then Aunt Amy crawled into the lodge and piled the rest of the flowers in the center. I started weaving in white and pink carnations. We whispered thanks to the flowers as we weaved them into the ceiling framework. The top of the lodge reflected the colors of the blankets below. We created a blanket of flowers above my head with colored blankets below me. It was so beautiful.

Aunt Kathy reached up to touch a yellow rose. "It reminds me of the moon when she is in full bloom."

Her words reminded me of the Yellow Moon Society that Dreams with the Wind was invited to be a part of in the vision I had. I looked at Aunt Kathy intently.

She caught my energy and said, "Tonight in your ceremony, travel on the winds, Wind Dancer."

A thought popped into my head, *had she been my aunt in that other lifetime?*

I wove the last carnation into the ceiling.

Mom whispered, "Aah, fill your lungs deeply with the sweet fragrance of life."

We all inhaled the mixture of spicy carnations and lemony spice roses and sighed.

"Now, Sage, let's get all your gear loaded into the lodge."

"Okay, Mom, my backpack is just outside."

Mom said, "To all my relations," and stepped out of the lodge.

My Aunts exited with the same words.

I stayed, and they handed me the foam pad. Grandmother had taught me that whatever direction I chose to lay my head would impact the ceremony—even how I slept in my bedroom at home. I chose west. This ceremony was about introspection, intuition, change, rebirth, and new life. In the morning, I was to birth myself out of the lodge like a butterfly emerging from its cocoon. Feet in the east, taking first steps to greet Grandfather Sun. A Rite of Passage from being a child into a young woman.

"Aunt Amy, please hand me my backpack. I need to unload it." I took my altar blanket out, which was near the top, and laid it next to the pad. Then I took other items out and used the pad as a staging platform.

Aunt Kathy stepped into the lodge, "To all my relations." She moved to one side, observing me. "Sage, when you place your medicine on the altar blanket, remember where you put things. It will be dark."

My mom and Aunt Amy were sitting close enough to the door to hear us.

"Thanks, Auntie. These are the hints I need." Aunt Kathy was always teaching me.

I took out the bright blue bag that held my lighters and gear.

"When you place things, tell me why you are putting them in the direction you have chosen."

"Okay, but I'm feeling pressured to get done, and I'm not sure in my nervousness that I'll remember."

"You have time, Sage."

That closed the door on my resistance. She never let me get away with anything, which I knew was good.

I took out my feminine fan. "These blue and green feathers come from a seed eater, a beautiful parrot. I placed it on the left, the feminine side of my mesa." I was given a large and small eagle feather at birth, and these feathers were made into a fan. I placed it on the right side, which is masculine. Next to the full eagle fan, I placed beautifully wrapped fluff feathers from the eagle. "These are the feminine within the masculine. How am I doing, Aunt Kathy?"

"Much better than you thought you would do. Keep going. This is fun."

"I'm putting the candle in the middle, behind my favorite baseball-sized crystal sphere. I'm placing it there because I want it to be in the center, balanced between the masculine and feminine. If I light the candle, it will shine through the crystal. I can then dream into the crystal, and it can take me inside, helping me with my vision quest. You know what I'm talking about, right?" Looking out the door, I saw Mom and Aunt Amy smile.

"Yes, Sage. We understand," Aunt Amy said.

"You've learned a lot," Mom added. "I'm proud of you."

I felt like I was on a roll now. I pulled out my small hand drum. "I will put it on the right side with my smudge and lighter—the spark of masculinity. Ah, corn pahoe for prayers on the left as it is feminine, too."

I pulled my medicine blanket out of the bottom of the backpack and spread it over my foam pad. I had a little pillow, too. *Not for sleeping*, I silently commanded myself. Now that my backpack was unloaded, I folded it up tightly and placed it next to the lodge wall, out of the way. Rising to my knees, I announced to all, "Everything is set. The lodge is ready except for smudging the whole area."

"Sage," Mom said, "you may want to take a minute and go down into your one-point and ask Spirit if you have everything you need."

I sat down, closed my eyes, and thought about my list. "I think I have everything."

Aunt Amy laughed. "What about your pee bucket?"

"Oh, my gosh. I forgot all about that! I need to ask Grandmother if she has a bucket I can borrow." I bounded out of the lodge. "To all my relations," I said after I was already a few feet away, but I kept moving. Next to the steps, going up to the pool, sat a bucket with a lid and some toilet paper. "How does she do that?" I said into the air. All three laughed. They, too, knew Grandmother had a special gift.

It was time for me to smudge the lodge. They stood off to one side watching me and talking softly as I got the big abalone shell out of the shed and filled it with sage, cedar, sweetgrass, and lavender. After using a lighter to get it burning, I used the eagle fan and smudged the outside twice and the inside twice, always circling clockwise. Two is the number for Grandmother Earth—I was birthing this lodge into my ceremonial space. When finished, I put the eagle fan and smudge back into the shed. I took a good look to be sure I remembered where the lighters were.

If I forgot anything, it was too late. The lodge was blessed.

Facing the lodge, I said, "The next time I stand here will be tonight when I'm ready to enter this womb." Saying this aloud made it real for my Rite of Passage Ceremony. "Close the flap," I said with confidence.

Aunt Kathy and Aunt Amy grabbed either side of the blanket and closed the flap door. We were all grinning as I led the way into the house where the activities were beginning to take place.

Chapter 5

Speaking The Unspeakable

My dad and uncles, Rex, Tim Fire Hawk, and Bruce Quiet Man, worked inside.

"Hey, Sage," Uncle Bruce said as I opened the sliding glass door. I ran to him for a hug and then gave Uncle Rex and Uncle Tim big hugs, too, which felt warm and reassuring.

The men were setting the space. There were two beautiful wool Pendleton medicine blankets on the floor in the living room with multiple designs in black, gold, red, and white. Staring at them, I wondered why they chose those blankets.

I heard Grandmother's voice inside my mind. *Look carefully at the little things, Sage, because it's the small things in life that matter.*

With everyone moving around me, I tried to remember the medicine teachings of the colors and directions Grandmother had taught me from her Metis medicine traditions. *Black is in the west—Grandmother Earth, feminine energy, the place of death, change, chaos, new life, and manifestation. Gold or yellow is in the east. Grandfather Sun rises daily in the east, bringing us hope and light—masculine energy. Red is in the south. Red is for protection and represents blood, the lifeforce energy. We always wrap the feather quills in red thread when making feathers into fans. It's the place of beginnings, trust, and innocence—the place of the child and our emotions. White is in the north. The winds and our minds are in the north, along with wisdom, knowledge, and harmony.*

Overwhelmed with emotion, I realized I needed to let go of my past to embrace my spiritual transformation—my Rite of Passage. I saw the story of my childhood in the colors of the blanket. When the light appeared and

Grandfather Sun awakened, I would leave the purification lodge renewed. Who I was as a little girl will have died, and, like a caterpillar, I would emerge as a young woman.

Can one ceremony really make such changes? Was it asking too much of myself to grow up overnight? I wondered. It seemed like a big order to me.

Grandmother's voice floated across the front room noise as she walked toward me

"So, the blankets talk to you! It takes a lifetime to grow up, but your little girl knows you will protect her. She will stand behind you, now. She no longer runs the show. The adult in you will begin making the decisions. The world looks different when you see it through the eyes of a young woman."

"Grandmother, what do you mean my little girl will stand behind me now?"

Come into my medicine room, Wind Dancer. You've asked a good question. Besides, you're in the way of what needs to be done—standing there with your mouth open, staring at the blankets.

I followed Grandmother Spinning Winds as she led the way into her bedroom.

"First things first." She sat on the floor with her back against the bed. She patted the space in front of her, where a medicine blanket created a comfy seat for me.

"Let's smudge ourselves with sage, cedar—"

"Sweetgrass and lavender," I chimed in, and we smiled at each other.

She laid her large, beautiful blue and green feather Quetzal feminine fan before me and handed me the abalone shell full of smudge.

I picked up the lighter, and as the herbs caught fire, I fanned them out to release the smoke. I blessed and cleansed myself with the sacred smoke and handed the shell and fan to her. Our eyes met, and it felt like we were hugging each other. She blessed and cleansed herself, then placed the fan and bowl on her mesa cloth.

"You are performing your Rite of Passage from little girl to young woman. It is the feminine energy of the bird world that you are needing."

I nodded and smiled shyly.

"Do you remember the teaching I gave you about the aspects held in your luminosity?"

I thought for a moment, and a vague picture came into my head. "I kinda remember."

"Okay, tell me what you kinda remember," she teased.

I closed my eyes and remembered that Grandmother had all her

Ceremonial Dance shields on her bedroom wall. I reached out to them and asked them to help me. Then I silently prayed, *"Great Spirit, help me remember the aspects of who I am."*

Smiling, I repeated Grandmother's words exactly. "The aspects of myself in my luminosity hold images and stories that represent me. They are inside my aura. I can't see them like my physical body, but someday I may be able to. They are real, but they vibrate very fast." I opened my eyes. "It's kind of like knowing that air exists but I can't see it. Okay so far?"

Grandmother nodded and brushed a wrinkle out of the folds of her blue, tiered skirt, waiting for me to say more.

I hoped to hear or sense something from inside. When nothing came, I remembered Grandmother had taught me that if I began speaking, the memories might pop up.

"The aspects of me can shift in my luminosity, so, at any given time, I may be seeing life through different eyes. My little girl will be my past, the adult I am becoming is the future, and my spirit masculine adult and spirit masculine child are always in the now. My little girl has been in front because I have been a child. Pretty simple."

I smiled at Grandmother. "When I had my first menstruation, I began the journey of becoming an adult, and what a journey it's been."

I closed my eyes again, and the words tumbled out. "With my Rite of Passage, I am to take steps forward as an adult, and my inner child will rotate behind my luminosity—not to be ignored, but not run the show either. This Rite of Passage Ceremony is supposed to keep my child behind me because it is my past. I don't want my child making decisions that need to come from a more mature side of me, like learning about relationships, sex, and intimacy."

I opened my eyes. "Was I close?"

Grandmother laughed, "You pulled that one off pretty well. Most of the time, when you think you have forgotten a teaching, you usually have it behind another thought. Want to know what I do when I am trying to remember?"

"Yes. I'll take all the help I can get!"

"Okay, Sage, it is one simple thing. Start talking and silently tell your brain to find, and you will access the knowledge. That's more important than me giving you more information. Learn how to access what you think you have forgotten! You remembered well and gave yourself a good teaching."

"Thank you, Grandmother. I'm glad you didn't let me off the hook."

Grandmother's face became quite serious.

I took a deep breath and tried to calm myself. I had no idea what was coming.

"Are you ready to speak the unspeakable to your parents? I have guided them to be honest and ruthless with you. Are you prepared to do the same?"

My inner voice said *Whoa. Honest and ruthless with me?* I was shocked and scared.

"Do you know why, Sage?"

My head moved back and forth.

"Hmmm," Grandmother looked at me intently, and I could feel her eyes searching my soul. Then she said, "Remember the times you came to me ready to run away, hating your parents—the times you cussed at them for grounding you because you were refusing to do your homework, and your grades were bad, just like your friends? Are those kids still your friends?"

"No, Grandmother, they're losers, but I thought they were cool. I wanted to do what they did."

Grandmother summed it up in a word. "Stupid. What about the time when you proved to your parents that you didn't lie to them, and it was their friend that had stolen their money? Did they ever really apologize to you? Do you still feel hurt that they didn't believe you?"

I nodded. I had to be honest with myself.

"Do you have anything you need to say to them? This is the time to speak the unspeakable across the talking stick. To clear any hidden, nasty little stinky, smelly, resentments, hurts, anger, or disappointment."

Do I have to do this in front of the whole family?

"Did they do the best possible job of parenting you? If you thought so, why did you come to me to learn about sex, the real nitty-gritty stuff, huh? Why didn't you go to them? Do you have anything you need to say about that?"

I was dumbfounded—boy, she had a good memory. I had decided not to speak about these things. It wouldn't do any good anyway, and now Grandmother was asking me to speak of them openly, in front of my aunts and uncles. I didn't know if I could do it.

Grandmother was looking at me. No, she was looking through me.

"You had better speak the unspeakable, Wind Dancer! This is your time to heal the little girl. Give her a voice and empower her. If you don't listen to her, if your parents don't listen to her, then you will continue to be a victim for the rest of your life."

There was silence as she let this sink in.

"I don't want to be a victim from my childhood."

Grandmother kept speaking as if she didn't hear me. "You can wait until you're forty years old to attend a workshop on healing the inner child, but I thought you didn't want to make the same mistakes that your parents made."

She had me. I said it, and now I had to walk my talk.

"Okay, I'll say what I'm afraid to say." I was prepared for some type of death ceremony, but I didn't want my parents to kill me.

Grandmother had that look in her eye. "You may be surprised by their reaction. They may be more grown-up than you give them credit for. You're not the only one I've been teaching!"

It was as if a light came on. Oh, my gosh, she has been teaching my parents all these years!

"Sage, wait here while I check on the preparations in the front room."

"Yes, Grandmother." I decided to dress in my old outfit, which I had put in Grandmother's room, the clothes of the child I was letting go of. It felt strange to be in my old clothes. It made me feel like a kid. I didn't know if I'd have the courage to speak to my parents. After all, they were my parents. I'd still have to live with them after the ceremony. Doubt flooded in when I put the clothes on. I was glad to know I'd be burning them.

I wondered if other people experienced their confidence waning when they wore certain clothing. I never liked the saying, "The clothes make the person," but maybe it was true. If clothes could make me feel "less than," then perhaps they could also make me feel "more than." How I dressed suddenly became important to me. Not just how I look on the outside, but how they make me *feel* inside. I promised myself that after the ceremony, I would go through my closet and try on every piece of clothing. I would keep only the things that made me feel positive and confident. I wondered if I'd have anything left to wear.

Grandmother came back into the room and stood quietly for a moment. "You learned a lot as a little girl. You will learn even more as a woman."

"Oh, Grandmother, I think it's already started."

We laughed, and I felt better.

"Be yourself, Sage. They are waiting for you. Let's walk this road together. The bridge you'll cross by yourself is your ceremony tonight."

I took a deep breath, remembered the pine tree, and felt calm.

My mother and father were sitting on the medicine blanket. A talking stick lay before them. There was a place for me to sit opposite them, and Grandmother sat in a low chair off to the side.

Around us sat my family. Grandmother Bebee had come in from California. I was pleased to see her and blew her a kiss.

My clan aunts and uncles and Grandfather Strong Bear were seated. I didn't see any of my friends. Then I remembered they were joining us after the ceremony tomorrow.

"Thank goodness," I said under my breath.

Suddenly, the room seemed very full. We were about to air our dirty laundry for the entire family to hear. This was no easy task; the first test of adulthood stood before me. I was glad my friends weren't here.

"Welcome, everyone." Grandmother Spinning Winds said as the respected matriarch. I noted her tone of formality and stature. "We are sharing in this special day, witnessing the ending of childhood and rejoicing at the first steps into conscious adulthood. Conscious adulthood," she repeated.

"Kathy Flowing Heart would you please start the smudge and pass it first to me." Grandmother then passed it to Mom, who smudged and handed it to Dad and me. I smiled at Aunt Kathy as she passed it around the circle.

"Since all things are born of the feminine receptive energy, one of the Sacred Laws, I am asking Rose, mother of Sage Wind Dancer, to pick up the talking stick and begin speaking what is in her heart. Speak the unspeakable to your daughter. For tonight, any issues with your child must be given away. A clear slate between you is necessary for her to step into adulthood in a good way."

"If you don't need the talking stick, then place it between you and Sage and speak over it. Everyone else will listen." This was spoken as a command. "If there is a disagreement between you and Sage, then I will ask for the talking stick format to be adhered to. It will be picked up. You will then speak in short phrases and hand the talking stick to the other. They will repeat the essence of what you said and hand it back until whichever one of you is holding the talking stick feels complete. Then you will repeat the process with the other person speaking the unspeakable."

Everyone was silent and listening intently. All of us, at one time or another, had used the talking stick. As I listened to Grandmother's instructions, I took a moment to breathe and gather my thoughts.

"If you don't need the talking stick," she said, "you can begin. You don't need to repeat the essence in this format, but if I see you interrupting each other or talking over each other, then I will implement the talking stick format. Do you understand? Are we in agreement?"

My mother and I nodded.

I thought this might be as hard for her as it was for me. I took a deep breath and tried to open my heart to hear what she was going to say.

"Rebecca Sage, I am very proud of you, sitting here in this circle, the Rite of Passage that you requested. There were times when I thought you were never going to make it. I didn't know if you were going to run away, or if I was going to ground you forever."

We both laughed, which seemed to ease the tension a bit.

"First, I want to apologize for not being a better parent, for not educating myself better about the responsibility of parenting. I especially want to apologize for not believing you when our friend stole from us and we thought it was you. I don't think I ever looked at you so that your very soul would know how deeply sorry I am. So, I do it now. I don't want there to be any mistrust or pain between us. I ask you; do you forgive me?"

I felt my mother's pain in the tears in my eyes. I realized she had been carrying things all these years, just as I had.

"Mom, I know I told you little white lies sometimes, and you knew it. So, I understand why you might think I would lie that time. I understand. Really, I do, and I forgive you. Will you forgive me for the white lies I told as I was growing up?"

"Rebecca Sage, you know I always call you Sage because it means wise, and you are wise beyond your years. Yes, I forgive you. It's a part of growing up, and I accept that. Besides, you didn't get away with much. I almost always knew when you were telling a lie because you don't lie very well. You are honest by nature. I should have trusted that." My mother glanced at my dad.

I took a deep breath, sensing that something bad was coming up.

"I have something else I need to say to you."

I saw the stress on her face and took another deep breath to calm myself.

"You are our daughter, and you have a stubborn streak in you. I think you get it from your dad."

Mom, Dad, and I smiled, releasing some of the tension.

"You get something into your head, and nobody can tell you any different. That's why your dad and I had to take such drastic measures when you started hanging out with those kids. You know, the ones that did drugs and dropped out of school."

"Grandmother mentioned something might be spoken about that today."

"I know you don't know this, but we did some detective research and found out that those kids were involved in a Satanic Church. They were stalking other kids to bring them in. We spoke to Grandmother Spinning Winds, and she confirmed it for us through her means. They were bad news, and so were the adults behind them.

"Grandmother found out they had quite a bit of dark power. It was so hard for me to let you explore and find that out for yourself. Something finally clicked for you, along with some tough love from us."

"Mom, I remember that they talked spiritual, but something was off. I felt it deep inside me, but I wasn't sure. I was curious, and they talked to my rebellious side."

"Thank you, Sage, for sharing that. It is good you recognize that side of yourself. It is not talking stick protocol for us to dialogue, but I appreciate your sharing."

I looked at Grandmother Spinning Winds and mouthed, "Sorry."

She nodded.

"Your stubborn and rebellious side almost got you lost. I know you can look back at it now and see how wrong you were and how your friends were not good people. But, at the time, you were beginning to buy into their whole world. It scared me. I thought I was going to lose you. Not just your love and respect, but your soul. I wouldn't have been able to live with myself if I had lost you to the dark. So now maybe you understand why your father and I were so freaked out, as you put it. We couldn't say anything."

I looked at Grandmother, and she nodded. It was okay for me to respond.

"But why, Mom? Why didn't you tell me?"

"Oh, Sage, do you think you would have listened? Think back."

I dropped my head, closed my eyes, and went inside. A question was asked, so protocol allowed me to answer.

"You're right, Mom. I would've told you that you were crazy, that you'd say anything to keep me from my friends. I would've hated you even more." I was looking at her with a twinkle in my eyes. "How did you and Dad get so smart?"

"We went to Grandmother Spinning Winds. She guided us just like she's guiding you. We had to make the final decisions, but she pointed out the boulders in the path that we were too close to see. You know what I mean, Hon?"

"Yes, I do. Thanks for the tough love. That's a good lesson to remember if I decide to have children, which I haven't decided yet. It's a lot of responsibility to raise children in a good way, and, boy, does having children mess up your romantic life."

Mom and Dad laughed and looked at each other with that knowing look, but I also saw something I hadn't seen in a while. I saw passion in their eyes for each other.

"I am complete," my mother said.

I reached out, and we hugged.

She looked at Dad, and he nodded.

He picked up the talking stick, and I thought he wanted to go into formal talking stick protocol where the essence is repeated. With a solemn look, he placed the talking stick between us.

"Since you mentioned it, I'd like to say something about our romantic life."

I had no idea what Dad was going to say. *Did I open up a can of worms or what?*

"Sage, I want you to know that your Mom and I wanted to be parents. We wanted a baby, and you were conceived in love and passion. We had a lot of good times. Then something happened that we weren't prepared for. No one talks about the changes people go through as they grow older and become parents. Jobs demand more, and responsibilities get larger. Having fun in many ways, including being sexual, gets put on the back burner.

"I have never been sorry we gave birth to you. There have been times when I lost connection with what was truly important—like making love and feeding our passion for each other. There were times that I blamed you. I wanted your mother to be my lover, not just the mother of my child, and she wanted me to be her friend, not just a frustrated husband. We made mistakes but attending the Spiritual Sexuality workshops helped us to turn our marriage around and put the passion back where it belongs. I know you didn't see this. You thought your mom and I were always too tired and didn't apply the teachings and training we received—what Grandmother is teaching you now—but it was the teachings that helped your mom and me to keep the spark alive and even nurture it. Now and then, it's been like passionate fireworks for us."

They looked at each other as if they were newlyweds.

He spoke with tenderness. "I see, now, how important it is for children to see the love and passion their parents feel for each other. It's natural and wonderful. I'm sorry I didn't show more love and affection openly to your mother. It would've been so much easier than trying to hide it. I hope this doesn't influence how you are with your future partners, especially if you decide to have children."

That was a lot. We reached out and hugged each other, rejoicing in the love that flowed between us.

"Dad, something magickal is happening in me. I am remembering teachings I got from another lifetime, teachings about sacred sexuality. Grandmother said she would guide me. I promise I'll be honest and natural and express my feelings to all my partners," I said exuberantly, "whether I have children or not."

Dad laughed, and it made me happy to see his open laughter—and he didn't say anything about me having more than one partner. I had many teachers in school, so it only made sense to have more than one partner to learn the lessons in life that were before me.

"Rod," Grandmother Spinning Winds said, "is there anything else you need to speak?"

He closed his eyes and went inside. Opening his eyes, he said, "Yes!"

Here it comes. My stomach dropped, and my breath became short and nervous.

"Though your mother spoke it, I will also say that I am sorry for not believing you when my friend stole from us. It was a hard lesson for me, too."

"Thanks, Dad. Hearing it from you means a lot to me." Oops, I interrupted, almost talking over what he was saying.

Grandmother Spinning Winds raised an eyebrow as if to say, *One more time and—*

I gave her and Dad a little smile.

Dad nodded to me. "Your turn, kiddo."

Taking a breath, I lowered my eyes, went inside, and felt the calm.

"Mom, I did tell you a few white lies. Dad, I told you less. Somehow, when you looked at me, I thought you could see right through me. I would get so nervous. Mom, you were a little softer on me, so it was easier. Anyway, I'm sorry. I know that a lie is a lie. I don't like it when my friends lie to me. It takes courage to be honest. Sometimes I feel my whole world will fly apart if I speak my truth."

"Well, Sage," Dad said, interrupting me. He looked sheepish and smiled at Grandmother.

She gave him the same look. "Remember not to interrupt each other or I'll have you pick up the talking stick and we'll go formal."

We nodded respectfully.

Dad spoke to Grandmother. "Yes, I have more to share."

Grandmother nodded her head, directing him to speak.

"May I speak my thoughts to you, Sage?"

"Yes, Dad. I would like that."

"It is challenging to speak the unspeakable. That's why people lie and cheat and hide their true selves. Sometimes it happens out of fear of rejection or losing someone they love. If they lie, they'll lose them in the long run anyway. Sage, don't settle for less in a relationship. Always speak the unspeakable. Then you'll grow together, no matter what."

I was listening intently, and my body told me that Dad was sharing deep wisdom.

"You won't always like what the other person says or even what they've done, but you have to let them do it. You'll both make mistakes but learn from them. Learn from them together. Honest communication, first with yourself, then with your partner, is the foundation for building a strong home. Just like we are doing now. Commit to speaking your truth. You can agree to confront each other, support each other, and grow into mature sacred humans. This is vital in all relationships."

Mom was looking at Dad the way one admires a beautiful work of art. Clearly, she loved him and respected him.

"Sage, you chose to be born through your mother and me, which means your contract with us is to be raised in the light. That's why we finally stepped in to guide you back to the light, with tough love, when you unconsciously accepted friends who were leading you into the paths of darkness. Remember, even though we are raising you to be very open and spiritual, even Jesus threw the money changers out of the Temple because their actions and their motives were wrong. Jesus said, 'Yea, so shall you do greater works than I.'"

My father had often shared his wisdom about spirituality versus religion, and I was paying close attention today.

"You know I have not raised you to be religious, but the original teachings of Jesus the Christ are profound. Don't throw out the good teachings with the dogma. Look for proper spiritual teachings like you found under the big Grandmother Pine Tree."

For a moment, I saw us sitting and talking beneath her out-stretched branches. I remembered the wisdom I received from connecting to Mother Father Nature through her as I had rested my back against her strong trunk.

"Sage."

My dad's voice jerked me back to Grandmother's living room.

"Sorry if I got on my soapbox. I just want the best for you. You must learn to listen to your inner spirit. The time has come when we can be a mentor, a guide, a family that will always love and care for you. Your decisions will fall more and more on your shoulders. The consequences and results will be the challenges and opportunities that will mold your life."

I started to pray silently when Dad prayed out loud. "Please, Great Spirit, always guide Sage Wind Dancer. Hon, I release you into the circle of yourself. I now stand as a proud father, seeing a very wise and beautiful young adult woman."

This statement of letting go was the hardest thing Dad had shared all day.

I had observed my dad with his friends before, and words of wisdom would pour out of him now and then. At those times, everyone listened—most of the time in agreement. Today, his words entered my soul and sang a new song inside me.

My dad closed his thoughts by saying, "Becoming an adult is a tremendous responsibility, not just for you, but in how you deal with others. You can be part of the solution or the problem on Grandmother Earth. It's your choice."

"Dad, at times, you really are a wise man. I can see why Mom loves you and looks at you with that look in her eyes."

"At times?"

We smiled at each other with so much love and joy I thought I would float away.

"Ho! I'm done," my father said.

With that, I said, "I guess it's my time to speak the unspeakable."

I extended both my hands and picked up the talking stick. I needed the extra strength of the great tree nation with the balance of the mineral and sweet medicine animal worlds, which were beautifully attached to the talking stick.

It seemed so much had been spoken. Even the things I was going to bring up were already resolved. What did Grandmother say to do? Give my inner little girl a voice and empower her.

Okay, little Sage, I said in my mind. *What do you need to say to our parents? I promise I will listen; I know they will listen, too. I'll hold the spiritual talking stick and place the physical one on the blanket between us.*

I heard my small quiet voice begin to speak aloud as tears fell down my face. Looking at my parents, I said, "I speak to you both. I am so much more than what you let me be. I have felt stuffed in a box that everybody had to approve of, but you never asked me if I wanted it. Who was I in all that? I now have to unlearn a bunch of stuff. Stuff handed down from your mothers and fathers. I love my grandparents, but it's still generations of thoughts and rules that may or may not be valid."

The floodgate was open now, and I encouraged my inner child to keep speaking her truth.

"I think a lot of what you did as parents, you just repeated how you were raised. Even though you stepped out of the norm, I mean, you're both freer than most of my friend's parents, you still didn't question why you taught me what you taught me. I need space to grow and explore who I am—not what others want me to be. I want you to see the real me, the natural me. I will be responsible. If I forget and blow it, I accept your guidance and strength in guiding me. I want more than anything to be me, and for you to see me and love me for who I am, and who I am becoming."

I took a deep breath, centering it in my belly, deep into my womb space. I asked myself what else I needed to speak. I felt a calm and deep love for my parents. *Do I dare speak my truth? Yes!* And my mouth began flowing.

"I want to be my best because I love you both. I want to truly see who you are. I want to see the two of you grow, also. I think you've been hiding a lot from each other and yourselves. Grandmother says we can always grow because we're not yet enlightened. I need for all of us to continue to become our true selves. There is still so much I can learn from you, but I don't want to learn old patterns that have not been challenged by the two of you to validate if there is truth being handed down from the generations behind us. I want to learn from your wisdom."

I stopped. My voice had gotten stronger and stronger. As I looked at my parents, I saw that they had tears running down their faces. I wiped the tears from my cheeks that had fallen nonstop since I began talking.

I was complete.

We moved together and held each other in a forgiving embrace. I felt the strength of family and love in this triangle. A thought popped into my mind: *This is the Sacred Hoop, generations healing together.*

If only everyone could be open-hearted and speak the unspeakable, any relationship could work. I bet life would be better if more people could speak the unspeakable and heal the Sacred Hoop.

I don't know who started to let go first. I think we all just relaxed and looked into each other's eyes. There was a smile that began on my mother's face, spread to my father's, and finished with me. It was a huge smile that filled the whole room.

I had no idea my little girl had so much to say, but she certainly spoke her mind. I quietly vowed to give her a voice to speak her truth and to listen with care. I made peace, not only with my parents but also with myself. It was a good day.

"Sweet family," Grandmother's voice gently weaved into our embrace, "it's time we pass the smudge again. Amy Singing Hawk will you light the mixture?"

The smoke began to spiral upward as the dried herbs caught fire. My aunt used the back of the lighter to tamp the flames. "Here, Sage, smudge yourself and pass it." Turning to the circle, she added, "Will everyone please smudge?"

I took the eagle fan, blessed myself with the smoke, and passed it to Mom. She did the same and handed it to Dad. He gave the bowl and a lighter to Aunt Amy, who walked it to the outer circle of the family. There was an audible sound of release as each person cleansed. The whole space was uplifted.

We all looked at each other and started to laugh. Then others joined us. The air was clear and fresh, like after heavy rain.

Chapter 6

Visiting Past Lives

Grandmother allowed the laughter to go on for a while, then her voice quietly penetrated the space. "It is now time for Wind Dancer to enter the Womb of Grandmother, the sacred purification lodge. We will say goodbye to her, for we will never see her again as we have known her."

The mood changed quickly from laughter to the quiet before the storm.

Grandmother continued, "Changes will take place this night. We will pray that Great Spirit will bless her and grant that she experience the vision that will guide her into adult life. With some luck, magick will happen tonight. If not," she teased with a glance towards me, "she may get bored sitting in a cold lodge waiting for dawn."

Everyone laughed but me. The humor seemed to help my family, but I felt rather solemn.

Grandfather winked at me and said, "Oh, don't be so serious."

I realized he was teasing, but I heard my doubt voice again. What if nothing happened? What if I fell asleep? What if I sat there all night bored?

Refusing to give in to doubt, I told myself I would do everything Grandmother taught me. I would create a sacred space and get rid of my doubt voice. I had everything I needed: smudge, fan, lighter, drum, and intent. If nothing happened, I would imagine myself with Grandmother in her medicine room, and I knew time would open up, and magick would happen.

Grandmother said, "Make a line, step into the silence, and follow me." She reached for my hand and pulled me behind her, *no escaping.*

My parents and the rest of the circle followed. We made a long snake walking to the lodge area. I looked at her pool and slide. I saw the image of Grandmother nude, laughing as she went down her slide and splashed into the pool. I felt better.

My feet walked, but my mind was talking to me. *No matter how old I get, my healthy inner child would always be with me. It was up to me to listen to her and treat her well. After all, she would hold my childhood memories—all the things I experienced and learned. Why would I want to get rid of her?*

When we reached the lodge, everybody made a semicircle around us. I leaned over to Grandmother and whispered, "Can I ask you a question?"

"Of course, Wind Dancer," she whispered back.

"I'm not killing my little girl, am I? I'm just putting her behind me so my adult can mature now. Like the roots of Grandmother Pine, I am growing above her. I keep thinking I have to get rid of her and grow up."

Grandmother looked at the slide, and a twinkle came into her eyes. "You know the answer to your own question, Wind Dancer. Don't ask questions when they are statements. Believe in yourself and in your wisdom."

"Believe in myself and my wisdom," I repeated softly.

"If I told you to kill her off, to get rid of your inner child, would you? Would your body-knowing listen to me or would you start questioning if Grandmother Spinning Winds had lost her mind?"

"Ah, so it's okay to question what my elders tell me!"

"Yes, Wind Dancer. Being an adult is finding and knowing the truth for yourself. Don't believe anything anyone tells you. Be an open cup. Receive their wisdom. Then find out if it grows corn for you. You will know truth in your body, not in your head."

"Grandmother, I know there's nothing for me to say. I know what you speak is the truth. I have to start trusting myself, my inner wisdom, more. I am ready to say goodbye."

Grandmother stepped aside so my parents could stand at the east door with me. Mother had tears in her eyes. Dad looked strong. I think he was being strong for me so that I could feel it. I did feel his strength, and I smiled.

"Tomorrow we will speak to a young adult and make new agreements about how we are to live together. For now, I embrace my little girl."

My dad's strong voice resonated in my soul.

"You look so young in those clothes. I let you go to find the center of your own circle, the very essence of who you are as a young adult."

Tears streamed down my mother's face. "Tears of joy," she said. "I prayed this day would come and feared it never would. Now it seems like just a minute ago I was holding you in my arms. Time goes by so fast."

I hope this night goes by fast.

"Every day is so important. This day is the most important day of your life, and I know there will be other such days, but we only have today. I love you, daughter of mine. I look forward to walking the road of changes with you."

I was hoping this ceremony would bring about changes at home.

Mom's tone changed. She became like a wise elder speaking to me. "Stay alert when the dream takes you. Sleep and wakefulness can become one."

She held me, and together our tears flowed. I felt my dad's arms around both of us. The two women in his life; he loved us so much.

"Thank you, Mom, Dad. You know I love you both."

Grandmother said, "It's time. Time to let the caterpillar crawl into her cocoon. We will see tomorrow the colors of the beautiful butterfly that emerges."

My parents stepped back. I looked around the circle. I smiled at each one—some with tears on their cheeks and others smiling, men and women, tears and joy. Grandmother picked up her Coatyl masculine fan made of beautiful eagle feathers. I had beaded the handle with a lightning rainbow peyote stitch. It was beautiful. She placed the feminine Quetzal parrot feather fan on top of the masculine one. It, too, had a lightning pattern of greens, yellows, reds, and the colors of the parrot feathers. Grandmother blessed me from head to toe and tapped my belly, my womb space, grounding me to my one point.

"Granddaughter, you are entering the Womb of Grandmother, in this sacred purification lodge. Many other women, for thousands of years, have entered into kivas, sacred caves, places within, to find their vision. Seek your vision, Wind Dancer, from who you have been, who you are, and who you will become. Embrace it firmly. It will guide you until you are twenty-seven years old. Then you will do another Rite of Passage to guide you for the next twenty-seven years."

My eyes opened wider, I'm sure.

"Yes, Wind Dancer, there are many Rites of Passages. Let us begin with this one. Goodbye, Granddaughter."

Grandfather Strong Bear had been standing silent this whole time, as he often did. Grandmother said she could feel his strength as it lifted her to do the work she had come here to do. He stepped forward and spoke of a vision—a *knowing* he had.

"Sage Wind Dancer, in another lifetime, you have sat before me in the Elders council. You have been a daughter to me. You have been a dear male friend that died in my arms in war. I now stand before you with an open heart and support you in this lifetime to continue the work your soul has chosen to do. When you know what that work is, I will support you just like I stand as the wind beneath Grandmother's wings. You are family. Nothing is ever too much to ask of me. Remember that in bad times as well as good. Have a good ceremony. May a strong dream carry you far and bring you back safely to us."

I looked deep into his blue eyes, noting his long hair braided with a traditional eagle feather hanging from the tie. "Thank you, Grandfather Strong Bear." I could not say much; I knew Grandfather had been one of those grandfathers in my vision, with the same blue eyes to his soul and the eagle feather adorning his braid. I knew what he said was true.

And the other lifetimes Grandfather spoke of, though I had no memory of them, I felt my body awaken to the feelings of truth, but what did Grandfather Strong Bear mean by 'return safely'? Could this vision quest be unsafe? After all, I was just in the backyard, in Grandmother's lodge.

These thoughts crossed my mind as I ducked to enter the lodge.

As I have been taught, I said, "To all my relations."

This would be my home from sunset to sunrise. I felt cozy inside. The flowers were so beautiful and fragrant.

Grandmother said, "Close the flap."

It became instantly dark inside, pitch dark. I held my hand before my face and could not see it. I took another deep breath of fragrant beauty and centered myself. This could be a very long night.

I fumbled for my lighter, remembering exactly where I had put it on my mesa, but in the dark, I still missed it. I felt around carefully so I wouldn't knock everything out of place, and I found it. I lit my candle, which created a warm glow. My eyes grew accustomed to the twilight as I sat before my mesa. It did feel magickal. My hand reached for the beautiful fan and abalone shell filled with the smudge mixture. Using the lighter, I let the flame nibble at the sage and cedar, which began to smoke, then the lavender crumbled with the flame. I loved the smell of these herbs when the smoke intertwined and blended. I kept the fire on the herbs until I could smell the distinct gentle fragrance of the sweet grass. Then I did as Grandmother had taught me. I called the powers of the winged one into the fan. The smell of each of the sacred plants awakened my senses. I fanned this smudge mixture around the lodge and myself.

As I have been taught, I prayed: "Sacred sage, help cleanse and banish any negativity from this space."

I doubt if there was any, but before a ceremony begins, one always makes sure it is a clean space.

"Sacred cedar, bring balance to me." I concentrated on centering myself, breathing deep and low in my belly.

"Beautiful lavender, bring me beauty in my ceremony, and long braided sweet grass, please bless this sacred space and help me seek my vision. I need your help, all of you."

The lodge was smudged, then I realized there was a lot of smoke in this small space. I could not open the flap or leave the lodge for any reason, any reason at all. I quickly put the smudge out as my eyes began to water. I placed the smudge, lighter, and fan back on the mesa exactly where I had placed them before so I could find them when I blew the candle out. I didn't want to use the candle if I could help it. The darkness held secrets I needed to explore.

"Oh, Sacred Ancestors, those who love me since always and for always, help me in my journey into womanhood. Show me what I need to see. Oh, Sacred Ancestors help me to open the inner gateways so that something *special* happens tonight."

I spoke prayers to all eight directions, but especially in the southeast of my circle where the ancestors—my ancestors—and the Little People reside.

I only wanted ancestors who were in the light to be a part of my ceremony. I faced the southeast while sitting in the lodge, and my voice became firm. "To all my ancestors who love me since always and for always help me to remember, help me seek my vision for who I am becoming as an adult, and help me remember who I have been. One more thing; help me stay awake. Thank You."

I think I prayed for a long time because when I was finished, I couldn't hear as much sound outside. Grandmother and Grandfather's home was in the suburbs of Flatrock, New Mexico. It was quiet and beautiful, and we could see the stars easily from here. There was some traffic noise, but once inside the lodge, the outside world seemed further and further away. I sat quietly, waiting for something, for anything, to happen.

I don't know how long I sat in the lodge. I held the cold crystal to my heart and felt my energy begin to warm it up. Nothing. I put it down. I reached for the top of the lodge and touched the roses and carnations. Each had a different feel. Rose petals were velvety soft, while carnations had pointy edges on each petal. In the dark, the feeling was beautiful.

I picked my drum up, asked for a song, and started drumming. Something welled up, and a melody with no words took me. The song slowly filled the lodge and wrapped itself around me. My voice became stronger and stronger and seemed to travel out the top of the lodge to the stars. Everything started shifting.

I was being carried on the wings of my song. I kept singing and singing, and the sounds took on meaning without words, not English words anyway.

I saw myself—a tall black woman from the Zulu Tribe. I was a dreamer woman. I was sitting in a small hut, off by itself, far away from my village. This was where I went to dream, to see the needs of the people, and how I could guide them. I saw huge ships with white cloth larger than clouds coming to our shores. I saw our people screaming and being herded onto these ships.

The further the ships traveled, the harder time I had connecting, but I felt the horror and shock of my people being captured and taken away. I cried out from the pain of wombs being violated. I felt their cries of death as they were taken further and further away. I ran back to the village to warn my people, but they didn't believe me. Tribes at war they understood, but canoes big enough to hold an entire village, and white-skinned men coming to steal them away—never.

They told me to return to my hut and let the medicine men dream for the people. I left the village rejected. In my vision, I saw myself living in my dreaming hut. The future of my people flooded into me. I didn't know what to do. The village had silenced my voice, yet I cried out in the night. I woke the lions with my sounds. I saw in my dream that the ships and village were gone. I had to know if I was crazy or if this were true. Did I foresee the future? I very carefully crept back to my village, and it was destroyed. I saw some of my people wandering about, hopelessly lost. The wives, husbands, and children had been stolen, all gone on the big canoes.

I went back to my hut. I tried dreaming with my people, but they kept going further and further away. Time passed slowly, lonely. For days, I ate little so as to dream deeper.

I saw more suffering.

Months passed. I walked and ate what I could as I continued to reach out to my people in the dream. Why was I saved? What was my purpose without my village?

In one dream, my captive sister came to me. She was in a strange land, wearing strange clothes. She wasn't happy, but she wasn't suffering. She was learning the medicine of the white man. He recognized her knowledge of plants and healing. He had bought her, and though he owned her, he was kind and was teaching her his medicine way. I knew I'd never see her again in this lifetime. I looked into her eyes and saw my Aunt Kathy Flowing Heart. Could they be the same person—these two women across time and space? I felt it in my body. Yes, they were the same.

My life was lonely in that lifetime. My village, my family, everything I had grown up with, all I knew had been destroyed. I lived my life learning and growing, but very alone. My African name came to me; it was Zama. Somehow, I knew it meant *to try*.

* * *

I sat up with a bolt. Had I fallen asleep? Had I been dreaming? Did I scream out in my sleep? I wondered if Grandmother's neighbors heard me. I remembered seeing Aunt Amy in the dream, but what did that vision have to do with my Rite of Passage?

It was my song. My voice took me into the dream, through the veil of remembering. Is this one of my medicine gifts? There was only one way to find out. I picked up my gourd and began to sing again to open my spirit to the song that wanted to be birthed. I sang and sang.

Nothing happened. Maybe it was just a dream, not real at all.

I recognized my doubt voice, my lower self, trying to run the show. So, as Grandmother taught me, I took a deep breath, then shouted out my doubt shout. Like a coyote, I howled three times. I shouted doubt out. I didn't care if the neighbors heard me.

I realized I could travel back in time and visit past lives, but what was this life to bring? Who was I to be in this lifetime? What was my destiny? I knew one thing, in my Rite of Passage heart talk, I had given voice to my inner child. Now I would give voice to my adult. I would never again allow a village or a town to stop my voice. I would speak out as Spirit determined, whether they believed me or not. I would not let my people down again. I would speak with such power and conviction that people would heed my words! This is what Zama learned in that lifetime.

Okay, I would try again. I smudged myself and picked the drum back up. It shouldn't matter, drum or gourd, but why push it? The drum worked the first time.

I began softly, allowing my hand to create a rhythm I was unfamiliar with, a rhythm and melody that sounded Japanese in nature, or so I thought. I closed my eyes to see if I could navigate the feeling that was emerging as I crossed the boundaries of time.

I was Kiyomi San, the head matriarch, responsible for training the Geishas. I held a high position in this dynasty, but I was jealous of my sister, who was the first wife of the emperor. It should have been me. I was older and wiser, or so I thought, but the emperor chose her, and she wouldn't listen to my counsel.

This temple was the most sacred training temple. Its beauty reflected what I taught. My life was full and abundant. I loved the young women I trained. They were all like my daughters, and I trained them in the sacred art of sexuality, politics, history, and culture. They learned the high tradition of the tea ceremony. To the gifted ones, I taught the way of the dagger and the fine art of poison. I was proud of my Geisha-trained assassins. Geishas held highly honored and respected positions with great responsibility. Our traditions were thousands of years old.

My sister, the empress, wanted to change it. She said it was demeaning. She said that my life's work taught women to be less than men. We would discuss and argue, but in the end, she was the empress, and the traditions were going to change.

I was angry and felt it in my whole body.

I didn't agree with her. Many of my Geisha daughters didn't agree either. They would never disagree with me because of the influence I had on them. There was one who was my best assassin and most beloved daughter, Sakura Cherry Blossom. She was invited to one of the sacred houses to entertain and present the beauty of her tea ceremony.

I instructed her to kill the head of that family, who was supporting my sister, in order to protect my Geisha daughters. But something went wrong, and Sakura Cherry Blossom was killed. My heart and spirit were broken. They knew the order came from me. I was only trying to preserve a tradition that gave women respect beyond that of the lowly wife.

The head of the guard, a very handsome man, came from the emperor to my temple court. I was waiting calmly, dressed in one of my high ceremonial dresses, white with hand-stitching, depicting a story of slaying the dragon. He had come to my temple often to see me. He was my consort.

With love and pain in his eyes, he said, "Kiyomi San, you can take your own life with honor, or I will take your life. This brings me no honor; it is my duty."

It was my choice. I sat under the bare branches of the tree Sakura Cherry Blossom had loved so much. She would play her flute for hours, and I would listen. Here I took my own life with the poisons I had dispensed to others. As I slipped into the arms of death, I saw clearly that I had crossed into the dark without knowing it, thinking that what I was doing was right. Change had to take place, and my death was a part of that change.

As I peacefully floated away from my body, accepting the pain I had caused others, I crossed into the other world to review my life.

* * *

I became aware of being in the purification lodge. It was like waking up into another reality.

Who is Sakura Cherry Blossom now? Do we know each other now?

I closed my eyes to try and recapture that lifetime. Suddenly, her spirit body stood before me in her youth and beauty, and I looked deeply into her eyes, the windows to the soul. There was Aunt Kathy Flowing Heart!

What does this have to do with my life now? I wondered. I was the head matriarch of a sacred temple who taught the Geishas spiritual sexuality. I was an African medicine woman and dreamer in another lifetime.

"Who am I now?" I asked with authority into the empty space of the Womb of Grandmother.

I felt the coldness of the night and wrapped my medicine blanket around me. I didn't move. I was afraid. The medicine blanket couldn't stop my inner fears. How could I be so wise and yet die for my blindness and pride? What if this same pride leads me on the wrong path in this lifetime? I had great power, and I killed a Geisha daughter, sending her to her death. I wept and wept till my body was trembling with my sorrow. Did I even want to see who I was this time?

I heard myself cry out, "Grandmother I am confused. Help me!"

I saw Grandmother's eyes appear before me. She said, *What are you seeking from me?*

"Oh, Grandmother, help me so I don't cross the line into the dark again," I said aloud though I only heard her words in my mind.

Granddaughter you have already been tested. You passed—with a little guidance from your parents. You were tested young, but things are moving much faster now. We can't wait until potentials are fully into their adulthood. We made a mistake and waited too long to test others. We realized how much time we wasted, especially when the dark force is seeking them out younger and younger.

"Grandmother, I remember when I was the matriarch of the Geisha Temple and my decision killed Aunt Kathy Flowing Heart."

Grandmother interrupted me, which she seldom does, *Yes, yes, I know. She does too. No big deal. Things happen. What are you learning?*

I was so surprised that they knew. My sobbing stopped, and I felt thrown back into the center of myself, clear and grounded.

"Grandmother, I want to learn the ways of Spiritual Sexuality. I am seeking it from you, a medicine woman, a firewoman, who teaches this sacred knowledge. It has been my path before."

Granddaughter, you have been a warrior in many lifetimes, both male and female, not always fighting but always a warrior. You will remember more tonight. You have chosen a warrior's path again. It's not easy. Testing and challenge will become close allies, comrades to you.

I wondered what she meant by that.

If you ever choose the easy path, your passion, your spiritual determination will leave you. You will become complacent in your life, and your spiritual flame will lessen. Your spirit will feel like it's dying. Never choose the easy, complacent life.

I saw Grandmother's wise face in the darkness.

Look for what is simple and flows, but not what is easy. Life will always present opportunities. Testing and challenge will teach you self-worth. Wind Dancer, life does not need to be hard. It can be simple but it usually isn't easy.

I wondered if I would remember everything that Grandmother had said. She shouted *my doubt shout* so loud that I thought a pack of coyotes was outside my lodge. I didn't think my doubt voice would ever return.

"Thank you, Grandmother." My eyes were huge, staring into the dark of the cold lodge.

She laughed. I could hear her as if I were sitting in her room.

My pleasure. It was fun. You ought to see yourself right now—pretty funny. You have much more to do tonight, and don't bother me. I want to sleep. Don't worry. I'll come if you really need me.

How does she do that? I wondered. *She just pops into my head as if she were sitting here with me. How does she know when to come?*

One of these days, I would stop asking that question, and I would know how she knows and how she does what she does. That *knowing* came out of my mind as a vow to the universe.

"I will be a medicine woman and a teacher of Spiritual Sexuality," I said out loud.

I hadn't even attended my first workshop. How did I even know what that was? But I knew. My body knew it was awakening to the memories of who I had been and how I could use ancient knowledge to accomplish what I was supposed to do in this lifetime.

Learn from the mistakes of your teachers, I heard echoing in my mind.

I guess I'm my best teacher because I sure made a lot of mistakes, I thought, but instead of feeling condemned, I felt encouraged. I had made mistakes, but wisdom had come from them. And then I realized my voice wasn't expressing doubt; it was sharing wisdom. Strength had blossomed from the truth of my vision.

Grandmother said that I had a lot more to do tonight. Time didn't exist in the purification lodge, and I had no idea how much time had passed or how much time remained before sunrise. I had never guessed that I might run out of time! Boredom was certainly not the problem at this point.

Grandmother, I shouted in my mind, *before you go to sleep, I have a question.*

How could I go to sleep with someone shouting in my head? I heard her answer.

Oh, I'm sorry, Grandmother. I wasn't sure you would be able to hear me call. Can I ask my question?

I'm awake now. You might as well!

Should I continue to seek out past lives, or should I seek a future vision? I said, concentrating so that I wouldn't lose our connection.

Use your name, Wind Dancer. There is no past or future—only now. It's all happening now. One lifetime on top of another—like a stack of records—old records, not CDs, not an mp3 player. Got the image? Use your name, Wind Dancer!

Thank you, Grandmother! Goodnight.

Good night, Wind Dancer.

Use my name, Wind Dancer, Wind Dancer, Wind Dancer. When Grandmother gave me my name, I was in her room. One travels back, then both become like one, yet neither is separate, yet both are individuals. Maybe I can dance the winds of time and see many lives simultaneously and get a thread of what they all have to do with this lifetime. If I can find the right thread, maybe it will weave through all my lifetimes.

This wisdom wasn't coming from me. I had no idea where these thoughts were coming from.

I suddenly felt pressed for time.

"Wind Dancer; is there a Wind Dancer song inside me?" I asked the dark space of the lodge. *What would happen if I unraveled that thread? Would I no longer exist? Would I disappear from this Womb of Grandmother's purification lodge, cross time, and never return? Is this what Grandfather meant when he said travel far and come back safely?*

Remembering Dreams with the Wind, I realized I may never want to return to this life. Maybe one of my other lives is better. I wondered how my family would know what happened to me. In the morning, they would open the lodge door, and only a wisp of wind would emerge. Would I leave them for one of my other lives?

This is my life now. I've just started, and I have work to do here. I'm in this lodge and the Rite of Passage Ceremony to remember my soul's purpose in this lifetime, not vacate the premises I chose to be born in. This body is pretty good. I like myself. I like my body as it's becoming a mature woman.

I voiced another vow to the universe. "Okay, decision made, I will travel the winds of time, and I will return here to this body and to this family."

I heard Grandmother's voice. *Thank you, Granddaughter. I was hoping you would choose to stay. You are remembering quickly, and there is still so much for you to learn. Dance the winds now. Gather the threads of your lives. Weave a new blanket called Rebecca Sage Wind Dancer.*

I closed my eyes, sent a kiss to Grandmother's cheek, and then a beautiful soft song came out of my heart and womb.

I was Dreams with the Wind, back in the kiva in my Rite of Passage Ceremony feeling all of the women who had done this ceremony for hundreds of years in this one kiva. It all seemed as if I had been here before. I had just returned from my vision quest and the initiation with the Grandmother Council into the Yellow Moon Society. They said I was to learn Fire Spiritual Sexuality Medicine. I was to tell the Grandfather Elders about my vision and leave nothing out.

I knew Grandfather Standing Bear would be sitting on the council with his deep blue eyes, long braided hair, and first eagle feather tied to his braid. I wasn't sure who the other grandfathers would be. But before I went into my kiva ceremony, Grandfather Standing Bear spoke with me and said he would stand behind me and speak for me if need be. He knew I was ready to work with a fire medicine man, but the final decision would be mine—if I expressed my maturity.

My heart opened to this wise elder, "Grandfather Standing Bear, I will do my best to show my wisdom."

As I stood before the Grandfather Elders, my heart pounded. I remembered to breathe as I waited for their final decision. Grandmother Seeks the Truth, who had been called in, nodded her head in affirmation. I felt my shoulders drop with relief, and I exhaled. I knew the eyes and soul of this Grandmother.

The elder Grandfather Standing Bear nodded his head, and the corners of his mouth took on a quiet smile. He said, "The Spiritual Elder Council and the Yellow Moon Society confirmed your initiation. The decision was made in your vision quest. You will be taught the Sacred Spiritual Sexual medicine. Our Grandmothers will teach you all they know. You will work with more than one fire medicine man to learn all the ways of men and you will work with fire medicine women to learn the ways of women. Speak up now if this frightens you. If you commit, it is your life's work."

"Oh, Grandfather, there is no doubt or fear in me. I am open to learning everything I can from my elders. I would be honored to make this my life's work. It is a gift to me that I may share with others."

Grandfather Standing Bear said, "You are known as Dreams with the Wind. May you always dream with the wind and birth yourself into womanhood, your spiritual sexual name is Fire Winds. You will not use it outside of your learning circle with the Grandmothers until you are initiated as a full Sacred Sexual teacher." Then the tepee flap blew open, and a gust of hot wind danced around me. I closed my eyes.

I realized I was sitting in the purification lodge, and I was overjoyed. I had been a dreamer before, and I had worn darker skin in another part of the Earth. I was a walker of the winds of time. I needed to go back. There was more. Something was trying to speak to me, to that other time and place. I closed my eyes and sang my song to find myself instantly standing before the elders. I lifted my head and felt my long black hair cascade over my shoulders. I had a big smile on my face. I could hardly contain my joy.

Grandfather Standing Bear and Grandmother Seeks the Truth stood on either side of me as we walked out of the teepee.

Bending to move through the open flaps, Grandmother went out first, then me. The rest of the Elder Circle followed and created a half-moon behind me, in front stood my tribe. A roar burst forth from all, including me.

It was a wonderful celebration. The word had already spread that I was to learn the secret ways of Spiritual Sexuality medicine. The eligible young men of the tribe gifted me. I was honored to receive so many gifts. I knew the gifting was an encouragement for me to look their way when I was ready to share a tepee. It would be some time before I did, and it would have to be the right man. My training would be for my entire life, and I would train others. My mate had to honor this way. The young men were trying to outdo each other. Their ponies would fly by with them doing tricks.

One quiet, strong young man walked up to me. I knew him as he, like all young men, had the duty to take care of the young girls in the tribe. It was part of their education in learning about the mysteries of women. He handed me a carved bone whistle with beading on it. It was intricate and beautiful.

"Did you do this beading? It is beautiful."

He smiled and almost blushed with pride.

"You deserve the finest. Your path needs to be honored as few are chosen to walk your road."

His eyes pierced mine for a split second. I looked down in appreciation of such an honor. I felt his soul and knew I would consider him when the time was right, and I was ready for a mate.

There was a moment between us. Time did not exist. I closed my eyes and felt Wind Dancer looking out through my eyes. She was me, here from another lifetime. I am awake-dreaming. Something magickal was happening as the tribe continued to celebrate.

"Dreams with the Wind!"

I was being called to come and enjoy the feast. The drum and songs were calling me. I spoke to myself, "Wind Dancer, we will meet again. We are sisters of the same soul journey. We are one—Dreams with the Wind and Wind Dancer. We have met on the winds of time."

* * *

I, Wind Dancer, took a deep breath and directed myself back into the lodge in Grandmother's backyard. I sat in the silence of the night and spoke the names of who I had been, Zama and Kiyomi San. I asked for greater knowledge of what I did in those lifetimes. I was looking for the thread.

Zama, a tall, dark, proud woman, looked deeply into the eyes of my soul. She smiled and spoke to me in her native tongue. I understood her because I was her.

"I taught the young men how to dream into the lion for their initiation into manhood. I directed them to become the lion, kill the lion, and receive its medicine. I guided them in the dream as they stalked the lion and took it down. I trained only a select few, and the ones I trained all lived to be great warriors."

I sent my voice out again in song, seeking yet another length of the thread of who I was and who I was becoming as Sage Wind Dancer.

A small Mayan woman, Itzel, showed herself to me. She was one of the few who escaped Cortez.

I saw Star Dreamer, from the Warrior's Clan, emerge from the Sacred Mayan Temple, running at full speed. He thrust a wrapped bundle toward me and asked me to hide it under my dress. He glanced behind him as I unwrapped the bundle. Star Dreamer took the cloth. I stared in wonder at the ancient Crystal Skull with a moving jaw, the most sacred object of the Mayan Civilization. Realizing the danger, I quickly positioned the skull beneath my skirt as if I were carrying an unborn child. Star Dreamer wrapped the cloth tightly around my belly to hold it in place as we ducked into the jungle and ran for our lives. If the skull fell into the hands of Cortez, it would be lost to the Mayan people forever.

I felt more lifetimes on the winds of change.

My name was Maltheo. I was a man, a confidant of Maltese who was the ruler of the Maltese people. As I saw Maltese in my vision, I recognized him as Thunder Wolf. I spent many years studying alchemy, deeply entrenched in my research. I often discussed my findings with Maltese, who warned me that I was stepping over sacred laws with my research, but I didn't listen because I was close to discovering a tincture to stop death. I even killed my lover, who was going to betray me. I thought I was justified because she was trying to stop me. I stepped into the dark.

As I, Maltheo, transitioned at death, I realized that Maltese was right. It is important to listen to the counsel of others. I was pulling the threads from times past, wisdom remembered, a soul always on the quest for knowledge.

I had many lifetimes involving Spiritual Sexuality. No wonder I knew things that were not from this lifetime but others. Thank God my parents did not squelch that. I could see that my commitment hadn't changed in all these lifetimes. It just evolved as I learned from my mistakes and developed different aspects of myself. I have been many things, but what was my destiny in this lifetime? What would be my destiny in the next? I had an overwhelming *knowing* that my work was not finished. I had to continue.

I heard myself breathe deeply.

Within the silence across time, in all my voices, I heard, "I commit myself to be of service, to learn all I can of the hidden secrets of Spiritual Sexuality, to speak truth, to keep and protect the teachings, and the children, for this and the next generations. I will learn the ways of a warrior. I will be strong and yet embrace my femininity."

There was another moment of silence, an eternity, and then something shifted. I felt calm and relaxed. I even laughed. I realized how simple it was and yet how challenging. It was a matter of greeting each day and never forgetting my intent. Never forgetting and always remembering. *What would that look like*, I wondered.

I sat for an eternal moment and felt the gate closing as I thanked the powers and sacred ancestors. I smudged everything as I had been taught and sat in silent gratitude.

I had no sooner completed this when the morning song began outside my kiva, the Womb of Grandmother birthing me. The song greeted the new day. I joined the outer song with my voice from within the lodge. We sang together until the song was over.

The flap opened.

Grandmother stood to one side of the door, giving me a clear view of Grandfather Sun coming up over the trees.

I crawled out of the lodge. It was cold, but I didn't care. There was a fire burning in the outdoor fireplace. Without hesitation, I took my old clothes off and threw them in the fire. I stood nude, watching them burn. I was lost in the warmth of the flames when Grandmother put a medicine blanket around me. We stood together until the last bit of clothing burned. We walked silently into the side door that led to Grandmother's bedroom. Her cats met us at the door. I went directly into a hot shower. It felt wonderful.

Afterward, I slipped into a bathrobe and knee socks, and Grandmother and I ate breakfast together. Never did cantaloupe taste so good! We were quiet for some time, drinking hot sage tea together. I didn't know what to say; so much had happened.

Finally, I said, "Thank you for my medicine name."

She smiled. "You're welcome. Your friends and family will be here at noon. You have plenty of time to take a nap if you wish and take the lodge down. Burn the flowers in the fire. Give them back to Spirit. Your mother is bringing your new outfit in plenty of time for you to prepare yourself. You know, curl your hair, put makeup on. There are some warm clothes on the chair you can put on to do your work outside. Let's have one more mug of tea, and then you can do what you want."

"I want to take the lodge down first and smudge everything. I feel very strong now."

Grandmother wrinkled her brow. "Oh, did you sleep all night, Sage? Not tired?"

"Grandmother, stop teasing. You told me not to bother you in your bedroom; you wanted to get some sleep. You told me to use my medicine name, so, I did."

Grandmother retorted, "Well, if you think I got any sleep you're wrong. I was called on the spiritual telephone line to confirm if a young Indian woman actually dreamed her vision of being initiated into the Yellow Moon Society or if she lied. I declare, I've got to train those Elder Circles to access this other dimensional knowledge on their own, disturbing an old woman's sleep for an obvious yes is ridiculous. They should have trusted her. She was the most promising student to learn the Spiritual Sexual Medicine. She had never lied to them about anything before, not even white lies."

I felt a little sheepish and looked at Grandmother through half-closed eyes.

Grandmother chuckled. "Some night's sleep I got, but that's ceremony for you."

At that point, I looked at Grandmother Spinning Winds and tried to figure out how old she really was. Was she sixty or two hundred and sixty? Had she lived all this time without dying, like in Biblical times? After all, she had just told me she was on the Spiritual Circle of Elders.

Grandmother's voice broke into my awareness. "You'd better get going on that lodge. You want time to nap and get ready for your celebration."

"I've already had my celebration, Grandmother, but this one will be nice, too. I think I'll invite Dreams with the Wind to join me, to see how we do it now."

"Who's Dreams with the Wind?" Grandmother asked and winked at the same time.

I skipped out the door in my sweats and boots. After all, it was December, and it was still chilly out.

I smudged the inside and outside of the lodge and then began to remove my ceremonial items, wrapping them carefully before placing them into my backpack. I took all the flowers out of the lodge and walked over to the fireplace and thanked the flowers before laying them on the hot coals to give them away.

I took a moment to warm my hands.

Next came the blankets. Shaking each one out, I folded them and placed them in the wheelbarrow to haul down to the shed. It took quite a few trips as I had blankets from inside and outside the lodge.

This was a huge job, and I was beginning to feel tired and could sense that I was moving slower.

I stood gazing at the heavy canvas, which still needed to be removed from the exterior of the lodge. When Grandmother came to help, I was so relieved! We folded the large canvas top together. She taught me how she liked it done so that it would be easy to unfold for the next lodge. It was like making a bed together after a warm night's sleep.

I silently admitted that it took two people to set up and take down the lodge.

"Sage, now that everything's put away and smudged, I suggest you sleep awhile. Crawl into my bed if you're tired."

"Grandmother, I'm pooped, and sleep sounds really good."

Then a thought occurred to me. Sleeping in Grandmother's room with all of her medicine—I hoped I could sleep and didn't go off on another dreaming quest.

Just then, I heard Grandmother's voice comforting me. *Don't worry, the room has an off switch. Besides, you're tired. You used a lot of energy last night. You'll sleep. And yes, I will wake you.*

Smiling because she had read my thoughts again, I turned towards the house.

See you after my nap, Grandmother.

Chapter 7

Finally! Honest Talk About Sex and Relationships

My eyes were still closed, and I woke slowly to the sounds of familiar voices filling the house. Grandmother had not come in to wake me, so I knew I could lie here a bit longer. I heard Grandma Bebee's voice, Aunt Amy Singing Hawk, and Aunt Kathy Flowing Heart. I heard the strong male voices of my clan, Uncle Tim Fire Hawk and Grandfather Standing Bear— *Oh, I mean Grandfather Strong Bear.* Then I realized their souls were one and the same.

My friends weren't here yet. Everyone was probably getting the space ready. I thought of the dresses I had seen in the mall and was excited to see which one my mother had bought for me. I sat up at that point, too excited to stay in bed any longer.

A beautiful white buckskin dress with beads and conch shells was hanging there for me to see, just like I had described to my mother from my vision. I jumped out of bed to feel and smell the leather dress. It was soft and smelled incredibly good. I loved the smell of leather.

Dreams with the Wind, this was your dress. I slipped it on, and it fit perfectly. There were also white moccasins for me to wear.

I looked in the mirror, and Dreams with the Wind looked back at me. So did Zama, Kiyomi San, Itzel, and Maltheu. All of me, male and female, stared back at me in my reflection.

This is my form in this lifetime. All of whom I have ever been—or at least the ones I met last night—were here with me, too.

I looked at the makeup bag and curling iron that Grandmother had laid out for me. I decided to leave my hair straight, but I put makeup on. I wanted my eyes to be as beautiful as Dreams with the Wind, and her hair was straight and shiny.

Just then, Grandmother opened the bedroom door and saw me in my beautiful new buckskin dress. Her whole face smiled as our eyes met in the mirror. There was a special moment between us, and my heart was open and filled with love. Time and space didn't exist. She saw who I had been and who I was.

I reached out to her. "No more white lies, Grandmother. Dreams with the Wind is teaching me. Dreams with the Wind never lied. Whatever happened to her, Grandmother?"

Grandmother Spinning Winds, her face still glowing, looked at me with love. "She is growing up, just like you. Remember, time doesn't exist, except in the minds of man. She is you and you are her, Wind Dancer. Your hair looks beautiful. I like it straight."

"The house is ready for your celebration, and almost everyone is here. I want everybody to be here and seated before you come out, You must make an entrance! This is a special occasion, and you must walk into your Rite of Passage like a queen preparing for her coronation."

A queen. I was just a girl yesterday. That wasn't my doubt voice. It was more like an inner acceptance of the knowledge I had gained. Maybe I did grow up overnight.

The doorbell rang, and we could hear a crowd of folks coming in. I was getting excited.

Grandmother squeezed my hands. "I need to check on things. I'll send my kitties in to visit with you and help keep you calm."

The house was filled with the sounds of people. When I heard the voices of my friends, I got nervous. What would they think? Grandmother opened the bedroom door, and both cats came in and walked right over to me. I began to scratch their chins and backsides as they purred.

I reminded myself to breathe slowly and deeply. My belly told me lots of food had arrived, and, boy, was I hungry! The cantaloupe I had shared with Grandmother that morning was delicious, but I was craving something more substantial. As I thought about being hungry, I realized I had an even stronger emotion. I was thankful—thankful to be alive. I was grateful for my parents, my clan aunts and uncles, Grandma Bebee, Grandmother Spinning Winds, and Grandfather Strong Bear.

I was in a quiet moment, a prayer of giving thanks, when my mother and father opened the door and stepped inside Grandmother's room. They paused for a moment and just looked at me. The smiles on their faces and the love in their eyes said it all. I felt such love and respect for them.

"Are you ready, Wind Dancer?" Mom asked. "Everyone is excited, and

Grandmother is having a hard time getting them to stay in one place."

"Yes, I'm ready."

Dad was beaming. "You're a beautiful woman, Sage. Please, lead the way. Walk into your womanhood, your Rite of Passage celebration."

I stepped into the hallway and cut through the kitchen. There was delicious food everywhere! Ignoring the growl in my stomach, I pushed the kitchen door open and entered the living room. Everyone stopped talking and looked at me. I could tell that no one had known about the white buckskin dress. My friend's mouths dropped open.

As usual, Grandmother Bebee spoke her thoughts, "You're a beautiful woman."

Everyone added the traditional 'Ho!' in agreement. My friends added a whistle and a 'Right on, girlfriend!'

After the smudge had been passed, Aunt Amy blessed me with the sacred smoke. A place of honor had been created by laying a beautiful medicine blanket over a chair surrounded by so many flowers that it looked like the roof of the lodge. I sat down, and Grandmother Spinning Winds began to dance chief the ceremony.

"Welcome, everyone, and thank you all for coming. Please, everyone, take a deep breath and go inside. Seek your quiet wisdom place. I am asking all the women to go deep within your womb space and share with Sage Wind Dancer the things you value about men.

Of course, Grandmother Bebee went first. "No matter how old you get, and I'm eighty-six this year, sex is always important. It makes you feel young and alive!"

Aunt Amy shared next. "I have never been married, but that hasn't stopped me from having men as friends and lovers. I value their opinions. It gives us the male perspective and helps us to have balance in our lives as women."

As my mother began to speak, I listened very closely.

"What I value most in a man is his self-confidence—not bravado—but true confidence."

She looked at my dad with love and respect in her eyes. I would remember that look forever.

Mom continued, "I value a man who has a willingness to grow and change in all aspects—emotionally, mentally, physically, spiritually, and sexually. A man who is not afraid of change is worth his weight in gold."

My aunt, Kathy Flowing Heart, said, "I value a man who is a good sensual lover with his body, his *Tipili.*" Looking at my friends, she added, "That's the ancient native term for penis."

My friends looked a little uncomfortable, but they were listening.

Aunt Amy smiled. "I value a man who knows how to be a good lover, too. It is important he not only knows how but that he enjoys pleasuring his woman with his fingers and his mouth. Oh, yeah, a man has to be good at oral sex and willing to learn. Every woman is different."

Mom winked at Dad again.

I was a little surprised at what was being said. I looked at my friends again, and Susie, my spunky friend with short, blond curly hair, looked excited to hear such honest talk. Cody, it appeared, had brushed his hair for the first time in months, and Michael sat tall and straight as an arrow. They looked like they were taking mental notes. I'm sure they wished they had pen and paper because this was important information for young men. Andrea, my sweet friend with long dark hair and a natural wave, was blushing bright red. Shane, the most mature-looking of my friends with his broad shoulders and short dark hair, was smiling.

My aunts looked at each other and started laughing—they had gottten on their bandwaggon—and everyone, joined in the laughter.

"Honesty and integrity are high on my charts," Grandmother Spinning Winds said. "No matter what my partner does, I want to hear it from him. I want the truth, no lies, and no white lies to protect me. I don't need protection. It doesn't matter if he has an affair, if he breaks a promise or if he lost his retirement due to a market crash. I want our relationship to be based on truth, the kind of truth that strips you of all your ego self-importance, to stand before each other naked."

Wow. Grandmother brought the whole group to silence. I knew she was talking about a lot more than standing before each other without clothes on.

Grandmother's voice was kind as she looked at my friends and said, "All right, Andrea and Susie, it's your turn, and it doesn't need to be in the order I spoke your names."

There was a sigh of relief from Andrea, and she blushed.

Susie jumped right in. "Though I like boys that are cute, what's more important is that they are nice, not mean, and that they treat me special."

Andrea spoke shyly. "I'm still pretty confused about boys, but I like boys that can dance. I love to dance and have been taking ballroom dance lessons. If ever I get married, I would want to be sure he can dance with me."

All my friends looked at her. None of us knew that about Andrea.

Michael said, "Guess I'd better start taking dance lessons."

Some of the men in the circle nodded, and there was laughter from some of the women. Aunt Amy said, "Absolutely."

Michael looked at the men and realized they were serious. "I have to learn how to dance?"

Once again, the group laughed and said, "Ho!"

"Ladies," Grandmother said, "it's time for us to listen to the men and learn from them."

I wondered how I was going to remember all that was being said.

Grandmother Spinning Winds read my thoughts. "Wind Dancer, you don't need to memorize all that has been spoken. As you enter into relationships, these values will pop out of your memory—not just from this lifetime, but from all lifetimes. Trust your womb space. Stay in the center of your own essence. Know that you will make mistakes in love. Mistakes are how we learn. As long as you learn from your mistakes, you'll do just fine. Try and learn from your mistakes the first time, so that you don't have to repeat them."

Once again, the adults laughed and wholeheartedly agreed.

"Men, please begin."

I was bracing myself for big breasts, a shapely body, and no fat. When I looked around the room at my aunts, mother, and grandmothers, they were calm. They knew something I did not. I felt an inner knowing and confidence from them.

My father took the lead. "I appreciate your mother's sense of humor. Whenever we begin to argue or when times are difficult, Rose has a way with her humor that makes things better. It's hard to fight or be stressed when you're laughing. Of course, everything that the women value in men, I value in women, especially a woman who loves sex. Hmm, delicious." He looked at Mom and smiled.

Clan Uncle Tim Fire Hawk took that moment of connection as his cue to begin. "I value women who are independent and self-sufficient but appreciate the help of a man. Combine this with being feminine and sensual and I'm all in."

Grandfather Strong Bear, hair braided with an eagle feather tied to it, nodded. "A strong woman is a gift. I value someone I can discuss ideas with, someone who challenges me to grow, and who always seeks *The More* for herself, inviting my strength to help her. It makes me feel good to have a woman who needs me as a man, honoring our differences and sharing, knowing we are equal."

Clan Uncle Bruce Quiet Man nodded his agreement. "This is not talked about, but it can make all the difference in a long-term relationship. I love women who love sex—not just for the man but because she enjoys it for herself. I value when a woman speaks up, who states what she wants and doesn't make me guess. She likes to try new things in the bedroom, front room, or outdoors. I value an intelligent woman; someone I can share my dreams and aspirations with. We can build together."

I was surprised that none of the men mentioned the shape of a woman's body or the size of her boobs as something he valued.

Clan Uncle Rex looked at me and smiled. "Aah, there is a topic none of you men have mentioned, and I think Sage needs to hear how we men feel about a woman's body. The shape of her body doesn't matter to me—if she has big or small breasts. What I value about a woman is that she loves her body and is proud of it—no matter if she is a little skinny-minnie or if she carries extra weight. And, of course, if you love your body as a sacred temple, you will take care of your body. If you have an eating disorder, anorexia, bulimia, or are addicted to food, drugs, or alcohol, you will find a way to heal the pain you are experiencing. This is true for any physical or psychological challenges. I prefer a woman with a little extra roundness. It feels good when we snuggle."

I remembered Uncle Rex was a psychotherapist and healer. He had worked with a lot of wounded women. What he valued in a woman is just what I needed to hear.

That seemed to trigger the men.

Uncle Tim Fire Hawk said, "I have made love to women with beautiful bodies, but they were terrible lovers. We had nothing to talk about. A beautiful woman often thinks she is unattractive. Most women are very hard on themselves."

Uncle Rex nodded. "Some of my best friends and lovers are attractive women because they make themselves attractive. They are really nice people, and that's what is important to me."

I was shocked. I thought for sure large breasts and small rounded butts would take a higher place on the list.

"I thank you, men, for your honesty," Grandmother said. "It's time to hear from the younger men in the room."

Michael had no problem speaking up. "I may not be able to dance, but what I like about girls, I mean women, is their warm heart. I can talk to women in a way that I can't talk to my guy friends."

Grandfather Strong Bear nodded. "That is true, son, but there are brotherhood groups, men's clans, where the men have learned to talk to one another, to be there for each other. You are welcome to join us for our next men's purification lodge."

"Thank you, Grandfather." For the first time, I saw something in Michael that had been hidden by peer pressure.

"I'm next," Cody said. "There's a lot about women that I love.

This opening comment received some exclamations of agreement from the men in the group, and the women beamed with the pride of being women.

Cody continued, "A woman's skin feels so amazingly soft. I love to touch them, and I appreciate when a woman is comfortable being touched. Just because I touch her doesn't mean I want to take her to bed. A lot of girls my age have one thing in mind. I just want to take my time, get to know her, feel safe, and touch her."

"Why, Cody," Michael said, "aren't you a softy? I would have never known it the way you go around school."

"I'm not in school, and we were asked to be honest," Cody said a bit defensively. "I'm saying it the way it is—what I appreciate about women."

Grandmother looked at Grandfather Strong Bear. He caught her direction and said, "Michael there is a time to tease and a time to be respectful. We've all been through it, hiding who we really are. High school is a hard training ground. Maybe you young men should be thinking about a Rite of Passage and joining the men's clan. Hanging with boys retards your naturalness about sex and women. You've got good heads on your shoulders. You're invited to the men's clan and purification lodge."

I was proud of my friends. I wasn't sure if they would make fun of my Rite of Passage, understand it, or just sit there like bumps on a log, but what they shared meant a lot to me.

Shane, who had been quiet and listening intently, leaned forward. "I'd like to say something."

Grandfather nodded.

"Being a woman today is much different than long ago. Women need to be educated, feel fulfilled in their work—be it as a wife, a mother, or a sexual teacher." He glanced at me for a split second. "When a woman has a destiny to follow, then she needs a man that can honor that. She will respect him, and he will honor her. Magick can happen between a man and a woman, but they need to go outside the box of their traditional upbringing. They have to find the truth of their relationship together, and honor the road that the Great Spirit puts before them."

There was a hush in the room as these words tumbled out of this young man's mouth. From his expression, it seemed as if he was wondering where the words came from, too. He smiled and said, "Ho!"

Everyone joined in with a resounding Ho!

Something happened, and I saw Shane through different eyes. I no longer saw my teenage friend but a young man, a potential life partner.

Who was he? Was I remembering Shane from another lifetime? In that moment, he stood before Dreams with the Wind, too.

What everyone shared was beginning to sink in. *Yes, my physical body is important. It's good to be healthy and attractive and to accept myself for who I am, but physical appearance is not the most important thing to these men, not even to these boys—rather, young men my age. You could've fooled me.*

Spreading her arms, Grandmother said, "Does anyone have anything they want to add?"

Then, like popcorn, words of wisdom jumped out from this person and that person.

"Be natural. Even farting in bed can be fun—big and little frogs."

"Honor the difference between men and women."

"We are different and equal."

"Speak the unspeakable to each other."

"Don't let too much time pass before saying what you need to say."

"Sex and love are different. If you can have both, that's great, but sex with friends can be great if you respect the person and are honest with each other."

Michael and Cody confirmed this with a strong Ho!

Susie and Andrea looked at each other. I knew we would be talking about this later.

"Loving someone is a choice you have to make every day."

"There are no guarantees."

"You have to work on yourself in a relationship. You can never change another person, only yourself."

After a moment of silence, everyone looked around the room, then broke out in laughter again.

"I guess there were a few more things to share," Grandmother said.

I closed my eyes and connected to my heart. How could I share what I was feeling? Would my medicine gifts show my deep appreciation for everyone and the wisdom they shared? How could I remember it all? Remembering seemed to be the theme from one lifetime to another, from one day to the next.

I looked into Grandmother's eyes, and everything disappeared. It was just the two of us in the elder Grandfather circle from my other lifetime. I was waiting for the Grandfathers to determine if I was mature enough to learn the Spiritual Sexuality Medicine. *Remember to breathe and speak my truth. Be strong yet humble.*

I was back in Grandmother's living room, and I saw the twinkle in her eyes. I looked into everyone's eyes that had come in honor of my Rite of Passage, and something passed between each of us. I looked back and forth between my aunts and said, "I am happy we are sharing another lifetime together. I love you both." They looked at each other and smiled, and I knew they were aware that this wasn't the first lifetime we had spent together.

There was so much love and support in the room.

I closed my eyes and invited Dreams with the Wind to join me, to help me.

"Mom, Dad, I know how hard you both work for us to have what we have. It is not time for me to go to work yet, but I can be a bigger help around the house. I will start looking for things that need to be done and do them without you needing to ask me. When you are both coming home late, I can cook dinner and start learning some of Mom's recipes."

Mom and Dad both smiled.

"I know I'm just beginning on this path into adulthood, so please continue to guide me, and I will try to be open to your suggestions. I'm seeing that you know a lot more than I ever thought you knew."

When everyone laughed, I realized what I had said and bowed my head. "I didn't mean to be disrespectful."

Dad said, "I know, Hon. My father became amazingly wise as I grew up, too."

"I love you both. Thanks for being my parents and for making this Rite of Passage possible."

It was time to share my medicine gifts. I was excited to see how everyone received them.

"Mom, I picked your favorite colors and made your earrings of purple, lavender, red, and yellow beads. Your tobacco tie is purple, too. I hope you like them.

"Dad, you were harder, but I know you love to hunt so I beaded the head of a deer onto a new leather scabbard for your hunting knife. I bet you didn't realize I borrowed your knife so I could measure the new scabbard. Your tobacco tie is wrapped in camouflage cloth."

He reached forward to accept the gift. "I really like it, and I've never seen a tobacco tie in camouflage before. It's perfect for me."

I sat up a bit straighter and brought my shoulders back.

"Grandmother Bebee, when I get to be your age, I'll be as flirtatious and outspoken as you are. You're a great role model for me. I know you love hearts and amethyst, so I want you to have this amethyst heart necklace. Know that you are always in my heart, even when we don't see each other."

I got up to present her gift and hug her.

With tears in her eyes, she said, "I love you, Granddaughter, and I always will."

I made feather gifts beaded with the lightning pattern on the handles for all my clan aunts and uncles. I spoke to each one, sharing what I had learned from them and the gifts I saw in them.

Looking at my friends, I wrinkled my nose and said, "You guys were the hardest."

"Andrea, Susie, I knew I could make lovely earrings for you."

I handed Andrea white and blue cut beads that glimmered beautifully against her long, wavy dark hair. "You can say a prayer with your tobacco tie and hang it from a tree in your backyard."

"Susie, with your short, curly blond hair, I picked black and turquoise beads and made them shorter." She took them out of the box, and her eyes lit up. "Hold them up to your ears," I said. "Yes, just what I had hoped for. They look great on you. And you can do a prayer with your tobacco tie, too."

Then I looked at my guy friends. "Dad helped me with yours, and I learned something about myself in the process. Dad took me to buy hunting knives to honor you as young warriors. As we picked them out, I realized I loved knives!"

Their expressions changed, and Cody and Michael said, "You like knives?"

Shane just smiled.

"Yes, there were so many beautifully hand-carved handles and metal blades of different shapes. There was one called Damascus steel, and it had a beautiful pattern right in the steel blade. One day, I'll have one of those."

I could tell the guys were being polite. They wanted to see what I gave them. I handed them a tobacco tie and their knives. As they opened them, the 'oohs' and 'thank yous' told me I had made good choices. "Dad thought these would be good for your first hunting knives."

My dad said, "In case your fathers have never gone hunting, or it's been a long time, you can learn how to handle those knives properly through the men's clan if you decide to join—with permission from your parents, of course."

Cody and Shane talked excitedly about going hunting, but not Michael. He looked down.

"What's wrong, Michael?" I asked

In a soft, embarrassed voice, he said, "I would love to go hunting, but I don't think my mom and dad will let me."

Grandfather spoke. "Yes, all of you will need permission from your parents first, but perhaps we could invite you and your fathers to experience a men's lodge first."

I nodded. I knew if the fathers would come to a lodge with their sons, going hunting would be a definite possibility.

Michael nodded. "That would be great, Grandfather."

I noticed that he used the term of respect rather than Grandfather's first name. He was learning.

"My dad would let me go hunting, but I don't know if I could get him to sit in a hot purification lodge," Cody said.

The guys had been looking at and fondling their knives during this whole conversation.

"I'm surprised how different you three look," Sage said. "I knew you were warriors at heart. If we lived in a different time and culture, you would have the training to bring out your strengths."

Michael sat taller in his chair, and I think he puffed out his chest a bit. He appeared more confident, stronger somehow. He was handling his knife as if he would go hunting someday.

Teasing, I added, "And those knives are to remind you to cut the bullshit out of your relationships with girls becoming women." I wasn't sure they heard me because they were absorbed in maneuvering their knives and testing their sharpness. It was obvious that they liked them, and I was glad.

"Thanks, Sage," Michael and Cody said one after another.

"It's the perfect gift," Shane said.

I walked over to Grandmother Spinning Winds. "Grandmother, please, stand up." I took her hands in mine, looked deeply into her eyes, and gently pulled her toward my chair of honor. "Will you sit in my chair of honor?" She looked at me with a question on her face. When our eyes met, she agreed. When she sat down, I sat at her feet. For an eternal moment, there were no words, just wisdom passing between us.

"Grandmother, from all who I have ever been, and from who I am becoming, I thank you. You are far more than what you appear to be. I hope that I can follow in your footsteps in all ways. I know I have much to learn and much to remember."

She reached out and touched my cheek with her soft hand, then rested it back on her lap.

"Thank you for healing the Sacred Hoop and healing me. All of who I am loves you. Dreams with the Wind is here and says thank you, also. It is you, Grandmother, who should be honored today. If it weren't for you, I would not be here doing this Rite of Passage." With tears of gratitude,

I handed Grandmother the gift I had made for her. It was a pair of brain-tanned leather beaded moccasins.

"I thought you could wear these at Ceremonial Dance, Grandmother. I took the pattern from your favorite talisman protection necklace."

The pattern was intricate and beautiful, and Grandmother touched the beadwork with fingers slightly trembling as if remembering something from a time long ago. Each bead was stitched with love and patience.

Her silence was huge in the space. No one spoke. I don't think anyone was even breathing. I laid my head against Grandmother's knee. I wasn't sure what was happening, but the worlds were shifting. Grandmother and I were in a different space, no longer her front room. I saw Grandmother, her tribe standing around her, singing an honoring song. Her first husband was high on the scaffolding, wrapped in his ceremonial robes for his journey into the great round. I saw Grandmother touch her heart and the talisman that hung around her neck. I knew without seeing that he was wearing moccasins with this symbol on them.

Tears ran down her face as she said goodbye to her first love again. I felt her sadness at losing the man she had lived with and loved for most of her adult life. I felt tears running down my cheeks, too.

Grandmother reached out and touched my head. We were back.

"Thank you, Wind Dream Dancer."

I realized that she thanked both of us—me.

"Grandmother, I saw your first husband."

"It has been a long time. I will remember, and my spirit husband and I will dance to the Tree of Life together at this year's Ceremonial Dance in the moccasins you brought back through time. Now our moccasins bear the same symbol—the perfect gift, Wind Dancer."

We opened our eyes and embraced, melting into each other. Then Grandmother stood and sat me in the chair of honor. Aunt Amy Singing Hawk handed me a Kleenex. I blew my nose and dabbed under my eyes to catch any black mascara.

I glanced around. It felt like Grandmother and I had been gone a long time, but everyone acted as if nothing had occurred. I felt confused, and then I realized that no one realized Grandmother and I were in an altered state. They just saw the tender moment between us.

How old was Grandmother? Which lifetime did we just visit? And why did I choose that design out of all the items in her room?

My internal questions were interrupted when Grandma Bebee said, "So, when are we going to eat all that delicious food?"

That brought me back into this time and space. I looked around and saw all the yummy food, and suddenly, I was starving. "Thank you, Grandma Bebee. It's time for the feast. Would you do the honors and begin?"

"I was waiting for you to ask, but first, Sage, you need to say a prayer over the food."

Me? I felt Wind Dancer, the new me, and shifted.

"I would be honored to say the prayer. Will everyone hold hands please?" Even my friends took each other's hands.

"Sacred sweet medicine animals and plant world, you have given your life that we might eat and merge with you. Thank you for your gift of life. Great Spirit, bless all who are here celebrating my passage into adulthood. May all their prayers be answered. Aho!"

"Grandma Bebee, may I serve you?"

"Thank you, Granddaughter. I want a little of everything, just a bite."

With that, I heard music—rock and roll—come over the sound system, and like a floodgate being lifted, everyone began talking, saying how hungry they were and how good everything looked. When the turkey came out of the oven, the house filled with the aroma of sage and garlic. I put a tablespoon full of everything onto a plate for Grandma Bebee: turkey, garlic mash potatoes, cranberry sauce, asparagus, buffalo stew, and a homemade biscuit. The apple pie would be for later.

"Thank you, Sage," Grandma Bebee said as I handed her the plate.

"I'm hungry, too!" As I filled my plate, I glanced around for Grandmother Spinning Winds.

She was still, unusually quiet, and holding the moccasins on her lap. She smiled up at me as she caressed the leather with her fingers. She then rubbed her tummy and headed for the countertop, where Grandfather Strong Bear put his arm around her waist and kissed her.

PART II

CHIEF THUNDER WOLF, PIERCING CEREMONY, AND THE ENERGY BREATH

Chapter 8

Shane

One day, I am celebrating my Rite of Passage, the next, we are back in school, and life is happening. The high school year flew by. My friends and I seemed closer, and we had lots of fun. I felt different—like something had changed—but it was subtle. I started dating Shane—kinda. Whenever we'd all get together, Shane and I would sit next to each other and talk a lot. We enjoyed hanging out with each other.

Shane and Michael came to a brotherhood purification lodge, but after telling Cody how hot the lodge was, Cody wasn't too sure about attending. They told him they were teasing, but I think Cody saw the truth in their teasing.

"The first lodge usually feels very hot until you get used to breathing properly," I assured Cody, "but then it feels like a warm blanket wrapped around you."

Even though lodges can be challenging, Shane said he liked them because they were spiritual without being religious. After that first sweat, he said he felt squeaky clean. Now, he wanted to do a community lodge where the men and women purified together, and he asked me to join him.

"I want to hear how the women pray differently than the men do. I'm sure the energy is different, too."

"It is different," I said. "I've done full moon lodges with women and the community mixed lodges, too. I think the mixed lodges have more laughter. Let's do the next community lodge together."

Then we talked about remembering.

"Ever since your Rite of Passage things have changed for me. I'm remembering my dreams, and I have thoughts that seem like someone else's because they're too wise to be mine."

We laughed.

"Sage, do you think we've had any past lives together?"

"Yes, I do, but I don't want to share what I remember. If you remember the same visions, that would be confirmation. Besides, we're here in this life together."

I liked Shane, and I saw him changing. He no longer cared what others thought, and he wasn't concerned with peer pressure.

He asked my dad to show him how to throw knives. My dad had special throwing knives, and Shane would spend hours in our backyard practicing. At first, I thought he was using that as an excuse to see me, but then I realized he was serious about learning.

Grandmother Spinning Winds had come over to visit one day, but I wasn't very talkative—Shane was in the backyard, and I kept looking out the window with a scowl on my face.

Grandmother shook her head and gave me that look that said she knew exactly what I was thinking. "Stop being a foolish little girl. You said you liked knives. Either go out there and learn how to throw them, or when he's finished, have some iced tea waiting for him and ask what he's learning. Men like women who are interested in what they're doing, even if they don't want to do it themselves."

"Thank you." I marched myself outside and asked Shane to show me how to use a throwing knife. We laughed as my knives bounced off the backboard and onto the ground. Finally, I threw one correctly, and it stuck. I whooped and hollered like we had just won the football game. It was fun, and, once again, I was thankful for the wisdom of Grandmother Spinning Winds.

In little ways, I thought, *this is how the Sacred Hoop is healed—the Elders teaching the next generations.*

* * *

Michael had asked Dad to teach him about hunting—everything he could learn without actually going hunting—so he spent time at the house practicing various skills. Dad shared with me how much he enjoyed helping Michael. I prayed that his dad would take him hunting or that they would join the men's clan and go hunting with the brotherhood circle.

Shane had been hunting with his dad and was intent on honing his skills. He and his father were planning a camping trip together later that summer. As for Cody, he seemed to be drifting back to the way he was before my Rite of Passage. He gave in to peer pressure and was doing stupid things like getting drunk at parties. If he'd participate in a purification lodge, he'd see that life could be different—more meaningful.

As for my folks, they gave me more freedom, which I loved, and more responsibility, which was good training for my adult life but not always fun.

"When you're living on your own, you'll have to do everything: cook, clean, work, and go to school," Mom reminded me. "So, why not cook some family meals as you offered during your Rite of Passage Ceremony?"

I didn't mind cooking. I was becoming a decent cook as long as I followed a recipe.

One day, my dad showed me how to change a tire.

"Your assignment is to change four tires this month. I want to be sure you can do it by yourself. Let me know when you decide to do it so I can be here if you need me."

Next, he showed me how to change the oil in his car. My next assignment was to change the oil in my mother's car with him watching and assisting if necessary. Changing the oil was a lot messier and more difficult than I thought it would be, but I did it, and that was cool. I don't know which I enjoyed more, being with my dad learning guy stuff or sharing time with Mom learning how to cook her favorite recipes.

* * *

One day, my mom disappeared for several hours. When she returned, I said, "Medicine talks with Grandmother?"

"You're starting to read minds like Grandmother."

My eyes must have popped open because Mom laughed.

Over time, I noticed a difference in my mom and dad. They were more affectionate with each other, and they seemed happier. I suspected they were applying more of the Spiritual Sexuality workshop training they had received in levels one and two!

Grandmother encouraged me to focus on school, studying, time with friends, and, of course, she had something special for me to set my sights on.

"Sage, you made those moccasins for me to wear. I want you to go to the Ceremonial Dance this year, too. I've been speaking to your parents about it. It would mean taking fourteen days off from work, which would be a challenge for your parents, but after your Rite of Passage, this ceremony is the next most important step in becoming a mature, healthy young woman. It would be great if you could attend as a family."

My parents liked the idea. Hundreds of people would gather from all over the United States, Europe, and the Scandinavian countries—non-Indians, of course. Thunder Wolf was the elder, and his wife, Quiet Owl, was the first woman in thousands of years to be chief of the Ceremonial Dance. Thunder Wolf was very proud of his wife, especially since she was not a full-blood Native American. She had studied and practiced for so many years that she had proven herself to the elder circle. She was well qualified to be the Ceremonial Dance Chief.

She was one of the reasons Grandmother insisted on me attending this ceremony. She wanted me to see how mixed-bloods can come together, embrace traditions outside their culture, and participate with the utmost respect and integrity.

"By the way," Grandmother said, "how is Shane? Do you think he'd like to come to Ceremonial Dance?"

It took me a minute to catch up. "I don't know, Grandmother, but now that you mention it, that would be great. I'll ask my parents if he can join us."

"Be aware, Sage. Sometimes we don't see the forest for the trees." Grandmother hadn't called me Sage in so long that I knew what she said was important, but I wasn't sure what it meant.

Grandmother added, "Ceremonial Dance is not until school is over. If you keep getting good grades, perhaps your parents will let you join me before the ceremony begins. I'll be going up with a bunch of other folks to help with the pre-work. There's much to be done the week before everyone arrives, and we need lots of helping hands."

"Grandmother, can Shane and some of my friends come up, too—the ones you met at my Rite of Passage? They'd be a big help."

"It's fine with me if it's okay with their parents, but they'll need to work hard, sleep in sleeping bags under the stars, and cook over an open fire. It's always nicer when there's a large group of people to help. It's a lot of work, but it's fun, too.

"We're the first to awaken the land from her winter slumber and prepare her for the people who will come to the Ceremonial Dance. All the jobs are important, especially making sure the latrines are composting and the shower house works, which sometimes doesn't happen until right before we leave the land. We may be dirty all weekend, but at least we get to go home clean."

"Oh, Grandmother, it sounds like a blast. My friends and I won't mind not showering for a few days. Can we brush our teeth, though?"

"I hope you will! Otherwise, you'll have Dance breath. Yuck!" Grandmother grimaced and then laughed. "The weekend before the Ceremonial Dance is very important. Sometimes we have only ten to twelve people helping when we could use fifteen to twenty."

"Wow, this sounds huge!"

"It is, Wind Dancer. It is."

"Grandmother?"

"Yes, little one."

"One last thing. How do I remember when I was a dancer before?"

"Do you remember what I taught you about awake dreaming?"

"Yes."

"For now, when you want to practice awake dreaming, ask to see yourself or feel yourself in your other lifetime. Do you remember how you first met Dreams with the Wind and the elder counselor in your Rite of Passage Ceremony?"

"Yes."

"That kind of concentration takes focused relaxation. Practice it on your own. Let me know if you remember anything. If you need help, I can help you, but first, try it on your own. And Wind Dancer, be open to how and when you can dream yourself back into remembering now."

That was an odd statement—be open to how and when I dream myself back into remembering now. I'd have to think about that.

Chapter 9

Remembering A Piercing Sun Dance

One Saturday, Grandmother called to invite me to join her and some of Thunder Wolf's apprentices to watch some medicine movies. This was the first time she had asked me to join her.

"You're invited to listen to the teachings and enjoy the movies even though you're not an apprentice. Do you want to munch on popcorn or do you have a sweet tooth?"

"Popcorn, please, and lots of it."

"You're like me. I'll bring four microwave popcorn bags."

I was grinning ear to ear.

Once we arrived, I discovered that everybody had brought popcorn and soda pop. I was excited as we prepared for a long afternoon of movies.

"I hope we see *Night of the Hawk*," Grandmother whispered to me. "There's a clip where Thunder Wolf points out two grandfathers who are his mentors in real life. One of his mentors is so big that you can't even see his face. All you can see is this large Indian."

"It was that way on purpose," Thunder Wolf added, overhearing Grandmother talking to me. "Billy didn't want his face to be seen. But those of us who know him can tell it is him."

We were all lined up in front of the microwave to make our popcorn.

"I don't like sharing my popcorn," Grandmother said.

She did love it. She could eat a whole bag by herself. I even got my hand slapped once for reaching into her bag.

"If you want more, make another bag, but this bag is mine. I only eat one, and it lasts all afternoon, but not if you mooch some of it."

I don't know if Grandmother knew which movie we would see, but the movie we watched triggered memories in me. The movie was a very old one. Thunder Wolf had three walls filled with home-taped and store-bought videos. It was as full as any video store. I stood with my mouth open, staring. He saw me and laughed, saying it was an assignment one of his elders gave him years ago. He had been tasked with copying every movie available on his movie channels for three months in addition to working, teaching, and having a personal life. It was designed to teach him how to deal with multiple topics and details without getting overwhelmed. He not only finished that assignment but kept it going. It was a cool video library.

"Okay, gang, everybody shut up." Thunder Wolf said in his best Drill Sergeant voice. "We have some newbies here, and I want them to understand the medicine in the movies."

Grandmother winked at me.

With old-fashioned sarsaparilla in one hand and a clove cigarette in the other, he bellowed, "Hey, where's *my* popcorn?"

He sounded like a military drill instructor. An apprentice jumped up and said, "Coming right up, Thunder, sir."

This was the first time I heard his shortened name. Everyone in that room might call him Thunder, but he was still Grandfather Thunder Wolf to me. He saw me looking at him with a puzzled look on my face, and he winked at me. From that point on, I wasn't afraid of him. I knew his bark was worse than his bite.

Everyone settled down on the worn brown couches or the floor with multicolored pillows of all shapes and sizes. A few apprentices preferred the straight-back chairs. Thunder Wolf announced that the movie was one of his older ones—*A Man Called Horse*—a cowboy and Indian story starring Richard Harris as a white man learning the Indian way.

I was glued to the television and listened to Thunder Wolf's side comments. A scene came up with what looked like a thousand teepees. It was beautiful, and I felt all warm inside—like I was visiting family I hadn't seen in a long time. Then it showed the white man doing a Piercing Sun Dance—as they called it in the movie. He was tied to a single tall pole, suspended by leather thongs, with sticks piercing through the skin on his chest.

Gasping, I felt a sharp pain across both sides of my chest. Panic welled up inside me, and I couldn't breathe. It was too much! I rushed out of the room and ducked into the bathroom. My emotions were overwhelming, and the aches on both sides of my chest throbbed. I headed back to the front room but couldn't make myself go in.

I stood against a wall with tears streaming down my face. I heard someone coming. Embarrassed, I wiped my eyes, but there stood Grandfather Thunder Wolf.

"What's wrong?"

Tears fell again without warning. "I remember. I remember when I pierced. I can feel the pain in my chest. I can't go back in there."

He looked deep into my eyes, and I felt a quiet calm come over me.

"There was a time when we pierced. We don't need to learn from pain and suffering anymore. Now, we learn from pleasure and knowledge. Some tribes still pierce, but we are a Dreamer's Ceremonial Dance path. Go back in and watch it, knowing you will never again learn from pain and suffering." He smiled, touched my shoulder, and continued down the hall.

I went back in and was transformed for life.

It took me days before I stopped feeling the pierced places in my chest and weeks before the image of that piercing was out of my mind. I had been a man in that lifetime.

On the way home from our movie day with Thunder Wolf, Grandmother asked me what I had experienced.

Of course, she knew something had happened during the movie and that Grandfather Thunder Wolf had talked to me. I explained what had transpired.

"Good," she said, "your remembering is healing you. It will benefit you when you do your first Dreamer's Dance."

"I don't have a clue how it will benefit me, but I trust you, Grandmother."

I was still overwhelmed by the pain in my chest. What helped me was seeing Thunder Wolf's eyes and hearing his calm, strong voice. I felt him look deep inside me, making me feel better.

I was a wreck standing in that hallway. I'll always be grateful for Grandfather Thunder Wolf's support.

Chapter 10

Magick at the Auction and Shane's Black Eye

It was time for our once-a-year School Art Auction Fund-Raiser, and it turned out to be another remembering time for me. It was the strangest night. I'm glad no one saw me or pointed at me and laughed. Shane was supposed to meet us there with his parents, but I didn't see him. I had a feeling something was wrong and planned to call him when we got home if it wasn't too late.

My parents went with me to the auction. They were always good about attending my school events. I felt lucky because half the kid's parents never attended their activities.

It was a Friday evening, and my parents said they might buy something for the living room. Dad had been measuring the spot. Many pieces were signed and numbered editions, which might eventually increase in value, but, more importantly, my parents always supported my school.

We went into the gym, which had been turned into an art gallery with auction seating for about two hundred people. Every year it seemed to get bigger. We were all looking at the offerings. I had some money saved from the odd jobs and babysitting I had done. There was a large print of a red-tailed hawk sitting in a pine tree with its wings out and tail feathers spread. The eyes glared intensely into the forest as if it spied a mouse it would pursue. It was beautiful. I loved that one. I saw another one I liked of two great-horned owls sitting close together on a bare branch. They looked like they were cuddling to keep warm. I knew when I got older and had a place of my own, I would want art pieces and paintings of wild animals and birds in my home. I saw my parents looking at two different paintings. They were pointing first to one and then the other as they talked. Dad pulled out his measuring tape. They looked up and saw me. I waved. Mom blew me a kiss, and dad gave me a salute.

I turned down another aisle filled with framed, limited editions, amazed at the variety of subject matter.

I shifted to another aisle, and then it caught my eye. I saw it sitting on the floor, stacked with other paintings, at an awkward angle. It was a Native American scene in a dark wood frame. The hues were beige and brown with occasional pastel strokes in the women's dresses. I couldn't tell what it was, but it had my attention, so I sat down on the carpet about two feet back and looked at it. I felt funny sitting on the carpet, but I didn't care.

Women in buckskin-fringed leather dresses stood behind young and old bare-chested braves—one woman for each brave. There was a tall, slender tree in the center of the circle, with branches only at the top and long tethers hanging off it. In the foreground, a medicine man or chief stood in front of a young brave with a beautiful young Indian woman standing behind him.

Then I saw it.

The chief had pierced the young man's upper chest with two skewers and was attaching the leather tethers to them. This was a picture of a Piercing Ceremonial Dance.

I froze as tears stung my eyes. I felt a tug, a pull across my chest. I looked at the other men in the picture. They were dancing, having already been pierced. They had long whistles in their mouths with fluffy feather plumes tied and standing upright on the whistle. Their heads were thrown back, pulling against the stressed leather tethers. Others danced forward toward the single pole tree. I saw all this. The women were standing back with shawls over their arms. I couldn't tell if they were dancing or standing behind the men, praying and sending them energy.

I felt myself saying, *no more pain, no more suffering*. I was remembering again. It was me. I had pierced many times in other lifetimes. My body was remembering, but now I was seeking vision beyond the pain, a way to dance and break loose from the ties of this world. I felt myself becoming calmer, unlike when I ran out of the living room at Thunder Wolf's home. I had gentle tears streaming down my face as I sat in front of this painting. I wiped them away and felt myself slowly calming down.

I had to have this print. I would look at the soft hues and the women's beadwork and remember that this was in the past. I don't need to learn from pain and suffering anymore. I can learn from pleasure and knowledge.

I got up and found my parents. My thoughts were faster than my words could come out. "Mom, Dad, I gotta have this print. Come, look at it. I was gone again, remembering. I've pierced. I've been a dancer at the Piercing Dance in other lifetimes."

"Hon, I see tears." My mother gently wiped away the moisture from my cheek.

"I'm okay. These are healing tears. I have a hundred dollars saved. I need that print. Can I borrow some more money from you if the bidding goes higher?"

"Are you sure, Sage? That's a lot of money. Whatever you borrow, you'll have to pay back. But you know that, don't you?"

"Yes, Dad, I know. It's part of my Rite of Passage and being an adult and remembering. I don't have to learn from pain and suffering anymore. I can learn from pleasure and knowledge! I really need that print, to look at it, to be reminded, and to heal."

Looking at each other, they made a non-verbal agreement. "Yes, Wind Dancer," Mom said with intent. "We see what this means to you, and we support you."

Dad added, "I suggest you don't bid too high. Don't get caught up in the excitement of a bidding war. Before the bidding begins, which is soon, put your energy into that print. Ask Spirit to help you. Say a prayer in your own words. Make it simple and powerful."

The print my parents picked came up before mine. Dad did the bidding, and Mom did the praying. They got the one they wanted.

Dad looked at me. "Breathe, Wind Dancer."

I was nervous because I had never bid in an auction before, but I was determined, and it was clear to everyone that the print was destined to be my painting. After a few bids against me, I got it for a hundred and twenty-five dollars. I thought that was way cool. Besides, the money was for a good cause, and I could easily earn the missing twenty-five dollars. My first numbered and signed print!

When the auction was over, I could hardly wait to hang the print in my bedroom, but for tonight, I put it on my desk and leaned it against the wall.

Sitting on the edge of my bed, I stared at the image of the Piercing Ceremony and felt a dreamy sensation come over me—I saw a future vision.

Many years had passed. I was no longer a child but a woman grown—a woman with a counseling practice. A native American man walked into my office. He gazed at this very same print, which I had hanging on the wall. He looked at me strangely, then back at the print.

"Do you know what this is?" he said.

"Yes, it is a Piercing Sun Dance."

He spoke softly. "I was at this High Ceremony. We allowed a photographer to capture the power of this Sun Dance."

He spoke the names of the medicine chiefs who ran it. They were familiar to me, so he was telling the truth. Having this connection authenticated by the Native man in the vision touched me deeply, both as an adult standing before the man in my office and as a teen sitting on the edge of my bed.

* * *

I must have slept like a rock. As I rolled over to look at my new picture, I felt an urgency to call Shane. I pulled my bathrobe on and dialed his number.

"Shane, I'm so glad you answered. I'm sorry I didn't call you last night. I felt something was wrong when you didn't show up at the auction."

"Yea, I can't talk right now," he whispered. "I'll call you when I have some privacy."

"You don't sound good. Will you be okay?"

"There are problems here at home."

That was the first time he shared anything with me about his home. I always thought he had a good family; he never complained.

"I'll send you a prayer. Call or come over when you can."

It was just a little prayer, but it made me feel better to do it. It was Monday in school before I heard from him. Our classes kept us apart until right before lunch break. When I saw him, I was shocked! He had a terrible black eye that was still in the blood red and purple phase.

He looked at me and smiled. "You should see the other guy."

I grabbed him by the arm. "Tell me the truth. Now!"

"Okay, but let's find a private place."

We sat in the stands, staring at the football field. The grass was thick and green except for the white stripes every ten yards. The excitement of the Friday night games began on Mondays. The school would be humming with excitement for the entire week. Whether you understood the game or not, the energy was in the air.

I understood the energy, which was a big contrast from the energy Shane was feeling.

It was lunchtime. I prayed that no one else would find their way out here. We were alone.

He unloaded like a dam of water bursting through its cement walls. I sat and listened and remembered to breathe.

"My father is an alcoholic. He has been sober for over ten years. I

114

remember when I was younger, Dad sometimes got loud and acted funny. I didn't know why back then, but I stayed clear of him. Mom told me to stay in my room and play. They would fight and yell, and it scared me. It had been a long time since he got drunk or even took a single drink, but something happened about six months ago. He didn't share it with me, but I could tell something was wrong.

He lost his job and started drinking again. The stress in the house has been really bad. It still scares me, but I don't hide in my room anymore. I'm not a kid Mom has to protect.

"Ah, so that explains why you've been spending more and more time with my Dad, practicing knife throwing."

I wondered if he was learning it for self-defense.

"This weekend, Dad went on a drinking binge and became violent. When he started verbally abusing and threatening my mom, I wasn't sure what to do. I couldn't allow him to physically abuse my mom. I would defend her no matter what."

"What happened, Shane?" I said softly, reaching out to touch his knee.

"Mom was trying to calmly reason with Dad, which made him even angrier. He pushed her, and she bounced off the wall, stunned. That was it for me; I stepped in and punched him as hard as I could."

Shane is slender but works out in the school weight room. He's stronger than he looks.

"We tumbled to the floor. Because he was drunk, Dad was numb to pain, and he kept fighting back." He touched his eye and smiled. "He got one good punch in." He sighed, and I saw that the memories pained him. "He wouldn't stop, Sage. I had to knock out my own father. Mom called the police, and they took him to jail."

"Oh, my god. I'm so sorry, Shane. How is your mother?"

"Mom wants to talk to a lawyer and force Dad back into a rehab program. She kept telling the police that he's been sober for the last ten years and a good husband and father. She said it over and over."

"I'm in disbelief that this crazy man is my father—the man who took me hunting last year."

Shane glanced around as if to see if anyone was watching. When he looked back at me, he had tears in his swollen eyes. I put my arms around him, and his entire body shuddered with the grief of this new reality.

"Shane, come home with me after school and spend some time with my dad. Now is when you need the men's clan to help you feel safe and protected within a circle of men."

He looked at me, and like a wounded child, he said, "Okay, Sage. I'll come."

"I will wait for you at the front gates. If you don't show, I'll go to your house and get you."

He smiled at me and gently touched my face. "Thank you. I really need you right now."

I touched his lips with my fingers, then kissed my fingers and touched his swollen eye. We hugged softly, intimately. This was the closest we had come to being boyfriend and girlfriend. It felt like the right thing to do.

When we walked through the door at my house, Dad was right there, almost as if he knew. Shane shared his whole story with Dad.

Dad called Shane's mom to let her know that Shane was with us and asked if he could spend a night or two. He offered to drive Shane home to pick up some clothes and whatever he would need for school. He also asked if it would be okay for Shane to participate in a men's healing lodge to help him deal with his trauma.

"Rod, I'm very thankful. I know Shane has been spending a lot of time over there. I'm grateful, and if Shane wants to spend a few nights and do the healing lodge, I'm in favor of anything that can help him. Maybe he'll be able to do his homework in a quiet home."

"I'll see to it, don't worry."

Shane and I looked at each other, relieved that he could stay—we could hear the conversation even though it wasn't on speaker.

"I don't think Shane and his father will ever be the same." A sob escaped from her lips, and then she broke down crying.

Dad, in his most comforting voice, assured her. "Shane is in good hands. He'll come through this a better man for the experience."

After the call, Dad turned to Shane and put his arms around him. Once again, Shane broke down with words of disbelief, but after a moment, he composed himself.

"All right you two, I've got some phone calls to make. Head on out and throw stars and knives at that board. Be careful—more careful than usual."

Dad looked straight at me; I was on duty.

Shane and I were still practicing our skills when Dad came out to watch. The stars were easier to throw than the knives. Knives were a challenge.

"You two are getting better. I've got the schedule for tonight. The brothers are going to Grandmother's and Grandfather's tonight at seven o'clock for the healing lodge. Fortunately, the lodge is still covered from a woman's lodge Grandmother did a few days ago, so that makes preparation easier, but there's still lots to be done. Grandfather Strong bear will chief the ceremony.

"Sage, you'll be helping Grandmother smudge the lodge at five o'clock. While she is Blessing and Awakening the lodge, you'll smudge the sacred rocks and be a rock carrier when we enter the lodge for the ceremony."

Looking at Shane, he said, "We call the heated lava rocks Sacred Rocks or Rock People. Grandfather Strong Bear and one of the men will arrive early and place the rock people with specific prayers in a tight medicine circle in the fire pit. Sage, I'm sure they'll allow you to add prayers for Shane's healing and for the Sacred hoop to be restored. Once the Sacred Rocks are in place, logs will be stacked teepee-style until no rock people can be seen. This is our to-do list before the ceremony."

Shane's eyebrows rose with surprise. "Wow, this is going to be interesting. I can't tell you how much this means to me."

Dad patted his shoulder. "You're a special person, Shane. You'll understand that tonight. So far, eight men have committed, even though it's short notice. There will be one man per direction, and the medicine wheel will be complete with you in the center of the lodge. Okay, Sage, it's almost five. You'd best head over to Grandmother's house. We'll meet you there later. Take a snack because there won't be time for dinner."

I didn't want to leave, but I had to help get everything ready.

Dad looked at me. "Don't worry, I'll take care of him."

"I feel better just being here, Sage Dream Dancer. I'll see you over there later."

I heard Shane use my medicine name, but it was different. Then I realized he had combined my names, Dreams with the Wind and Wind Dancer. He never knew my other name. *How did he do that? Was he even aware of what he said?* As I left, I wondered if I had known Shane before.

I was not in the lodge that night, so I can't tell what went on inside, but it was a long sweat lasting over two and a half hours. Over sixty rocks were called in, and that's a lot. At one point, Grandmother was sitting in front of the lodge door smoking her pipe as a guard, and I thought Shane was dying from the anguished primal scream that came out of him. Then there was laughter, and all the men sounded their warrior cries. I thought the top of the lodge was going to come off.

Grandmother caught my gaze. "Don't imagine, just listen and watch."

Soon after, the lodge door opened, and a new Shane emerged.

Standing taller than I had ever seen him, he led the men to the pool and jumped in, whooping and hollering with the brotherhood spreading out to join him.

Grandmother and I closed down the fire, and Grandfather asked her to pour the last six buffalo horns of water for the ancestors and add her heart prayer to the completion.

I was looking at the men and Shane. It was like I had never seen him before. I was looking at a man. A man birthed into his power, supported by other men. The Sacred Hoop was being healed again.

"Grandmother, the Sacred Hoop. Look, look at Shane."

"Yes, Granddaughter, you have seen the Sacred Hoop in the healing of this young man."

"I want to be a part of this, Grandmother, forever—healing the brotherhood." Grandmother looked at me strangely. I had seen that look before. She was gleaning me, seeing into my luminosity, and gaging the law of probability for my future.

"There are many ways of healing the brotherhood. You will discover your way, but you have made a good start. You brought Shane to the men's clan."

Shane spent the night. We talked for a while, but my father said Shane needed to take his awakening into the men's clan, into the dream, and seat it firmly.

We gave each other a hug that was difficult to pull apart from. We smiled at each other, and Shane kissed his fingers and placed them on my lips. We parted, and I went to bed. I felt myself take three deep breaths, and then I was fast asleep, dreaming of warriors wearing armor in a distant land.

* * *

The days and weeks passed with life seeming to get back to normal. Shane's father willingly went into an alcoholic forty-five-day rehab, which included attending AA meetings. His mother had shared with my dad how thankful she was that their insurance covered his treatment because it was very expensive.

When the forty-five days were over, Shane's father returned home. They attended family counseling at the rehab center, and Shane's father continued AA meetings. Shane and his mother attended Alanon meetings to receive help and support also.

Shane joined the men's clan every time they met and was sweating in the lodges regularly. He told me it would never be the same between him and his dad, but something good had come out of it. He had found his manhood, and he would always protect the feminine. He had found his spiritual home with the brotherhood clan, and his parents were dealing with their problems in a good way.

Chapter 11

Teach Me To Breathe Into An Energy Orgasm

Between school, my friends, getting better grades this semester, and my excitement about going to Ceremonial Dance, I didn't have much time for what started this whole journey. Every time I asked Grandmother about sex, relationships, and energy, she kept guiding me to remember when I was initiated into the Yellow Moon Society and my Spiritual Intimacy training when I was Dreams with the Wind many lifetimes ago. She gave me a workbook for a Spiritual Sexuality workshop and said it would help me when I got old enough to attend—I had to be eighteen to attend. I had lots of questions after reading it, but Grandmother took me back to breathing. She said I needed to learn how to do the Energy Breathing technique.

We set a date for my first lesson for the following week.

I couldn't wait to learn how to breathe. Sounds funny, but breathing is somehow a key to learning about sacred sexuality. Grandmother said not to eat a big breakfast, so I had some fruit and hot peach tea and then scooted over to her place. Everything was green and alive as I walked, skipped, and ran to her house. Her cactus blooms were just beginning to peak out of their tight green jackets.

We went to Grandmother's medicine bedroom, where her ceremonial medicine blanket was spread out on the carpet with the usual pillow for me to sit on. Grandmother sat in her favorite low-back beach chair with her medicine blanket doubled up on it to make a soft seat for her. She started with a story of how she learned the Energy Breath technique, which helped her discover her life energy expressed with passion.

"Sage, learning how to breathe properly during lovemaking is a key to being a good lover and having great orgasms."

"Grandmother, I've been doing the self-pleasuring exercise almost every day. It has really helped me relax, let go of stress, and get me energized in the morning before school or after school. Also, I discovered it relaxes me at nighttime to sleep better. I discovered I can set my intent and my orgasm changes. How can a breathing technique do all that?"

"For now, Sage, Wind Dancer, the breathing with self-pleasuring and moving energy through your chakras is what is important. Not how it works. You have a body knowing of all the benefits you have gotten from doing this practice. Do you want to learn more about the Energy Breath?"

"Oh, yes, absolutely. Please tell me, how did you learn?"

"It took me nine months, practicing three times a week before I got proficient in the Energy Breath technique. And then I only got the energy up to my throat chakra. The first time I got the energy to go all the way out the top of my head, I was demonstrating it in a Spiritual Sexuality workshop. Thunder Wolf was teaching Level One in Michigan, and I was one of three people back then who knew how to do the Energy Breath technique. I was the only female available to travel with him, and he needed one male and one female to demonstrate the exercises. It was my first time on a plane, but off I went to Michigan with Thunder Wolf and Bobby to demonstrate the exercises and Energy Breath in front of a whole group of folks who were attending the workshop.

"Thirty-four years later, I still remember that evening. I was lying in the middle of the room on a beautiful ceremonial medicine blanket. By that time in the training, other exercises had been practiced so everyone was comfortable being nude or the shy ones wore a sarong. So, I was nude, breathing, and pulling the energy up. Just rolling my belly muscles, inhaling, and squeezing my PC muscle, the pubococcygeus muscle. You know which one that is, don't you, Wind Dancer?"

"Yes, Grandmother, you told me and taught me to do the Kegel exercise."

"Yes, that's right. So, as you inhale, contract your PC muscle and pull it up and then exhale and relax, sometimes pushing that muscle down to be sure you are fully releasing the tension. And continue doing this. When it really gets going, you are breathing like in lovemaking—fast and passionately. You don't think about your breath; you just breathe. It's really easy. I don't know why it took me so long to learn it."

Grandmother was in her memories, sharing out loud. "I saw it done once by Suzie Shy Fox, who was an apprentice and partner of Thunder Wolf in his younger days. That was when I first entered the medicine—when I was thirty-eight. I was attending a weekend workshop with Thunder Wolf. I didn't believe what I saw at first. I thought she was faking it. Any woman can fake an orgasm. Faking anything is stupid unless you have the intent to fake it till you make it. Now, that's different. You are striving for excellence with that attitude. To just fake it so you don't hurt someone's feelings or disappoint someone is stupid."

"Grandmother, you are so blunt about your opinions, and this obviously is one of them. I would never fake an orgasm. I want to learn how to have them, all of them, for real."

"Good, Wind Dancer. Good!"

"Suzie Shy Fox was not faking it either. I saw her energy move up and out. She was gone. Thunder Wolf was describing what Shy Fox was doing, looked over at her and said, 'Yep, she's gone.' When he said that, it confirmed it for me."

I realized I was gone because my thoughts went back to what Grandmother said about demonstrating at the workshop. "Grandmother, you were doing the Energy Breath nude in front of everyone?"

"Granddaughter, everyone was nude. Now, mind you, we don't begin with everyone taking their clothes off! That would be too shocking and very inconsiderate for the folks who are shy. After all, most of the American culture thinks that if you are nude, it means you are having sex. It doesn't. You can go to any beach in Europe, and everyone is topless. It's no big deal. And what they wear on their bottoms is about the size of a band-aid. The American culture is still puritanical. Too bad that some of the naturalness of the Native culture didn't rub off on those pilgrims.

"So, yes, Wind Dancer, after we have created a safe environment with boundaries, when it's time to do an exercise, we invite everyone to get out of their cloths and put on a sarong or robe. It covers them without any constricting clothing. We're not there to embarrass anyone but to set them free. The body is the most beautiful creation of Great Spirit. Why must we be ashamed of our bodies? Religions say we should be ashamed and cover ourselves. Great Spirit did not say that."

"Wow, Grandmother that's great. I'm not saying it would be easy for me, but I do enjoy swimming and going on your slide nude. It's no big deal for us. So, I guess with agreements of being respectful of each other, it would be the next step in free expression."

I was surprised at what I had said. *Is that Dreams with the Wind talking?* That sounded like a teaching from my memory.

"Yes, Wind Dancer you are remembering teachings from that ancient lifetime. Though you know this to be true and respectful, you'll get some good arguments from a lot of your religious and social leaders. They'll fight you tooth and nail to prove sex is sinful unless you are properly wedded.

Some religions teach that you should only have sex for procreation. It's appalling that this is still taught in some religions. If we followed that line of thinking, we would be no different than the animals on this planet. The last time I looked, animals don't have free will, only humans, and animals don't have erogenous zones."

"What do you mean, Grandmother? Do you mean they don't feel pleasure? How could that be?"

"Animals mate when the female is in heat, producing pheromones to alert the male of the species that she is receptive to procreation. Males don't go into heat. They can mate year-round. For some mammals, like the big cats, it can be painful. Research has recently shown that female animals have a small clitoris, but it is unknown if it produces pleasure. The penis of many male animals looks like a large pencil with no distinct head. We would be overrun with the animal world if they experienced pleasure year-round.

"There are two main exceptions to the mammal world. One is the dolphin, which is in an orgasmic brain wave state all the time. Their penis, as I described, has with no distinct head, but science has proven that their brain waves are very evolved. Can you imagine being in an orgasmic state all the time—a bit overwhelming, huh?

"The other exception is the Bonobo Monkey. They discovered the Bonobo Monkey uses orgasms to keep the peace in the group. Remember, there is a difference between orgasm and ejaculation. All mammals ejaculate to reproduce. It seems that the Bonobos are always masturbating each other, and when two males start getting aggressive with each other, the females break it up by backing up to them and offering themselves."

"I bet we could stop a lot of wars if we used that technique," I said with a belly laugh.

"Sexual frustration is the biggest cause of aggression in men and women—just my opinion for what it's worth."

"It's worth a lot, Grandmother!"

"Sage, I think you should research this band of monkeys. Remember, don't believe anything anyone says. Find out for yourself if it is factual or not."

"Okay, Grandmother, that sounds cool. Maybe I can turn it in to my English class for one of the papers I need to write. You know, two birds with one stone."

"That's good, Wind Dancer. I'm sure your English teacher will get quite an education from reading your paper—maybe even enjoy it. Do you think she'll have you read it to the class?

"God, I hope not!" The thought of reading it to the whole class almost made me change my mind.

"You said that other than dolphins and this band of monkeys, humans are the only mammals that enjoy sex?"

"Yes, that's right. Animals only have sex for procreation. When we show too much passion, many religious folks say stop acting like an animal. Boy, do they have their story mixed up. Many think that as you get older and can't make babies, you're supposed to lose interest in sex. They have their heads up their you-know-what. Ask any man over sixty-five if he still wants sex. If he doesn't, he's the walking dead. Women tend to buy into the sex-has-died story more so than men. Menopause means change, but it doesn't have to wipe out your common sense or your desire for sex and intimacy. Besides, the biggest sex organ you have is between your ears."

"What do you mean, Grandmother?"

"Wind Dancer, remember! Your state of mind is what keeps you sexually active until you're old and gray and beyond. Having lots of sex with lots of orgasms and intimacy is what keeps people young. Orgasms rejuvenate the body at a cellular level. Researchers even have articles, now, that validate what the ancients have known for thousands of years. You can look this up, too. Just look at the 1999 version of Real Age where the statistics show the average American has fifty-eight orgasms a year. If they were to double that, they would increase their life span by one and a half years. Look it up, don't believe me! I'm sure there are more current statistics."

"I wonder how long the bonobo monkeys live if they are having lots of orgasms."

"That's a good question. Maybe you can find the answer when you do your research. Add the facts for the human mammals, too. Having sex is good for your health and longevity, and it's fun. You feel a heck of a lot better afterward.

"Sage, people are so uptight around their bodies that it's a wonder they can relax enough to even have fifty-eight orgasms a year. Nudity without intercourse is one way to free the mind of all the lies, dogma, and indoctrination that have infiltrated and annihilated the God-given beauty and naturalness of the human form.

"So, yes, Wind Dancer, there is appropriate nudity in the Spiritual Sexuality workshops. This is why you not only have to be eighteen or legal age to attend, you must be mature enough. That was a long answer to a short question."

"Grandmother, is this like Dreams with the Wind standing before the Elder council asking permission to learn the Yellow Moon teachings?"

"Yes, but modern people don't understand that. Some individuals, no matter what their age, don't grow up. Everyone goes through an interview before they are accepted into the workshop. You, Sage, will not be able to attend until you are eighteen and mature enough. Everyone is screened before being accepted—if they realize it or not.

"So, back to answering the question inside the question—lying nude, demonstrating my first full Energy Breath demonstration. There I was, lying on the floor, doing my breathing and moving the energy up into my solar plexus or heart chakra. Until that night, I had never gotten the energy all the way up through my crown chakra at the top of my head. I was worried that I wouldn't be able to show the full demonstration, but Thunder Wolf assured me.

"He said, 'Spinning Winds, you just breathe and get it up as high as you know how, and then I'll guide you the rest of the way.'"

"I said, 'Okay, but how about we cheat a little and you pull me up and out.' His expression said no chance. He said he'd guide me verbally, and I'd do just fine."

"Sage, don't look at me that way! I have a sneaky side, too, but Thunder Wolf was right. I didn't need to cheat. It was the first time I assisted in a workshop. When the time came to teach everyone the Energy Breath technique, he asked us all to get nude. He didn't want me to feel uncomfortable with others dressed. 'No lookie-loos,' he would say. So, everyone just slipped out of their clothes, which they were used to doing by now, and took them into the other room. They returned wearing Sarongs. Furniture was moved back, and everyone either sat or stood so they could see. I lay down with my legs up and knees bent, about hip-width apart, creating my gate.

"I began breathing. I took deep breaths, pulled the energy up, squeezed the PC muscle, then exhaled and relaxed. As I found my rhythm, I began to feel the energy tingle in my first chakra, my *Tupuli* or sacred cave. I felt my second chakra, the space above the hairline, begin to fill—a warm, sensual, gentle feeling in my womb. It was easy after nine months of practice. I felt my second chakra stronger than ever before. I moved the energy up to my belly. I felt sensuously hungry and wanted more. It felt like I had an invisible spirit lover teasing my body into waking up and feeling passion. As I moved the energy into my heart chakra, I made sensual sounds, which meant that the energy was moving into my throat chakra, too, but first, I had to build it stronger in the heart chakra space. I had gotten this far before, but I had never gotten the energy above my throat chakra. I was now making guttural, throaty sounds, moaning my desire with each escaping exhalation of my breath.

"Then I heard Thunder Wolf say, 'Spinning Winds, lift your arms above your head.' That opened my rib cage, and I made more sounds. 'Now, out the top of your head,' he said. Then in a commanding voice, he said, 'Think Stars.'"

"That was all I needed. When I lifted my arms, I could feel this stream of energy going right up the center of me, through my heart chakra, and like a rocket ship blasting out the top of my head into the atmosphere. I was thinking stars. I made such a sound I could have sworn it was someone else. It was a primal scream of pleasure when the energy burst out the top of my head. I did a body arch like a backbend and was pushing the top of my head into the carpet. I exploded into an energy orgasm that shocked me and I think everyone else. I had never experienced anything like that in full physical lovemaking, let alone the energy work I had been doing, and it went on and on and on. I couldn't believe it.

"I later asked Thunder Wolf if he had pulled me out. But he said that I did it all on my own, that I had just needed a little coaching. So, yay for coaching. It was amazing. I had never experienced anything like it before.

"Sage, my sex life was never the same after that. The Energy Breath changed my life, not just my sex life, but every aspect of my life. I was able to access that kind of energy anytime I desired or needed to."

"Grandmother, you didn't touch yourself at all?"

"That's right, no physical touching—just breathing, muscle control, and sensuous imagination."

"Wow. How does it affect a man? Does he get an erection?"

"When men learn how to do this, they seldom get an erection or ejaculate. They go into full body orgasms, multiply orgasms, so deep and strong it rumbles their soul. It is shocking to most men that they can have such a fulfilling intense orgasm without an erection or ejaculation. But once they have done it, they say it is a tossup as to which feels better, intercourse or energy course. Both can be shared with a partner, and doing both regularly becomes the norm."

"I can see how important it would be to learn this, and most of the world doesn't even know about it. Are the workshops being taught outside the United States, Grandmother?"

"Yes, by word of mouth, they are being introduced into many other countries."

Grandmother reached for a glass of water, and I shifted positions on my medicine blanket, waiting for her to continue.

"Now, that we have looked at the big picture let's start with the 'one to the many.' You will be the one learning this breath. It's part of your training and will make all the difference in having a happy, healthy life, whether you have a partner or not. This breath is great for people who are celibate, single, with a partner, or who are young and not yet sexually active with another. This is especially good for adults who are not getting their physical needs met even if they are in a relationship. Men and women need to feel the aliveness of sexual, sensual energy running through their bodies."

Grandmother was giving me another Spiritual Sexuality teaching. I sat up, tried to relax, and listened deeply. I wanted to absorb it all.

"When a man is hungry, a woman can tell, and she won't get near him with a ten-foot pole. Ask any adult male. It's like having a stamp on your forehead that says, 'I'm horny.' They will never get laid. If they knew how to breathe, they could take care of themselves and eliminate the yucky hunger from not making love. This is true for men and women. Wind Dancer, if you desire to learn something, no matter how long you have to practice it, you can learn it. All things are possible! And guess who tells you that?"

"I don't know."

"If you can believe, all things are possible to him who believes, Mark 9:23. This is also one of the Sacred Laws in the shamanic tradition."

"Sacred Laws?"

"Yes, Wind Dancer, Sacred Laws are at the core of all that exists."

"I think I'm going to have to learn about sacred laws. It sounds pretty important."

"Good answer. But for now, let's stay focused on the two topics we have going, Spiritual Sexuality and the Ceremonial Dance, which are totally separate from each other but part of this shamanic path. Just know there are fewer Sacred Laws then manmade laws. They make sense, and you don't need a lawyer to understand them."

"Grandmother, if all things are possible, I'm going to hold that and see Mom, Dad, and me going to Ceremonial Dance."

"There you go, Wind Dancer, you've got it. Apply the law to know it. Let it teach you. Practice seeing and feeling what you are asking Great Spirit to manifest for you. Let it teach you. If it doesn't happen then, perhaps it wasn't meant to be. You need to check if your little 'me' ego was involved in the asking. Are you ready to begin?"

"Yes, I'm ready to practice the Energy Breath technique. I'm going to learn it no matter how long it takes."

"You'll probably be one of those lucky ones that learn it the first time you try it."

After Grandmother's story, I was excited, and I did pick it up quickly—

the first time I tried it. I had the energy running through my whole body.

"Wind Dancer, let go. Stop controlling your body, flow with the energy. Let your body feel how alive it is."

After a few verbal pushes, I guess I got a little angry and decided to just go for it. All my inhibitions dropped away, and I was breathing and moaning and feeling my whole body in such passion; I couldn't believe it.

"Wind Dancer, make sound. Let it go into your throat. Good, open, let the sound be louder. Lift your arms over your head. Imagine the stars."

I felt like a pressure cooker ready to pop.

"Okay, now exhale and tilt your head back. Open your neck and throat, make sound."

A loud moan escaped my mouth, and I felt energy fly out the top of my head. Talk about intense. I just kept going until I heard Grandmother's voice.

"Wind Dancer, keep breathing and begin to slow your breath and focus on bringing your energy down into each chakra. Never stop breathing at the top. Always slow down, and like a plane, bring it in for a gentle landing. Seat it in your first chakra, ground it down."

I lay there in amazement. What had I just done? "Did I do the Energy Breath, Grandmother?"

"Yes, Sage Wind Dancer, you experienced the magick of breathing with intent."

This was amazing. I think the excitement of learning and then Grandmother's story had me on the edge. I had tasted something beyond my imagination, and I wanted more. I would not give up until I knew how to do this anytime and anywhere. One question bothered me, and I finally asked.

"Grandmother, if I could reach such powerful orgasms by myself, could I experience this with a partner, too?"

"Yes, of course, and you'll need to teach your lovers how to breathe. The men you choose to be in your life will be very lucky because you are responsible for your own orgasm. Your body will be more alive, so a sensuous touch of your neck or on the palm of your hand can bring you to an energy orgasm. You can teach them how to have full-body energy orgasms, too."

"Remember, Sage, most young men are *Tipili* focused. You know, first chakra, Mr. Happy—their package."

I must have looked uncomfortable.

"Granddaughter, get used to the common everyday words we use to describe our Sacred Sexual Self. You don't need to be uncomfortable.

Remember, Great Spirit made men. So, don't get mad at them if they seem single-focused. It's just the nature of the male species. It helps them survive, provide, and populate the planet. You'll have to be strong. Teach them how to have full-body orgasms. Share with them the self-pleasuring exercise I have you practicing. It'll help to relieve some of their urgency and make it easier for them to learn the Energy Breath. That is one of the reasons you were able to do the breath so easily. You had already been practicing moving the energy from your vagina, inside your body or first chakra to your solar plexus or heart chakra in that exercise."

"Oh, my God, Grandmother, you're right. Now that you mention it, I remember feeling energy going up my belly. It was like a stream of warm water running up my body, filling me with passion from my pussy, my *Tupuli*, to my heart chakra."

I was so excited to be putting two and two together.

Immediately, I did it to show Grandmother that I was doing it right, and she smiled.

"I was already learning the Energy Breath Orgasm by self- pleasuring then backing off four times before letting myself orgasm on the fifth time. Oh, my God, I know you told me, but I didn't understand. Sometimes it was really difficult to hold back and make myself build the orgasm up five times. I remember you telling me I was healing myself: emotionally, mentally, physically, spiritually, and sexually. I could feel that.

Grandmother, I did just what you had me do today with the Energy Breath, and, boy, on that fifth time, when I let myself have the full physical orgasm, it was intense. I made sounds and tilted my head back, just like you told me. I heard you say imagine stars. Wow, I was out there. When I did that, my energy just flew."

"You taught yourself well, Wind Dancer. That is why you could do the Energy Breath today without any physical touching."

"Something else, Grandmother. I just started doing this. I don't remember you telling me about it, but I love to keep pleasuring myself even after I get so sensitive. The pleasure just keeps going and going."

"Ah, now you are pulling from your past life and training. I never spoke this to you. It may seem normal, but once a man or a woman has an orgasm, they usually get super sensitive and stop their pleasure. You discovered how much pleasure and heightened state of energy you can achieve after an orgasm. Good for you, Granddaughter."

Chapter 12

Learning From Dreams With The Wind

"Wind Dancer, do you want to visit Dreams with the Wind and see what else she and you are learning? You seem to be connecting easily. You're just not realizing it."

"Right now, Grandmother?"

"No time like the present to slide into the past and bring knowledge back into the future."

"Do you have time? You said you are running a lodge today."

"You know I play with time. Thirty minutes is all you will need with Dreams with the Wind."

"That's not much time! Will you call me back?"

"No. You're responsible to set your inner clock. Trust yourself. You'll know. Now, stop asking questions. Laydown and go."

"Just like that? No drumming or story or—" Grandmother cut me off with her look. I lay down and closed my eyes as she scolded me.

"You're wasting time that doesn't exist. That was your last clue."

In a tone I have only heard when Grandmother is using her pipe, she commanded, "Be Gone from this Space, I command it to be so, it is so, and it will continue to be so until you chose to return. Ho!"

I was gone as if falling into a dream so vivid that one remembers it their entire life. I was visiting myself through the eyes of Dreams with the Wind.

Dreams with the Wind flung the tepee flap open, and as I stepped into her world, I whispered, "May I join you for a while?"

"Welcome, sister Wind Dancer, I was wondering how we are doing in your time? How much you must be learning."

"I was thinking the same thing. That's why I'm here, to learn from all that you have been learning."

We both laughed, and I relaxed, giving myself to this wonderful, ancient time.

"We will see what this day brings us. I always begin my day by greeting Grandfather Sun and take into my body the energy light of Spirit. I will show you."

I felt us merging into one with awareness of each other.

Standing outside the tepee, I turned to face the early morning sun and felt the warmth soak into my leather dress and caress my face. Lifting my arms above my head, with my palms to the sun, I formed an arrowhead with my void-element thumbs and pointer fire-element fingers touching.

The sun was in the middle of this arrowhead, shining directly into my third eye that sees other worlds. My palms became warm and began to tingle with energy. Slowly, I opened my arms and felt energy between my hands. The wider I made my arms, the larger the energy became. My arms felt like the wings of a soaring eagle, filled with energy. I brought them down, bringing all that energy into my sacred Tupuli, up my centerline of life, and over my heart and face—energizing my eye that sees other worlds. I flipped my palms back out, forming the arrowhead again to capture more of the sun's energy that is freely given to our world. I repeated this several times until I felt calm, filled with love for life, deep inner peace, and tranquility of mind. I was in Great Spirit's arms.

"Good morning, Great Spirit. I have a visitor with me today. I listen to your guidance as this day unfolds. I choose to live my life guided by you. Aho!"

"That felt good," Wind Dancer said.

"I do this every day, and sometimes as the sun is setting, as that is also a powerful time. Now, let's see what is calling today."

I became aware of the morning activity, and others coming out of their tepees to greet Grandfather Sun. The village seemed to come alive with sounds of laughter and talking. I loved the smell of burning wood.

A young warrior approached. "Good morning, Dreams with the Wind, you have been up early."

He is so handsome, strong, and gentle, I heard Dreams with the Wind say in my mind.

"You have learned many songs on the flute I carved for you. I enjoy listening to you play," he said.

"Good morning, Cloud Walker. It pleases me to have my songs dance on the winds or sing with the birds. Your gift is more than the beautiful beadwork or your time in carving the flute. Your gift is the words you share from your heart." She spoke boldly and lowered her eyes.

"May I touch you, Dreams with the Wind?"

She nodded.

Reaching out, he gently caressed her hair and tucked a strand behind her ear.

I felt it as if he were actually touching me. He *was* touching me as I am Dreams with the Wind in this ancient lifetime.

"I'm glad you are considering me," he said.

We looked up, and our eyes met. A depth of communication took place— my soul's desire for a partner to support my chosen path was strong. Our smiles touched each other until we laughed. Our laughter danced on the morning breeze, joining the sounds of our tribe.

The laughter became a moment of truth. We opened our palms for Cloud Walker to place his palms on ours.

"I will always speak what is in my heart, guided by Great Spirit," Dreams with the Wind said. "It is not always easy to say or hear, but I will get stronger as I gain age and wisdom. I must have a man who will never stop growing and will always speak the unspeakable."

Time stood still—the now, the future, the waiting.

Cloud Walker smiled at us and brought our hands together, and placed his hands under and over ours—supporting and protecting. "Time will tell, one day at a time, whom you will choose."

I felt the energy he was sharing with us. Our hands began to tingle. I felt the energy moving through his body into ours. He, too, was learning the energy ways. My body started to vibrate with the intensity of awakening.

Cloud Walker moved his lips, "Be joyful today. Dance with this energy. I give it to you freely, like Grandfather Sun."

He then softly released our hands, and we put our intent into the Earth to stand alone as our body embraced this energy sharing.

As he walked on to his next journey, Dreams with the Wind said out loud, "Always speak the unspeakable; ask for what I desire; give permission for what I desire; be patient, and the world will open into other worlds."

Dreams with the Wind had no sooner said this, and I was back in Grandmother's room saying the exact same thing.

"Perfect timing, Wind Dancer," I heard Grandmother's soft voice say.

"And it appears you brought back very good lessons. Always speak the unspeakable; ask for what you desire; give permission for what you desire; be patient, and the world will open into other worlds."

"Grandmother, did I say all of that? I was there one moment, and then, like someone flipped a light switch, I was here."

Smiling with her soft grandma's heart, she said, "One of you said it, and I heard it. When you are steady on your feet, remember to put your energy down into Grandmother Earth, like Dreams with the Wind told you, and then drink a glass of water. It will help you settle. Walk home with your eyes and ears wide open."

She stood up.

"Remember, you can start practicing your energy breath. It is good for many things."

* * *

The rest of the day melted into a wonderful exploration of all I saw and heard. Life was wonderful, and I loved my tribe of friends and family. The next day brought the challenges of life, and I forgot to go out and greet Grandfather Sun to start my day.

I practiced energy breath, and to my surprise, I barely got the energy to my belly. How could I be flying one day and crashing the next? I immediately called Grandmother.

As soon as I heard her voice, I blurted out, "Grandmother, I lost the Energy Breath. I only felt it in my belly. I couldn't get it up to my heart chakra or my throat. I felt nothing above my belly!"

"Now is the time to breathe and practice till it's as natural as sneezing. Get off the phone and go try again."

From that day on, I greeted Grandfather Sun every morning and practiced the Energy Breath when I got home from school—until I had it down. I switched to self-pleasuring at night before I went to sleep, telling myself to relax rather than energize myself. I was learning that my intent is everything.

* * *

"Can I share this with my friends?"

I wanted to share this with my friends, but Grandmother warned me that teaching sexual practices was a very touchy subject, and my friends' parents may not like it. It was like having a special gift I couldn't share with anyone.

I went against Grandmother's advice and told Susie about the breathing I was learning to do.

Her words imprinted on my brain. "You are too far out for me. I'll learn about sex the old-fashioned way. Breathing into an orgasm—yeah, right!"

132

I thought about telling her about the self-pleasuring technique, but one day she was feeling blue and told me her mother had said that anything to do with sex at her age was wrong. I guess Grandmother was right. I decided not to mention my training to anyone, not even Shane. Boy, did I feel lonely, the oddball-out. So, I decided to just have fun with my friends and not teach them what I was learning. They were my friends, and school was more fun with them than without them.

Chapter 13

Teachings About Ceremonial Dance

My first sight of Ceremonial Dance land was on the final work weekend before the Ceremony began. For months, there had been other work weekends dedicated to specific areas. This weekend, a huge amount of work got done before everyone arrived. My friends, Andrea and Shane, were able to join us. I was secretly hoping Andrea would learn something positive from Grandmother about sex.

I was glad it was okay with Grandmother for me to bring two friends. We had to get out of school early on Friday as the drive would take six hours with stops for gas and food. We were supposed to leave at noon, but it took Shane and Andrea longer than expected to get to Grandmother's house.

Standing in the driveway, Grandfather gave us all hugs, saying, "Have fun and try not to get too many blisters."

Andrea, Shane, and I looked at each other, wondering if he was kidding or warning us. Grandfather leaned over to give grandmother a long, warm hug. "Deborah, drive carefully, and watch out for the other guy. Call me when you stop to eat and when you get safely on the land."

He held her the whole time, and she melted into him. They kissed, and then he gave her backside a pat. "In you go. Off with you all. You want to get to the land no later than dusk."

I loved Grandmother's four-door truck. I climbed up front with Grandmother, and Shane and Andrea were talking in the back seat. We went through Los Lunas, which was beautiful. I love getting out of the city. I knew this was the perfect time to ask Grandmother about the Ceremonial Dance, but not until we were on a straight road with hours to go.

"Hey, you two, would you like to hear Grandmother tell us about the

135

Ceremonial Dance?"

They both said yes, and two pairs of arms rested on the front seat as they leaned forward to listen.

My questions started flowing. "Grandmother, how many people will be attending?"

"Around one hundred seventy-five to two hundred."

"Will everybody stay in local hotels? Where do we go to the bathroom, and are there showers?"

"Sage, take a breath and slow down."

Where have I heard that before?

"There are showers, but we might have to wait till Sunday before the shower house is up and running with hot water. They built a new shower house this year with eight shower stalls and one big stall with two shower heads—large enough for two people. Couples can jump in together, save time and water, and scrub the red dirt off each other's backs."

"The shower curtains need to be hung and cleaned because they have been sitting between work weekends for the past four months. It takes a lot of volunteers to get the land ready. That might be a good job for you two, Sage and Andrea."

"We're here to do whatever jobs need to be done," Andrea said enthusiastically.

"Shane, you are a strapping strong young man. You'll be asked to help with the heavier jobs."

"I'm good with that." His smile was broad, and he sat a bit taller.

"That's a good attitude. Thanks. It will be fun. To answer your other questions, we had porta potties delivered, and there are composting toilets. Those are the ones we will use this work weekend. As for hotels, there are a few small country towns about thirty miles from our location, but no hotels out there! We have sixty acres. Like the old days, they put up teepees, only we call them tents nowadays. We'll create a tent city. Have you two ever camped out before?"

"I have camped with my family," Shane said, "and I really like it. Especially at night, looking up at the billions of stars. So much better than a ceiling."

Andrea's experience was closer to home. "When I was in grade school I used to sleep in a tent in our back yard, and we had a fire pit."

"Close enough," Grandmother said. "I'm sure you'll enjoy being out in nature. We have pretty much tamed the land. It's not the same as having a bathroom down the hall, but down the road will have to do."

"Will we have time to walk the land with you, so you can point out where

Tent City and some of the other spaces are?" I asked.

"I don't know which jobs you'll be asked to do, but anyone can answer questions. Just ask.

Just ask for what I want, I heard in my head.

"Will all two hundred people use one small shower house? It must take all day for them to shower," Andrea said.

"Good girl," Grandmother said kindly, "you were listening. Yes, it takes all day and evening, too, meaning people spread their shower times throughout the day so they don't have to wait in line—though that happens after the purification lodges. I have never understood why after every pore in your body is open, and you are sweating squeaky clean, people take showers."

"Should we have brought up soap, shampoo, and conditioner?"

"Yes, but it all needs to be biodegradable, which is easier on the land. You can use mine when we clean up on Sunday. I keep it all in a waterproof bag. That's what the dancers do. The shower floor gets pretty wet and dirty. So, when you're done, you'll want to slip on some flip-flops. Did you bring them?

"Ahhh, I did, but I forgot to tell Shane and Andrea. Sorry, guys."

They looked at each other. "I have sandals," Andrea said.

"I brought my flip-flops," Shane chimed in.

"Good." Grandmother said. "We'll be taking turns showering on Sunday, too.

Sage and Andrea, you can undress in my tent and leave your clothes there. Just slip on your bathrobe and flip-flops and grab a towel. We girls will shower at the same time, and there may be one or two other women there as well. The men will give us privacy. When you're done, if you feel shy, pull the towel into the shower stall, dry off, then put on your robe and flip-flops and we'll go back to my tent. Keep something clean to wear for the trip home; you'll feel better.

"You might feel shy, but you don't need to feel embarrassed. It's part of your life training. Nudity doesn't mean sex. It means you are nude inside the shower house, getting ready to take a shower and wash all the red dirt off your body. Don't buy into the guilt-blame-shame trip about how you think you're supposed to look."

"Okay, Grandmother." I turned to Andrea and said, "Grandmother teaches us about the beauty of who we are right now. There is nothing dirty about our bodies except the red dirt." We smiled at each other.

"You girls will be fine. Shane, you'll be working until the last push on Sunday. You can have the tent to yourself, but there will probably be other men showering when you do, just like in the high school gym. No big deal.

"Hey, let's drink some water. Will someone, please, open a bottle for me? There are bottles in the back door pockets. Help yourselves."

There was silence as we enjoyed the water sliding down our throats.

"Would you like to hear about the purification lodges on the land? Andrea, I know you've never done a lodge with the woman's circle. Maybe after seeing them this weekend, you'll decide to join us."

"I would love to hear about them. This is like going to another country and having a personal guide telling us about the special things to see."

Shane drank more water. "Grandmother, are we going to be stopping soon for gas and a bathroom break?"

"I could use a bathroom stop, too," I chimed in.

"Okay, guys. Can you last another twenty minutes?"

The three of us looked at each other and nodded.

"Yes," I said. "We're fine."

"Good. There's a small town ahead. I'll start the story of the purification lodges, and we'll see if I can finish it in twenty minutes. This year, we have nine lodges. Eight of them are in a large circle with the doors facing each of the eight directions of the medicine wheel, and the ninth one is a center pit lodge that sets outside the circle."

Nine lodges, wow! I thought to myself.

"There's a big fire pit in the center of the eight lodges where they heat over four hundred rock people at one time."

"Wow, I thought sixty rock people were a lot," Shane said in amazement.

"Yes, four hundred rock people, and everybody purifies themselves. We do this every evening, four days in a row, before entering into the Ceremonial Dance."

"Dance, Grandmother?" Andrea said.

"I thought it was a ceremony, not a dance," I said, echoing Andrea's question.

"Sage," she said with a little extra twang to my name, "you still have a lot to learn. The learning begins this weekend for all of you. It's a different world, a different culture, and a beautiful one. You'll get to experience some wonderful people coming here to awaken the land and prepare it for the ceremony. We are doing this because those who fly in from around the world can't do it. No one gets paid—except for the joy of being here together and sharing a weekend under the stars."

"I like the sound of that," Shane said from the back seat as his hand touched my shoulder.

"The nightly lodges help the soul to pray, and the heat relaxes tired muscles from a hard day's work," Grandmother added.

"Will there be a lodge this weekend?" Andrea asked.

"No, we are repairing and preparing lodges for the ceremony. If we did a lodge, who would want to go in?"

"I would. Something inside me is kinda scared, but something else feels warm and comforting," Andrea admitted.

"Well spoken, and thank you for your honesty. Yes, the Womb of Grandmother is very warm and comforting."

Grandmother pulled up to a gas pump. "We're here. Shane, would you do the honors? Here's my credit card."

Andrea and I made a beeline to the convenience store and found out that the bathrooms were on the outside of the building. When I came out, I saw that Shane was still pumping gas. I went over and placed my hand on the pump handle, slightly touching his hand. "Go. I've got it."

Grandmother moved the truck when I was finished pumping. She had purchased fruit and string cheese, which she placed into a small ice chest and told us to help ourselves or go in and buy something. While she went to the restroom, we munched down on apples and cheese.

When she returned, she said in a commanding voice like Thunder Wolf's, "Hey, where's my apple and cheese? Rip the top off the string cheese so I can squeeze it out and drive. There's a roll of paper towels back there. Give me two."

"Yes, Ma'am," Shane said, diving into the ice chest and handing it to her. We ate for a few minutes and then got back on the road.

After her last bite of apple, Grandmother picked up where she had left off.

"Sage Wind Dancer, this is your first year, so you'll be a helper. This way, you can see what the Ceremony is all about. Next year, you can dance."

"I'm not going to be part of the ceremony, only a helper?" I realized my tone showed disappointment, but I couldn't help it.

"Wind Dancer, even the smallest job is important. This one ceremony does more to help heal the planet than all the other individual ceremonies put together. Your job, whatever it is, will help make this happen." Looking at me sharply, she said, "If you have a good attitude, it will happen in beauty.

"We still have a few hours of driving left. Why don't we stop for dinner around five o'clock or did you just kill your appetite?"

I don't know who spoke first, but we tumbled over each in expressing our agreement to stop for dinner.

"We are getting into some pretty country," Grandmother said. "Let's relax for a bit and chit-chat. I like listening to country music."

That was my clue, and I turned the radio on. It was already on her favorite country pop station. We settled into listening and admiring the scenery as we flew by. Grandmother put the petal to the metal as we talked about school and other items that popped into our heads, and Andrea fell asleep.

After a time of radio music, Grandmother said, "Are you ready to hear the story of Ceremonial Dance? It may help you to understand the importance of your giveaway of being a helper this weekend."

"Yes, Grandmother, I'd love to listen to your story," I said.

"Me, too," Andrea said, waking up.

"Don't leave me out. Someday I may want to join Sage and attend."

I heard Shane's words, both spoken and unspoken. I turned and looked at him. It was a two-second, deep look, and he smiled at me.

"Grandmother, the more I know, the more fun it will be," I said.

She looked at me funny, and a little smile crossed her lips. "This Dance has been taking place on Turtle Island, South, Central, and North America for a long time. It was so long ago that the Bering Straits were still connected to the continents, which lead to Asia. DNA has been found in the South American indigenous groups that have genetic similarities with Australasians, indicating that the descendants of the first Americans mated with Australian ancestors at least fifteen thousand years ago. Researchers are still figuring out how the land masses facilitated that Australian connection. That's a bit of history for you—the short version. Remember, don't believe me; look it up for yourself. It might make a good school report."

Glancing at me, she said, "Wind Dancer, do you remember what Metis means?"

"I think so, Grandmother. Does it mean mixed blood? A lot of people from different bloodlines married each other and eventually, they are like one people."

"Yes, Metis means mixed ancestry and interracial marriages. Almost all of us on the planet are Metis at this point. This Dance has its own history. There are the Dreamer's Ceremonial Dances and Piercing Ceremonial Dances. They are very different. Both still exist today."

"What is a Piercing Ceremonial Dance, Grandmother?" Andrea asked.

"It's where the men have two wood skewers placed under the skin on their chests or in their backs, and they are attached to the Ceremonial Dance pole—not a living tree—and they dance themselves into a trance until they throw themselves back against the leather tethers that are tied to the pole in an effort to break the skin and free themselves. It is considered an act of power to be able to do this. They dance from sunrise to sunset and then sleep through the night and begin the next morning."

I heard Shane say, "No way. Not ever. I get it, the trance and an act of power, but I wouldn't do it now or in future lives."

I turned around and saw him massaging his chest where the skews would be placed. Was he having a past life memory like I had? Was he Cloud Walker?

I added my voice to his. "Something in me knows, as a man, I would never pierce again in any future lifetime. What of the women? Do they pierce?"

"No, granddaughter, but those who are called to will have pieces of skin cut away from their upper arms. It is *not* our way. Thunder Wolf taught us that we don't need to learn from pain and suffering anymore. That was the old way."

I was listening attentively as Grandmother continued.

"By permission of his Elders, Thunder Wolf is the first to offer the non-piercing Dreamer's Ceremony to non-native people who have apprenticed under him and the teachings. The people who attend are so dedicated that this is the nineteenth year they have honored this Ceremonial Dance tradition. Thunder Wolf is quite proud of his people. You don't have to be a full-blooded Native American to understand the power of two or more gathering in prayer. There's a group in a Scandinavian country in their ninth year of dancing.

"This planet feels the power of the Ceremonial Dance prayers. Grandmother Earth hears her grandchildren's prayers for clean water, clean air, and world freedom—not world peace, mind you—world freedom. You can have peace under a dictatorship, but true world freedom, where men and women have autonomy and individual rights—as in our Bill of Rights and the Constitution. Now, pay attention to the words of the Declaration of Independence.

> "When, in the Course of human events, it becomes necessary for one people to dissolve the political bands which have connected them with another and to assume among the powers of the earth, the separate and equal station to which the Laws of Nature and Nature's God entitle them, a decent respect to the opinions of mankind requires that they should declare the causes which impel them to the separation.
>
> "We hold these truths to be self-evident, that all

men are created equal, that they are endowed by their Creator with certain unalienable Rights, that among these are Life, Liberty and the Pursuit of Happiness. —That to secure these rights, Governments are instituted among Men, deriving their just powers from the consent of the governed,—That whenever any Form of Government becomes destructive of these ends, it is the Right of the People to alter or to abolish it, and to institute new Government, laying its foundation on such principles and organizing its powers in such form, as to them shall seem most likely to effect their Safety and Happiness.

"Prudence, indeed, will dictate that Governments long established should not be changed for light and transient causes; and accordingly all experience hath shewn that mankind are more disposed to suffer, while evils are sufferable, than to right themselves by abolishing the forms to which they are accustomed. But when a long train of abuses and usurpations, pursuing invariably the same Object evinces a design to reduce them under absolute Despotism, it is their right, it is their duty, to throw off such Government, and to provide new Guards for the future security.

"I could go on, but I think you got the point," Grandmother said. "By the way, do you still study this in school?"

"I don't think we study it the way we should," I said. "I can't even remember what we learned. I wish you could come to school and teach us. Wouldn't that be great?"

"It would make our history come alive instead of just reading words in a book—boring!" Andrea said.

"You know, Wind Dancer, the Talking Leaves, which the Constitution and Bill of Rights are known as in the native world, were formatted or taken from the ancient Cherokee Council of Law. The Cherokee Nation lived in peace and freedom for over two thousand years abiding by the Council of Law."

"Grandmother, why don't we use the Council of Law now?"

"It would be the best thing that could happen to our planet, let alone the United States if we went back to the original Council of Law, but big government and big business would never allow it. There would have to be another revolution before it would happen, or a collective internal awakening of the soul's relationship to Spirit with 144,000 people in each of the Eight Great Powers of the world stepping up as Rainbow Warriors. Some people will never wake up until they are recycled through death, change, and rebirth."

In the silence that followed, I shifted space and time into the future.

I was familiar with traveling into my past lives. Grandmother spoke about prophetic seeing into the future, but she never taught me how to do it. How this came to me, I don't know. I just knew in my being the truth of what was being shown to me as Grandmother spoke.

The planet moved into a very dark time. It is darkest before the dawn as we're moving into the fifth world of humankind when Great Spirit would heal the whole planet after enough people woke up. The people need to see and feel the evil that has penetrated deep into our Grandmother Earth for thousands of years and every aspect of society, including blinding our souls and hypnotizing our minds. The people had to protect Grandmother Earth, the sacred hoop of generations, and honor the sacred law of 'Do Nothing to Harm the Children.'

I heard myself say, "Do nothing to harm the children," as if I were coming out of a dream—not quite asleep or awake. Realizing it, I said, "Grandmother! Your story took me into the future. It's hard to believe what was just shared with me."

"Don't talk about it now, Sage. Let it sink in." She looked at me, and I understood. This was not to be spoken about in front of my friends.

I saw Shane and Andrea look at each other and brought the talk back to the Ceremonial Dance. "The depth of this Ceremonial Dance story is fascinating and much bigger than I thought. A council of law, two thousand years of freedom, our Constitution based on it. Tell us more about the Circle of Law, Grandmother."

"It's too much to go into it now, but I can see your interest, and that's a good thing. One day, we'll begin your education regarding the Council and Circle of Law."

"All right. It feels a bit overwhelming right now anyway."

Shifting the energy, Grandmother said, "I don't know about the rest of you, but my stomach is talking to me. We're almost there."

"Mine, too," Shane said just as his stomach growled.

Everyone laughed, which relieved the awkwardness of the moments before.

Soon, we were driving into town and pulling into the restaurant.

"We have time to stop for dinner and dessert, and we'll still make it to the land before dusk. I'll call Grandfather to let him know we're in good shape and hungry."

A patty melt on rye with dill pickles and sweet potato fries never tasted so good. We enjoyed our meals with lots of exciting discussions and were on the road again.

Chapter 14

Work Weekend, Here We Come!

Finally, we turned off the two-lane country highway onto a dirt road. The sign for this road was small, consisting only of numbers. Grandmother slowed down to avoid the potholes and large rocks.

"Grandmother, how do you remember all these back roads? It's a good thing it's still light out, otherwise this road would scare me."

"Don't worry, I've been driving out here for over twenty years. I know the way, even in the dark, but the potholes and rocks are different every year because of the rain and winter weather. Sometimes the locals grade the road, and then it's easier to drive on."

Coming up over a rise, we saw the land for the first time, and it's difficult to describe my feelings. It's immense. Grandmother pulled to the side of the road and stopped on the hill, which overlooked the entire valley.

"Look, kids. You asked me to show you where everything would be set up, but this is a better story. You can see the whole layout, including the big mesa standing as a wall of protection on the south side." Pointing, she said, "See where we turn onto our private road? It takes us past the security gate and the big house on the left, where we have meetings and the sand painters create their magick away from the wind."

"It's beautiful out here," Shane said.

"Yes, it is. Now, look off to the right. That's our Ceremonial Dance Arbor. It holds up to two hundred dancers. See the earth house? That's our medical space. The tepee is not up yet. As the road curves to the right, you'll see a big open space where the large Capitol Tent will be set up. That's our general meeting place. Beyond that, see the box trailers?"

"Yes, Grandmother, we're following you," Andrea said.

"They hold the supplies for setting up the Ceremonial Arbor. Across from the box trailers is the shower house and a few yellow porta potties for this weekend. Can you see where my space is from here?"

"Is it next to the big space with Astroturf? Do you have a carport roof?" Sage asked.

"You got it. I prefer to sleep under the stars this weekend, so that's what we'll do tonight. Let's head down before it gets too dark."

"Thanks for the visual tour," Shane said. "Being up on the hill gave us a great view of the land and this beautiful sunset. I have to admire God's artwork."

I looked at him. *I need to get to know Shane better, and I will this weekend.*

We took a few moments to take it all in before heading into camp.

The sun had not completely set when we arrived. As we explored the beautiful surroundings, Grandmother introduced us to the other Wolf Tribe workers. Some were eating their dinners while others sipped on hot coffee and talked. They told us how happy they were to see three strong young workers.

One of the women, Sally Sees the Thunder, said, "There are more people coming tonight, and some will arrive first thing in the morning. We'll start very early in the morning, so get your rest tonight."

Everyone laughed and nodded. Early to bed was the theme.

As we walked back to the truck, Grandmother said softly, "The heck with the compost toilets for tonight unless you need to go number two. You know what that means, yes?"

We nodded. Grandmother had told us the rules. It's okay to pee on the trees and bushes, but take a plastic bag for toilet paper.

When we returned to the truck, Grandmother directed us like the head Chief.

"Get the tarp from the back of the truck and spread it out, then your sleeping bags. We'll sleep in the ceremonial area because it's already cleared of all the cactus and plants. Someone, please grab my foam pad, pillows, and sleeping bag. I don't do the hard ground anymore at my age."

We threw a big plastic tarp on the ground and set our sleeping bags and backpacks on it. We spread out Grandmother's thick foam pad, unrolled her sleeping bag, and gave her the big pillow. Heading off in separate directions, we took a trip to the bushes.

When we returned to our sleeping bags, we took off our shoes and hung them on a bush so that spiders or scorpions wouldn't crawl into them and critters couldn't carry them away. We crawled into our sleeping bags and talked quietly as the night closed in around us. We were tired. Between getting up early for school, driving for six hours, and visiting, we were looking forward to being prone and watching the night sky.

As the stars came out, the Milky Way showed itself. I'm always amazed by the trillions of stars that blanket the night sky. When I felt my nose getting colder, I pulled my sleeping bag and colorful native-design fleece blanket around my neck and face and snuggled in with a contented sigh.

"Look, a shooting star," Andrea exclaimed as she pointed to the east.

There was more soft talk, but my eyes grew heavy.

The next thing I remember was Grandmother's voice saying, "Grandfather Sun is up, and we have breakfast to fix and lots of work to do."

It was about 5:00 am, and it turned out that we had gone to bed around ten o'clock the night before. I had thought it might be difficult to get up that early, but it was easy to wake up because the sun wasn't hiding behind dark curtains.

Work wouldn't begin until six.

"Open up the camp stove," Grandmother said. "Put water in the tea kettle and get it going. We need some hot tea or cocoa. Bundle up, so you don't get chilled. It'll warm up later."

Grandmother's ice chests held the cold fruit, coconut milk for cereal, yogurt, almond butter, and jam for bread. Shane boiled the water, and Andrea filled the cups with hot water for steaming teas and hot chocolate. It all tasted wonderful.

It was a busy Saturday with everyone working on different projects and helping each other with whatever was needed. Everyone welcomed Andrea, Shane, and me as if we were long-time family. Everyone was friendly and open-hearted. It felt like the village of Tepees I visited with Dreams with the Wind.

I liked seeing the Ceremonial Dance land before all the dancers arrived. It was so quiet and beautiful on the high plains. Rabbits were abundant. We were told to walk around any rattlesnakes we saw and to tell someone so they could be gently moved to the outskirts.

I got blisters on my hands, and Andrea got a blister on her little toe.

We met up near our camp around noon.

"Grandmother, can we put lunch together?"

"Let's take a look at those blisters first. Sage, get my first aid kit out of the truck. It's behind the front seat. Shane, open up the four-foot table, please."

Grandmother brought out prepared sandwiches while we retrieved the medical supplies.

"Good, you found it. Andrea, you first. Let's see that toe. First, we'll clean it with an alcohol swab. Then we'll need to prick it with a pin to release the fluid, but we'll keep the skin over it. It won't hurt."

Andrea made an exaggerated face.

"You'll live," Grandmother teased. "Next, some antibiotic cream. Up here, and working in the dirt, we need to be careful. Here, wrap this Band-Aid around your toe. Sage, let's look at your palm. Okay, same procedure. Clean it first."

Grandmother was proficient. I needed a bigger Band-Aid because it was on my palm.

"Grandmother," Shane said, "how many sandwiches did you bring for us?" He had pulled out the chips, a bag of red grapes, paper towels, and the drinks.

"There's enough for each of you to have two. And you can start. Don't wait for the blister sisters."

We all laughed, and in moments we were digging into a delicious lunch of chicken salad sandwiches, fruit, chips, and Powerade with electrolytes.

"Grandmother, this is so good," I said. "Thank you!"

We cleaned up lunch while Grandmother relaxed.

We rested a bit, but when we heard the drum, we knew it was time to go back to work. Andrea was limping a little, and my palm was sticky from the Band-Aid moving around. I used a pair of Grandmother's gloves, which helped a lot. I can't remember ever working so hard. Shane worked all over the land helping different crews. He was tall and strong and never got tired. He seemed to be shining. Being in the men's clan had changed him. I saw him taking on responsibility with pride. He seemed so happy. I hardly saw him that first day.

Andrea and I helped Grandmother put up the major camp she uses when on the land. She arrives early with a group of other leaders, so she camps for thirteen days. Wow, talk about set-ups. Grandmother first had us put down Astroturf over her whole space, which was covered by a carport with an extended roof. She had a big twelve-person tent and a complete kitchen set-up. It was tucked behind an L-shaped fence that protected her from the high afternoon winds. She outdid my parent's camp ten-fold.

"Grandmother, is this all just for you?"

"This camp is for Grandfather Strong Bear, me, and all our medicine. We also hold staff meetings here. Now it's time to help set up the ceremonial space, which is where we slept last night. We need to move our gear from there into this tent for now."

When we arrived at the ceremonial space, the team leader approached.

"Are you ready to create magick? Time to earn our keep! A lot happens in this ceremonial space, so as we put it together, let's keep our minds and talk positive."

The team leader lit the smudge and passed it around the circle before we started working. We all said our names again, and I tried to remember all the folks I was meeting. We were all assigned tasks, and we all worked together. It took hours to put the 60" x 20" canopies on the top permanent structure.

The structure frame was cemented into the ground. We wrapped shade cloth around the poles, laid Astroturf, and nailed it down. Then we moved to other crews that needed help. Since we all split up, Grandmother told us to meet back at the large ceremonial space when we were finished.

Later that evening, when Shane and I returned to camp, Grandmother was waiting for us. Andrea was lying down, and Shane and I sprawled out on the Astroturf.

"It feels good to be off my feet and on my back. Aah!" Shane sighed.

"Grandmother, this space is huge," Andrea said.

"Yes, it is, and the canopy protects us from the hot sun and rain. The shade cloth allows the breeze to come through, which helps to cool it down, and the Astroturf keeps us out of the dirt."

"What, exactly, will happen here?" Andrea asked.

"Andrea, since you and Shane have not been introduced to what the Ceremonial Dance is all about, I'll give you the big picture. Nearly two hundred people from around the globe come for this ceremony with the intent of praying for the world. Most are dancers, drummers, singers, kitchen chiefs, and, of course, there are children and teens and our medical healing team in case they are needed. There's a job for everyone. About a quarter of the participants come here before the dance to help get everything ready. This is the specific space for ceremonies and medicine talks. We have a full ceremonial crew, five medicine chiefs, a medicine elder, and eight advanced apprentices who use these shaded spaces. This is a time when the participants can do some of the other ceremonies they need as apprentices, and there are meetings to teach the first-time dancers the protocol.

"The dancers bring their shields to hang in their arbor space, and sometimes they need repair. This space is used to prepare all the sweet medicine totems, which are placed on top of the purification lodges and in the Ceremonial Tree you have been walking past—the big tree in the center of the circle of trees and the arbor framework."

"Wow, this is a busy place," Shane noted, and Grandmother agreed.

"In my space, I have two folding six-foot tables and six chairs. We often meet to repair medicine items, review the next big ceremony, or use our laptops to record how we can improve what we are doing. The second one is for my kitchen. I have a camp stove for making hot tea and coffee after the lodges when the camp kitchen is closed, and we are meeting again. I like offering hot drinks and snacks after dinner. It gives us chiefs a boost of energy.

"Grandfather built this L-shaped wood fence to protect us from the wind. This fence has withstood fifteen winters and is still strong, just like me—a little weathered but as good as ever. It becomes a very attractive spot when the wind and rain spirits let us know who's boss," Grandmother added with a twinkle in her eye.

I was getting a deeper understanding of Ceremonial Dance and seeing how playful Grandmother could be. I was beginning to recognize her teasing.

Andrea was very appreciative. "Grandmother, I can see how big this land is with the buildings, the Ceremonial Dance space, and camp spaces. When everybody's here, I imagine it's amazing. I wish I could come back for the full ceremony and be a helper with the children's camp."

"You're welcome to come back, Andrea, but you need to speak to your parents, of course. If they'll consider it, you and your folks can come to our home, and I'll explain more to them."

"Wow, thanks. Can I ask one more question?"

"Of course, you can, dear."

"When do we eat dinner? I'm really hungry."

Grandmother laughed.

"We're starved too! Can we have a snack before dinner?" I added.

"We can quit now. Almost everyone quits working around 6:00 pm. It's close enough. No showers, though. Sorry. The showers need more work before turning on the propane hot water heaters. We have cold water in the two deep sinks attached to the outside of the shower house. It's really cold, but we all could do with some washing up."

We beat the crowd there, and it felt wonderful after being sweaty and dirty all day.

Afterward, Shane said, "I could eat a whole cow."

Grandmother glanced up and said, "We're having steak tonight. Maybe you're becoming psychic, Shane." She winked at me, and I smiled back.

We decided to snack while preparing dinner. Grandmother and I would do the cooking, and Shane and Andrea would clean up. I was quite happy with that plan.

Dinner was delicious. We grilled steaks, wrapped potatoes and onions in tin foil, and cooked them under the coals. Grandmother had brought a big salad from home and had it in a plastic bowl. She said we should save some for lunch the next day, but I guess she forgot how much kids can eat. Finally, she told us to go ahead and finish it up, and we did. We also finished off the last of potatoes, and not a scrap of meat was left. Grandmother laughed and said not to worry; she had brought plenty of food.

Cleanup was easy—I'd forgotten we were using paper plates. Shane and Andrea had boiled water for the items that needed washing, and both volunteered for the task.

Andrea sighed as she submerged her hands in the soapy water. "Aah, I'll never take hot water for granted again."

"At least, let me rinse," Shane teased.

"Okay, but I'm taking my time washing these bowls."

They laughed, and I couldn't help but smile, too.

I looked at my hands and saw dirt beneath my nails and red smudges on my skin, despite my cold-water scrubbing. "Let me know when you're finished," I said. "I want to wash my hands before you throw that water out."

They were kind enough to give me a turn before the water grew cold, and I plunged in with the same contented sigh Andrea did. The warmth felt so good, and one dab of soap let me clean up to my elbows.

"Grandmother, do you want a turn?"

"Maybe a quick one," she said.

While she washed up, I put on sweatpants, a turtleneck, and even a sweatshirt.

It was getting dark, and Grandmother had the Coleman lanterns glowing brightly as everyone began to gather at her camp.

We put on more hot water for anyone who needed hot tea or cocoa. Some folks didn't bring a camp stove for this short weekend. They knew Grandmother would have enough to share, and it was a tradition to gather at the end of the day.

Everybody started talking, laughing, and storytelling about other Ceremonial Dances. I did a lot of listening.

Martha Star Light caught my attention and said, "Sage, you may want to sit at the Children's Fire on the East Mesa. Especially on Friday night. It's a magickal place. Everyone is amped because it's the last night of dancing our prayers. The dancers get a second wind, and most everybody is up and dancing to the tree. When the drum goes down at 2:00 am, the arbor is quiet. The dancers are deep in dream time. There are two volunteers per shift to keep the Children's Fire going all night. You can sit next to the rock circle and feed the fire, but remember to keep the flames low. You can see the ancestors dancing and hear the drum and spirit songs whisper in your ears."

Someone heard her and said they had sat at the East Mesa for many dances just to feel the magick when all was quiet.

When Bobby started to share with a pronounced Australian accent, everyone quieted down. "I remember the first Dances at Silver Creek, California. It was a much smaller space, and we only had about forty dancers. The arbor was smaller, thank God. It was not wrapped in shade cloth, like we do now, to provide protection from the sun. It was built like the older style arbors with brushes cut and woven to provide shade."

Looking at Grandmother, he said, "Deborah, you remember. You were there. I think out of this group, we are the only ones who were there." A bunch of us would climb into a big truck and drive to the overgrowth to cut truckloads of bushes with our machetes for the arbor crew to weave into a wall around the entire arbor. We weaved them above us, too—like a lean-to. Wow, did my legs get scratched up. I was younger and too inexperienced to wear long pants."

Everyone laughed, then Bobby continued. "The best thing about the brush arbor was the fragrance of the freshly cut bushes. I can still smell it when I think about it. At night, when the drummers sang their last song at 2:00 am, and we crawled into our sleeping bags, the fragrance took us into the dream. Most of us slept on the ground."

Bobby looked at Grandmother, "There were a handful of wise ones, including Thunder Wolf, who had cots with soft three-inch foam pads to make sleeping more comfortable."

Grandmother smiled. "Yes, when I think about those early days, I smell the strong, beautiful fragrance of mother nature. The take down was almost sacrilegious to me. I could have lived there, though the rain dripped right through onto our gear. We used plastic tarps to protect our stuff. When the dance was over, we cut the twine that held it all in place, and, like peeling an onion apart, we stuffed truckloads of brush back into the bed of that one big truck and hauled it to the ravine where the landowners asked us to dump it. Wow, how the dust and dirt flew! We were filthy, and there was no shower house in those days! My camp had one of those hanging shower bags that captured the heat during the day. You could stand under it and wet down, close the spigot, soap up, and open the spigot again to rinse, but you had to be quick!"

Bobby laughed. "You had a fancy camp. I just jumped into the pond. No soap, just a washcloth to scrub the dirt off. During the buildup, I could come by your camp, and you always gave me a nice, hot cup of coffee.”

“Yes, I can still see your happy face.”

Bobby smiled. “You’re a doll. I could always count on you for my morning coffee. Is there any more coffee, now?”

Everyone laughed.

Grandmother looked at us, and Shane and I popped up.

“I’ll get more water,” Shane said. “I want another hot chocolate.”

“Me, too,” I added. “Anyone else ready for more?”

There were several takers. I loved our camp. It was filled with friends.

“Back then, did everybody have to cook all three meals for themselves, build the arbor, and purifications lodges before the Ceremonial Dance began?” I asked.

Bobby and Grandmother looked at each other and smiled.

“There was one large lodge,” Grandmother said. “We put twenty people in one, and when they were finished, there was a second round for the other twenty. As we got bigger, we had to build a second lodge.”

Bobby nodded. “As the tribe gained more apprentices, we had to move to the far side of the meadow, to the larger tree, where we could build a larger arbor, which meant a greater distance to the center Tree of Life and back to our personal shield spaces. The first year, there was a lot of grumbling. Then we started challenging each other from across the arbor to see who could get to the tree first. We forgot about the additional length we were traveling with every prayer.

“Covering this arbor took a lot more brush, so we finally decided to use a shade cloth. It was expensive to buy but wise in labor cost.”

Grandmother nodded. “There are so many wonderful memories and stories. I wish I could project them from my memory into a hologram for you all to see. We need to capture this somehow. If only we had been recording it all these years, but this always happens. Over a campfire, at the end of a workday, the stories are here because we are here. What will happen when we are gone? How are you going to know the beginning of our spiritual path with heart? The heart is in the stories. They need to be saved somehow.”

Julie Walks Tall said, “We have heard the assignment. The seed has been planted. Let’s all dance it to the Tree of Life and see it happening.”

There was a resounding ‘Ho’ of agreement followed by Julie saying, “For now, let’s focus on tomorrow.”

The discussion turned to what needed to be accomplished before leaving. The plan was for everything to be completed by one or two in the afternoon, at the latest. Most people had to go to work the next day, so it was important for everyone to get on the road early. Everyone agreed they had done a good day's work, and someone said having three extra helpers was very much appreciated.

The three of us said, 'Thanks!' simultaneously and then laughed.

Robert Thundering Dove said, "Shane, you can come up any time. It's nice to have a strong young man to help with the heavy stuff."

"Thanks, I might just take you up on that. I like being here. I'll sleep tonight. That's for sure."

That seemed to be the signal, and everyone stood and headed toward their camps.

Shane, Andrea, and I decided to sleep under the stars again and spread a tarp in an open space near Grandmother's camp. Shane had placed his sleeping bag next to mine, and Andrea was on my other side. He held his hand where only I could see it, and we held hands. My arm was cold, but I didn't care.

The stars seemed so bright and close. We tried to stay awake to see some shooting stars. The three of us whispered until we could barely keep our eyes open. At last, we saw a shooting star streak across the star-filled sky. We echoed one last sigh of appreciation for the beauty around us, then, with a simple good night to each other, we let our eyes close for the night.

Shane squeezed my hand and gently released it.

Chapter 15

Mama Cougar and Spirit Hawk

Sunday morning was quiet, and the stars still twinkled in the sky. As much as I dreaded it, I took a quick trip to the bushes. It was cold, and I quickly snuggled back into my sleeping bag to get warm. Shane was sound asleep. He looked peaceful—like a young warrior. I felt my heart open and gently touched his face.

I looked over at Andrea, and she was awake, too. We couldn't see Grandfather Sun in the sky yet, though his power was beginning to bring a crescent of morning light to the sleeping desert. After about ten minutes of whispering, we pointed to the outline of a small mesa. We quietly slipped out of our sleeping bags and dressed in double layers. The cool air felt good because we knew it would get hot by 9:00 am. We rolled our sleeping bags and stuffed them back into their little carry bags to prevent any scorpion surprises!

We grabbed two apples and headed for the Mesa.

Grandmother said there was an easy walking path behind the mesa that the Dog Soldiers and security team used during the Ceremonial Dance. She said you could see the entire valley from there. According to one of the stories from the night before, it was a popular place for dancers to meet before the ceremony, and a great place to see the sunrise or sunset. Andrea and I intended to visit the mesa and return before the camp awoke.

Our apples were delicious. Every bite was loud as we crunched our way to the apple core. We looked at each other, and with a bit of mischief in our eyes, we threw the tiny cores as far as we could. Some rabbit would have a nice breakfast treat.

"Let's get to the top," Andrea said with more energy than I'd ever seen her have before. "I want to see Grandfather Sun as his body peaks out from behind Grandmother's mountains."

I looked at her with surprise because what she said sounded so natural, but it wasn't the high school Andrea I knew.

The air was crisp and quiet. We started to talk and laugh and then stopped. It seemed more respectful to be quiet.

Grandmother had told us there was a mother cougar that lived out here. Her tracks were visible in the dry mud on the outskirts of the camp. The caretakers of the land occasionally saw her, but when folks began coming up to prepare the space for Ceremony, they thought Mama Cougar had retreated into the open country.

This morning, she must've been curious because just as we topped the mesa, we saw her sleek, beautiful body escaping down the other side of the plateau. We gasped and stood in surprise and a little bit of fear. It may have been unwise, but I ran to where she had disappeared and was thrilled to spot her sitting beneath a tree staring back at us. I waved at her and smiled. I felt stupid after doing that, but it seemed the most natural thing to do. Andrea had stepped back, but my whole focus was on Mama Cougar. It was like Mama Cougar was in my mind and knew I meant her no harm.

We looked at each other for the longest time. I could feel the strength of her muscles, shoulders, and legs, which were capable of quick, powerful movement. It was my body, sleek and long, and my mind at peace and curious about these two-legged ones. I sat looking back up at myself as she sat inside me looking at herself. I don't know how much time passed; it could have been an hour or a second. It seemed like time stood still. Was I dreaming in my sleeping bag or was I looking at myself looking at Mama Cougar?

Grandmother jumped into my mind. She was awake and wondering where we were. Then, she knew we were on the mesa. For a moment, I was confused because Grandmother was seeing Mama Cougar through my eyes. I don't know how I knew this; I just knew. Then, I felt the connection between the three of us break, and Mama Cougar trotted down the hill until she disappeared into the high plains scrub brush.

Andrea spouted, "I was so scared, but excited, too! I kept thinking, what if she runs up the hill after us? You were the brave one."

"Did you see her looking at us, Andrea?"

"She was looking at you, not me, and I was glad. I was hiding behind you! I didn't want to be her breakfast."

"She wasn't going to eat us. We were just getting to know each other."

"You're weird."

That was not the first or last time I'd feel different than my friends. They always accepted me, but, clearly, my world was different from theirs, and I wouldn't have it any other way.

Andrea's fear melted into excitement. By the time we finished talking and laughing, we realized that Grandfather Sun was lifting himself into the sky. We were making so much noise that we didn't realize Grandmother and Shane had joined us on the mesa. They were greeting Grandfather Sun as I had done in my Rite of Passage Ceremony. We quietly approached them, lifted our hands, and formed a triangle with our void-element thumbs and pointer fire-element fingers touching. We extended our arms and placed Grandfather Sun in the center. I closed my eyes and still saw Grandfather Sun shining through my triangle and touching my forehead third eye. I slowly opened my arms until it felt like I had a beach ball full of energy in my arms. I then brought that energy into my body.

I started at the first wheel, my first chakra. I felt warmth and tingling in my sacred genitals and lifted the energy all the way up to my belly button, then to my heart wheel or chakra, and up to my throat wheel. When I reached my forehead, I rotated my hands back out again to capture more of Grandfather Sun's energy.

Shane said, "Wow, what a rush!"

Grandmother nodded. "Yeah, you can get so high and light you might just be able to walk on the clouds. I've seen old ones who got so high they stepped off the side of a cliff and floated to the bottom where they continued walking."

I looked at Grandmother. It was as if she were talking to us from a trance. I felt myself being pulled—pulled to the edge of the mesa. I stepped into her world. I thought she would step off at any moment, and I would step off with her. I felt her waiting. She whispered, "Not yet, Wind Dancer. You need to dance and build your personal power first."

I shook my head a little and Grandmother laughed. I looked at her with my mouth open. "How do you know what I'm thinking? "

Slowly, as if in a song, she repeated my name, "Wind Dancer." With a big smile, she added, "What do you think your name means?"

"I guess I'm learning." I sang my name over and over. "Wind Dancer, Wind Dancer. Oh my God, do you mean?"

Grandmother laughed, pointing at the expression on my face. She couldn't stop laughing, and I finally joined in. I understood what my name meant, and maybe someday, I could float off a cliff, land on the ground, and walk softly on.

I know my friends must have thought we were crazy. Andrea was back three feet from the edge and looking scared. "Were you going to jump?"

I laughed and almost said yes, but I knew she couldn't see and feel what I had just experienced. "No, of course not, silly. I was just feeling what it would be like to be a bird and be able to fly or walk on clouds."

Grandmother and I giggled.

Shane stood quietly at the edge, breathing in the morning energy with his eyes closed. He was in another world.

Grandmother gently called to him. "Shane, Spirit Hawk, are you flying?"

A smile came over his face, and he opened his eyes.

"Yes, Grandmother, I was flying. Like the red-tailed hawks I see near my home."

"Shane, your medicine name just came: Spirit Hawk. If you choose to accept it, take a moment after we have left and announce it to the Four Directions. Each time, say it with a voice of power, 'I am Spirit Hawk. This is how I will be known in the Universe!' Feel yourself soaring on the winds. Feel the freedom and joy."

With that, we all stepped to the edge and began to laugh, except Andrea.

I tried to be serious. "Birds aren't afraid to stand on the edge of a cliff. Come and join us, Andrea."

"No way! I'm afraid of heights and totally forgot how high we were until we got close to the edge of the mesa."

"Okay, but you've got to face your fears sometime." I couldn't resist teasing, "We can hold hands and jump off together."

She looked at me with exasperation. "You're nuts. Let's go down, I'm hungry."

Grandmother agreed. "My belly's so hungry it thinks I cut my head off."

At that point, Andrea led the way down the path as fast as she could.

I yelled after her, "You must have mountain goat medicine in you."

She yelled back, "I've always liked mountain goats. They can go places I'm afraid of."

Grandmother looked at me with a knowing look. "And what sweet medicine animal do you have in you?"

"Oh, Grandmother, Mama Cougar was on top of the mesa just as we arrived this morning. She was beautiful. She ran off the cliff, and I followed her."

"Oh, you ran off the cliff before I got here?"

"No, Grandmother, I didn't mean I ran off the cliff. I stood at the edge. She was hiding under some scrub tree, but not really hiding. We looked at each other for the longest time. I felt her inside me, and I was inside her. I felt you, too, when you were wondering where we had gone. And you were inside me looking at Mama Cougar. Were you a little confused at first, Grandmother? That's what I felt. Was it accurate? Did I really feel you inside me looking at the cougar? I would love to be a cougar."

"You are Wind Dancer. Mama Cougar gave you some of her medicine. And, yes, your skills are improving. When I saw Mama Cougar, I had to determine if you were in danger. Remember cougars can be protective if they have a cub nearby."

"Oh, I totally forgot about that. I was so excited to see her after the stories last night that I wasn't thinking. I acted on instinct."

Grandmother had an inquisitive look on her face.

"Did I say instinct? Wouldn't instinct make me afraid of her?"

"No, Wind Dancer, not necessarily. Common sense would tell you to be cautious, but true fear only comes when you sense you're going to be attacked. Besides, you greeted her, and she was as curious about you as you were about her."

"I felt stupid waving to her and saying 'hi'."

"That was kinda silly, but your greeting was from your heart. That's why she opened herself to you. Your fibers spoke to her. You slid into her on your fibers, and she slid into you."

"Wow, I can use my fibers to connect with animals?"

"With sweet medicine," Grandmother reminded me. "Always be respectful and call them by their full name."

"Yes, Grandmother, Mama Cougar deserves the utmost respect."

"Let's speed up. We had better get down the hill before Andrea beats us to the ice chests. She has mountain goat in her."

Grandmother turned around and looked at Shane. He was still on the cliff's edge with his arms out feeling the winds. She spoke silently into Shane's mind, but I heard it as well. *"Spirit Hawk, introduce yourself to the universe then come on down for breakfast."* In a stronger voice, she added, *"No flying today."*

Andrea was pulling out the breakfast food and placing it on the table.

"What kept you two? I'm starving. Where's Shane?"

"He'll be down soon. If he doesn't decide to fly away," I said.

Grandmother gave me that look. I shrugged my shoulders and was saved when we heard a warrior whoop and holler from the top of the mesa.

I thought Shane might have jumped, but Grandmother said, "He likes his name."

I was having a hard time comprehending everything that had happened that morning, so I just said, "I'll boil some water for sage tea. I think Shane will need lots of food this morning."

We worked hard that Sunday.

The showers were up and running with hot water, and wow, it felt good to be clean.

Finally, we all left for home at around two o'clock that afternoon, inside the time frame we had agreed upon the night before. While driving home, Andrea and I told Shane all about the cougar, and he told us how much he liked his medicine name. He was looking forward to sharing it at the next men's lodge where he would announce himself for the men and Great Spirit to hear. We talked until we reached the hamburger restaurant, which Grandmother turned into without hesitating. We were pretty talked out at that point, and I could hear my stomach growling, or was it Shane's?

Grandmother pointed to a table and said, "I need to wash my hands and call Grandfather. He likes to know when we are at the restaurant. He tracks us for safety."

"We all need to wash up again," I added. "The showers were great, but I feel like I have enough red dirt on me to take a few more showers."

I never appreciated a real toilet, running hot water, and air conditioning like I did that day. It was still hot outside. We had worked hard, and we all ate big meals.

The six-hour drive went fast because after eating we all fell asleep except Grandmother, thank goodness, since she was driving. Grandmother later told us she listens to music to help keep her awake. We hit the late afternoon heat of Flatrock Valley, and the weekend seemed like a dream, but I knew we would be returning for Ceremonial Dance in less than a week.

I had lots to do to be ready.

PART III

CEREMONIAL DANCE

Chapter 16

Ceremonial Dance Begins!

Mom and Dad were very busy between working and packing for our Ceremonial vacation. Grandmother wanted us to go up two days before everybody arrived on Friday. Mom asked all sorts of questions about the land. I told her it was hot, windy in the afternoon, and wonderful.

My parents were excited and concerned that I had encountered a cougar. Dad said he was going to bring his rifle and handgun. I told him Grandmother said any weapons on the land must be Blessed and Awakened in a special Pipe Ceremony so that the individual will realize that weapons are tools and must be used to protect life and defend it. When everyone is in the dance, all weapons are kept in a lock box to keep them safe. Only the security team, which is composed of highly trained individuals, carries weapons.

Dad pointed out that we were in New Mexico, an open-carry state. "If I want to carry my gun in my holster, I can."

I knew Dad was going off on one of his tirades about Second Amendment rights and how we are losing our freedom in the United States because of people not understanding what our forefathers learned. He believed that people have the right to defend themselves. He could go on and on. I almost knew it all by heart.

"It's in the Constitution," he said.

"Dad, you know that Grandmother, Grandfather, and Thunder Wolf feel the same way about gun rights as you do." That seemed to calm him a little. "Also, I talked with the cougar. She won't be anywhere around when all of us two-legged ones show up."

He looked at me, a little amazed. "The next time I go hunting, I'll take you along to talk to the animals."

"Sweet medicine animals, Dad, and would you really? I'd love to go with you. We could find the right deer or elk that is ready to share its life with us."

"You've been hanging out with Grandmother a lot, haven't you?" He chuckled. "Don't let my teasing get you. I'm proud of you. I think Grandmother Spinning Winds is training my young lady to be a medicine woman—and in this day and age! What a career."

When Dad said I was his young lady, I realized he didn't call me his little girl. Wow. I stood a little taller. And then I realized what else he said: Grandmother was training me to be a medicine woman. Yes, she was! Had I been a medicine woman before? How would I make a living as a medicine woman?

Dad's concern crept into me. I thought for a while and realized that Grandmother and Grandfather had a nice house and two big trucks. She loved her full-size, fire-engine-red Ford truck. It was an American-made truck; no cars for her. She always had things to haul around, like purification lodge rocks, and she often needed to pull a trailer for items like lodge trees. She seemed financially comfortable. I'd figure it out. Right now, I am still in high school and going to my first Ceremonial Dance.

One afternoon while eating lunch together on the school bleachers, I asked Shane, Andrea, and Susie if they would like to come to the Ceremonial Dance. Susie said thanks, but her idea of camping was in a hotel.

"I'd love to come and help in the children's lodge," Andrea said, "but my parents have already made vacation plans for us. Do you think I could come next year, Sage?"

"I don't see why not. We just have to plan early enough, and your folks would still need to visit with Grandmother. You could stay with us if your parents don't want to come."

"I have to stay home," Shane said as if ashamed. His dad was having a hard time now that he was out of the rehab program, and Shane was concerned for his mother.

I gave him a big hug and told him he'd be missed. "I'll say a prayer into the Children's Fire for you."

"Speak my medicine name, Spirit Hawk, into the fire, and maybe next year, I'll be able to go, too."

The school bell rang, and Susie started down the bleacher steps. With a glance over her shoulder, she teased, "Hey, you two, don't be late for class!"

We hugged again and held each other for a few moments. He kissed his fingers and placed them on my lips. I wanted him to kiss me, but the moment was gone.

We were home only three days before we were on the road to the land for our eleven days of Ceremonial Dance vacation. It felt good to know where we were going. I guided my parents to the restaurant where Grandmother took us during the work weekend. We ate a hearty meal, and I tried to answer my mother's questions between bites.

"Time to get on the road," Dad announced when our plates were clean.

Jumping back into the truck, I said, "This drive is even more beautiful now that I know where we are going."

When we finally arrived, it felt like the land had her arms wide open for us. It was a shock to see how many folks had already set up camp. Even two days early, the quiet, sleepy land on the work weekend had transformed into a small community. It was no longer the quiet sleeping giant I had seen the previous weekend.

Tent City was bigger than I imagined, and it wasn't even half full yet. People had set tents up everywhere, or at least it looked like they did, but it was well organized.

There were designated camping areas for tents, trailers, car camping, and motor homes. Festive colored flags marked the different areas, which made it easier to locate people. It looked like the pictures I had seen in my history book about the Renaissance jousting festivals with colorful banners flying in the wind.

Some of the volunteers I had met the previous work weekend had stayed during the week to meet the tent company, who always arrived first. They erected a circus-sized tent two stories high. The community called this tent The Capitol because it was so big and white. This is where everyone gathered for camp meetings and protection from the sun, wind, and rain. It was filled with tables and folding chairs so that everyone had a place to sit and relax. Here, the caterers set up their cooking stoves and ovens and parked their refrigerated truck at the back door of the tent.

Mom, Dad, and I set up our camp near Grandmother's tent, so we could spend a lot of time with her. She filled me in on what was happening as we prepared for the ceremony.

Mom and Dad were on the Dog Soldier crew. The arbor building crew was the largest work crew with about forty people. As Grandmother had shared with me, the dancers who were attending the ceremony for the first time were the ones who built the arbor. Other dancers who liked that crew would also volunteer. In the center of the arbor was the Ceremonial Dance Tree with a large trunk split into two large limbs, creating a large 'Y', representing feminine energy. This tree is called the Tree of Life. It is this tree that the dancers move to with their prayers. The tree absorbs all their energy prayers and sends them out into the universe.

The arbor would be completely wrapped with shade cloth, which would wrap around the structure and cover the heads of the dancers. During the ceremony, this is where the dancers sleep and dream at night. Its primary purpose was to provide shade. It wasn't much protection from the dirt whirlwinds or rainstorms.

Participants choose their work crews—first, second, and third choices on their registration forms. I was most interested in the ceremonial activities. As a teen, I was able to serve as an apprentice to the ceremonial staff. All teens choose an area where they want to apprentice. This allowed them to work and learn so that when they got older and returned to Ceremonial Dance, they would know where they wanted to focus their energy.

The ceremonial crew always arrives early. They perform special ceremonies before everyone arrives on the land. The first ceremony is called Walking the Good Red Road. They bless the road everyone drives on, beginning about two hundred feet from the official entrance, where the security team lives, all the way to the East Gate of the Ceremonial Dance Arbor.

Grandmother suggested I watch this ceremony, and she went with me.

The Good Red Road ceremony was simple and beautiful. No wonder something special seemed to happen from the moment people arrived on the land. Most people never even knew this took place.

At the end of this ceremony, Grandmother said, "There is a small Ancestor Dance Circle away from the main population. It's set high on a hill where the ancestors can dance before joining us in the Ceremonial Dance event. Thunder Wolf taught his apprentices that some ancestors were not sure they wanted to come and dance, so this allowed them to dance and pray and come to a good decision. "I wanted you to be on the land a few days early so you can see all the ceremonies that take place here. You can help, observe, and remember. Remember, the smallest job can have unintended consequences if it isn't done with respect."

"Thank you, Grandmother. I am remembering all you have told me about what is going on right now. Guess it's time to get back to work. No matter how small, I will do it like when I help you with the purifications lodge."

She smiled and gave me a nod.

"There's a job waiting for you. Go back to the ceremonial space, the large one we call The Garden, and you can help with the Ancestor dance wheel. One of the medicine people is waiting for you to help."

I ran to the ceremonial space and found Bobby Sees the Rainbows, whom I had met during the work weekend. He greeted me with a smile and happy hello. He asked me to help him carry bottles of paint and water up the hill.

I loved his Austrian accent.

As we walked, he began to teach me. "Every year the forked sticks for the Ancestors Circle have to be repainted and new feathers and tobacco flags added. After being out in Mother Nature all year, some of those old feathers only had a few spiney, short feathers left."

The new feathers were beautifully wrapped and represented the four directions wheel of this tradition: red for south, black for west, white for north, and yellow for east. We spent hours preparing it for the ancestors to dance. When it was finished, we smudged and sweet grassed the ancestor dance circle to bless it awake.

This happened early, too. None of the dancers came up here. Bobby told me that only he and one of the other chiefs in training come during the dance to do a ceremony for the ancestors. I felt very privileged to be able to help prepare this space.

The ceremonial crew was busy preparing various special places for the dancers to visit before the dance began. One of my favorites was the miniature world shrine. Once the Mother Gaia or Mother Earth shrine was ready, everyone was required to visit her and pray for the next generations. There were miniatures representing everything that is wonderful about being in the physical body as a sacred human being. It was so beautiful I could have stayed there for hours, but I could only manage short visits because I was busy with the ceremonial crew.

Sherpas, modeled after the Tibetan guides who carry the belongings of travelers, were a small crew of volunteers who helped the participants take their belongings to their campsites once they arrived on the land. They used wagons and wheel barrows to help with this process. The crew chief was happy to have two extra volunteers—my mom and dad, who also served as Dog Soldiers.

One of the largest crews was the purification lodge crew because all nine lodges had to be covered, made ready, Blessed, and Awakened for the ceremony. Josh, who I met at the teen camp, apprenticed here. He was cute, and I was getting to know him.

The sandpainting crew produced amazing ceremonial pictures with colored sand, which are placed in front of each lodge and on the East Mesa.

The American flag flew at the top of the east entrance. Flags representing all the dancer's countries of origin were strung corner to corner, touching each other across the whole bottom of the upper east structure. The Eight Great Powers flags were flying in the center of the arbor, on the Grandmother Tree of Life.

All the personal shields of the dancers were to be secured in the front of their arbor sleeping spaces, and the big lodge shields were tightly secured on the vertical East Mesa because of the high winds. They did not want flying shields in the heavy winds. The sweet medicine animals were respectfully attached to the Grandmother Tree. I loved the energy of the Buffalo head, the eagle at the top of the tree, and the wings of a hawk, which came from New Zealand—Grandmother had brought them back in her luggage when she had discovered them as road kill. There was a deer hide, an otter hide, and more. Just like the purification lodges, the whole arbor had to be Blessed and Awakened, but it took twenty or more apprentices to do it.

This was huge beyond anything I could have imagined. This land became a village with everyone having a job, sharing mealtimes, renewing friendships, and coming together to pray for our planet, freedom for the people, and themselves.

Like Grandmother said, she couldn't have put it all in words. I needed to experience it for myself.

Needing a few minutes of rest, I wandered back to Grandmother's tent. "I'm glad we came up a few days early. I like helping you, Grandmother."

"Sage, you are young, but the ceremonial staff could use your help in preparing for the different ceremonies. You have learned a lot working with me at home."

In other words, I was a gofer—go for this and go for that, but I didn't mind the little jobs. Everyone was welcoming, kind, and supportive. I was learning about ceremony, so I swept the spaces and helped lay the mesa blankets. I got water for the south and earth for the west elemental bowls. I lit the candle for the east and put pahoe—blue cornmeal—in a bowl representing the wind in the north, just like in my Rite of Passage ceremony.

I hardly saw my parents because our schedules were different and the ceremonial crew was busy with the various ceremonies that took place when the camp broke for a meal.

"Sage, you can share a meal with your folks if you like or stay and help with the specific ceremonies," Grandmother said.

"I want to stay and help, but do we get to eat lunch?"

"Yes, of course, silly. Our crew goes early to the kitchen. Get a plate and bring it back. We can't take the people away from their work crews, so at mealtimes, they are given a half-hour to eat, then they come here to The Garden."

"Why is it called The Garden?" I asked.

She smiled. "Because so much growth takes place here, and the green Astroturf makes it look like grass. My handle is even Garden Mama because I oversee the Garden! Silly, but why not? While participants eat their lunch in the Capitol, you'll be helping set up the space. Eat as you can or save it till after the ceremony is over."

"Think I'll eat on the run. I can't wait or you'll hear my stomach growling over the drum. Grandmother, before it gets too busy, can I go over to the purification lodge area and check it out?"

"Yes, Sage, just tell the dance chief who you are. There'll be one day in which the teens can choose a different crew to apprentice with. Ask him if you can apprentice there."

"Okay, thanks."

My little girl felt like skipping, so I skipped to the lodge area. We—me and my inner little girl—were happy.

The dance chief wasn't there, but I took a few moments to look around.

The lodge area fascinated me. It was quiet and beautiful. The seven chakra-colored round pavers were clean and began behind the lodge and led to the opening of each additional lodge. The sweet medicine on top of each lodge was different, and I didn't know what it meant. It all had meaning—that, I knew. There was so much to learn, and a huge crew had been assigned here. I have never purified four days in a row.

We were in the high desert with temperatures ranging from 95˚ to 114˚. Everyone was working hard all through the day and then purified every night. The medic team kept reminding us to drink lots of water and take electrolytes. I left the area but planned to return when the dance chief was present to ask if I could apprentice there.

There was one purification lodge for the teens and one for the children. The children's lodge is held during the light of day, using very small rock people. They light a candle so the children can see each other and feel safe, and the dance chief tells them an inspirational story.

The teen lodge is held in the evening and runs like a regular adult lodge.

We had already been on the land for a few days, and I had lost track of what day it was, but tonight was the teen's night for purification.

When it was time for the teen lodge, we met at The Capitol in our bathing suits and wraps. Josh sat next to me. We had been chatting here and there in between our busy schedules.

We were early and had some time to talk before everyone else arrived.

When all the teens had gathered, the dance chief took roll call, and then we walked down to the lodge area. We had towels to sit on and medicine gifts to give to the fire crew and dance chief, like when Grandmother runs a lodge in her home.

Josh and I stood together in the line. I was blessed into the lodge, and Josh followed and sat next me. Most of us had been in a purification lodge before, so the dance chief made it nice and toasty. The rock people were glowing orange hot, and the steam rose like clouds as the water was poured over them. Our pores opened, and we sweated the dirt from our bodies.

Our prayers were guided to reflect the intent of the Ceremonial Dance, which included a tradition of four rounds of prayers. First was a prayer for ourselves, then others, then giving away what was stopping us from getting what we prayed for—like laziness, procrastination, or anger. The last round was done in silence while twenty buffalo horns of water were poured on the hot rocks, and we thanked the twenty powers of the universe. Josh's prayers were powerful and honest.

When we stepped out of the lodge, the night was cool and never felt so good. We all laid down on our bellies to be sure we were grounded. I turned over and looked up at the stars—there were so many stars. The Milky Way was right on top of us.

As I gazed at the stars, my mind went through my day's journey. Josh had shared with me that this was his last time in the teen lodge. We had both been so busy that we only had time to talk when we met at the teen lodge in the morning before going to our prospective crews, when we had lunch or dinner, or we ran into each other while on an assignment. We always stopped to talk for a few minutes. It's amazing how much can be shared in a short time.

I didn't want to go to bed. I wanted to talk with Josh. He was so handsome.

The teens began gathering their belongings and heading back to their campsites. When Josh stood up, I didn't wait another second; I invited him to my parent's campsite. He smiled and reached out his hand to help me up.

We walked back to camp, made ourselves comfortable beneath the blanket of stars, and talked the night away.

I didn't care if I missed breakfast because I stayed up so late. I really liked Josh, especially after the teen purification ceremony. His prayers impressed me. Most of the boys I knew were shallow, except for Shane. They didn't want to show their emotions or talk about things that were spiritual or different. Josh seemed confident, and yet he was vulnerable and honest. There was something about him I needed to discover.

The moon was shining on the mesa where I had seen the cougar. I told him the story.

"Sage, do you want to go up there when we have some time off? Maybe we can find her tracks."

Sage smiled. "Sure. I've heard that Mama Cougar sometimes comes close to drum camp since it's on the outskirts of all the activity."

Josh's eyes sparkled. "Let's look for her tracks there when we have time off together. Should we ask our dance chiefs if we can have after lunch and ceremonies off?" He looked at me for what felt like a long time,

"We can ask, but that might be difficult to make happen."

"Yeah, no kidding," he chuckled, and I gave him a big smile.

Josh told me about his Rite of Passage and Vision Quest Ceremony and that he was being guided at home by a medicine man. He learned that women do their vision quest in the womb of the lodge, but men needed to be with Grandfather Sun.

"Our vision quest is out in the open," he said. "When I came back from it, I did a lodge with all the men. What followed was a gathering circle with everyone. I learned a lot from what the men and women shared. They helped me understand what is important about women, being in a relationship with a woman, and what women like in a man."

"It sounds like the Rite of Passage I had. Was it in the Metis Tradition like this Ceremonial Dance?"

"Yes. Attending this dance is completing the ceremony. I am dancing my first dance this year."

"That is so awesome! Being of service in the ceremonial crew is part of my Rite of Passage, too. I'm coming back next year so I can dance."

There was a moment of quiet between us. Our eyes were speaking, seeking. Then I think we both felt a bit awkward.

"Sage Wind Dancer, I have a question. I'm curious. Since your Rite of Passage do you find that you look at the guys in school differently? Because I really look at the girls differently. They all seem immature and shallow, interested only in talking about who was dating who and what they are going to wear. I decided to wait for someone special who doesn't think I'm weird because I'm different."

A shiver ran up my back. I wondered if it was the cold night air seeping in or if it was what Josh had shared.

"I have felt the exact same way. I decided to keep my training to myself and just let the friendships be. Especially with those who attended my Rite of Passage."

I thought of telling him about Shane but decided not to. I was scared Josh wouldn't want to spend time with me.

"Thanks for sharing. Somehow, not being alone makes it easier."

Another shiver ran up my back.

"Can I keep you warm?" He smiled as I moved closer, and he wrapped his arm around my shoulders. I was shivering.

"Oh, I know what you need. Body heat is the best way to get warm."

I wasn't sure what he was going to do, or if I was going to stop whatever it was. I had never felt my belly and heart be so excited before. Josh unzipped his big jacket and said 'climb in.' I slipped one arm around his waist, behind his back. His body was like a furnace. He took my other arm and wrapped it around his front side and pulled his jacket around both of us. Within minutes I was toasty. I don't know if it was his body heat or my body awakening. We didn't talk; we just held each other.

I had never felt so safe, more at peace, or more turned on in my entire life. I didn't want to leave his arms. Looking up, I pulled away a little, hoping he would kiss me.

Josh looked at me and caressed my face. "You are a very special young woman and beautiful, too. You have a great medicine name, Wind Dancer. Will you show me how to dance on the wind?"

I smiled at him. I wanted to say, *yes, but first, you have to kiss me*, but I didn't have the nerve. Besides, he may think I was too forward. Instead, I said, "When I learn how to dance on the wind, I will show you. It may take a few years."

"I plan on dancing next year, too. Shall we make a date?" he said.

"Yes. I'd like that very much."

Reluctantly, we agreed it was time to go to bed.

My thoughts were flying high. How was I ever going to fall asleep?

I shouldn't have worried. I was no sooner feeling the warmth of my sleeping bag when my eyes fluttered shut. Somewhere between falling asleep and dreaming, Grandmother Spinning Winds spoke to me in the in-between state.

You better not be late tomorrow morning. We have a big ceremony to prepare. And by the way, don't forget, women are supposed to lead. Men show respect and wait for an invitation to kiss them.

As I drifted off, I was once again wrapped in Josh's arms, telling him that I wanted him to kiss me. He smiled and said he'd been waiting for me to say that. Then his lips touched mine, and I felt an electrical bolt go through my body like an instant Energy Breath. I was no longer in the dream. I was panting and feeling what could only be a whole-body orgasm. I was very aware that the sleeping bag was now, all of a sudden, too hot. I had been practicing the Energy Breath since Grandmother told me how important it was to learn how to breathe, but she never told me this could happen. My body finally relaxed, and I never slept so deeply and peacefully.

Would the real thing feel this good? I wondered. Before the dance was over, I intended to find out. I was going to ask Josh to kiss me, but when and where? I needed privacy, perhaps when we looked for Mama Cougar's paw prints. Then sleep took me.

I dreamed of Shane. He was fighting with his father. He spoke to me in my dream, clear as can be. *I wanted to be there with you at Ceremonial Dance, but I had to stay.*

Somewhere in my dream mind, I knew I had to talk to Grandmother about Shane and Josh.

Chapter 17

Serving as an Apprentice

The next morning came quickly. I sprinted up to grab a breakfast plate and took it back to the ceremonial space so I could get instructions on what was needed for the ceremony and eat breakfast at the same time.

Grandmother looked at me with a raised eyebrow. "Are you going to use a fork to write down what you need to do?"

I realized that my breakfast would get cold before I could finish it, and lunch would taste very good today. "I was up late last night."

"Sage, didn't you get my dream message last night?"

"Yes, Grandmother, I did, and I'm not late!" I looked away because I'm sure I looked sheepish. I knew she was talking about not being late this morning, and about it being my responsibility to ask for the kiss. I picked up my pen and paper.

The day was flying by. It took all morning to set up the Garden for the adoption ceremony. There would be thirty-six apprentices attending this ceremony. Three ceremonial spaces called mesas were needed. The ceremony would begin with a beautiful story of the lineage of the ancient Metis tradition. Next, the Ceremonial Medicine Elder, who I was surprised to learn was Grandmother Spinning Winds, would tell of Thunder Wolf's family lineage.

When the time came to dress for the actual ceremony, I wore clean clothes, and Grandmother loaned me one of her ribbon shirts to wear.

I felt so proud of Grandmother as she stood up to speak and everyone fell silent.

She wore full ceremonial attire: a tiered layered lavender skirt and matching cotton calico shirt with ribbons of the four directions attached. She had an eagle feather tied into her hair, and she was wearing a beautiful, beaded Ceremonial Dance belt that she had made.

"I know your apprentice guides have described this ceremony to you," she said. "There is no rush to do this ceremony. Please take a moment and go deep inside. Is this your path of heart? If yes, then please join us. If you are not sure, then please wait."

All but one decided to do the ceremony. The woman who decided to wait asked if she needed to leave or if it was permissible for her to stay and observe.

"You are welcome to stay, and if, before the last person is complete, you change your mind, and you know in your heart that this is your path, you are welcome to step in."

"Thank you, Grandmother," the woman said respectfully.

The adoption began with a Pipe Ceremony led by one of the senior apprentices sitting at a mesa. Three apprentices moved to the south of a mesa and began by smudging themselves and praying. They stated out loud what they needed from their new adopted family and what gifts and talents they had to offer, and then they shifted to the next direction. Another apprentice joined the others, working each direction until all four directions—south, west, north, and east—were filled.

Grandmother taught me never to share the specifics of a ceremony because it's important to experience the ceremony firsthand, but I was fascinated by the mechanics of how it operated. When all three mesas were filled with apprentices working each direction, the energy became very powerful. People blessed themselves, and some sang songs that had no words but came from their souls. Others were taking their Ceremonial Dance vows to protect the women, children, and the people's freedom. Of course, there was more to it. I understood why Grandmother said you need to partake in the ceremony to understand the whole alchemy.

Upon completion, one at a time, the apprentices sat in front of the dance chief of each mesa and received an eagle whistle blessing, then they went to Grandmother Spinning Winds to receive something to add to their protection bundle. She shook their hands, and others reached out for a tear-filled hug as she welcomed them into the family as free-thinking, autonomous individuals.

I heard her say, "Never give your power away. The power is in the teachings, not the teachers. Challenge the teachings and make them your own. Don't believe what someone says. Find out for yourself."

This truly was a family coming together—willing to work, pray, and help each other. I wished I could go back in time and live as we once did, as a tribe on the land, with ceremony a natural part of our everyday life. At the end of the ceremony, several of us were in tears.

When the adoption ceremony was over, we carefully took the mesas apart and put everything away. The mesa dance chiefs thanked me and the other ceremonialist-in-training for doing a good job. I felt proud and realized how a small compliment went a long way.

This was a perfect time to talk to Grandmother. Everything was done. We were on a break, and I had a plan.

"Grandmother, can I work with the Purification Lodge crew for a day if the fire chief allows me to?"

She raised her brow. "Could it be because a certain young man works there that you want to spend a whole day there?"

I felt my face go red. "I have to admit, the thought crossed my mind, but I also want to learn how these lodges are different from the one in your backyard."

She nodded. "You may, and today works best because our schedule is light. Be sure and let the other ceremonial chiefs know that you won't be helping them for the rest of the day. But first, ask Grandfather Strong Bear if you may apprentice. He's the Ceremonial Dance fire chief."

All these years of knowing Grandfather, I never knew he was the Ceremonial Dance fire chief for nine lodges. At home, I thought Grandmother was the head, but I was mistaken.

When I spoke with Grandfather a short time later, he said, "The lodge in our backyard is Grandmother's, and I honor that. She's a fire chief also. I support her when she asks for help, but she calls the shots on her lodge. I'm chief of the Ceremonial Dance purification lodges, and I work with the ceremonial crew."

"Wow, that's cool, Grandfather. Can I apprentice here for the rest of the day to learn about the lodges?"

"Yes, Sage. Your work with Grandmother will have helped prepare you."

"Thanks, Grandfather. Here is some tobacco."

He smiled and received my gift. "Our schedule is very different from the ceremonial crew schedule. We are on a break now, but we'll be going into high gear soon." He raised his eyebrows to make his point, as I was glancing around, not giving him my full attention. "What or whom are you looking for, Sage?"

"Is anyone else apprenticing here?"

"Josh, but he decided to apprentice with the ceremonial crew today."

Grandfather looked at me—or right through me. He saw my disappointment and distracted me. "The initial preparation work is complete.

The lodges will remain covered for the entire ten ceremonial days. There is prep work each day. The cold stone children must be taken out of the rock pit, and the wood must be stacked close to the rock wall. We pray over the rock people as we lay them in a ceremonial medicine wheel. Next, the wood is piled on top, creating a tepee structure covering every single rock person. Over four hundred, you know!"

"Four hundred rock people?" My voice rose quite high in disbelief.

"Yes. We have to feed six to nine lodges, depending on how many people we have at any given Ceremonial Dance. We need forty-five to sixty stone children per lodge. You can do the multiplication. There's plenty of work to be done, Sage. You are welcome here. Josh apprenticed to the ceremonial crew for the afternoon, so having you here makes up for his being gone."

I'm sure my face dropped with disappointment.

Josh and I hadn't talked to each other, so he didn't know I was coming to apprentice on his crew and vice versa. We'd have a good laugh about this later, but for now, I longed to spend time with him—even more than I realized.

Grandfather put his arm around my shoulders. "Ah, is that why you wanted to apprentice here?"

"Partly, but I want to learn more about the lodges. Do you have time to answer a few questions, Grandfather?"

"Better ask now because once things get rolling, it'll get pretty hot and busy around here. A four-hundred-stone fire puts out a lot of heat. Be sure you come back tonight with long sleeves, long pants, and boots—tennis shoes if you don't have leather boots. Now, what is your question?"

"You said the initial preparation work had been done. What was it?"

"When you came up with Grandmother last week, what did you see here?"

"I saw the wooden frames of the lodges with dried brambles and weeds covering the whole area inside the lodges and all around. There was a year's worth of dead growth on the ground."

"What do you see now?"

I looked around and felt stupid. It was as clean as if someone had swept the earth. I had been so busy with the ceremonial crew that I'd had blinders on. The lodge space was beautiful. The lodges were covered, and there were sand paintings representing the nineteenth Ceremonial Dance in front of each lodge. There were eight lodges, one for each of the compass directions of the medicine wheel, and the ninth lodge—representing the center of the wheel—built this year with a central pit. All the other lodges had rock pits on the right-hand side of the door. This, and other alchemy placed under the poles and rock pit made these Healing Lodges.

"Grandfather, how does one learn what to put on a lodge and all the ceremony involved in it?"

"Wind Dancer, if someone wants to learn, they must discover if this is their path of heart. If it is, they apprentice. They prove their integrity over time and increase their knowledge. There are vision quests, gateway ceremonies, teachings from the wheels, and keys to learn. The medicine way and its lineage are highly respected and protected from being misused.

"The Hopi Prophecy," Thunderwolf said, "says the men who are white skins in this lifetime were full-bloods and walked the good red road in other lifetimes, and many full-bloods in this time were the violent white Indian haters in other lifetimes—a reversal of experience. So, skin color doesn't matter. It's your heart commitment to being a Metis Warrior from one lifetime to another that matters.

"That explains why most of the people at the Ceremony are non-natives. No matter your skin color, it's the heart and integrity of the teachings that are first and foremost. It takes a long time to learn the Way of the Purification Lodge or the Way of the Pipe. It's not about learning one thing, but many things."

"I'm beginning to understand the depth of this path and the ancient lineage teachings. Thank you, Grandfather."

"Be my shadow today, Sage. Just like at Grandmother's lodge, all the same things need to happen. Instead of one lodge dance chief and three rock carrier assistances, there are nine lodge dance chiefs, two assistants for each lodge, twenty-two rock carriers, and four rock pullers. The lodges were already Blessed and Awakened with a special alchemy."

I was beginning to understand that there was ceremony inside ceremony in every aspect of this annual celebration.

"Sage, this is the third night of sweats. All the rocks have been taken out of the lodges and laid out. You can smudge all the rocks, all four hundred. Say a prayer for the rock people to be clear from last night's sweat."

I picked up the blessing fan and big abalone shell filled with smudge and was ready to light it.

"Sage, ask all four hundred rock people to do a major giveaway, and go into the fire for a total of five times."

To my surprise, the rocks—or rock people, as I was taught to show respect—didn't seem to mind. They even talked to me, saying, *Hey, child, we're here with the sole intent to hold the heat so you can purify and come into alignment with us and the other worlds of Grandmother Earth. We wait all year for this. We all want to go into the fire.*

I have heard sweet medicine animals talk in my head like Mama Cougar, but I never heard rocks talk to me before, and they all seemed to have their own personalities. How was I going to explain that to my friends? I decided against it. They already thought I was strange, and now I was even talking to rocks!

Grandfather was in my head just like Grandmother. *Sage, use their proper name. It will make more sense for you to talk to rock PEOPLE.*

Yes, Grandfather, I responded in my mind.

When I was done, I went over to Grandfather. "What else can I do?

"Before the fire crew arrives, scoot to your tent and put on long pants, socks, and boots. You have hiking boots, right? Tennis shoes will melt if you are too close to the fire pit."

I didn't answer him. I knew I had to wear my tennis shoes.

"You'll need a long sleeve shirt, jacket, gloves and hat," he repeated. "Bring a bottle or two of water. Grab yourself a snack. You'll get dinner with the first half of the crew and bring it back here later. I'm sure you'll be starving, so grab that snack now."

The fire crew started to arrive, and they sat with Grandfather under their gathering tree.

I joined them after most of them were present.

Grandfather announced, "Hey, everyone, we have a new apprentice for this afternoon and evening. This is Sage, my adopted granddaughter. She has already smudged the rock people. Please go around the circle and speak your names. We'll see how many she can remember."

He looked at me and winked. Thank goodness he was teasing.

Most of this crew had experience from the other annual Ceremonial Dances.

Grandfather Strong Bear asked for a wood platform to be laid. Once the platform was set, Grandfather began the prayers with the first seven rocks, calling in the powers of the Four Directions, the As Above, the So Below, and the Dream. That made seven. Then he called in the twenty powers that make up our universe. It was like listening to a poem, a beautiful poem about our world. Grandfather put the energy of each power into the twenty rock people. Then the fire crew and I added a silent prayer for each of the four hundred rock people.

Grandfather gave us a nod; it was time to cover the rock people.

We alternated layers of rock and wood until you couldn't see even one rock face. The pile was high! It looked like a big tepee.

We circled the fire and began singing a song I didn't know. It was a fire song to call the spirit of the fire into the rock people and sacred wood. Grandfather took the bag of smudge consisting of sage, cedar, sweet grass, and lavender and sprinkled the mixture over the entire pile with additional prayers. Then, from the four directions, the fire was lit. South for Trust and Innocence, west for Introspection and Intuition, north for Wisdom and Knowledge, and east for Enlightenment and Illumination.

Grandfather stepped back to see which side of the fire caught quickest and which side had a difficulty lighting—everything had medicine and a teaching to it. Yes, the wind played with the fire, but there was more to the medicine than how the wind affected it.

The fire crew sang the flames into power, and the whole camp could hear the song.

Everyone knew they would purify themselves that night in preparation for the Ceremonial Dance. I heard people say the wet heat relieved them of some of their aches and pains from the day's physical labor.

When dinner break came, I was starving, just as Grandfather had said. I went to get dinner with the first crew. The lodge crew ate dinner in shifts because once the fire started, it must always be attended.

After dinner, the people began to gather in the Capitol with their towels and medicine gifts. People signed up beforehand if they wanted to purify with friends or partners. Some years, lodges were designated for specific intents, and you signed up for those specific lodges. For example, whichever Gateway you were in, all those apprentices purified together.

While the people gathered, the lodges were fired, meaning, two red-hot rock people were placed in the fire pits with a sprinkling of smudge to purify the lodge.

The lodges were ready!

I was down by the fire, keeping warm, as line after line of dancers came down from the Capitol to the lodge area. There was soft talking or silence. The energy of the space had changed, and the air was filled with excited expectancy. The lodges filled with people being blessed into the space. As dance chiefs called for hot rocks, and the rock carriers delivered them, the lodges hummed with slowly rising heat.

Calls came from one dance chief and then another, "Close the flap, close the flap."

It became pitch black in the sacred lodge, the Womb of Grandmother, except for the glow of the orange rock people. You could hear the dance chiefs calling in the powers as they poured a buffalo horn of water onto the hot rock people, and the rock people sang a sizzling song. It was beautiful.

The people in the lodges said 'Ho,' a throaty sound in recognition of the prayers being said. Then the voices of each lodge burst forth as individuals stated their prayers for themselves. It was one of the most powerful experiences before the dance—nine lodges, all praying at the same time.

It was midnight before the second round of lodges was over. Once the last person left, the lodge flaps were closed again to let the ancestors purify.

The dancers were squeaky clean and relaxed back in their camps for a peaceful night's rest.

What I liked best about the whole experience was watching the four rock pullers step into the fire circle to pull the rocks out on their pitchforks. Man, that fire was hot! Those four rock people kept all twenty-two rock carriers busy. They knew what they were doing, and most had been on the fire crew for several years. Yes, they wore gloves, long sleeve shirts, jeans, and leather boots, but they were aligned with the fire. I saw why Grandfather told me to wear boots if possible, and I was determined to buy some for future lodges—on and off the land—as there were a few times when I felt like putting my feet, tennis shoes and all, in a bucket of cold water to cool them down. I hopped around like a fool because, suddenly, my feet were burning.

Grandfather told me to stay back. I stayed out of the way, but the fire kept pulling me toward it. I wanted to learn how to walk into the fire pit like they walked in and pull a red-hot glowing stone person out of the four hundred.

The fire crew and Grandfather Strong Bear were tidying up the shovels, pitchforks, and dying embers, and blowing out the Children's Fire lanterns that sat near the sand paintings in front of the lodges.

Grandfather saw me and said, "It's okay for you to go to bed. It's been a very long day. You did a good job, Sage."

"Thank you, Grandfather." My smile was as big as my face could hold. I was bone tired, but very happy. He had instructed his crew to return at 7:00 am to begin preparations for the next day's sweats, so I quickly made my way back to camp.

Once snuggled into my sleeping bag, I dreamed of sacred lodge fires. I even dreamed I was a rock puller, picking up the hot glowing stone people with my bare hands. It was a cool dream.

When I woke up, I had a blister on my hand, but I just figured I got it from working at the lodge fire the night before—though I didn't remember burning myself. I was working with the ceremonial crew again and excited to tell Grandmother Spinning Winds about my experiences and my dream.

"Fire is an expression of our sacred sexuality. It's spiritual fire medicine that you are learning. I understand why the lodge fire draws you. Maybe one day, you'll be here running a lodge. We'll see." She teased me with that knowing look.

Did she just say I might be dance chiefing a lodge someday? That was a mustard seed planted, followed by my inner thought, *Yeah, right, in about twenty years.*

"Picking up hot rocks with your bare hands was pretty brave of you, in the dream," she said. "And by the way, Josh did a very good job with the ceremonial crew. I'm sure you two will have lots to talk about. I guess you didn't talk about spending time in each other's apprenticeship programs."

"Grandmother, I'm realizing how important communication is. No, we didn't share our intentions. I'm learning the hard way. It was really awesome apprenticing there, though. I thought we were busy in ceremonial crew, but, wow, the lodge crew has to get up early and stay up late. They burn it at both ends. I don't know if Josh and I will be able to find time to talk or do anything else together until the dance is over."

"Do anything else, like ask him to kiss you?"

"Grandmother," I said, a little embarrassed.

"Life is full of opportunities, and most people miss them because they're afraid to ask for what they want. Remember, asking doesn't mean you'll get it, but not asking is a sure way not to get what you desire."

Chapter 18

The Cougar, Josh, and Me

Everything was humming along with the arbor preparations, ceremonies, people working and laughing, and the drummer's songs thundering over the land as they practiced. I loved hearing the drum.

The ceremonial crew had a quiet afternoon, so I took the opportunity to talk with Grandmother about Shane and Josh.

"Grandmother, I want to find Josh and spend some time with him, but I had a dream about Shane fighting with his dad. He told me he wanted to come to Ceremonial Dance and be with me. Was that a dream—the part about him fighting with his dad, or did I actually see what is happening with him? Is it too late for him to come?"

"Wind Dancer, I don't know if it was a dream or if you're tapping into Shane's matrix, but he won't be allowed on the land without an invitation. I believe it was a dream of Shane's wishful thinking and your confusion about your feelings for Shane and Josh. Put yourself in his shoes. Would you rather be fighting with your dad or spending time with a beautiful young woman?"

"Oh," I said, feeling stupid. "The obvious sometimes escapes me. Grandmother, I'm feeling something with Josh that I haven't felt with Shane. It's such a strong pull! I have to find out what it is. But what about Shane? I'm not sure if I feel guilty or exactly what I'm feeling."

"If you don't know what you feel, be honest. Tell Josh you have a male friend that may be more than a friend. When you go home, speak honestly to Shane about your feelings for him and whatever you discover with Josh. It's not hard to be honest. You just have to accept the consequences of how they will respond. There's always a risk in being honest, but if you find someone who's willing to be honest also, that makes for a good relationship.

"You can tell white lies to try to protect them, but in reality, you're only protecting yourself, which backfires in the end. The next time you talk to Dreams with the Wind, ask her for a few words of wisdom. She's had lots of young warriors interested in her. Remember, her life was dedicated to becoming a sacred sexual teacher and healer."

I was momentarily speechless as I thought this through. Maybe it was simple in theory but not in application. How can you be totally honest about your feelings when you are unclear about how you feel?

"Thank you, Grandmother. May I have the afternoon off to look for Josh? Maybe I'll even find myself."

"Sure, Sage. We'll talk later."

I told my folks I was going to see if Josh wanted to go for a walk.

"Okay, Hon, but don't go too far." Dad gave me that look. "You know the cougar sometimes comes in to see what the ruckus is about. I don't understand this cougar because human noise usually sends wild animals as far away from us as possible."

"Okay, Dad."

I was walking toward the lodge area when I ran into Josh. He looked surprised to see me, too.

"Hey," I blurted out. "Were you coming to find me?"

"Yes."

Almost simultaneously, we said, "Can you take the afternoon off?"

We laughed and started walking and talking non-stop. We didn't discuss where we were going. We just headed down the dirt road that took us past some of the larger motor homes and toward the drum camp. The drummers were practicing in the Capitol, so we were guaranteed almost total seclusion.

It was easy to talk to Josh. I told him how much I loved the lodge area, especially the fire, and he spoke about the ceremony he assisted with and how it was like being in the purification lodge space. We laughed about going into each other's apprentice areas only to find the other one gone.

To my surprise, he said, "Communication. If you want something to happen, you've got to talk to each other!"

We laughed again, and then my belly got tight. I wanted to know if a physical kiss would feel the same as the dream kiss. I had to find the courage to speak, but it was difficult. As much as I wanted it, I knew the time wasn't right yet. I wondered if it would ever be right.

I suddenly realized he had stopped talking and was looking at me.

"Lost in your thoughts?"

"How did you know?"

His face was soft, and his smile gentle. "Your silence when I asked a question."

"I'm so embarrassed. What did you ask me?"

"It wasn't important." He held out his hand. "Can I hold your hand while we walk?"

"I'd like that."

I was relieved. He was still interested, and so was I.

I looked into his eyes, and, for a moment, nothing else existed. "Josh, I have to share something with you, and it's really hard."

"You have a boyfriend at home?"

I was shocked. "No. Maybe. I don't know." My words came tumbling out like a fast-moving stream. "Shane has joined the men's clan. I like him, and he's special. I have never kissed him, but we have hugged. I think we are best friends, but sometimes it feels like more than that, and it feels like he wants more. So, I don't know what we are."

He was still holding my hand.

"I've never felt what I'm feeling with you. I need to discover who you are." *Talk about being honest. Wow, that just rolled out of me.*

He smiled. "I would like that, too. It sounds like Shane knows what he wants. You're the one that has to decide what you want. My uncle said women do the choosing, men do the hoping to be chosen."

We continued walking. I was quiet, somewhat in shock, and thinking.

I felt the weight of the world on my shoulders. I had shared so much, and it seemed easy. Josh was okay with me not knowing how I felt about Shane, but how would Shane feel when I told him about Josh? Maybe I didn't have to tell him. Perhaps nothing would happen when I asked Josh to kiss me.

Would I have to tell Shane if Josh kissed me?

I heard Grandmother in my mind saying, *Stop thinking, and be with Josh NOW!*

How does she do that? I wondered for the thousandth time. Then I looked at Josh, and everything else melted away.

We looked for cougar tracks far outside the drum camp perimeter.

Josh pointed to the sky. "Look, a red-tailed hawk is circling above our heads. I love watching them. I'm a red-tailed hawk in Sun Bear's Earth Astrology."

I watched the lazy circles the hawk was making. "Their red tail feathers are so beautiful. They're my favorite, too. Shane's medicine name is Spirit Hawk."

Now, why did I say that? It came out so easy.

"That's a strong name," Josh said.

"What is your medicine name?" I couldn't believe I hadn't asked him! *What was wrong with me?*

He looked at me and must have seen something in my eyes.

"Please don't be upset with yourself. This is your first time here, and we've been busy with only moments to connect. I don't think you're going to believe this, but after my Rite of Passage and Vision Quest Ceremony, I was given the medicine name Walks on the Wind. I was blown away by your name, Wind Dancer. Maybe that's why we have a connection."

I didn't know what to say.

He pointed to the red-tailed hawk again, and we laid on our backs to watch it. We would've stayed longer if it wasn't for the stickers prickling our backs, but after a few minutes, we got up and brushed each other off. I felt that energy start to flow again, and I liked it!

Looking into my eyes, he said, "Let's walk out a bit further. I thought I heard someone in drum camp, and I don't want our quiet time to be disturbed."

As we walked further from camp, Josh glanced behind us now and then.

"What are you doing?"

"When we walk back, it will look different. I'm getting landmarks so we don't get lost."

"I remember this teaching from Grandmother, but it never dawned on me that we could get lost so close to camp. I'm glad you're looking because I think we've walked farther than I realized."

The sun was going down, and it was behind us, so the lighting was perfect. I saw a blur of movement off to the east. "Oh, my goodness! There she is—Mama Cougar."

Josh looked where I was pointing. It took him a second, but then he saw her. "She might have cubs to protect."

"Let me check." I closed my eyes and imagined myself inside of her and her inside of me. It took a moment, but then we connected. I was watching us through her eyes. I opened my heart to her, and our thoughts mingled. *She doesn't have cubs this year.*

I could hear Mama Cougar's thoughts. *I recognize the female scent. This human girl is different. She's my ally. I'm curious about the male scent, but I'm not in danger. These humans are safe, and my belly is full. I feel like playing and bouncing.*

"Sage? Sage?"

I heard Josh calling me from a long distance and right next to me. I didn't want to answer. I wanted to stay in the cougar and roll and tumble.

He called me again. "Wind Dancer."

Hearing him speak my medicine name broke through my thoughts, but we, the spirit of the cougar and I, decided to pounce on him. As I did, I heard a growl come from my mouth. The next thing I knew, we were tumbling on the ground, rolling around, mindless of the stickers. I nipped at his ear, growling. He was surprised but immediately got into the action—we were two cougars playing. After a few moments, we looked up and saw Mama Cougar jump onto something imaginary, roll on the ground as if connecting with us, and then she trotted away.

"What just happened," he whispered.

I was panting from the strenuous play and looked into his eyes. "I entered her, and she entered me. She's my ally, and she—we—wanted to play."

I was on my back, and Josh rested partly on his arms and partly on me.

"I want you to kiss me," I said easily and naturally.

A quiet expression came over him, and he softly touched my face and lips. It was so gentle I could barely feel it, yet I felt electric shocks coming from his fingertips. I touched his face as if discovering true masculinity for the first time.

As his lips brushed mine, a moan escaped me. My lips parted, and I felt his breath. I saw only him as his lips kissed first one side of my mouth, then the other. I arched my back as he kissed my neck and explored my throat and earlobes.

He slowly brought his lips back to mine, and the tips of our tongues touched. I felt energy running up my spine and belly, and my body shuddered beneath him.

"Aah," he moaned.

I felt an Energy Breath orgasm building as my breath and body started doing what I had trained them to do in the privacy of my bedroom. Josh began breathing with me as deep rolling waves of energy moved up our bodies.

We looked deeply into each other's eyes and began to laugh. He rolled so I was on top of him.

I grabbed his arms and pinned him down. "Got you!"

We began breathing again, and deep rolling waves of passion moved through us.

The spirit of Mama Cougar was still in me, and my dominance felt powerful. I brought my mouth to his neck and began kissing and biting him.

Now he moaned with desire.

Then I felt Mama Cougar's gentleness and kissed his face and lips, almost purring. He gently met my tongue with his, and there was a new dance—a slow rhythm of breathing and exploring each other for the first time.

Passion surged within me like a tidal wave that I could ride the crest of forever.

I felt another flash of the cougar and rolled him on top of me. His body's weight on mine felt natural.

His kiss became more passionate, seeking my response.

I opened to him as I had opened to Mama Cougar. I went inside of him and invited him inside of me—a spiritual connection for spiritual lovemaking.

I became lost in the passion of our kisses—we were hungry for each other. I experienced every type of touch from soft and gentle to strong and urgent. I had never felt this before. Our bodies were electrified by the Energy Breath of orgasms and desire.

I realized I had my answer. As my body arched in the most intense Energy Breath orgasm I had ever experienced, I whispered, "The dream and the physical can be the same."

We were breathing loudly, moaning our pleasure, as our bodies arched away from each other, yet we were connected at the belly. Had someone taught him the Energy Breath? How had he known to do this?

I heard Grandmother's voice in my mind: *Stop thinking and stay present. Experience the greatest of all gifts—love and intimacy.*

"Thank you, Grandmother," I responded silently.

I looked into Josh's eyes and saw my own as he looked into me. An eternity passed, and we smiled.

He gently touched my lips and caressed my face. "I knew you were different—special."

I smiled. "I've been wanting you to kiss me since the first night we talked."

"I know, but I've been taught to let the woman lead, so I waited for you to ask or say it was okay."

His honesty encouraged me to share more of my feelings.

"I was scared the dance would be over, and we would never have experienced this."

Josh nodded. "I thought I felt this energy, but I wasn't sure it came from you. I was afraid you wouldn't ask me—that I would never know."

I was still vibrating.

We became aware of the time and the cool air. Josh kissed my lips, which sent a shudder through us. We looked into each other's eyes and realized we could do this for a long time. We laughed and stood up, hand-in-hand, and walked toward camp.

The talk was quieter, and we seemed to float into camp. As we approached my tent, he said, "What did you mean the dream and the physical can be the same?"

I hesitated but decided not to let any opportunity pass me by. "I was tired the other night, but before I fell asleep, I was imagining you kissing me when we sat together—my arms wrapped around you and your jacket pulling me close, keeping me warm. I went into an Energy Breath orgasm that was off the charts, and I never even touched myself."

His eyes got bigger. "Sage, that's why I had to kiss you before the dance was over and we were in different states. That night, as I lay in my sleeping bag, I imagined kissing you. I so wanted to, and then a flash of energy belted me. I had never experienced anything so intense. I've been going crazy ever since wondering if it was real or just my imagination. After today, I know it was real. Everything I experienced with you today was real—more so than anything I've ever experienced before."

"Wow," I murmured, "we shared that being in separate tents across the distance. That's really cool. What we experienced today was magickal."

We reached out and kissed each other with a soft, gentle, passionate kiss that went down to my toes. It was the most natural thing to do, and we didn't care that we were in camp.

My father walked up and smiled. "I guess my young woman is growing up."

Josh and I pulled apart, a little embarrassed.

"Never be ashamed to show affection in public," my dad said. "We need more of it in our lives. TV programs show violence. We should see more intimacy and loving-kindness.

"Don't worry, Hon, your mother and I saw it coming before you did. Josh, you're a very nice young man. You're welcome to come and visit us when you can and continue your friendship with our daughter."

"Thank you, Mister..."

"Call me Rod. Oh, by the way, Grandfather Strong Bear is looking for you. And Grandmother is looking for you, Wind Dancer. Something about a cougar. Have you seen Mama Cougar?"

"Yes, Dad, and she doesn't have cubs this year. I better run and see about Grandmother."

"Wait!" Josh said. He gave me a tiny peck on the forehead. "See you tomorrow—for a moment or two, at least!"

We smiled, and I was off before Dad could corner me about the cougar.

Chapter 19

Monkey Climbers, Shields, and High Winds

Grandmother listened attentively as I explained about finding Mama Cougar, how we had shared thoughts, and how I pounced on Josh. I told her I finally asked him to kiss me and that it wasn't difficult once the moment was right.

"And the Energy Breath?" she said, leading me to share more.

"We experienced the power of the breath when two people do it together. It was amazing!"

I must have been talking fast because Grandmother smiled and let me talk myself out, and then she suggested I take a breath.

"You're becoming a woman, Sage. What are you going to tell Shane?"

My exuberance faded, and I became quiet. "I might need some help with that. Grandmother, can I have two friends?"

She looked at me or, rather, through me. It felt very strange. Finally, she said, "Some women and some men can be with more than one. It takes maturity and honesty—no lying, and no cheating. It goes against societal norms. It was more common in ancient times and for specific purposes. Let's just leave it at that. You have two young, vulnerable men in your life. You have to make some decisions."

The sun was lower in the western sky, and it was getting cooler. We could smell the kitchen preparing dinner for more than two hundred dancers, drummers, hungry kids, and teens.

"Let's go eat," Grandmother said.

"Yes! My stomach is growling."

After dinner, an evening of teachings, and another lodge, I headed back to our camp and crawled into my sleeping bag. I was ready to sleep and dream of Mama Cougar and Josh.

"Hey, sleepy head. Time to wake up," my dad said as he gently shook my shoulder. "You slept a good eight hours. You should be feeling as playful as Mama Cougar, but you'll need a good breakfast before working with the ceremonial crew today."

"Good morning," I said with a yawn. "Thanks for waking me. Breakfast sounds good, and I'd like to eat it while it's still hot."

I wondered how they found out about Mama Cougar and was surprised that Dad wasn't upset.

As usual, I dressed in layers, mindful that though it was chilly at night and in the mornings, it was blazing hot during the day.

After breakfast, Grandmother and I walked over to the Dance Arbor in silence.

The arbor was coming together. The crews were preparing to attach the medicine to the vertical East Mesa when we arrived. My tumble of romantic thoughts rolled into the recesses of my mind as I began to count the spaces measured for one hundred and seventy-two dancers.

The Drum Arbor was also decorated with medicine. It featured a drum large enough for twelve to fifteen drummers to sit around with space for another fifteen singers behind them. A special ceremonial handmade quilt measuring ten by fifteen feet hung on the back wall. The year and number of the Ceremonial Dance were sewn onto the quilt with buttons. This year was 2001—the 19th dance.

The vibrant colors of the arbor made it look so festive and inviting!

Grandmother and I began walking clockwise around the arbor. Next to the Drum Arbor was the Healing Arbor, both of which had grass growing in them—beautiful, lush green grass. The rest of the arbor floor was dirt, raked and re-raked to clear it of weeds, pebbles, and small rocks. It was the dream of many dancers to one day have grass covering the entire arbor.

Twelve living trees formed the outer arbor ring. In the center stood one large tree—the Ceremonial Dance Tree of Life.

"Grandmother, "Who takes care of the land?"

The trees and the land are nurtured, watered, and taken care of by Tommy and Beth, a wonderful couple who live here year-round, and the land committee, who assist them regularly."

"Wow, a lot of people are involved. It must take a tremendous amount of work. The arbor is huge!"

Grandmother smiled. "It takes the tribal village working year-round to manage this beautiful piece of earth. The dream is that one day the arbor will hold up to three hundred dancers. The living trees were planted when they were young and ten-feet tall. Now, they're thirty feet high and provide a partial shade canopy during the dance.

"There's a lot of wildlife here, too. Come on more work weekends, and you'll see lots of rabbits. In the winter, herds of antelope graze on the grass, and garter and rattlesnakes visit when the heat of summer warms their bodies and the land is quiet from human feet. There are bobcats, lynx, and a kestrel hawk that nests in the corner of the East Gate under a big shade tree. Have you seen the nest?"

"Yes, Grandmother, every time I have a task up this way, I stop to look at the baby birds. They've been growing quickly."

Grandmother scowled. "Unfortunately, everybody else has been doing the same thing. Mama Hawk abandoned them."

"Oh, no! What will happen to them?"

"Your father helped the medical team by going off land to hunt a jackrabbit. The medical team cut the meat into small pieces and is feeding the baby hawks three times a day. In the time we're here, they'll grow into strong fledglings. If Mama Hawk doesn't return, they'll be taken to Albuquerque and given to a wildlife rescue group for hand-raising until they can be returned to the wild."

We had traveled almost the full way around the inside of the arbor. There were over forty people still working on it.

Grandmother pointed upward. "The green cloth provides shade for part of the day. It's wrapped around the sides and over the top of the lean-to dance structure. There's space for one hundred and seventy-two dancers to place their cots and medicine items into spaces like slices of a pie. There are fifteen drummers, ten service dancers, and a few volunteers who come up to help during the dance. There are caregivers for the kids and teens lodge with six Dog Soldiers to do tasks like keeping the Water Sanctuary clean and full of water. As you know, your parents serve as two of those Dog Soldiers.

"Teen volunteers help with whatever needs to be done. One important task is to make sure the Children's Fire on the East Mesa never goes out. There's a teen and an adult present for the entire three-and-a-half days at the Children's Fire."

"The cooks will prepare three meals a day for the drummers and everyone outside the arbor. The dancers can smell that food when they're fasting, but most of us aren't affected."

We were standing in the northeast section of the arbor, and I glanced around. "Grandmother, where will they hang the dancer's shields?"

"See those ten-foot bamboo poles by every arbor space? The shields will hang high, all around the arbor."

"Do the colored ribbons represent the directions?" I asked.

"Yes, they are hung from the two-star poles in each cardinal direction—south, west, north, and east. The bamboo poles are tied together so they are long enough to attach high in the center ceremonial Tree of Life and reach all the way to the lean-to structure. The cardinal poles hold energy, the non-cardinal poles move energy, and there's one pole for the non-cardinal directions. Do you remember the colors for them?"

I nodded.

"Very good. Now, look into the upper-most part of the Tree of Life. Do you see Thunder Wolf's eagle at the top of the tree with the Eight Great Powers flags?"

I tilted my head back and opened my mouth in awe. "Yes, Grandmother. Why is the eagle in that clear box? How did they get it up there?"

"We have skilled monkey climbers who use ladders to hang all the medicine in the tree."

"Monkey climbers?" I laughed. "That's an odd name."

"That's our affectionate name for the young men and women who do this task. When the winds stir up, it can become quite dangerous. They are very skilled and hold on tight. They are often in the tree for hours.

"We almost lost our eagle one year as he was secured to a branch without protection. From that dance on, we protect him so his spirit will fly forever."

We continued walking around the inside of the huge, one-hundred-and-fifty-foot diameter circular space until we came to the exit. As we stood outside the arbor looking in, Grandmother grew silent for a few moments.

I waited.

"Sage Wind Dancer, look with your eyes and fibers and remember. Take this all in. There is much work to do to complete the east vertical and ground mesas. When this is complete, connect to it. Throw your fibers into this space. In other places and times, this looks different."

I felt a tap of spirit.

"Know this," she said, "so you will know which ceremonial Children's Fire you are sitting at—Dreams with the Wind's or Wind Dancer's."

I looked at Grandmother and could sense she was dreaming of other times.

The vertical East Mesa flew the American flag at the top.

I saw another flag—the flag with the golden rays of the sun shining around Mother Gaia. This flag represented the Metis Golden Age Prophesy, which opens the next phase of Grandmother Earth's evolution, which takes us into the fifth world of humans coming together in unity by 2054. I glanced at Grandmother, pleased that I had remembered her teaching. The Wolf Tribe flag hung next to it. It was just like Grandmother described, but no words could do it justice.

Seeing all the smaller world flags strung in a long line representing the dancers and their ancestries was amazing. The lodge leaders brought their lodge shields from around the world, which would soon hang on the vertical East Mesa in order of longevity. The very first shield would be the Wolf Tribe, and then Grandmother's. It was surprising to realize how long she had been here.

Everything on the upper vertical East Mesa had to be wired into place to withstand the gale-force winds, which could blow in at any time, especially in the afternoon.

"Look at the vertical East Mesa," Grandmother said. "The same monkey men and women who climb into the Grandmother Tree of Life, climb twenty-foot ladders, walk onto tied narrow platforms of bamboo poles, and hang on with their feet and legs while they fight the winds and wire everything down."

"Wow, that's incredible," I said. "I'd like to watch them do that."

"Good, because that's your job this afternoon. Here they come now, back from their yellow banana breaks."

"Their what?" I said, wrinkling my brow.

"That's our nickname for the outhouse. Has a rather nice ring to it, doesn't it?"

I laughed.

The ceremonial crew was gathering to complete the vertical East Mesa.

"Sage," Grandmother said, "go sit on the tarp with the painted buffalo skulls and sacred medicine items for the lower East Mesa. Don't let anyone trip on anything, and secure the shields if the wind picks up. I have other responsibilities this afternoon. I'll meet up with you later."

I moved out of the runway and sat about twenty feet back.

I watched in amazement as the monkey climbers attached the lodge shields to their proper places. As the afternoon wore on, the winds began to stir. At first, I was grateful for the breeze, but the gusts grew stronger, and the dust from the arbor floor began to rise. Soon, the edges of the tarp fluttered.

The pitching winds caused my hair to whip about, so I twisted it into a long, thick braid to keep it away from my face. Shielding my eyes, I saw other women doing the same.

Despite the dust, I glanced around at the ceremonial crews—they were racing against time—you could see it in their faces, yet they continued to handle the medicine items carefully. The vertical mesa had to be complete before the lower mesa ceremonial pieces could be placed on the ground below. They couldn't risk something falling or breaking a ceremonial lineage item.

Suddenly, there was yelling in the arbor, and people ran toward the East Mesa. At first, I couldn't see what was happening, but then I saw a giant dust devil that looked like a small tornado inside the arbor. The people on the ladders grabbed the cross poles and prepared for impact. The wind hit so hard that I had to close my eyes against the flying particles of cutting sand.

The tarp fluttered violently, and the edges lifted in various places. Shields and ceremonial medicine items began shifting from their places. I threw myself over the tarp, hands outstretched, to grab what I could and add weight to the tarp. Two women saw what was happening and laid over other portions of the tarp. Others ran to help hold the ladders so that two people supported the base of each ladder.

Someone yelled, "Look out!" as a large shield flew off the vertical mesa.

The monkey climber had tried to hold it, but the wind wrenched it out of his hands and spun it from the gate like a frisbee. One of the larger flags ripped, and dust and dirt filled the air.

Through squinted eyes, I saw a coil of rope get sucked into the funnel and fall back out. Loose items flew in every direction. It was a dangerous situation, but everyone did what they could to limit the damage.

Within moments, the funnel passed. Fortunately, the monkeys were unharmed, and everyone on the ground was safe. The vertical East Mesa structure was undamaged, and only one shield and flag needed repair.

Now, I understood why it was important to guard the tarp. We placed heavy rocks on all four corners and in the spaces between the medicine. Others secured the remaining loose items, and extra people came to help finish the vertical East Mesa.

Volunteers climbed up the ladders to hand shields and flags to the monkeys. They couldn't assist in attaching the medicine to the arbor itself because the bamboo could only support the weight of two climbers at a time, but it did speed up the work.

Finally, they finished the vertical East Mesa and preparations could begin for placing ceremonial items on folded medicine blankets on the lower East Mesa. Soon, the entire arbor would blossom into a beautiful mesa of powerful objects that told the story of the Wolf Tribe and its lineage.

Sage Wind Dancer, I heard in my mind. *My responsibilities are keeping me longer than I anticipated. You were brave during the storm, and I'm proud of your work. I'll be back with you soon.*

Thank you, Grandmother. Experiencing the buildup of this once-a-year ceremony is beyond anything I thought possible.

I might have shared more, but her voice was gone.

The ceremonial crew placed the final item on the ground, inside the East Mesa. To the left quadrant was a huge covered sand painting that represented the intent for this year's dance. I had asked about it earlier, and Grandmother told me it would remain covered until the start of the dance to protect it from the weather. I hadn't thought much about it at the time, but after experiencing the storm, I was glad it was protected.

Grandmother said it took five days and six people to create the sand paintings for the purification lodges and East Mesa, and the artisans put prayers into the sand as they created them. I was looking forward to the unveiling.

Across from the sand painting, on the right quadrant, was a large mesa cloth bearing the colors of the eight directions forming a circle. As in my Rite of Passage, all the medicine wheel colors have meaning. As I watched the crew members place special crystals and statues representing the Eight Great Powers on each color, Grandmother approached from the east.

"Shall we continue our tour?" she said.

"Yes, but I just want to say, that wind was something else!"

Her eyes twinkled. "All in a good day's work."

I pointed to the mesa cloth. "Grandmother, what are the Eight Great Powers."

"I've been waiting for you to ask that question. Your interest is progressing."

"I want to learn as much as I can. After all, I did apprentice to the ceremonial crew," I teased.

Her eyes sparkled. "The Eight Great Powers represent nations from around the world. Many dancers fly here from other countries. We place statues that symbolize those countries or linages, and the crystals charge the energy."

As we talked, the fire crew came to lay the wood for the Children's Fire, which was in the middle of the East Mesa inside a stone ring, below the sandpainting on the left and the mesa cloth on the right. Grandmother reminded me that the wood would be lit at the beginning of the dance and kept burning continually for entire three days and nights, plus an additional night for the ancestors to dance their energy for the manifestation of what had been prayed for self, life, and others.

"Another interesting feature about the Children's Fire is that once the dance begins, everyone on the land may stop by, take a pinch of tobacco, say a prayer, and put it into the fire as they walk in and out of the arbor."

I felt another tap of spirit and saw myself here.

"Yes," I said, "this is where I will be. I want to help keep the fire and watch the dancers." I said a silent prayer for Shane Spirit Hawk.

Finally, the lower mesa medicine was in place, and the ceremonial crew had cleared away all the tarps, boxes, and equipment and cleaned up the dust from the windstorm.

I had thought we would be heading back to camp, but I was in for another surprise.

The dancers began to gather at the East Gate, chatting excitedly about the arbor and its transformation.

"Grandmother, what's going on?"

"The second roll call of dancers. The first one took place when the dancers gave their medicine blankets and tobacco to the Ceremonial Dance Chief, as is tradition. Look, they're holding their personal shields. All one hundred and seventy-two shields must be hung at the top of the ten-foot bamboo poles, on the left side of their individual arbor spaces. See? The ladders are being placed around the arbor. They'll be asking for volunteers. Do you have the energy to help hand up shields?"

"Yes, Grandmother. This is cool."

"After the shields are secured, then the arbor will be Blessed and Awakened. It will be hours before this is accomplished. Do you remember me telling you about this?"

"Yes, I've been excited to see this final stage of the process."

"First, we must answer the roll call. The dancers who are chiefs will enter the arbor first after our names are called. We proceed to our designated arbor spaces where our names are attached to poles. We'll sit on Grandmother Earth, holding our shields.

The dancers will be called in to choose their lanes according to the number of years they have attended—the most senior dancers first and progressing downward. A dancer can save a space for their partner if they enter the arbor first. Finally, the first-year dancers come running in to select from the remaining spaces.

"We don't Bless and Awaken the arbor until after the shields are hung and the family lineage medicine pipes are cleaned and made ready for this year's Pipe Ceremony. After the Blessing and Awakening, we invite the ancestors to dance first."

"So, the ancestors dance first and last. Right, Grandmother?"

"Yes. They will fill the arbor, especially on Friday night. The East Mesa is a front row seat. You'll be able to see Josh dance from there also." She winked at me. "Just remember to keep the fire burning. There's a lot to do when you are helping at the East Mesa. Those instructions will come later.

"They just called my name." She smiled and yelled, "Ho!" Turning to me, she said, "Come on, we can go in. You're not a dancer, but you can come in with me."

She started walking around the circle to her arbor space, holding her shield and talking quietly. "I'm one of the old-timers. I was at the first Wolf Tribe dance in the US. There were only twenty-seven of us back then."

When we reached her spot, we sat on the Astroturf that covered the southeast quadrant at the request of the senior chiefs. As they called the chief's names, this quadrant filled up. We sat in silence, but others whispered as they watched the other dancers claim the spaces and directions they desired to dance from during the ceremony.

"We are designated in the southeast quadrant of the arbor because we need to be near the Healing Arbor," Grandmother whispered.

"Grandmother, there's Josh! He's running to a spot in the northwest of the circle."

Once everybody was in the arbor, they conducted another roll call. The dancers had chosen their spaces and temporarily tied their shields on the correct posts.

Once this roll call was complete, everyone was released. Grandmother and the dancers left, and I spent the next two and a half hours helping to hang the shields. Josh helped, too, so we got to spend some time together. There was a lot of silent eye communication, smiling, and laughing with everyone. As we left, we picked up bits of wire and removed the ladders.

The Ceremonial Dance Arbor was finally ready.

Dog Soldier guardians stood watch in front of the gates so no one would enter until everyone arrived for the Blessing and Awakening.

As we walked out, Josh said, "When's dinner? I'm famished."

"Me, too!" said about ten people around us, and we all laughed.

This is a great family, I thought to myself.

Yes, it is I heard Grandmother say in my mind.

I laughed with the wonder of all that I was experiencing.

Chapter 20

Challenges Before Opening Ceremony

Neither Josh nor I were participating in the Blessing and Awakening Ceremony, so we went to the Capitol, piled our plates high with food, and took our meals to go. The fire crew needed Josh's assistance, so after a quick hug, he headed down to the purification area, eating along the way. Since I needed some warmer clothes before heading back to observe the ceremony, I went to my tent to enjoy my dinner at a more leisurely pace.

After dressing in layers, I headed back to the East Gate. Grandmother arrived a bit later.

Seeing that I was taking notes, she said, "Sage Wind Dancer, don't write about the Blessing and Awakening as it is High Ceremony. Some things are better left for an individual to find a path with heart, study, and learn the sacred ways."

"Thank you, Grandmother. I understand. It's not secret, it's sacred, and must be learned in a proper way, with elders."

"Yes. If anyone feels the pull of this ancient lineage, which helps to heal ourselves, the people, and our Grandmother Planet, they will find a path with heart, maybe even ours, and will step in."

"I'm realizing how privileged I am to be here and to witness all the ceremonies. Thank you." I threw my arms around her, and she hugged me, too.

The Blessing and Awakening would take nearly three hours. Afterward, the crew and twenty-five ceremonialists would eat their dinners, which would be kept warm in the ovens, before heading into the last round of lodges. It would likely be midnight before they headed back to their tents.

* * *

The next morning, I was up early. It was easy to rise with the sun after being on the land for eight days. They announced in the Capitol via the whiteboard, where they posted all announcements, that the arbor seal would be opened in a special way at 10:00 am. The dancers could enter and place their cots and medicine, but no water or food would be allowed in because once the arbor is Blessed and Awakened, it is a dry arbor.

People must follow protocol when entering the arbor, walking clockwise with their gear, not turning their back to the Tree of Life, and backing out when exiting the arbor. All of this was explained in the first-year dance meeting, but I, of course, learned it from Grandmother.

There was another meeting for dancers who wanted to dry fast. Dry-fasters were usually experienced dancers, but first-year dancers were occasionally inspired to try. Apprentices who decided to dry fast had been talking with their apprentice guides and preparing themselves throughout the year for this event.

It was hard to imagine going without water for three and a half days!

When I arrived at the arbor, I quickly saw that before anyone could enter and look for where their shields were hanging, they had to get past the Dog Soldiers, who vigilantly asked, "Do you have any lip gloss in your pocket, water bottle, food, or even a protein bar in your backpack? You can retrieve them when you come out."

I saw many people taking items out of their pockets.

A second dry-faster meeting would be held today near sunset to remind dancers how to dry fast and the pros and cons of doing so. The healing team would tie ribbons to the dry-faster's poles so they could check on them throughout the dance. Any non-dry-fasting dancer could step out, as needed, to drink in the Water Sanctuary outside the arbor.

Most chose not to dry fast, but five to ten people usually danced without pain, suffering, or water. Grandmother Spinning Winds and Grandfather Strong Bear had done it many times.

I sat with the Dog Soldier or ceremonial person as they changed shifts to get their bedding, ceremonial clothes, chairs, and personal pipe bags into the arbor. I noticed when people were in the arbor, they obeyed protocol. They never turned their back to the Tree of Life. Even when they left, they backed out of the East Gate. It seemed so natural.

I felt a tug in my spirit; Grandmother needed my help. I half-walked, half-skipped to her camp. It reminded me of skipping to her house for my medicine talks.

"You need me, Grandmother?"

"Can you help me move my belongings to the arbor, please? Grandfather

Strong Bear is preparing the lodge area for the final Going-in Lodge, and he still has to get his gear moved."

"Of course, Grandmother. How can I help?"

We filled the wheel barrow with her sleeping bag, pillow, blanket, rain gear, rain boots, and smaller bags of soft items. Next, we used her cot to create a long, flat shelf where we stacked her foam pad, and long clear plastic box, which held her beautiful ceremonial skirts and ribbon shirts.

As Grandmother placed her folding chair at the top, she said, "Grab those bungee cords. Let's go longwise over the top first, then we'll use three more going across."

Once her ceremonial items were secure, I gazed into the clear plastic box and wondered why she had packed so many clothes. She must have seen the question on my face.

"I'm not going to sweat and dance in the same outfit for three and a half days. I change my undies and ceremonial attire."

"Got it, Grandmother. I'm making mental notes for when I come back to dance next year."

"Oh, you've decided before seeing the actual dance?"

"Josh and I have a date to dance together."

She smiled. "You push; I'll guide us."

"Grandmother, are you sure you don't want me to ask a Dog Soldier to help us?"

"They're busy. Besides, I've been doing this for nineteen years, and I'll probably do it for nineteen more."

"You probably will, and I'll be here to see it!"

We slowly pushed the wheelbarrow up the road, along with the other hundred and seventy-plus dancers.

As we approached the entrance, a Dog Soldier greeted us. "Hello, Grandmother Spinning Winds and Sage. Do you have any gum, cough drops, water, Chapstick, protein bars, or fruit? We're hungry!"

We laughed.

I patted myself down to be sure nothing was tucked away in my pockets. "Sorry, you'll have to wait for lunch," I teased.

We continued into the arbor and to Grandmother's dreaming space. The green Astroturf that covered the southeast quadrant looked peaceful and inviting.

"Wow, this is nice, Grandmother. If it rains you won't get muddy."

"Yes, and when the wind blows, it helps keep the dust down."

"Grandmother, do I need to keep my front to the tree when we are unloading?"

"Step in here, and I'll give you a little teaching. Just leave the wheelbarrow there. This space we are under is nice and tall, right?"

"Yes, even a tall person can stand up straight."

"The lean-to is where the cots, chair, medicine bags, and clothes go. It represents our everyday life. Our homes and our box of limitations. This is the third dimension, mundane everyday reality. With the proper attitude, it could be where we dream a new dream for ourselves. Just like you have been doing."

I looked out and saw lots of dancers moving in.

"In here, you can move any which way as you help me set up my home space, my piece of the pie, as long as you are inside the lean-to space. Once you step into the dance area, where the wheelbarrow is right now, you need to take care not to turn your back to the Tree of Life. The dance space is fourth dimension."

"I'm looking with soft vision, but I don't see any change. I don't see any wavy energy lines."

"Sage, we haven't begun dancing yet. People are putting their focus on their tonal everyday comforts like cots and pillows. We are getting everyone in the proper protocol because it will change during the dance from what you see and feel now into a very altered space."

"Ohhhh," I said, grasping the difference.

"The dancers can awaken themselves into becoming forth dimensionally determinant. This is when they can dance their dreams awake, making major positive changes in their lives. Don't worry about what you did or didn't understand. It will land somewhere in your consciousness and make sense sometime in your life. Help me unload the wheelbarrow."

"It would be easier if I wheel it in here since nobody else is unloading near you."

"That's my girl—if you can maneuver it without turning your back to the Tree of Life, which may be easier said than done. Give it a shot."

I took advantage of the extra room to get the wheelbarrow inside the third dimension tonal space. We unloaded it to one side, set up the cot and chair, and then everything else seemed to have a home in the narrow strip.

"Sage, take that medicine bag with all my doctoring tools into the Healing Arbor. Don't walk all the way around. Walk in the tonal space, then facing the Tree of Life, scooch around the wall. Put my bag with the others that you will see there."

That took me two minutes.

"Okay, now crawl to the head of my cot and place my ceremonial pipe bag there."

"Ouch! I hit my head on one of the thick tree trunks!"

"Sorry. It's a lean-to structure. Not much head-room in the back."

"Grandmother, where do you put your pipe together? There's no room."

"I sit on my cot or move my chair and sit on the ground, like the other dancers."

"Okay, that makes sense. I'm surprised all your stuff fit. I didn't think we'd find space."

"I've been doing this for many years. Now, put the bag of ceremonial manuals behind my chair, and place the box of ceremonial attire under the cot with the rain gear on top, so it's easy to get to in a flash storm."

We finished putting the final touches on her home space by covering her cot and medicine blanket with a waterproof cloth in case it rained or the dirt blew in before the dance began.

Other dancers were still moving their gear into the arbor and creating their home spaces.

I pulled the wheelbarrow out and started walking clockwise around the arbor, greeting folks as I passed. I backed out of the entrance as instructed. It felt good that I remembered.

I took the wheelbarrow back to the Dog Soldier house so others could use it.

The night before, when everyone was at dinner except the Blessing and Awakening crew, they announced that the fourth purification lodge, the Going-in Lodge, was at 10:00 am and noon. "Don't be late," they said, "and don't miss this lodge or you can't dance!"

There were two-time slots for dancers to put their gear inside arbor: before the lodges and from noon to 3:00 pm. In between, the Dog Soldiers closed the entrance and stood guard. Dancers would meet in front of the East Mesa for roll call, dressed in full ceremonial attire and ready to begin the dance by 4:00 pm. They were to form a line that would circle counter-clockwise around the outside of the Arbor.

Things were moving fast. I wanted to connect with Josh, but I was so busy helping the ceremonial crew and Grandmother that I didn't see him. I had hoped I might spot him in the arbor setting up, but I didn't. He was dancing his first dance, and I wanted to tell him—I don't know what I wanted to say, but I knew I wanted to hug him.

Lunch was served at 1:00 pm, the last meal for three and a half days and nights. That sounds like a long time to go without food to me. I was glad I wasn't dancing this year. I got to eat regular meals, or so I thought.

Lunch was a buffet of salads, chicken, and everything left over from the week before. It looked appetizing, but I didn't eat, even though I was hungry. I kept looking for Josh.

No doubt he was busy bedding down the lodge area, just like I was helping with the last-minute things with the ceremonial crew. The wind and rain had been so bad the night before that we had to cover the East Mesa, the ceremonial items, and the Eight Great Powers mesa. Because everything was covered, we needed to uncover everything and clean it up again. Once the dance started, we wouldn't have to keep everything spic and span, just protected in case of gale-force winds or rain, and the mesa blankets brushed off as best we could.

I walked over to the lodge area, but Grandfather Strong Bear and his crew were gone—probably eating lunch. That reminded me of how hungry I was. I joined the camp at the Capitol and noticed people's plates were piled high in preparation for the fast.

"Hey, Grandmother," I said as she walked into the Capitol.

"Did you find Josh?" she said.

"Not yet. I want to wish him a strong dance and give him a hug."

"I saw him. He asked me to tell you that he's been looking for you. Sage, so that you know, this first Ceremonial Dance is very special for him. There will be an honoring dance for him since he went through his Rite of Passage and this is his first-time dancing as a young man, a warrior. It will take place on Saturday, the last day of the dance."

Now, I really wanted to tell him I would send all the energy I could muster. I headed to our tent to change clothes and ran into my mom and dad.

"There's our long-lost daughter. Ceremonial has been keeping you busy."

"Oh, Mom, Dad, these are the best days of my life. Thanks for bringing me here."

"The dance hasn't even started yet."

Dad winked at me, and Mom held out her arms for a hug. I held her tightly, too.

"I'm due at the East Gate," I said. "I'm on the crew to keep the Children's Fire burning throughout the dance. I need to put on some clean clothes and take a warm jacket. I plan to stay as late as I can to see the star nation people dance above, and the dancers running to the Tree of Life below."

"We are helping with the Children's Fire also. We have a late-night shift."

"That's great, Dad. Maybe we'll pass each other—shifts in the night."

"The song and poetry of this ceremonial time has clearly touched your heart with humor," Mom said as they headed toward the East Gate.

I smiled as I watched them go, happy to have a few moments with them before ducking into my tent for a quick change.

I grabbed my jacket and dashed off to the East Gate.

It was 4:00 pm on Wednesday. I needed to be there when the dancers gathered. Would I find Josh? When I turned the corner of the medical tepee, I saw many dancers dressed in full Ceremonial Dance regalia with every color imaginable—ribbon shirts and fringed skirts with beautiful Pendleton medicine blankets thrown over their left shoulders. Friends took pictures, and dancers greeted each other. More and more dancers came until the line was halfway around the arbor.

An order went out, and everyone lined up. The oldest male and the youngest female dancers were at the front. It was their honor to pull the male and female ceremonially-painted buffalo skulls. First, they would circle the outside of the arbor, then the inside to begin the ceremony. Harnesses were placed around the horns of the buffalo with straps over the dancers' shoulders. Chief Thunder Wolf, the lineage elder and Ceremonial Dance sponsor followed the dancers. Next came the dance chiefs, Dena Quiet Owl and Bobby Sees the Rainbow, followed by the Spirit Father, Thomas Running Bear, and Spirit Mother, Martha Star Light. She held Grandfather's and Grandmother's ceremonial items.

Grandmother Spinning Winds held the family Wolf Tribe ceremonial item, and the assistant to the dance chief, Julie Walks Tall, carried the large lineage crystal. Next came the dancers with the greatest number of years, and lastly, the first-year dancers. The long line, referred to as the tail of the sacred snake, wrapped almost halfway around the arbor. All waited for an official roll call, and then the drum would announce the commencement of the dance and the lighting of the Children's Fire.

I was looking for Josh in the crowd but still couldn't see him. I had to stay on the East Mesa to light the Children's Fire when the drum sounded. I only had a few minutes and desperately wanted to run down the line to the first-year dancers and find him. How did this happen? The dance was about to begin, and I didn't even speak to him. I was so torn. I didn't want the dance to start without connecting with him.

The drum and opening songs began with passion, and I immediately lit the fire. It took off, singeing the hair of my hand, and I jumped back. The eldest man and youngest woman started to pull the skulls. The procession slowly began to move. I looked frantically around, but there was no one to take my place. Then I saw Grandmother waiting for her first steps. She looked at me sternly, and I heard her clearly in my mind: *Don't you dare leave your post.*

I sank in despair, a feeling I didn't expect to begin the dance with. I looked at Grandmother, and she mouthed, "Wait. He'll come to you."

I felt a glimmer of hope, but then, to my surprise, I felt tears well up, and I started to beat myself up for not planning to meet Josh before the dance began. Communication breakdown again. "Damn," I muttered under my breath. When was I going to learn?

The line was moving faster now. Grandmother was halfway around the outside of the arbor, and the line was still coming.

Then it dawned on me; if I didn't pay attention, I would miss Josh as he walked by.

All the dancers had whistles in their mouths, blowing a high, shrill, eagle-like sound. The feather fluff plumes were lifted high and moving forward and backward as if the blessings had begun. The dancers looked magnificent in their wrap-around and Navajo tiered fringed skirts and ribbon shirts. It was as colorful as a rainbow river. The drummers sang loud and strong as the processional moved around and more dancers came into view—but where was he? Where was Josh?

I saw my mother and father standing with the dog soldiers and other helpers. My father pointed down the line—he had spotted him for me.

I looked at the fire; it was burning strong. I walked to the edge of the East Mesa and saw him. He looked so handsome, I gasped. He was truly a warrior, and he was looking straight at me. I gave him a bright smile as I took in his ceremonial attire.

He looked taller, his shoulders broader in his black fringed skirk with a red and orange design like flames lapping up from the hem. His ribbon shirt was bright red with a lightning bolt going across it with ribbons of the four directions, red, black, white, and yellow, sewn down the sleeves and on the collar. His medicine blanket, also black and red, was hanging over his left shoulder.

I took another glance at the fire and ran up to him. At least I could walk with him for twenty steps. "Josh, I'm so sorry I didn't ask to meet you," I blurted out.

He looked into my eyes. "I know. Me too. We were so busy!"

"I didn't realize how fast everything would be today, and I really wanted to see you."

We were almost out of time. I had to leave him; the line was beginning to move faster. Josh leaned down and kissed me.

"Josh Walks on the Wind, you are a warrior!"

He smiled at me, and I was happy to have had a few moments with him.

We were in front of the East Gate. I walked back to my post near the fire and saw that a Dog Soldier had stepped in to take my place as guardian. I felt sheepish, but I would've done it again. With a smile on my face and tears in my eyes, I watched Josh march away in the procession.

The dog solder smiled at me, "Do you want me to stay so you can grab another kiss when they come around again?"

The light bulb went off in my head—they walked around twice. I get to see Josh again.

I smiled shyly and couldn't help feeling embarrassed. "Yes, please. Thanks for offering—just in case"

We stood together as guardians of the fire.

The buffalo skulls were coming into view, and I overheard someone say, "The head of the snake has almost bit the tail."

There was a gap in the processional of about twenty feet. I saw the two dancers pulling the buffalo skulls speed up to catch the end of the line before it passed us again with plumes blessing everyone standing on the sidelines. This was the nineteenth dance. There were tears in people's eyes. I could tell they remembered other dances and other times.

I acknowledged the dancers as they passed by. The immensity of the Ceremonial Dance sank into me; all these people were going to dance their prayers to the Tree of Life—prayers for self, life, and others. Prayers to heal the planet.

Then I saw Josh again. The dancers in the processional walked in twos. The woman next to him was a young woman in her early twenties. She looked beautiful and was also a first-time dancer. I felt a surge of emotion. Was I jealous? Was I envious? All of a sudden, I wished I could be dancing next to Josh.

I felt Josh looking at me, and I met his gaze. He started walking so that he could pass within inches of me if I came to the front of the East Mesa.

I felt myself hesitate. *Was I jealous?* I asked myself again.

I quickly moved to meet him.

He said, "Next year, we'll dance together." He brushed his lips on mine. The woman next to him smiled at me so sweetly that I felt my heart open to her. I smiled and wished for her to have a good dance also.

I moved back to the fire and smiled at my co-guardian. I mouthed thank you, and she nodded. I stared into the flames while hearing the whistles all around the arbor. My thoughts went to Grandmother's talk about jealousy. I never wanted to go there. I preferred to feel the sisterhood. I thought Josh and the woman he was walking with would dance next to each other in the arbor. That would mean their cots would be next to each other, falling asleep and waking up next to each other in the arbor. Was I jealous or envious? I slept next to Shane in my sleeping bag, and I liked that—looking up at the stars and being close.

What about Shane? I realized that Josh wasn't jealous of Shane. He permitted me the space to discover my feelings. Was it possible to care for more than one person and in different ways? I felt a deeper appreciation for Josh.

I wanted to ask this sister to take care of him. Not that he needed it, but that was my feeling.

Just then, I saw that the whole processional had snaked around the inside of the arbor, and the tail of the snake—where Josh and the beautiful maiden walked—were close to passing the East Gate again. I stood up and moved to the edge. As they passed, I put up my hands, palms out, as if I were holding plumes, and blessed them. I felt free inside and energized. It was as if I had passed a huge final exam. I wouldn't understand this till much later, but that's precisely what I had done.

Once all the dancers circled the inner arbor twice, the buffalo skulls were pulled out of the East Gate. A Dog Soldier helped take the harnesses off the dancers, and they hurried into the arbor, to their spaces, to get their pipes ready for the collective opening Pipe Ceremony.

I'm not allowed to go into detail about the Pipe Ceremony, still, it was amazing to see over one hundred and seventy-two pipes raised in honor of the two Sacred Laws: All things are born of the feminine sparked by the masculine, and let nothing be done to harm the children of the planet.

Chapter 21

Magick in the Ceremonial Dance

I felt the excitement build throughout the arbor as the clock approached 6:00 pm. With the Pipe Ceremony complete, the dancers stood beside their poles, below their shields, waiting for the drum to sound. They carried feathered plumes in their hands, tethered to their little fingers to prevent them from falling to the ground if they dropped, and they held whistles between their lips.

Then it happened! Four strong beats thundered from the drum, and the dancers ran to the Ceremonial Tree of Life.

The wind shifted, and the smoke from the fire obscured my vision. I lost sight of Josh!

It was a blur of skirts blowing in the wind, whistles piercing the air, and flags whipping. Wave after wave of dancers ran to the Tree of Life with a long, single blow on their whistles, giving away their prayers and sending their energy into the tree with their feather plumes, then dancing backward toward their shields, blessing themselves as they moved, making little tweet-tweet sounds on their whistles. How they avoided running into each other was amazing.

The fire seemingly licked and jumped to the rhythm of the drumbeat.

The sun was setting, and as the smoke cleared, I saw the first stars of the evening appear. Then I saw Josh make a run to the tree—and I mean run. There was a man on either side of him. One appeared to be in his thirties, and the other was older, perhaps in his late fifties. All three ran to the tree, blessed it, then ran backward as fast as they could, repeating it over and over. ·

I wasn't surprised that Josh was running like the wind, but the fifty-year-old? Wow. I wondered who would give up first. I think they were challenging each other, and I couldn't take my eyes off them. Something magikal was happening in the dance arbor, or did it just appear that way because I watched them through the fire?

I felt a shift of energy. It was a slight shift, like when I'm in Grandmother's room taking a journey into remembering. I wondered if I could travel back to Dreams with the Wind and still hold my space at the fire.

I was remembering another time, a past time when there were brotherhood and sisterhood societies, men of different ages training each other and creating warriors they could trust their backs to. Then, to my astonishment, Josh stopped at his pole, took his plumes and whistles off, and collapsed into his chair. The two other men laughed and challenged each other to the tree. This went on for another thirty minutes.

"Are you ready for a dinner break?" one of the Dog Soldiers asked.

I looked to see a man in his early thirties. "Oh. Already? I love it here, but I *am* hungry. I'll be back as soon as possible. Is it okay if I stay even after my shift?"

"Definitely. Glad to have the extra help."

Dinner was delicious, as it always is when one is especially hungry. I didn't talk or visit. I ate my dinner and hurried back to the fire.

There were always two people at the Children's Fire. We were available to assist a dancer who wanted to sit with the lineage items, to ensure they didn't trip, especially the dry-fasters.

I reached for a piece of wood, said a prayer for Shane Spirit Hawk, and gave it to the fire. I planned to speak many prayers for him over the next three and a half days.

I had invited him to join us at next year's dance.

That'll be interesting, Shane and Josh at the same dance ceremony. Oh, my.

Just like Grandmother said, the fire called to me. I discovered I could feed the fire, look into the dance arbor, and see almost all the dancers. It was as if they were sliding back and forth on an invisible thread or fiber. Then a light bulb went off in my head, one fiber to the tree and one in their shields. Seeing it, I understood what Grandmother had said.

It suddenly dawned on me that Josh wasn't next to the beautiful young woman. He was between two men. I had gotten upset for nothing. I wondered if jealousy was like that—getting upset to discover it was all my head. It was a good lesson. Maybe it was a lesson I'd remember—unlike remembering to communicate clearly. As I watched the fire consume the wood I had just offered, I wondered if it was all part of good communication.

The drummers were strong, with voices piercing the night.

The hour grew late. A handful of dancers were resting on their cots, but most stayed up that first night rejuvenated by the night-time breezes. They took turns sitting, praying, and dancing until the drum stopped at 2:00 am.

Two Dog Soldiers and my mom and dad came over.

"Hey, Sage, time to get some sleep. We'll take over for the rest of the night. We took naps."

I hadn't realized how late it was. I thanked them, gave them hugs and kisses, and blew an imaginary kiss across the arbor to say good night to Josh.

I floated around the large arbor, past the Water Sanctuary, shower houses, and yellow banana porta-potties, making a stop before going to Tent City. I entered my tent and crawled into my sleeping bag. Before I could count to ten, I fell asleep, feeling the sounds of the now-silent drum vibrating deep inside me.

The drum started the next morning at 6:00 am, its gentle heartbeat waking the dancers. I know because I woke up at five-thirty, dressed, and was on my way to the Children's Fire. I was quite awake for having gone to bed at 2:00 am.

I met my parents along the way as the Dog Soldier I'd be joining had already relieved them of their duties.

"Good morning, Mom and Dad. The tent is already getting hot, sorry. Don't know how you're gonna sleep without sweating miserably."

"Good morning, Hon," they said simultaneously, their voices resonant in masculine and feminine tones.

"There are tricks to getting cool," Dad said. "You can shower first, then lay down on your wet towel. It helps keep you cool when you sleep."

"It also helps to sleep nude with a damp sarong over your body," Mom added.

"Good to know," I said. "Sleep deep and wake rested."

Dog Soldiers could shower during the dance, so they were off to shower and bed, and I was off to the East Gate.

"Breakfast isn't ready yet," I told my hungry stomach. "We have to wait."

I got to the East Gate in time for the opening Pipe Ceremony. Most of the dancers were sitting in chairs in front of the East Mesa, inside the arbor.

The two senior leaders, Medicine Chief Grandmother Spinning Winds and Paul Gray Eagle, were sitting on blankets at the front of the east lower mesa waiting for stragglers to move out of their arbors and join the rest of the dancers. I saw a ceremonial chief walking the circle, encouraging them to hurry up.

The Elders had their large lineage pipes before them.

Grandmother picked up the microphone. "Good morning, dancers!" she said with energy and joy. "It is our first whole day of dancing in the nineteenth Ceremonial Dance. Are you ready?"

The dancers responded with a resounding "Ho!"

"There are some protocol reminders this morning, and an invitation to sit with the lineage ceremonial items up on the East Mesa. There are Dog Soldiers here to assist if you need it. Connect your energy to the items and the dancers who were here before you, adding your prayers to our linage. Remember to take your whistles and plumes off when you stop dancing, and tie them to your pole."

Gray Eagle spoke into his microphone next. "We will honor the powers of the Four Directions and add a special intent for this first full day of dancing."

After the prayers were spoken, everyone concluded with a loud "Ho!"

"Dance your dreams awake, and have a great day!" Grandmother said. "Please, go back to your spaces and get ready for the first dance."

By 6:20 am, everyone was up and dancing, sending prayers to the people of the world and the children of the planet for clean water, food for all, spiritual accountability, freedom for all countries, and dream visions for themselves. These trips to the Tree, carrying prayers, would go on for another twenty hours, minus necessary breaks, until 2:00 am when the drum went to sleep.

I wanted to stay at the Children's Fire the whole time, but once I smelled breakfast, I took my turn at the Capitol. I surprised myself by eating a big plate of scrambled eggs with cheese, toast, almond butter, jam, potatoes, and apple juice. Then, I went back to the fire and stayed beyond my shift.

I finally needed a break from sitting in the hot sun and went to the Capitol to get a late lunch. It was so pleasant in the shade that before I knew it, I had fallen asleep. I don't know how long I was out, but I was dreaming about the fire and felt the pull of the East Gate and the drum calling me back to my post. Even when I wasn't needed, it was where I wanted to be.

The day flew by. To the relief of the dancers, some clouds gathered in the afternoon. I, too, was glad for the cloud cover and thankful it came without high winds.

I watched Josh and the other dancers moving through the day's heat, dancing, lying on their cots, holding their crystal dreaming spheres and crystal skulls, drifting into altered spaces with marriage baskets over their three-wheel or belly, smoking their pipes, and seeking a vision.

Dancers visited the Water Sanctuary more regularly, and the dry fasters began to dance differently—having had no water for over twenty-four hours. They danced in a trance-like state, some hugging the Tree of Life, flooding the trunk with their tears as they released their emotional pain from childhood or tragic events. Then, having given their burdens away, they stood tall and danced backward with arms high in the air.

With the cool of the evening, more dancers walked to the Ceremonial Tree, offered a pinch of corn pahoe with their prayers, and released it. By the time the first stars were visible, the energy picked up, and the arbor became crowded with dancers rhythmically moving their prayers to the Tree of Life.

As the cool air settled in, you could see the relief on everyone's faces. By 1:00 am, a handful of dancers had crawled into their sleeping bags seeking that deep dream space. My nap helped, and I stayed awake until the last drumbeat. The other two Dog Soldiers were present, which was lucky.

It was almost 2:00 am, and Josh came out to visit one of the yellow bananas. We talked for a few minutes under the gorgeous sky with the Milky Way flowing across the universe.

He took my hand. "I never knew entering this ceremony would take so much energy. The brothers on either side of me are guiding me. I can't believe how strong they dance. I am learning so much. I have been dancing prayers for my birth family and my medicine family. One of my prayers is that we get to see each other over the rest of the summer and perhaps during the winter holidays."

"That's my prayer, too. Thanks for telling me. I've been watching you dance."

"Yes, I feel it and wondered if you could send some Mama Cougar energy to help me dance strong."

With my eyes sparking like the stars above our heads, I said, "I'll do better than that. I'll image kissing you and running Energy Breath with you."

"I like that." He squeezed my hand. "I gotta pee really bad."

We both laughed

"Me, too, now that I think about it. I'm heading to bed soon, so I'd better do it now."

"Shall we?" We walked hand in hand up the little hill.

Other dancers were also making their last trip before settling down for the night.

The drum softened into a two-beat rhythm.

The gentle voice of the drum chief came over the speakers. "Good night dancers. Sleep deep and dream strong."

I headed off to my tent, and Josh returned to his cot in the dance arbor with all the other dancers. I have no doubt we were asleep before our heads hit the pillow.

* * *

It was Friday morning, and I was up early again and at the East Gate. The light of Grandfather Sun greeted us all. Martha Star Light and Thomas Running Fox, two of the funniest medicine people I have ever heard, led the morning ceremony. They had all of the dancers laughing at themselves. They were going to create a new corporation called CDP—Ceremonial Dance Products. The latest rage was red socks permanently stained by the red dirt of the land, stinky breath in a bottle, and tarp juice. We all laughed because when it rained, dancers would stand under the dripping tarps and open their mouths for a drink. This is a big no-no according to protocol. Everyone got the message and agreed—no more tarp juice drinking.

It always rains during the dance—sometimes a little and sometimes a lot.

The shade cloth let the rain drip through, so everybody needed water protection over their sleeping bags and cots. Everyone was prepared to put on rain gear and keep dancing. Some dancers let themselves get wet because it felt good—instant air conditioning when the rain stopped.

Nothing stops Ceremonial Dance—not rainstorms or smoke from nearby fires, which in some years was a challenge.

Friday was long and hot. More dancers went to the Healing Arbor for crystal doctoring, eagle fan clearing of their energy, or having a medicine talk with a healing chief. Some dry-fasters decided to break their fast. I'd see them walking slow and unsteady to the Water Sanctuary, sometimes with a Healing Dance Chief next to them for support, then thirty minutes later, they were running to the tree, rejuvenated. *That's the magick of water.*

They drank regularly after breaking their dry fast and danced stronger and stronger. Seeing the miracle of water rejuvenating the dancers was amazing.

I had to take more breaks out of the sun, too. I sat in the Capitol and talked to the drummers who were on break. I was interested in learning the dance songs and sitting on the drum. They said I could learn the songs, but I had to dance four times before I could be a drummer.

I was sitting on the porch of the Capitol when the late afternoon clouds finally showed up. It was a huge relief to everybody. The winds picked up, too, which helped cool us all down.

My jacket and rain poncho were tucked in a corner of the Capitol. I carried them down to the East Gate in case a storm hit, and extra hands were needed to secure fragile medicine items and cover the mesa with a tarp. Hopefully, the wind spirits would stay as a strong breeze and not increase into a windstorm.

As the sun set, it cooled off, to everyone's delight.

Friday night was the last night of the dance. I wondered if Dreams with the Wind had ever attended a Ceremonial Dance.

Then Grandmother's voice spoke into my head. *"Tonight, is a good time to travel and find out. The energy will be hitting its peak. You can dance on the winds of the collective energy."*

Thank You, Grandmother. I'll take your direction, I said in the silence of my mind. *Do you want me to tell you before I try to dream out?*

Grandmother almost shouted in my head. *"TRY to dream out! Good luck with that intending. I will know IF you are gone."*

She rebuked my doubt voice, and I got the message.

I decided to wait until my relief team came to the East Mesa, so I wouldn't have duties and could dream into Dreams with the Wind's lifetime.

My partner left, and the next team came. I told them I would stay but desired to sit with my back to the fire and gaze into the dance arbor.

Teasing me, one Dog Soldier said, "If a storm hits, shall we tip you over and cover you with the rest of the ceremony items?"

I laughed. "That might be a good idea because I may be here in body only. They looked at each other and nodded. "Yep, we get you, Wind Dancer."

The last full day is powerful, especially Friday night. The drum crew performs the Eight Great Powers songs to show respect for the eight powers that hold a lineage. You would think everyone would be dog-tired after dancing for three and a half days, but the dancers were raised from their tiredness by the energy of the drum and the power in the songs. The arbor was full of running dancers. I saw the center tree become the Tree of Life. It was as if white light energy were shooting out the top of the tree into the universe. The Tree of Life had its own aura—every leaf was alive, every branch.

I had never seen life so vibrant. I was mesmerized. It looked like there were more and more dancers, but they were fuzzy, like looking through a thin veil.

Grandmother Spinning Winds walked by.

"Grandmother," I said loudly to get her attention, then brought my voice down as she joined me on the East Mesa. "Look into the arbor. Am I seeing things?"

"Yes, Wind Dancer. You are seeing a lot of dancers."

"I'm seeing more and more dancers—more than those in the arbor."

Grandmother pretended to squint and looked hard into the arbor. "Yep, a few hundred ancestors are dancing with us. We invited them. It's the last night, after all."

My mouth must have dropped open because she reached over and touched my chin as if to close my mouth.

"Wind Dancer," she said with authority, "the time is now."

As she turned to leave, I heard the inner command as I gazed into the arbor and saw the ancestors dancing in the spaces between dancers. There were more dancers in the shadows, whistles blowing, and movement to the Tree of Life.

Chapter 22

Two Ceremonial Dances—Simultaneously

The drum song was different.

Deep and powerful male voices beat out a rhythm. No women were singing at the drum.

I was gazing into the other dance, and I saw the dancers, the men strong, running to the Tree of Life on this last night. The tree was different, and the arbor was different. Only men—where did the women go?

I heard Dreams with the Wind say, "Welcome Wind Dancer. I have been trying to connect with you. I was wondering if you have ever attended a Ceremonial Dance."

"I said the same thing to Grandmother Spinning Winds about you. She suggested I join you, but her directive had no doubt voice. I could not try. I had to determine, and so I am here. Dreams with the Wind, may I join you?"

"Yes, of course, and thanks for sharing your teaching. I will not use the word try again. I'm glad you succeeded. To answer your question, women do not dance in our Ceremonial Dance. Are they allowed to dance in the future?"

"Oh, yes! At least, in our Dreamers Dance. We don't pierce."

"We are not a Piercing Dance either. That is not our tradition. We no longer need to learn from pain and suffering."

"That's what Chief Thunder Wolf teaches, too."

Dreams with the Wind was silent for a moment. "I will remember his name, Thunder Wolf, in my soul. He must be a powerful chief to bring this knowledge to his people."

"He sits on the elder council as one of the youngest chiefs. He is a dreamer and a warrior. I love him. He teaches me like a granddaughter more than an apprentice."

We sat in silence, watching the dancers. I looked for Josh Walks on the Wind, as I always did, but I could not see him.

"Are you looking for someone special, Wind Dancer?"

"Yes, Dreams with the Wind, but he's not at your dance."

"Are you sure?" she said with a twinkle in her eyes.

"No. If you and I can be in two lifetimes at the same time, maybe he's here, too. Do you have anyone special yet?"

"Not yet, but there is one brave that is beginning to speak to my heart. He made me this whistle, and look at the beadwork."

Our hands moved the whistle around and gazed at the beautiful beading. It was very intricate. We can't play it here on the East Mesa, at the Children's Fire, but I am holding it and sending energy to help him dance strong. This is his second dance. He is becoming a strong warrior. I can see it as he travels through his ceremonies."

"Have you had time by yourselves? Have you held each other? Are you learning the energy breath?" I asked.

"I am learning the energy breath of life," said Dances with the Wind. "I practice it daily, especially out in nature. The trees love to share energy with me. I wrap myself around the truck of a smaller tree and breathe with it. Sometimes, I rest my back on a larger tree and introduce myself. I ask permission, and I invite the tree person to breathe life into me, also. It has been amazing what I am learning."

"Wow, I've never done that. Grandmother has me learning about my own body with self-touch and breath."

"Oh, I am practicing with self and breath, too. I discovered one day while sitting with Mother Nature to use my breath like the winds, and magick happened. I really connect to the tree nation people."

"Do you think it would be okay for me to explore that?" I asked.

"Wind Dancer, that is not a question for me to answer. You need to answer that for yourself or ask Grandmother Seeks the Truth."

I just realized something; our lives were intermingled. Dream with the Wind spoke of Grandmother Seeks the truth. I spoke of Grandmother Spinning Winds. It didn't matter if they were the same souls or not. We had wise grandmothers in our lives who gave us teachings and wisdom. The Sacred Hoop was connected for some of us through the ages.

"Dreams with the Wind, where is this brave, and what is his name?"

"His name is Cloud Walker. Let me find him. There are so many ancestors dancing right now."

"At our dance, too. It's the first time I have ever experienced something like this. There are no friends that I can talk to about this—except maybe Shane. He's special. So is Josh."

"Oh, Wind Dancer, there are two young braves that speak to your heart. Perhaps, that's part of your medicine—the heart and soul to love more than one. It is unconditional loving that allows us to be trained as teachers of spiritual sexuality."

We were thoughtful as our eyes continued to search the dancers.

"Dreams with the Wind, I see that we are here to teach each other. It's for me to remember and for you to dream ahead."

Dreams with the Wind said, "I am being taught that we can bring other lifetimes together in the one we are focused in and capture the talents, skills, and abilities that we once possessed by remembering many lifetimes. This is how we become more in Great Spirit's world." She suddenly jumped up and pointed, "There he is." Then, almost embarrassed, she quickly sat back down. "I forgot we are in the East Mesa and must always be respectful or we will not be permitted to sit here after our time with the fire."

"We are respectful on the East Mesa, too," I said.

"Do you see him, Wind Dancer?"

"Yes, let's both send him energy."

"Cloud Walker is dancing strong. There, see how he leans into the tree. He is gathering energy from the tree person. I think he is feeling our doubled energy. Look at him running backward and, again, another prayer run. He is looking at us."

He stopped dancing and put his plumes and bone whistle on his pole. He was looking our way with great intensity, and then we watched him leave his space and walk around until he backed out of the entrance.

We stood up and backed out of the East Mesa. We moved toward each other, away from the fire light.

Dreams with the Wind smiled and looked into his eyes.

Cloud Walker's voice was deep and resonant as a whisper left his lips. "I felt you so strongly; I had to come to you. Are you safe? Do you need me?"

Our hearts burst open.

Dreams with the Wind spoke for us. "We are safe. My future self is here with me. Her name is Wind Dancer. We have been dreaming together since our Rite of Passage ceremonies. Together we sent energy for you to have a strong dance. I am sorry if—"

Cloud Walker pulled her into him and said, "I am proud to have you both in my life. Welcome Wind Dancer and Dreams with the Wind. You dance in my heart. Quaheystamaha."

The three of us from different lifetimes embraced, and the energy started running. We held each other. Dreams with the Wind and I poured energy into Cloud Walker. His body began to vibrate with the intensity of an energy orgasm. We all began to laugh, then shooshed each other, which made us laugh even more. Dreams with the Wind and Cloud Walker moved closer, and their lips touched for the first time—another moment in eternity. He moved quickly back into the arbor for the last runs. I don't think his feet were even on the ground.

I asked Dreams with the Wind, "Can you come forward with me so we can share this energy with Josh?"

"Yes, for a moment in timelessness, as the drum is about to take the dancers into the dream."

Chapter 23

From The Past Into The Future

The drum and the Children's Fire were calling me back. The drum hit the four strong beats, and the last song slowly brought the dancers to quiet movements to and from the tree. The voices of men and women sang the closing evening song.

I was sitting on the East Mesa with my back to the Children's Fire, gazing into the dance arbor, watching the ancestors and dancers slowly take their final evening prayers to the Spiritual Tree of Life.

"Dreams with the Wind, are you with me? Do you hear the men and women singing on the drum? Do you see our ancestors dancing, and the men and woman dancing together?"

"Yes, I would never imagine such a thing could be. The song is beautiful with the women's voices weaving around the stronger tones of the men's voices. I feel the beauty and power here. It is different yet the same in many ways.

"Where is your brave, Josh Walks on the Wind? It is interesting how similar our names are."

"He is dancing from the northwest, and there are men dancing on either side of him. He is looking at me."

I lifted my hands as if sending him energy. He nodded to me and took one slower run to the tree.

"Yes, Wind Dancer, I see him. He's a handsome brave and looks to have good energy, even at the end of a full day."

"Would you like to meet him?" I said, feeling a sense of unexpected pride.

"Yes, I would. Do you want us to share energy with him?"

"Yes, Dreams with the Wind. He still has tomorrow to go before our dance is over. It would be a nice burst of energy to carry him through. He might have a hard time going to sleep tonight though."

We watched him complete his dance, though the drum was still going. He walked around the inner circle and backed out of the arbor, never turning his back to the Tree of Life.

"Ah, we follow the same teaching. We never turn our backs to the tree that gives life," Dreams with the Wind said.

We stood up and walked backward out of the East Mesa. Josh was off the path, standing in the shadows. I moved into his open arms.

"Josh, there's someone I want you to meet."

My eyes never left his. Time was evaporating for us. "She has traveled here from my other lifetime. She is me, back then. Her name is Dreams with the Wind."

Josh looked a bit confused and stood silent with his arms around us. "Did you just say, Dreams with the Wind?"

I nodded. He released the hug and gave us a little room.

"Interesting our names are so close. Perhaps she could teach me how to Dream, and when I learn, I can teach her how to Walk on the Wind."

The three of us smiled.

"Hello, Dreams with the Wind. I am Walks on the Wind. I guess you just heard me thinking out loud."

Dreams with the Wind spoke to me, and I spoke her words.

"Hello, Walks on the Wind. When you learn to walk on the wind, I would love to learn your medicine. I'm learning to dream ahead into your time and Wind Dancer is learning to remember from my time. We are like sisters. One soul sharing multiple lifetimes and gathering knowledge from them."

I spoke softly. "It is getting late, Josh."

The drum stopped, and the Drum Chief's voice came over the microphone. "Good night, dancers. Dream deep and wake rested for our last day together."

"Josh, would you like an energy hug from us?" I said.

"I would be honored."

He took my hand and moved us further into the shadow of the arbor. He opened his arms, and I felt us both embrace him as he wrapped his arms around us. We relaxed and melted into each other. The familiar tingle of warm energy began in my womb, and I enjoyed the feeling. It started to move up as I took a breath and began to flow on its own. I felt my body shudder and Dreams with the Wind moaned with the added energy. The three of us pulled closer, and I was aware of her spiritual body almost taking form.

"This feeling is amazing," Josh moaned. "Please, a few more breaths together."

Our breath sent energy flowing up our chakras—our wheels of light. Our bodies shuddered, my legs got weak, and then the energy flowed out the top of our heads.

Dreams with the Wind whispered, "I am leaving. This energy is perfect to take me home. He is a wonderful brave. Thank you for this journey into my future. My soul will remember all I have seen."

Then she was gone, and my legs became even weaker. Josh Walks on the Wind held me to him and grounded us down using our breath, directing it into our first chakras.

"Are you alright?" he asked.

"Yes, with a little help from you. I need to ground this energy into Grandmother Earth. To get my land legs. Dreams with the Wind went back home. That's when my legs started giving out."

"Feeling the energy of the two of you is difficult to put into words. I don't think I can. Not now anyway. Thank you for sharing this tremendous gift of love with me. I felt the shift when she left. I'm so glad we met, and I've had this time with you—who you are now and who you were then. May I kiss you?"

"I would like that." I spoke with my eyes and with a voice that sounded different to me, more mature.

He kissed m and we hugged again.

Slowly releasing each other, I said, "Good night, Walks on the Wind."

"Good night, Wind Dancer."

I floated on the wind to my tent and lay awake for a while, feeling the magick of the evening before I fell asleep.

The next morning came fast. Dena Quiet Owl, Thunder Wolf's wife and dance chief of this year's event, and Bobby Sees the Rainbows led the morning ceremony.

Dena spoke first. "Today is the last day of the dance. You have all danced very strong. Your energy went out the top of the Tree of Life and brought energy to all those we prayed for. It has touched the people of our planet.

"We will dance until noon today. We'll be doing honoring-dances and ask that you dance in between these. We will also be holding a water ceremony to honor those who have dry fasted. This will take place at 8:00 am, so keep up your prayers and energy for the dry fasters and those we will be honoring this day. Bobby will share this morning's Pipe Ceremony."

"Thanks, Dena." He took a pinch of tobacco, along with Dena, and added specific prayers. "We will now honor the Four Directions and set our intent for this last ceremonial day of prayers."

After smoking the sacred pipes, everyone spontaneously said, "Ho!"

As the morning dance prayers continued, the Dog Soldiers took down the lodge and personal shields.

Every lodge leader danced their lodge shield to the tree. Dancers took their personal shields to the tree. New ceremonialists stood at the center tree while the more seasoned dancers danced to them and blessed them with their feathers. In honor of the veterans, Thunder Wolf danced to the tree with the other dancers who had served their countries. Tears stung his eyes as he spoke about his lost buddies from the Viet Nam War.

Then I heard Josh's name being called.

"Everyone, please, stand at your arbor space."

I stood up on the East Mesa, near the Children's Fire.

"We honor this next dedication dance to Josh Walks on the Wind, who has gone through his Rite of Passage into manhood. This is his first Ceremonial Dance, and he has taken his place in the warrior clan. He'll take two runs to the tree with everyone joining him for the second run."

My eyes were glued to him as he put his bone whistle into his mouth and held his feather plumes very high. When the drummers hit four beats hard, he ran to the Tree of Life with all his strength and pride, blowing the bone whistle into the air. The song carried him. Everyone blew their whistles and made high trill sounds from their arbor spaces in praise and support of him. It was magnificent! Then the men on either side of him joined in, as did all the other dancers.

When they reached the tree, the men stood behind Josh, protecting him so that other dancers did not crush him in their exuberance. They let their whistles fall to their chest and continued their warrior whoops and hollers. Josh joined them as the whole arbor danced to him, blessing him with their plumes, whooping, and trilling. Gradually, the swarm of dancers began to dance backward, and Josh followed suit with the men on either side of him. He was beaming, and I was so proud of him.

Another name was called—Heart Song. It was the young woman who had walked into the arbor with Josh. Though she was older, she too had gone through a Rite of Passage. This was her first warrior dance after entering the women's clan. She was given the same honor but with a different song meant for women. After dancing the first dance by herself, the women on either side of her danced to the tree with her. They were undoubtedly teaching her how to dance just as the men had helped Josh.

I realized that next year, that could be me, and I felt an inner excitement deeper than anything I had ever felt before.

There were other dedication dances, and before we knew it, the time had arrived for the water ceremony, which broke the dry fast. The Dog Soldiers came in with blankets, which they spread out from the Ceremonial Tree into the south of the arbor. They placed buckets of water and a chair for the dance chief at the edge of the blankets. Dena Quiet Owl invited the dry-fasters to join her on the blanket for the water ceremony. She did a special honoring and passed bowls of water to each dry-faster and encouraged them to drink their fill.

All the other dancers sat in their arbor spaces. When the dry fasters began to drink, all the dancers stood up and shouted and applauded in recognition of their going without food, water, suntan lotion, lip protection, and hats for more than three and a half days. These men and women were truly Ceremonial Dance Warriors.

At the end of the dance, Dena Quiet Owl and Bobby Sees the Rainbow walked around to shake the hand of every dancer, thanking them for their prayers and strong dancing.

I watched Josh as he waited for the dance chiefs to come around to him. He seemed to be glowing, but he wavered a bit. At one point, he leaned up against his shield pole.

When the last person shook the dance chief's hand, an announcement came from the Drum Arbor asking everyone to get their pipes ready for the closing Pipe Ceremony.

Everyone sat with their pipe mesas, and the dance chiefs led everyone in the final prayers of appreciation for all the powers. I heard tears in Dena Quiet Owl's voice as she spoke of appreciation from the ancestors and the dancers. She closed the entire ceremony by saying, "*In honor that all things are born of the feminine sparked by the masculine. Let nothing be done to harm the children. We take these pipes apart.*"

Everyone in the arbor took their pipes apart and put them away in a sacred manner. The lineage pipes, I was told, were kept together until the following year's Ceremonial Dance.

As I watched the end of the dance draw near, I realized that more had happened than I could ever share. So many precious moments stood out in my mind, like when the children came into the arbor to dance. They brought so much joy and energy with them that even in the heat of the day, all the dancers got up to honor the little ones. Some would dance to the tree with them, and some, after being outrun by the older children, would patiently assist those same children to walk-run backward so they didn't fall down.

At the end of the dance, the medicine people worked with otter skins, fans, and gourds on the dancers needing physical healings, and there were healings at the Spiritual Tree of Life. Now, I understood why Grandmother only gave me a short description of the Ceremonial Dance. How could words capture the energy and magick that happens at such a gathering?

I was jarred out of my contemplation as the dancers began to move out of the East Gate towards the ice-cold watermelon that lay waiting for them in large tubs of ice. I wanted to join them, but my co-guardian and I had to remain at our post. We had to keep the Children's Fire burning.

I saw Josh dip his hands into the ice and take two big pieces. He stepped away from the tubs to allow others to move forward as he bit into one of them. He walked over to me as he took another chomp of the red, juicy, cold melon.

"You've got to taste this," he said as he offered me the other piece.

"Thanks. I haven't fasted, but I spent a lot of time in the sun. This is really yummy!"

We slurped the juice into our mouths and smiled at each other.

"Want another piece? I do."

"Yes, but I have to stay here."

"No worries. I'll get more, but I'll have to weave through the crowd this time."

Dancers were removing their gear from the dance arbor.

The Ceremonial Dance was over. Part of me was sad, wishing we could live together as a tribe again.

I spotted my parents serving as Dog Soldiers, helping some of the dancers. They stopped to hug me. I held them tight, and for a sacred moment, I knew they were my tribe, along with all my clan aunts and uncles.

"Sage Wind Dancer, we have a lot to share, and we want to hear about your journey to the other Ceremonial Dance," Dad said. "We'll have lots of time to chat on the way home."

How did they know about that? Oh, Grandmother, of course.

"Sure, Dad. I'm happy to share. We, Dreams and I, learned so much."

"Dreams, aah, so you did get to know each other better. Is that your nickname for her now?"

I smiled. "Yeah, I guess it is."

"We're on duty until everyone leaves the land tomorrow. We'll see you at the feast tonight or at the tents later."

"Tonight, everybody will be showered, clean, and dressed in their best," Mom said. "You may want to wear that sundress you brought for this evening's festivities, and for Josh, too."

I blushed. "Yes, I want to look especially nice tonight. I think I'll wash my hair, too. It needs it."

I felt sadness sweep over me as I watched my parents walk away. The dance was over.

Shaking it off, I reminded myself that the arbor had to be cleared so the ancestors could have their last night of dancing.

The Coming-Out purification lodges were to begin in two hours, at which time the dance arbor would be sealed until the following morning when it would all be taken down in a day. It took so many days to set everything up, and now it would all be taken down and put to sleep in less than twelve hours? I couldn't even imagine that.

Josh was heading my way with more watermelon when a man approached him and gave him a big hug. They walked over to me, and Josh handed me another piece of watermelon.

"This is my father."

The smile on the man's face as he looked at Josh told me he was proud of his son.

"Dad, this is my very special new friend, Sage Wind Dancer."

We looked into each other's eyes and smiled at each other.

"I know, Son, I've been Dog Soldiering with her parents. They're great people. We talked about our two families getting together for a camping trip later this summer if you guys are up for it."

"Wow, Dad, that would be awesome!" Josh said.

"Yeah, how did you guys know?"

"We parents are pretty smart that way."

We laughed, and he opened his arms for us.

The tribe is here, I thought as he released us.

"Hey, Dad, we sure could use a wheelbarrow."

"I'll get one and meet you at your arbor space."

As he left to find a wheelbarrow, Josh said, "Wind Dancer, before we all get busy with the closing lodges and festivities, I want to make clear plans for us to spend as much time with each other as possible."

"Definitely," I said with a smile.

"I'm not going to let this last day and a half get away from us," he added, and we hugged.

"Ditto. I want to be at the festivities after the feast, but I'm having a difficult time leaving the Children's Fire. Would you like to take one of the two-hour shifts with me?"

"I don't care where we are; I just want to be with you. Sitting quietly by the Children's Fire after my belly is full sounds wonderful—except for one thing."

I was afraid he had other commitments.

"We're not supposed to kiss inside the East Mesa."

I smiled. "I'll ask Grandmother Spinning Winds if it would be okay now that the dancers are gone. Maybe the ancestors won't mind, and we can make plans for next year's dance. I really want to dance next year, but I see we'll be across the arbor from each other since I'm a first-time dancer."

"I'm a second-year dancer, remember? I can dance anywhere there's an open space in the arbor. I can dance near you—maybe even dance a few runs with you."

"Agreed! Let's make tonight last as long as we can."

We hugged again, and then Josh went to meet his father.

I was relieved from my post so I could help Grandmother remove her gear from the arbor. A Dog Soldier gave Grandmother a wagon this time, which was easier to load and pull.

"Grandmother," I said, suddenly receiving the answer to one of my prayers. "I know what I need to say to Shane. If he's okay with it, we can all come to the dance next year. He and I as special friends, and Josh and I as whatever we will be. I think Josh and Shane will like each other, don't you?"

With a twinkle in her eye, she said, "Time will tell, Wind Dancer."

My heart danced as I reflected on all that had transpired.

I am Wind Dancer and Dreams with the Wind. I was remembering the past, yet my life was just beginning!

Glossary

Aho or Ho! A sound or exclamation which means one is in agreement with the speaker.

Alchemy: A simple way of thinking about alchemy is to relate it to a recipe. The proper ingredients mixed in the appropriate order with the proper heat will produce the intended outcome each time. For example, a perfect recipe for a fluffy cake will produce a flat cake every time if you fail to add one essential ingredient—baking powder.

Transmutation is the keyword characterizing alchemy, and it may be understood in several ways: in the changes that are called chemical, in physiological changes such as passing from sickness to health, in a hoped-for transformation from old age to youth, or even in passing from an earthly to a supernatural existence. Alchemy should always have the intent to be positive, never involving degradation except as an intermediate stage in a process having a happy ending.

Body Knowing: Also known as a gut feeling. A sense of knowing something without knowing how you know it. Your Soul resides within the temple of your body and is talking to you. Listen to this guidance.

Ceremonial Dance: An annual dance ceremony attended by people from around the world in the summer months across North, South, and Central America. It is a wonderful opportunity for people, tribes, and families to gather and unite in sending prayers for the planet, self, and others.

Child Shield – Inner Child: A Shamanic teaching. Within our luminosity are vortexes of energy referred to as Shields: child, adult, spirit child, spirit adult, and spirit elder. A shield can protect the individual or block them from seeing life accurately. Seeing life through the eyes of your child shield or your inner child, which is better understood in the psychological field, can be a benefit when, as an adult, you desire to play. There is a time and a place for your child, but not when making important business or life decisions.

Clan Aunt or Uncle: This is a person who is not a blood relative, but a friendship or mentoring relationship has developed. There is respect and love between the two people. They become a part of your Clan or your family. There can be a formal adoption ceremony or an informal agreement that happens naturally.

Corn Pahoe: Corn Pahoe is the actual pollen from the corn husk and is considered sacred. As a substitute, pollen can be brushed from any flower. Blue corn meal harvested on the Hopi land can be used as well. In a medicine wheel, it is placed in a small bowl in the north, representing the winds. Pahoe is taken on the winds.

Crystal Skull: Mitchell Hedges Crystal Skull with a movable jaw: The legend foretells that one day the ancient elders will transport it from the museum and place it within the circle of eleven skulls with movable jaws. Each skull came from a different planet and holds the knowledge of each planet. They were given to the young Earth to help it evolve into maturity. They are protected by the Circle of Ancient Wise Ones.

It is now called the Mitchel Hedges Crystal Skull. Anna Mitchel discovered it as a child while at a dig with her father. The native people named her its guardian since she found it. Thunder Wolf went to visit Anna to 'glean' the crystal skull before she donated it to a museum. He asked if she would return it to the ancient ones and assured her of getting it to them. It had power connected to the Sirius Star System. She had no idea what she held and wasn't spiritually trained. As an old woman, she donated it to a museum.

Doubt Shout: Our doubt voices are loud in our inner dialogue. They undermine our confidence. There is a ceremony to acquire a Doubt Shout that rids oneself of this negative internal tug-of-war. The shout can be done in the silence of your mind or out loud.

Eight Great Powers: These are forty-one cultures that are placed in a medicine wheel teaching. They represent the development of the Earth, with each culture providing knowledge that works, whether it came from your tradition or another. It doesn't matter if the knowledge is ancient, it's still applicable in these modern evolving times.

Kiva: In ancient times, a kiva was a round room. More recently, kivas are eight-sided rooms built underground and used for sacred ceremonies and council gatherings. Kivas are usually accessed by climbing down a ladder from a hole cut into the ceiling. The entrance is kept covered so no light enters. Some more modern kivas have steps leading down with a door that shuts tightly so that no light enters.

Maltese: Maltese was one of Thunder Wolf's past lives as a leader in Roman times. Sage remembered her role as a man in that lifetime. The name Maltese also refers to an ancient culture.

Maltese historical civilizations: ancient Greeks, Phoenicians, Romans and Arabs. After the Bronze Age tribes, the next inhabitants of the Maltese Islands were first the Ancient Greeks in 700 BC, then the Phoenician traders, followed by the Romans.

Medicine Name: A name that helps an individual to grow and actualize their potential. The first medicine name given is usually at the birth of a child. In the Metis modern world, the first medicine name may be when one steps onto a shamanic path and apprentices. One's name can reflect maturing over time and changes with a Rite of Passage ceremony. If one belongs to a group like a brotherhood or a sisterhood clan, or a secret society, they may be given a name or do a vision quest to receive a name from Spirit that resonates with that group. This individual may be known in these different gatherings by only one name. If you don't know their specific name, that group may not know whom you are talking about.

Metis Golden Age Prophesy: This coincides with other spiritual paths teachings. We are leaving a dark cycle of 2000 years of being influenced by negativity and Satan. We are waking up to the battle between darkness and light. We are moving into the next 1000-year cycle where the light force energy will permeate the entire Earth. 2054 is when the spiritual gates will open for us to step into the Golden Age the fifth world of humans in unity—Humanity. We have been living on the razor's edge since the Mayan calendar ended on December 21, 2012 with the gateway slowly opening.

Mother Gaia: Gaia is life, the very soul of the earth. Many believe she is a goddess who inhabits the planet, offering life and nourishment to all her children. In ancient civilizations, she was revered as mother, nurturer, and giver of life.

Nagual: Spiritual Realm

Orgastic: An energy state of full body—emotional and mental—arousal that often does not involve an erection or vaginal arousal for women. This state can be experienced for long periods of time, solo or with a partner.

Quaheystamaha: (Qua-Heysta-Maha) "You Dance in my heart."

Rainbow Warriors: Men and women who know they are a part of something larger and make the decision to be an active part of the solution. Their souls are hungry to learn, grow, and challenge themselves to become the best they can possibly be. That means getting out of their comfort zones and challenging everything they know. They have to let it all go in order to discover *The More* and search for *Truth* again. These are men and women of *The Light*, being of service to humanity—humans in unity. We need 144,000 awakened Rainbow Warriors in each of the Eight Great Powers to bring freedom to the people of the Earth as free autonomous sacred humans.

Smudge: A mixture of dried herbs that, when burned, creates a smoke that one can bathe in by using their hands or an actual feather fan to sweep over the entire body, luminosity, or to cleanse a room. Sage banishes negativity, Cedar brings balance, Sweetgrass blesses, and Lavender flowers bring beauty.

Since Always and For Always: A power statement used in ceremony. For example, "To all my relations who have loved me since always and for always."

The More: This is a phrase to indicate no matter how evolved we become there is always THE MORE. A higher state of consciousness, a more benevolent state of mind. Never settle for…. Always go for The More. Don't be lazy or complacent with your soul's evolution. Go for The More.

Tobacco Tie: Tobacco is considered a sacred herb. It is given as a sign of respect or appreciation for what that person has done for you. One can give a whole pouch or what is called a tobacco tie. One takes a pinch of tobacco and puts it inside a square piece of cotton or natural cloth approximately 2x2 inches or larger. A prayer is put into that pinch, and the corners of the cloth are pulled up and twisted. A string or piece of yarn is tied around the twist to prevent it from opening.

To All My Relations: We say, "To all my relations," before entering the purification lodge. A deeper understanding includes all we have been from previous and future lifetimes, those who have been blood relations, our awakened selves, and the entire family of humanity. We are all interconnected at the Quantum level.

Tipili: Male Genitals, Penis, Sacred Snake

Tupuli: Female Genitals, Vagina, Sacred Cave

Tonal: Day-to-day, ordinary life

Yellow Moon Society: Yellow Moon Society teaches spiritual sexuality, keeping the Sacred Hoop unbroken. In modern and indigenous cultures, secret societies hold the precious knowledge of their lineage. Those entrusted with responsibility must be very selective about whom they train to carry on the lineage and keep the knowledge safe, uncontaminated, and alive for seven generations and beyond.

Multiple societies and councils meet to help guide the movement of our planet, including Warrior, Healing, and Spiritual Sexuality societies. Unfortunately, there are also societies and councils of darkness that actively enslave the people of the planet. Rainbow Warriors battle this evil enemy.

Zero Chiefs: The names given to men and women who explored the history of what happened in the beginning of our planet. They discovered the universe has inter-relationships with all things through mathematics. There are twenty sacred powers that make up our entire universe. The numbers 0 to 20 represent *The Everything*. Zero (0) is the potential of all forms of all things. It is a system to understand order in the universe. Because they discovered and taught this, they were honored with the name Zero Chiefs.

Sage's Names In Modern and Ancient Times

<u>**Modern Times**</u>

Rebecca Sage: Rebecca: Hebrew meaning Bound to God; a knotted cord, representing beauty in the old testament. **Sage:** Wise one, prophet, from the sagebrush plant, sage used in smudge banishes negativity.

Wind Dancer: The wind element sits in the north of the medicine wheel. The wind represents the mind, wisdom, knowledge, logic, balance, and harmony. To be mentally open and flexible like the wind. All things are possible. To dance on the winds of time, moving from lifetime to lifetime. Eventually, with training, learns how to literally dance on the wind, above the physical realm, or on the spiritual plane.

<u>**Sage in her PAST LIVES, in Order of Discovery**</u>

Dreams With The Wind: To remember one's dreams. Spirit guides us in our everyday life and supports the Soul's development through the dreamscape that needs to be understood by interpreting the symbols and stories using the wind-air element, which is the mind—wisdom, knowledge, logic, balance, and harmony.

Zama: To Try. She was a member of the Zulu tribe.

Kiyomi San: Kiyomi means pure beauty, strength, and heart. San means someone with a higher status showing respect and being polite. For example, Mama San.

Sakura – Cherry Blossom (Sage's Aunt Kathy in Modern Times): The flower of spring, the beauty of nature, the renewal, the ephemeral nature of life. (something that lasts a very short time)

Itzel: Moon Goddess, she of the rainbow, associated with stars, sky, and heaven. Origin is native American-Mayan.

Maltheo: Matthew is a name inspired by the Greek name Matthaios, which is itself a variation of the Hebrew name Mattityahu, meaning "gift of Yahweh."

Additional Acknowledgements

Jan Orsi: Creation Story
A special note of appreciation for my dear friend, Jan Orsi, co-author of Song of the Dear, The Great Sun Dance Journey of the Soul, for her permission to print her version of the Creation Story, which is found in the first chapter of this novel. Thanks, Jan! You dance in my heart! Aho!

Wendy Carter: Author and Editor
Thank you for helping me actualize the dream of sharing my knowledge through the written word. Over the past twenty years, I have worked with two other professionals—Laura Bush, author, coach, and publisher, and Bettina Steinle-Vossbeck, publisher and editor—who have helped me get my novel to the point where we began our journey together. It was a pleasure to be guided and educated by your vast, well-earned knowledge. Any author, published or beginner, would benefit from your tutoring and dedication to excellence. Blessings for all you are and all you do. May it be returned to you ten-fold.

Kirk Cameron: Monumental DVD
Appreciation for his work in Search of America's National Treasure. A ninety minute true story about the pilgrams. Our families are worth fighting for.

Geno E. A.
For twenty years, I have been working on my novel. It has sat on the floor and on a shelf in my mind as I rationalized my procrastination by blaming others. We shared lunch, and you said the right words at the right time. "This knowledge needs to be shared, and it doesn't matter what you call it. Our beloved nagual wants these teaching out to help heal the people of our planet. Do it." Thank You, Geno, my friend.

Note From the Author

It has taken twenty years to produce this novel. Like many aspiring authors, its many versions sat piled in a box at the foot of my bed, awaiting moments of inspiration when I'd add to the latest draft and then abandon it once again to the demands of a busy life. But the dream of sharing my growing knowledge of the shamanic world never left my consciousness. Eventually, this desire—one aspect of my true calling—burst through the many ways I justified procrastination, and I began writing and rewriting my novel with renewed determination. After five long years of concentrated effort and professional guidance and assistance, I am delighted to release it into the world.

Initiation into Spirituality Sexuality is a sharing of thirty-nine years of my life, woven with threads of fiction, as I discover a Spiritual Shamanic Path, participate in vision quests and intense training, awaken my Sacred Sexuality, and become a senior teacher of ancient sexual practices and traditions. Many of the stories, such as past life visions and dry fasting for 3 ½ days in high ceremony, are shared from the depths of my personal experiences.

My greatest decision in life was to create an active daily relationship with a Higher Power. I make time to connect first thing in the morning, before coffee or work. It's my time to listen for that quiet voice or soft nudge of God's guidance and direction. Whether it's emotional, mental, physical, spiritual, or sexual—I listen. It sets my day.

I'm about as retired as I can be and still engage in private practice full-time. I enjoy counseling couples and individuals through the challenges of Marriage, Relationship, and Sex in traditional and open lifestyles, and I love facilitating workshops, yet, if I had I died before sharing my knowledge through the written word, I would feel as if a large piece of my life's purpose were not accomplished. I have to write—*from the one to the many.*

If I am sharing new thoughts and a deeper understanding of who you are as a sacred sexual human being, or if I'm affirming what you know to be true inside your own soul, then I am happy. Sometimes we need to hear from another source before we give ourselves permission to be our true authentic selves.

It is my hope that you discover your soul's desire and your heart's dreams, and never give up on manifesting them! Aho!

In Beauty and Strength,
Ina Laughing Winds

About The Author

Ina Laughing Winds has a M.A. in Transpersonal Psychology with an active private practice since 1985, counseling adults and teenagers. She touches thousands with her counseling, radio shows, international workshops, and seminars. She supports healthy relationships between adults of all ages and guides parents in helping their  teenagers to become responsible, mature adults. Ina is also an ordained metaphysical minister, advanced hypnotherapist, and spiritual healer.

She is a published author, including a DVD, a CD, and her book "Improve your Sex Life and Relationships One Bite at a Time." She wrote monthly articles for Quest and Playtime magazines for ten years, providing teachings on improving relationships and understanding male and female differences and how to navigate them.

Ina is featured in two documentaries: The Good Sex Guide, UK, and Sex TV, Canada. She's a presenter in the DVDs: "Journey into Self Discovery" by Nick Karras and Beck Peacock and "The Sacred Prostitute / Magdalene Unveiled," by Kenneth Ray Stubbs Ph.D. which explores Sacred Sexuality with a Rabi, Christian Minister, Tibetan Lama, and Shaman. Ina Laughing Winds presents internationally as a teacher of Shamanic Wisdom and facilitates workshops and seminars.

She began her Shamanic Spiritual Path in 1982 and is a senior teacher. She has been a teacher of Spiritual Sexuality workshops for thirty-nine years. Her life includes performing at Carnegie Hall with the Carolyn Eynon Singers, competitive handgun shooting, where she met her husband in 2002, and street self-defense martial arts training. She dances like no one is watching when a band is good and there's no one to dance with. Ina says, Ina says,

"The best rewards in my 73 years of life are the warm relationships and the positive changes I have shared in."

Contact Ina:
Questions about the book,
ina@spiritualsexuality.com | www.spiritualsexuality.com

Workshops, Seminars, or Sessions: (Office or Zoom)
ina@talktoina.com | www.talktoina.com